Vision

Enchantment

by Mary J. Dressel

PublishAmerica

Baltimore

ISBN: 1-4241-5203-8
PUBLISHED BY PUBLISHAMERICA, LLLP
www.publishamerica.com
Baltimore

Printed in the United States of America

Dedication

I dedicate this book to the men in my life. For you, Chris and Jim, who encouraged me from the first scratches in a yellow notebook to the finished manuscript. You watched each revision, and knew the pain of each rejection. Before my eyes, you grew into men, but still, you would not let me give up.

To the first man in my life, my dad, Ernest F. Hahn, for never letting me believe it when I said, "I can't do it!" Chuck, my brother—because you know what it's like to face obstacles and still win. John, my dear husband—Even though you came into my life long after this writing was over, you taught me what it means to challenge myself, and you take pride in showing me new ones each day! Without you, I wouldn't have a whole add-on family to love. Most importantly, you have shown me that a person can get through any challenge in life, if they just don't stop trying.

Acknowledgment

It's difficult to acknowledge only a few people, because so many of you were involved with me in some way while I wrote this book. I'll start with my friends who read the rough drafts in various stages, and gave me suggestions to make it better. Sonja Sluder—whom I've known forever. You were the first to read it, and you said, "Forget the book, I want the movie!" Elly Eddington, my most avid reader friend and neighbor who kept on me about writing. Constantly! That's a good thing. Ron Rowe, for your all important 'Man's Opinion.' You really got on my case about my hero! Because of you, I made him a gentleman; well kind of. A special acknowledgement goes out to Margaret Frazier, my best friend for life. What would I do without your prayers and confidence for all these years? You told me I would lose my God given talent if I didn't use it. I sent this manuscript in one more time because of you. You, and that little whisper from God. For the people who helped with my photos, Taylor, Jim and Chris. Acknowledgement also goes to all my other friends and co-workers, both old and new, who never hesitated to ask if I was still writing and told me I better not quit! I can't begin to name all of you, but you know who you are. I sincerely thank you all!

Prologue

April 1882

Quinn Matheson wasn't a weak man. Not until he saw the bruised body of his child beside him. Not until he held the broken body of his wife in his arms. His fingers caressed the soft hair of his freckle-faced son as life slipped away from his young soul.

It happened so fast. Was it a bear in the shadows? A bear that spooked the horse in the foggy night, sending the carriage, and the lives in it over the hillside?

He slipped in and out of consciousness, weeping hysterically when he had a lucid moment. His pain was great, both in his heart, and his soul. He knew his life was over. His own wretched body told him that. "Breathe," he told himself. "Help will come, breathe…"

Quinn could hear the whinny of the horses as the wagon came closer. Mr. Tucker, their neighbor, was making his daily trip to the barn across the road. On this dreary morning, the fog lifted early. His eyes rested on the tracks in the muddy road. He stopped the horses, listening. The crows were cawing at their usual pitch, warning him away from their young. He cocked his head to the side, still listening.

"Here, over here… Please, help me."

He appeared at the top of the hill overlooking the horrible sight. As quickly as he could he descended the hillside, slipping nearly all the way down. "Oh, mercy be, Quinn. What has happened?" He knelt down, holding Quinn's wounded head in his hands, scanning the area, seeing the woman and her son.

"Tell Eryn we love her," begged Quinn, grabbing his coat sleeve.

"I'll tell her. I'll tell her…"

"Tell our beautiful daughter we love her." His breaths were ragged, words barely more than a whisper. "Oh, the pain…"

He clutched his wife's hand.

Mr. Tucker rested the boy's head in the crook of his father's arm. "Hush, don't talk, you need your strength."

"Tell her—tell Uriah…to take care of our little girl." His breaths were short, raspy, but he continued the struggle, looking to the murky sky as he spoke. "Tell her—we love her. Love our Eryn.…"

* * *

Rain clouds loomed overhead like a dirty blanket. A large crowd stood around the graves of the Matheson family. The red haired girl leaned against Uriah. Her great-great grandfather took her gloved hand to his cheek.

They were all she had left, and it was more than a seventeen year old girl could deal with.

Tears didn't fall this day. Sobs didn't shake her shoulders. Her beautiful eyes only stared. Stared through the black veil to the small grave of her brother. Her body yearned for the comforting touch of her mother…the tender smile from her father.

Uriah's arm tightened around her. Gently, and sympathetically he drew her head to his chest as he glanced at the old grandpapa. Unlike Eryn, Grandpapa's agony was obvious. Large tears escaped his eyes, and he openly wept.

"…This is a sad day for Enchantment," said the deep voice of Preacher Dan. "A lot has been taken from this town." He looked at Eryn. "This young lady is our responsibility now. We should help her in any way we can." He closed his Bible, walked to the graves and dropped a white rose bud on top of each one.

"Quinn Matheson and his family will be sorely missed...."

* * *

"Eryn, let me in to see you, please." Uriah pounded on the door of the lonesome house. She refused to let him in.

"Go away. Just go away," she said, sniffling. "I don't want to see anyone!"

"Please let me in," There was no answer. Willy, the old Collie, sauntered up to Uriah, nuzzling his pointed nose into the palm of his hand. His tan hair was knotted and dirty. Uriah went to the barn and scattered corn for the chickens. He picked up Willy's brush and brushed out his matted fur. Sitting on the dirt floor, he dropped his head into his hands, and wept.

* * *

The sun was rising on yet another morn. One more day of agony for his beloved. He would wait forever if he had to. Wait for her to deal with the tremendous loss that faced her. But today he would barge through the door if she didn't let him in. Today he would make her see him. Make her go into town to stay with her great-great grandfather. It wasn't good for her to be alone.

He knew it was too early to ride across the field to her. Later, when the fog lifted he would prepare some food, make her eat. They could talk of their wedding. She always smiled when she talked of marrying him.

Slowly the fog burned off and the forested mountains stood majestic over the foothills. The ground sparkled with the dew that moistened it. It was early spring and the day would be hotter than usual, he could feel it.

He hitched the horse to the wagon to carry supplies to the forest. His lean body glistened with sweat, his hair sticking to his skin as he swung the ax. Uriah liked hard work. So much that time slipped away from him. The sun was nearly overhead. It was time to see his beloved. With the wagon full of wood, he decided to take it back before he went to her. Splashing water over his body couldn't hurt either.

With a clean shirt and a basket of food he made his way through the plowed field. When he arrived at her house he was glad to see her Grandpapa. At least he could take her back with him today.

Upon seeing her, his arms immediately embraced her. "Eryn, Eryn—I've been so worried about you."

Her eyes were swollen and streaked with red. Willy nuzzled against her, but she gave him no response.

"I'm sorry, please let me get through this pain...I just want to be left alone until I don't hurt anymore."

"Yes, but let us help you. This is not a time to be left alone." He held her tighter, inhaling the fragrance of her hair.

"I want my Eryn girl to come to town," said the old man, "and stay with me."

"Yes. Yes, of course, that would be best." Uriah held her at an arms length, looking directly into her eyes. "Eryn, you know it would be best. Let me take Willy. I'll come back and feed the animals."

"I don't know. I need to stay here," she said, her head down, hiding her emotionless turquoise eyes. Strands of long waves hung knotted down her back. Her slight frame looked frail.

"Listen to me, girl. Let us do the thinking for you right now. You're suffering inside. Suffering so much."

Looking back at him, her eyes filled with tears. She looked into his amber colored eyes, and out of habit, pushed his hair behind an ear. "I know you're right, Uriah. But, don't make me leave my parent's house. I *need* to be here! I need to be close to them." She left his arms and went to the window.

The smell of pipe tobacco lingered. Uriah recognized the aroma of Mrs. Matheson's bread. Did Eryn smell it everyday too? No, he wasn't going to let her stay alone, not one more day.

Grandpapa cocked his head toward her, motioning for Uriah to go to her. He lit his pipe, whistled for Willy and went outside.

Uriah put his arms around her and she rested her head against his chest. He held her while she sobbed. His eyes closed, and he remembered the sight of her in his bed, the feel of her skin against his. Was it only four nights ago! That same sight and same feel of her aroused him, even now as he remembered her passion. The scent of her enticed him, reminding him of only a short time ago. Was it only a short time ago, that her world fell apart? He so wanted to make it right for her. So wanted to take her in his arms and love her as he did, a short time ago.

He glanced at the dress hanging in the parlor, then back to Eryn. When she looked at him, he saw something was lost. One more glance at the dress caused his heart to sink. Would she ever wear it to the alter to marry him now? Yes, he would see to it. He would.

"Will you go with him? If not for you, do it for him." He pointed to the side of the barn. "Look at him, he needs you, too."

Wiping the tears away with her fist, she sniffled one more time. "I'll go."

Together they packed a few items of clothing and personal belongings. Although it was against her will, Uriah persisted, refusing to accept no for an answer.

He helped the old man up, then lifted Eryn into the carriage. "I'll see you later this evening." Caressing her fingers, he brought them to his lips, craving the love that was hidden beneath sadness. "My work needs to be finished, then I'll come."

"Come, sup with us tonight, boy," said the old man.

"I'll be there before sunset."

"Uriah, don't come tonight." she said, without looking up. "I just want to be left alone with my pain." Casually, she touched his arm. "Alone, don't you understand!"

The old man sat beside her in the carriage. "I have invited him, Eryn girl."

"Please, Grandpapa, grant me this tonight."

Uriah took her hand, trying to read her eyes. "Don't shut me out."

"I'm not trying to, I'm really not. Please, not tonight."

A myriad of thoughts raced through his mind, but he would do as she asked. Only for tonight, he would let her be. If he had to take her home with him tomorrow, he would do that. There had to be a way to ease her pain.

* * *

Although the day was as warm as the morning promised, a sudden fog settled over the fields. Wild daisies and buttercups seemed to have bloomed overnight.

A sound rang out. Thump! Crack! Thud! Uriah was stacking the wood he chopped earlier. He was so busy he hadn't noticed Eryn until she was practically in front of him with a glass of cool water.

Bending down, he snatched a bunch of daisies from the ground, handing them to her, smiling his famous smile. "I love you, girl."

Her arms went around his neck, clinging tightly. "Uriah, I love you so much…" She pressed her cheek against his chest, ignoring the sweat. "But—"

"Don't talk right now, girl. Come inside with me."

"No, no, I can't."

"Why?"

"Uriah, I…I can't." She stood back from him, the words lingering inside her mouth, not wanting to be heard.

"Come inside with me, I need you. You need me, too."

"No, I won't be coming to see you again."

"What…"

"Don't try to change my mind. Grandpapa has a…a—"

"What do you mean, don't try to change your mind? I *love* you, you have to fight to get over this."

"I'm going," she said, as she slowly turned from him, handing him the flowers. "Don't try to find me."

"Eryn—"

Walking away, she glanced back at him, hiding the tears as she wept. Was leaving the right thing to do? "Yes," she whispered. Grandpapa knows what's best. "He knows," she said, all the while doubting her decision to leave. "He knows a place where I'll forget my pain…forget everything."

Yes, Grandpapa knows best, she told herself.

She so wanted to turn and run to him, let him take her into his house and do what he could do so well. But she couldn't, for Grandpapa was waiting, waiting. Faster now, walk faster she told herself. Don't look back, but she had to look back, just one more time she had to look back. The sight she witnessed tore her heart apart. Uriah, her knight, stood staring, watching, crying. The daisies, one, two, three, slipping from his fingers, falling to the ground. One more glance. "Good bye, my brave knight, good-bye… I will always love you," she whispered, as she climbed into the carriage.

Two Months Later

His age was a mere twenty years, but age had nothing to do with his shattered heart, for he was a broken man. His hair, as flaxen as the wheat fields around him, slipped through his trembling fingers. Sitting on the steps of the gazebo, he waited. As he looked to the sky, sunlight reflected off his misty eyes. Holding his head in his hands he wondered why she left him…disappeared, vanished.

The clippity clop of a horse drew his attention, and when he looked up, he watched Grandpapa lower his old bones to the ground. Bent and frail, he hobbled over to the young man and put his bony hand on his shoulder. "I know where she is, Uriah—It'll be a hard thing for you to understand, boy, but I can take you through the, the—the door to the future—where I took Eryn. I can help you find her, but first we gotta have us a talk…you gotta know what it's like a century away, boy."

Chapter 1

The trip seemed endless as Eryn drove away from the western sky. The narrow, two-lane road followed the Allegheny River, twisting and climbing through small towns. Alyce, her first born twin slept in the seat beside her.

Sometimes, and this was one of them, she had the feeling someone was calling to her, calling *for* her, but it was a familiar feeling, one she had for the past twenty years. The past twenty years was all she remembered of her life. Somehow, the memory of anything before that had slipped away. Ever since then something deep inside her yearned for fulfillment, craved a kind of satisfaction. She had no idea what it was. Now, she thought of her husband, Taylor. Taylor, whom she married twenty years ago, and who left her ten months ago. Silently, she made a vow to find him, and to find *whatever* it was that was calling to her.

Darkness was falling as the sun dropped in the sky. A sudden fog ascended from the valleys, making it difficult to see through the mist. For some unknown reason Eryn was afraid of the fog. Although Alyce awoke and offered to drive, Eryn still held some control over her fear, declining her offer, but a few more miles the fog worsened, as did her anxiety. Like a Godsend, a sign appeared telling them a town called Enchantment was only four miles ahead. As they approached, the fog began to subside. A long, dangerously steep hill led them into town.

Slowly driving through, they both admired the look of Enchantment, enjoying the candles burning in windows of the old homes. Ahead on the left, an old book store advertised classic books, and Eryn knew she would visit there before leaving.

On the right they spotted an inn. Before Eryn pulled in she was embraced by a sudden chill. Glancing around she felt something familiar, but didn't know what the feeling was. Alyce, on the other hand, jumped out, paying no attention to her mother's state, and grabbed her luggage. Eryn sat a moment, exhaling long and slow, glad to be off the foggy highway. Tilting the rear-view mirror upward to get a look at the town, her eyes deceived her, for it no longer looked as it did. This charming little town was no longer set in the present. Through it she saw a park with a gazebo, a fountain, dirt roads, and carriages. The buildings were wood clad, but painted in drab colors. She tilted the mirror a bit more, confused when she saw the eyes of someone looking back at her. Amber brown eyes, eyes she had seen before.

When Alyce opened her door the mirage disappeared. Blinking her eyes in bewilderment, Eryn looked again. Everything returned to normal. She turned around quickly, curiously looking out the rear window, then back at her daughter.

"Mother, you look like you've seen God, what is it, what's wrong?"

Eryn stepped out and walked to the rear of the car. There was no gazebo, but the fountain *was* there and working. The roads were paved—carriages a thing of the past. She walked back to get her things from the car. "Let's go inside," she said, "I'm more tired than I thought." As they went through the door, Eryn turned to look again, shaking her head, wondering about her vision.

They entered through a long hall creatively decorated with simple, antique wood furnishings. Candles glowed in the hallway, that led to a small mahogany desk. As she walked toward it the clerk raised his eyes, staring at her with a look…a look so seductive, it caused tingles to tiptoe down her spine. She didn't notice his face turned pale and his knuckles turned white as he gripped the edge of the desk.

In a flurry he went to meet her—so wanting to take her hand, taste her lips, touch her soul, but he didn't. Still, he escorted her to the desk, not removing his eyes from her beautiful face.

"You don't remember me, do you," he said, his voice quivering.

Carelessly, she fumbled through her purse for her credit card, cautiously glancing up at him. Her legs trembled at seeing the way he surveyed her, his eyes narrowing, saying something only he knew. When she gained the courage to look at his face, she saw something she didn't understand. Amazingly, his eyes were amber, and her trembling legs weakened.

Something about him was familiar, she thought, but she said, "No, I'm sure we've never met…" Looking into his eyes brought a calmness to her being, even as he continued to stare. Why would this man cause this feeling inside her? She stuck her credit card back in her purse, pulling out enough cash for the rooms. Too much information could be acquired from a credit card, and the look in his eyes told her he wanted to acquire every bit of information he could, and that unsettled her.

"Go to the stairway and turn left at the top," he said, before his lips curved into a smile. A slight southern accent, yet a little eastern, too, could be heard in his now composed voice. "My name is Uriah, Uriah Prescot, if you need anything."

A familiar chill engulfed her—the longing in his eyes, why was it familiar too? What was happening? If I need anything, she thought, I won't call you…*or will I?* She pulled her stare away from his before she picked up her bag, thanking him as she walked away. Alyce waited at the stairs, taking the key from her mother.

"We have adjoining rooms. It seems they only have single beds left."

Alyce looked at her mother with a questioning frown, but when no explanation came, she headed up.

Before Eryn stepped up she glanced back at Mr. Prescot, watching as his tongue gently moistened his lips, before he said, "Maybe I'll see you at check-out, Ms. Matheson…I mean, Ms. Sterling." He moistened his lips again. "If not before."

"It's *Mrs.* Sterling," Eryn said. Her tremble was obvious as if a gentle breeze blew across her shoulders. As she ran up the stairs his chuckle repeated itself through her ears. The hall was quiet, giving up the sound of a creak on the stairway. She couldn't get inside fast enough. While she leaned against the heavy door her breathing slowed down.

The room looked cozy and warm, her confused feelings forgotten. She untied her shoes, kicked them off, and sat on the four-poster double bed. As she looked around she realized why she felt so reassured. Her favorite colors were used to decorate the room. The carpet was soft, a thick plush, teal in color. The color that made her feel good. A friendly, romantic color. Looking around she noticed candles were everywhere. One picture on the wall attracted her attention. To her surprise it was the same park she *thought* she had imagined. She summoned the vision from her memory, recalling each and every detail. Yes! It was the same. Satisfied with the semblance of it, she closed her eyes for a moment.

She thought of her best friend, Beth, and decided to take back some truffles she saw through the gift store window downstairs. She laughed aloud when she imagined what Beth would say about watching her weight, but she didn't need to worry about a piece of candy now and then.

As she took off her socks and started to pull off her sweat shirt there was a knock at the door. Unexpectedly, her fear returned. "Who is it?" she asked, cautiously.

"I have a complimentary gift for you, Miss Sterling," said a woman's voice.

Eryn walked over and peeked through the peep-hole. There stood a young girl wearing what looked like a uniform. A warm smile met her as she opened the door, and to her surprise the girl was holding a tray with a box of Swiss Chocolates and a single white rose.

"This is beautiful," she said, taking the flower, "my favorite color of rose! Thank you."

"Well, someone here thinks you're special, Miss Sterling. Mr. Prescot likes to make some of his guests feel at home. He owns this place so he can do...whatever!"

She took the tip from Eryn, leaving quickly. Eryn sniffed the rose, twirling the stem between her fingers. While she enjoyed its fragrance that familiar glint of sorrow played on her mind. Reality returned to her upon hearing voices in the hall.

When she looked through the peep-hole she held her breath, for it was he who made her heart throb a little too much. The same young girl stopped to talk to Uriah Prescot. Uninterested, he put something in her hand and turned to walk away from her, but she grabbed his arm. The girl smiled at him, but he pried her hand away, laughing the laugh that Eryn was beginning to know.

"My, but she looked like a sweet little thing," Eryn whispered. She took a long look at this man called Uriah Prescot, feeling more secure behind her closed door, knowing she had not seen him before, yet, a hint of familiarity was surely there. A very strong hint that spread a feeling of warmth all over her. Why? she wondered. His hair was blond, quite thick. It was long and tied back at the nape. Her weakness for long hair on a man was showing.

Standing there, his broad shoulders leaned forward as if he was trying to hide his tallness. His jaw was, model-type square, very touchable. A small jagged scar ran across it. Why did she have the sudden urge to trace it with her fingertip? It was obvious his chin needed a razor taken to it—his beard probably growing since yesterday. A darker mustache was in need of a trim, but it was his eyes, his golden, cat-eyes, that rattled her soul.

The man's frame was on the thin side and he was remarkably tall, about six foot three. Even though his physical appearance seemed unkempt, Eryn approved of his expensive taste in clothes. He wore a brown suede jacket that stopped at his narrow waist. A coral cravat was neatly tucked inside the opening at his neck. Kind of old fashioned like, she thought. His tan trousers fit loosely, but on him they looked…suggestive. His plain, brown pointed-toed boots had no shine. He could have been great looking, and except for the clothes, it almost seemed like he didn't care about what he looked like. She had to wonder about the man, but at the same time she felt excited about him!

One glance toward her door caused Eryn to jump back as if he could see through the thick oak, yet, she couldn't resist the urge to look out one more time. While he still looked her way, the resonant sound of her thumping heart burst through her ears. He stopped looking and started walking toward her door then suddenly turned and went back the other way. There was no reason to distrust him, albeit, the mere sight of him manipulated the rhythm of her pulse. Maybe she would remember something about him soon.

She went back, sat on the bed and again smelled the alluring scent of the rose. Her daughter's face rested on her mind. Of the two girls, Alyce looked more like her, with her dark hair, and petite features, but Eryn was the only one in the family who could claim the turquoise eyes. They could never figure out who Avis looked like, with her light hair, and darker eyes. Although Alyce was going away to college to live with friends, a good move for her, Eryn would miss her. As if she knew she was being thought about, her daughter knocked on the adjoining door and walked in.

"Hey, I didn't get any candy and flowers!" she said.

"I'm not sure I wanted to get them. They're from the owner of this inn. Something about him makes me nervous."

"Mother, *you* are too suspicious. I see how men look at you. You look young enough to be my sister, and that's probably what everyone thinks. I mean, look at you, you're beautiful. Enjoy it."

"This is not suspicion. I don't know what it is, but I don't think I like him." Or what he does to my insides, she thought. "And thank you, sweetheart, for the compliment."

"Oh, Mother. Now, about dinner—I need some food before I faint," she said, pretending to fall over.

"Call room service. I'm too tired to go down to eat," she said, shaking her head. I think I'll take a bath, then call Beth," said Eryn, heading toward the bathroom. "It'll feel good to relax."

"I'll take a shower and order dinner soon. How's that sound?"

"Great! Something lite for me, please."

Eryn lit two candles in the bedroom. She was looking forward to a hot bath as she dropped her clothes. Before she sank down in the bubbles she lit the candles. Stretching out, she let her wavy, chestnut colored tresses fall over the back. One glance at the wilting rose on the vanity brought thoughts of Taylor.

The candlelight and the hot water made her sleepy. As her eyelids became weighted she closed them, but those amber brown eyes took residence somewhere behind her own orbs. She quickly opened her eyes, realizing the warmth of her body, and she shivered a little, but it wasn't a shiver from being cold. It was more like a trembling, the feeling she had when she woke in the night from that heated dream of a stranger. She closed her eyes, trying to remember the look in the eyes of the apparition that loved her. She imagined the tender touch that expertly drove her to ecstasy…this man without a face…but she forced herself to think of the man she married. "Okay, Taylor," she said. "I have to think about you. Sometimes it hurts so bad and I should miss you."

But again, she closed her eyes, remembering *his* touch. She pictured his eyes, the eyes she would never forget. She thought about the visions she had seen in the mirror but wasn't sure now—not sure she really saw anything.

Her thoughts went back to Taylor, remembering their years together. Eryn was only about seventeen years old, and twenty year-old Taylor taught her to be a woman, whether she liked it or not. "He didn't intentionally abuse me, he really didn't." She tried to convince herself one more time.

Through the blur of tears she stood up and reached for a towel. Beneath the door to the hallway was a shadow. It lingered there for a moment then moved away. She barely dried herself before running to the other room to fetch her robe.

Alyce came into Eryn's room and room service followed shortly. After they ate dinner Eryn stretched out on the bed, Alyce on the carpet. "I thought they only had single beds?"

"That's what he told me downstairs," said Eryn.

"Sure, you just wanted the big bed!" she teased, jumping up, standing with her hands on her hips.

"Trust me, Alyce, I'd much rather have the single bed." Eryn looked saddened by the comment.

Deep furrows appeared on Alyce's forehead. "Mother, are you feeling better now?" She sat back down on the floor, raising her eyes to meet her mothers. "You look like you're worried about something."

"I spent some time thinking about your dad, that's all."

"Will you be okay without me?" she said, getting up.

"We already had this conversation, sweetie. You know I will be. You're not that far away if you get homesick."

Alyce sauntered over to her mother. "Well, I'm going to bed now. I stayed up most of last night. Thanks for the going away party, Mother," she said, before she hugged Eryn and closed the door to her room.

Eryn put on her night shirt, but she wasn't ready to sleep. Remembering her students' papers in the car, she knew she had to check them. She promised the kids she would have their grades by Tuesday. On went her jeans and shoes, then she ran out the door.

The minute Eryn stepped into the parking lot she realized she forgot her keycard. Plain old keys, she would have remembered, but a keycard was supposed to be safer. She wasn't feeling secure at the moment. She ran to her car and rummaged through some papers in the box on the seat. Finally, she found them and her novel, and pushed the lock down on the door. As she turned to go back inside, she caught the silhouette of a man looking out a window on the second floor. He turned away, but she recognized the long hair and broad shoulders. With homework and red pen in hand she walked to the front desk and explained her embarrassing situation.

"Could I see some identification, Ms. Sterling?" the lady interrupted. "Anyone could just come in here and say they were someone else. I need to see some identification!" said the desk clerk.

"It's Mrs. Sterling, and when you let me in I *will* show you some I.D.."

"It's against our policy," the clerk said, as she looked at the title of Eryn's novel—*Hot Hotel Nights.*

Eryn blushed and said, "I'm a fifth grade teacher, I have work to correct. Never mind that. Will you please call my daughter in room 214?"

"That won't be necessary," said Mr. Prescot, as he eyed Eryn with those disturbing eyes, smiling a pleasant smile at the clerk. "I'll handle this, Mrs. Karrly. I checked Miss Sterling and her daughter in earlier."

"Well, I was only doing my job, Mr. Prescot. We can't let just anyone in here," she said, looking at Eryn with accusing eyes.

"Come with me. I'll let you back in your room." His gentle fingers took Eryn by the arm and led her to the stairway. When he bent forward, making a bowing motion, indicating she should go ahead of him, his silky hair fell from behind his ears. He took her by the arm once again when they reached the top.

Trying to ignore his fleeting touch, she was relieved when they reached her door. "Thank you, Mr. Prescot," she said, pulling her arm away, noticing she had to tug to get him to release her. Why was it familiar, the way his hair fell from behind his ears?

He took a keycard from his inside jacket pocket, slid it through the lock and opened the door for her. Eryn took a step inside, thanking him again. As she reached for the door her shirt slipped, revealing a bare shoulder. His eyes fell to the smoothness of her slightly tanned skin, lowering them even more when he realized one full breast was nearly exposed. Nervously, her fingers fumbled as she tried to pull the shirt back up causing her to drop some pages of homework, and her steamy novel. They both bent over to pick them up, and again her shoulder became bare. Quickly, she stood up, reaching for the folder. He looked at her lips, moistening his own as he bore his wanting eyes into hers.

Again, Eryn felt that shiver. She grabbed the papers and book. Let his mind wander! she thought, trying to hide her blushing cheeks. "Good night, I'll remember my card the next time," she said, closing the door.

He straightened his shoulders, quickly sticking his foot in. He leaned into the room and with the same awry smile, he asked, "Do you need me to check your room? You are in here alone...right?"

"No thank you," she said quickly. "I feel perfectly safe."

He stood there, watching, thinking, wondering if she really could remember nothing.

She stared right back with a look of defiance, casually closing the door on those craving eyes. As she slid the dead bolt across the door jamb she heard him laugh as he turned away.

He left her nervous, feeling out of control, and she didn't like that. She leaned against the door, refusing to let herself cry. Why did she feel so defenseless? And warm? Warm in places that hadn't been warm for some time.

Chapter 2

Uriah Prescot leaned against the wall when he left her room. Thankfully, it was there to hold his quivering, lean frame. He remembered back to many years ago. The same woman who walked into his inn this night was the same woman who walked away from him a long, long time ago. Was it really twenty years ago? *Twenty years plus a century?* She was but a girl-woman then. The sea-blue eyes were the same, but he didn't see the love in them, the love that was once for him. Yes, she had grown into the beautiful woman he knew she would. And he loved her as much as he did on the day she left.

The girl opened her door and came face to face with the man in the hall. They exchanged glances and he felt drawn to her. She looked to be around twenty years old and resembled her mother, and he saw something familiar in her eyes. She went back inside her room and he allowed his pulse to return to normal.

Eryn had returned. But she didn't remember him. It didn't matter— his Eryn, his Sweet Eryn had returned.

* * *

Eryn, her restlessness finally calmed, settled down with the papers to grade, and candy she received earlier. She forgot all the strange happenings as she became engrossed in her students' work. After awhile she put the corrected papers away and opened the trashy novel.

Finally, she turned off the light and snuggled under the covers. She thought of her daughter, hoping she would do okay. Her transfer went through at the university. Alyce, and her sister, Avis, missed Taylor in a way, but the home atmosphere was much calmer now. As she lay in bed thinking of him she could again feel his hands, smooth, manicured hands that sometimes hurt her. But at times her body became confused, still yearning for him…for someone. She began to drift off to sleep, and from somewhere in the night, and somewhere in her dream, the eyes, the amber brown eyes were smiling at her…but on this night they had a face, and long blond hair.

* * *

She had a restful night, but somehow knew she had dreamed. She couldn't recall exactly what it was, but there was an inkling of remembrance. As she brushed her hair, pulling it back she sensed something unusual. It caused her to remember a part of her dream. There was a table in a café; yes, she was sitting across from a man. If history proved her right, she was adequately dressed for the nineteenth century. Her hair looked quite red, pulled back, cascading in curls over her shoulder. It was the look in her eyes that captivated her even in the dream. They seemed to hold a tremendous longing for the man she spoke with.

As she continued to think, she dropped her hair, looking closer into the mirror, not really seeing herself but remembering more of the dream. She took leave of her present surroundings, forcing herself to remember. The man had large hands, and in his left hand was a ring. Yes, it was the ring she had specially made for her husband. His face was shadowed and in the shade she couldn't see the color of his hair. The dream was otherwise so vivid! She shook her head to bring her thoughts back to the present. The feeling of being drawn into this wouldn't leave her.

* * *

While they sat in the dining room, Eryn tried to explain what she saw the night before, leading up to her dream.

"That's impossible, Mother. It must have been the fog and the tiredness."

"But I can't explain these feelings," said Eryn. "I can't figure it out."

"We miss Dad. But we'll get over it; he probably already did."

"No, it seems like there's more to this than just him."

Alyce reached across the table, putting her hand on Eryn's. "When you aren't in this mood, you do seem happier. Isn't it really better? Better without…"

"Please don't say it, young lady!"

"Are you sure you'll be okay with me at school? Maybe I shouldn't go now."

"I'll be fine," she said, picking up her napkin. "I know you need to be away, I understand. I get like this sometimes. I think I dreamed about him last night." Or someone, she thought. "Let's eat."

* * *

After returning she would browse around some of the boutiques, and explore the tiny book store she saw on her way through town. After reading that novel last night she wanted something a little more refreshing and up to her standards. Maybe she could even find the classic she searched for. This could very well be the store to find it in.

Before popping a chocolate candy into her mouth, she was startled by a knock at her door. She asked who it was, walking over to look through the peep-hole.

"I've come to take your luggage, Mrs. Sterling," said a man from the hallway.

She peeked through the door then opened it. "I'll be returning later this afternoon, but you may get my daughter's luggage. She's in the next room."

"My pleasure! I've seen your daughter."

25

Eryn saw his smile and liked him right away. "Here, let me give you a tip anyway," Eryn said.

"No, thank you, Ma'am. We don't accept tips."

"But the girl did last night…oops! I don't want to get anyone in trouble," Eryn said, frowning.

He threw his hands in the air. "New people are hard to train. Room service know they aren't supposed to accept tips. That's why he continues to pay so well." He started to walk out. "Mr. Prescot will have to know about this. I wish it wasn't me that had to tell him. He usually hires good people."

"Wait! It wasn't room service. Actually, she refused the tip I offered. It was the girl that brought the complimentary gift…you know, the rose and candy."

He spun around, his eyes narrowed. "Mrs. Sterling, we—I don't know how to say this, but this inn doesn't give complimentary gifts. The *owner* gives gifts."

Suddenly she felt that chill again, as she pointed to the half eaten box of Swiss chocolates and the wilted rose. "Last night a young girl brought this. After she left I looked out the door and saw her talking to Mr. Prescot. I thought it was a nice gesture."

"Mrs. Sterling," said the young man, "just between us, and I do mean between us. The gift might not have been given with good intentions. Like I said, there's no policy about complimentary gifts."

"Whatever do you mean?" asked Eryn, now a little baffled.

Before he closed the door, he said, "Never mind that. When you come back later, please use your dead bolt. I'll get your daughter's luggage now."

Chapter 3

It was a splendid fall day and the town was preparing for a festival. As Eryn walked down the main street she headed toward the historical part of town, learning that it was founded in 1795. She browsed in and out of buildings. There were at least twenty different styles of Victorian architecture. The small book store was a little farther, but when she got there it was closed. A quaint little tea room looked inviting so she entered and ordered a scone with a pot of tea. The book store would be opened soon; she would wait.

An elderly lady was the only other customer. Her smile was friendly and Eryn wondered why she would be eating alone. She looked to be around seventy. Her gray hair was yellowed in places and twisted into a bun with a pretty silver comb adorning it. She looked to be tall and slightly plump. Eryn could see a large brown mole on the left side of her forehead. Beneath her stylish spectacles were soft, brown eyes.

Suddenly she appeared in front of Eryn. "Forgive me for asking, dear, but do we know each other? My mind isn't what it used to be."

"No, I don't think so," Eryn said. "I'm just visiting your beautiful town."

The waiter brought her Earl Grey tea, asking if she was changing tables.

"No," she said, turning toward her own table.

"Please, sit here," Eryn said.

"Won't it be a bother, Miss?"

"I'm here alone anyway, I'd like the company. Please sit down."

She accepted and the waiter refilled Eryn's teapot too.

"You're very kind. My name is Hanah Grace."

"I can see why you come here. It's cozy and relaxing. I love places like this. Hi, my name is Eryn, Eryn Sterling," she said, extending her hand to introduce herself.

"Are you new to our town, Eryn?"

"No, I'm not. I was driving through last night. The fog was so thick I could barely see to drive. I never liked the fog. I have a room at the Enchanted Inn."

"Yes, that Mr. Pres…Prescot owns that inn," stated Ms. Grace in an accusing tone.

"I met him last night," said Eryn.

"Well, you watch yourself with him, dear. I've heard a story about that man."

Eryn tried to hide her strange feelings for him, hoping this gentle stranger couldn't read her eyes.

"You look awfully familiar, Eryn. Are you sure we haven't met?"

"I really don't think so. I've never been here before."

"I've seen your face somewhere, but they do say everyone has a look-a-like." She continued, "How long are you staying, and if you don't mind my asking, what brings you here alone?"

"I think I'll be leaving tomorrow, but I'm not sure," said Eryn. "And I don't mind you asking. I took my daughter, Alyce, up to the campus. She decided to live on her own for awhile."

"Oh, just one child?"

"Alyce is a twin. Our first born. They're not identical. Avis is a photographer with a famous travel magazine. She travels all over the world."

"What does your Alyce go to school for?"

"She wants to be a bio-chemical engineer…like her father. How long have you lived here, Ms. Grace?" asked Eryn, trying to change the subject.

"Oh, I was born here. I know 'bout everybody here, 'cept for a few newcomer's, and that Mr. Prescot." She put her hand on top of Eryn's, patting it. "Good Heavens, it's time for me to leave. You remember what I said about watching yourself, dear. You be careful now."

She took her cane from the back of the chair and stood up. "It has been such a pleasure to meet you. I wish I could remember where I've seen you."

Eryn knew it was about time to go back to the book store so she stood with her new friend. "Wait," she said, "let me walk you to the door."

Eryn went on toward the book store, but remembered her package. She turned so abruptly that she ran head-on into Uriah Prescot who had been directly behind her. He was so close that she had to put her hands against his chest to keep from pressing right against him. After a half-hearted apology she attempted to go back into the tea room.

He took her arm as she passed him, holding her for a moment, looking into her eyes. She was mesmerized by the stare, feeling him drawing her closer, both physically and mentally. Finally, she tugged her arm away, lowering her eyes to prevent him from seeing the surrender that she had no control over.

Her package was still by the chair, and as she bent over to pick it up, something caught her eye. As she turned to look toward the reflection, she saw a chime hanging in the corner of the front window. It dangled, barely making a sound when the door opened and closed. Why hadn't she noticed it before? Walking over for a closer look, her hair stood on end, knowing she had seen it before. She stared at it a few minutes longer, so sure it was the same chime that was in the dream she had the night before.

A movement on the outside drew her attention, and when she looked up she saw Uriah Prescot staring through the window at her. The look on his face was one of total suffering, one that made her heart flip. He turned and left as quickly as he appeared.

* * *

The store didn't fit in its surroundings. The rest of the town was kept up nicely even though the buildings were old. The book store was tiny and dilapidated. Directly to the right of it was another large home. The book store itself looked like it could have been an entrance way or foyer to a larger house. The front was in the shape of a round tower, only about twenty feet long and about fourteen feet wide, two stories with a tall steep roof. As Eryn walked closer she saw another room was added to the back.

Inside, there was a strong wooden door that separated the two rooms. Although it looked gloomy from the outside it was quite nice inside. It had the smell of old books—kind of musty, and leather. There was a cranberry scent coming from a large candle, but the smell of pipe tobacco overpowered everything. Two chairs sat around a wood table. A candy dish filled with chocolate drops sat next to a Tiffany lamp.

Old photographs hung crooked on the walls. One in particular drew her attention. It was considerably large, and must have been tinted with color. When she looked close at the picture of the young girl she felt kind of eerie, for it resembled her. "Maybe that's why I looked familiar to Hanah," she whispered.

The girl was swinging on a tree swing with someone pushing her from behind. Her long, red hair was blowing in the breeze, and she was leaning back with her eyes closed, a child's smile on her face. A tall, genuine windmill sat in the background.

She was delighted to be among such history; she felt at home. Walking around, she noticed new best sellers, as well as, old classics. Her hopes of finding her missing classic grew.

The clerk came out of the back room, dropping some books as he quickly shut the door. "Afternoon, Ma'am, I didn't hear the bell," said the older gentleman.

"Hi. I'm not sure I heard it either," said Eryn, as the old man went over to see if it was working.

He opened and closed the door several times and sure enough, no ring. "Will you hold this stool for an old man?"

"Why don't you let me do it for you." Eryn stepped up on the stool, straining to get the hook over the door. "There."

"Why, thank you, Mrs. I need to hear that because I spend a lot of time in the back room. I have my old favorites back there. Ya know what I mean? My private collection of classics."

"I love old books!" She jumped and clapped her hands like a child being given a piece of candy. "That's why I came in here. I'm interested in the late 1800's. Eighteen eighty-two to be exact." Her hands were still clasped in front of her.

"Well, Missy, that's around my favorite time, too. I wasn't even a spot on the globe at the time, but I think it was a grand time to live. Ya know what I mean?"

"Yes, I do. Is this your building, Mr....?"

Just then four children ran inside the door, laughing and pushing. The old man went to the counter and took out a round glass bowl filled with gum balls. He let the boys reach inside and choose their own color. He mused up one boy's hair, and laughed with them.

Soon it was quiet again, and he came back to Eryn, never forgetting her last question. "Most folks call me Emmet, Emmet McDanil."

"Have you lived in Enchantment long?" asked Eryn, as she accepted some of the chocolate drops he offered.

"Oh, my, I was born in the house that used to be attached. That was...let me think," he said, as he squinted his eyes and scratched his head. "That was 19—, well, a long time ago, Missy! You new here?"

"My name is Eryn Sterling, and I'm only traveling through. I stopped last night; it was the fog. I think your town is beautiful!"

"Thank you, Eryn Sterling. We like it here and we all try to keep it up, but I ain't as young as I used to be so I have it hard sometimes." Another group of kids came in the door, and once again, Emmet gave them gum balls.

"You must know Hanah Grace," she asked, walking over to the counter.

"We go back a long ways, me and Hanah." He motioned for her to wait one minute while he walked to the door with the kids. "How'd you come to know her?"

"I met her a little while ago. Very nice lady."

"That she is," he said, as he walked over to a book shelf. "That she is."

"Do you think I could go in your back room to see your special books?"

"No, no. It's in a shambles now, my dear. It's not meant for visitors," he said, as he motioned for Eryn to follow him to the decorated corner.

"Please sit down and I'll bring you one special book." On his way to the back room he stopped and looked at the picture of the girl, scratched his whiskers and shook his head, then left.

In the furnished area she sat down, waiting as he backed into the other room, keeping an eye on her. She thought it very strange that he didn't want her to go with him. Maybe he worried she would damage his books. After all, they were his private collection. She popped a red M&M in her mouth, knowing she would respect his request and wait for him at the table.

He looked to be in good shape for a man his age, probably around five foot nine, thin, about 145 pounds. His hair was gray but still had a touch of black at the crown. When he walked he leaned forward just a bit. She noticed that his hands were large, his fingers long. His skin was very smooth.

He stumbled through the door with a large, dusty, hard bound book under his arm and a few smaller ones. Eryn got up, dashing over to hold the door open, but he quickly squeezed through it, nearly dropping the books. Was he trying to prevent her from seeing in the back room? They went back to the table and Eryn began to turn the pages of the old, worn book. The first thing she wanted to see was the year the book was printed and soon found her answer as Emmet began to tell her about it.

"This book was the first and only one my granddad gave me as a boy. I was...let me think. Must have been 'bout ten years old."

Eryn found the page as he was talking, showing him the date.

"He gave this one because—well, look at the writer's name," he said, closing the book, showing Eryn the cover.

"Oh, it's written by—Emmet S. McDanil. Is this your grandfather?"

"Yep, that it is, my dear," Emmet said with great pride. "He wrote these stories for me," he said, reaching for an M&M. "Look on the next page."

As Eryn read the words she glanced up at Emmet, observing a look of sadness. "Is something wrong, Mr. McDanil?" she asked, touching his shoulder.

"Yep, and no, my dear. You see, my granddad died just after he printed this. It was in the house attached to this one. He burned in the fire..." His eyes trailed off to the floor. "That part is sad for me, but the memories of him make me happy again." He stood up a moment, looked at a photograph on the wall then sat back down beside Eryn. "The night of the fire he brought this book to me and asked that I read it, but I was a sleepy lad, falling asleep before I finished it. My old granddad died that night."

He put his head in his hands and Eryn felt a sudden closeness to him. "If I had read it, I could have saved him! He wrote about the fire." He stared directly at Eryn when he said the words.

"What did you say? How could you have saved him?"

"You won't understand."

"Why did you bring me this book if it's so sad for you?"

"I got to show you something," he said, taking the book from her. "First, take a look at these."

He took the large book from her hands and she accepted the others without question. Thumbing through one, she felt a familiarity about it. "These books aren't quite as old are they? I may have seen this one before."

He didn't seem to be listening.

He startled her out of concentrating on what she was reading. "Do you have children, Mrs.?" he asked when he took a comb from his pocket, combing his coarse hair forward from the top of his head.

"Yes! I have twin girls."

"Twins? Are they at home with your husband or here with you?" he asked, while he looked into her eyes.

"Well, one is at college and...why do you ask me this?"

He gave a nervous laugh, motioning for her to continue with what she was reading. She did continue but was interrupted again. "What brought you here last night, Mrs. Sterling?"

"Oh, it was so foggy, I could barely see the front of my car. Luckily, this town was close enough to be a refuge. Why do you ask me these questions, Mr. McDanil? Please tell me."

"Where's your man, Eryn?"

"He's... He's missing," she said, avoiding his eyes.

"I knew it as soon as I saw you." He turned to the table of contents in the large book, looking for a particular title. As he turned to the page indicated he looked Eryn right in the eyes, and said, "Mrs. Sterling, my granddad titled this book plain old, True Stories, because he was a very special man. You see, and you might not understand. I'm not sure I did 'til you walked in. I knew it was you right off! My granddad had visions, he saw things others didn't."

Eryn secretly thought of her own vision.

"He know'd what was going to happen. Don't ask me how, he just did. I never knew it 'til I read the book." He placed the book on Eryn's lap and pointed to the page, telling her to read. Emmet got up and walked to the pot belly stove, pouring two cups of tea.

Eryn looked down and read the title, *One Enchanted Foggy Night*. She quickly thought of the fog the night before. As she read, she came to a part that sent a cold chill through her. She questioned Emmet as he handed her the cup of tea. "How can this be? What does it mean?" she asked, as she reread it aloud:

"It will be a night in early fall. A fog, a terrible, terrible fog will bring an unknown lady, a sad lady, to Enchantment. Her hair will be the color of roasted chestnuts, and her eyes will be like no other eyes you have seen. They will be the color of tropical waters. She's alone and searching for someone. You can help her. She went through childbirth once, but bore two. She will find trouble and be with the wrong man. You can help her...."

The cup in her hands began to tremble. Emmet took it. She leaned back on the recliner disbelieving what she just read. He took the book from her, but she reached out for it in vain.

Then, almost without realizing it, the door opened and Uriah Prescot entered. Emmet shoved the book on the bottom shelf of the table, getting up as quickly as his porous old bones allowed. Mr. Prescot looked at Eryn in a way she couldn't comprehend. He frowned at Emmet, taking him by the arm. "I want to talk to you about a trip," he said, leading him away from Eryn.

Eryn was not a bit pleased with the way he came in and startled the old man. She was shaken from what she read and his behavior was too much for her. All she could make out was a nod from Emmet and a definite no from Uriah Prescot. It was obvious they weren't coming to a compromise. She jumped up and walked toward the two men, noticing he still held Emmet's arm.

Touching his hand, she said, "Mr. Prescot, I don't know what's going on here, but what gives you the right to barge in like this?"

"You're right *Ms.* Sterling! You *don't* know what's going on so please stay out of this, Madam."

He was like a different person from the one she met the night before. Why the strange behavior? "I think you should leave, please, Mr. Prescot."

Eryn was surprised when he left Emmet's side and came up to her, leaning close to her face…with his damn beautiful eyes too close! He took her by the shoulders, speaking in a low voice. "When are you leaving?"

"To…yes, tonight." She wasn't intimidated easily, but something in his eyes and the way he asked confused her beyond reason. She didn't know if he asked because he wanted her to leave, or because he truly wanted to know. He loosened his hold on her, but was still too close, and he smiled with that cute crooked smile again. Even though she was unsure of him something warm rushed over her body. Oh, that familiar touch!

"Well, if you need anything—or anyone, let me know." His darkening eyes burned straightforward into her soul. "I'll be more than happy to oblige you." Slowly, intentionally, the tip of his tongue stroked his bottom lip. A half smile appeared and he deliberately reached over and touched her face. A recognizable look of yearning outlined his handsome features. He ran his fingers softly down her neck, mischievously playing with her collar. Boldly, his fingers found her top button and he unbuttoned it so easily she hardly knew it. That wistful look he carried grew more intense.

She reached out to remove his hand, but he took her fingers and leaned closer, his breath against her ear, whispering, "I'll see you before you leave." Then he glanced at Emmet, leaving only the fragrance of his aftershave in his wake.

Eryn and Emmet stood, staring at one another, both stunned. "Mr. McDanil, I know it's not my business, but what's going on here?"

"Mrs. Sterling, it's better that you stay out of this. He's a strange man, that one."

"But what upset him so much, and what did I have to do with it?"

"It's nothing," Emmet said, but didn't sound very convincing. "Please sit down and finish your tea. He won't be back. His point was made."

"Mr. McDanil. How did you know I was Mrs., not Miss Sterling? I didn't say one way or the other."

He picked up the book from the table, and said, "I read the end of the story."

"What does that mean? There's a thousand other women that could have been written about."

He repeated, "I read the end of the story."

"You can't leave me hanging like this, Mr. McDanil. Please tell me something."

"You must leave town. You must leave tonight and don't come back!"

"What? Why not?"

Emmet stood there and closed his eyes. "Your hair is brown, like chestnuts, you have twins. Your husband is gone. Look at your eyes, they're beautiful. You must leave!"

Eryn looked at the book, remembering.

Emmet, his eyes still closed, bowed his head. "I think it's time to talk, but not now. I have to go over this myself first. I don't mean to leave you waiting, but please try to understand. Let me find a way to tell it. Eryn, stay somewheres else tonight."

"Please tell me something. Anything?"

"No, can't do it right now. Please go and let me think. Remember— stay at another inn tonight. Tomorrow is another day, Missy. We'll talk then."

Eryn looked in his eyes, knowing he wouldn't budge in his thinking. When she got up he took her hands in his.

"Don't be alone with him. He may only bring you… Never mind. I can tell you, you'll be happy again one day. Trust me." He opened the door for her. "I know you don't want to go, and I wonder myself if you should." As she stepped out, he said, "Eryn, if…if somethin' should happen to this old man, your answer can be found in my back room."

She looked at him with questioning eyes and started to reach out for the book in his hands.

He looked back at her, slowly closing the door. "I doubt my own thoughts about letting you go, but it's best this way."

She waited for a moment, hoping he would change his mind, but he didn't open the door.

Once again she looked at the western sky, seeing the same beautiful gold and pink hues along the horizon. It had been a little more then twenty-four hours since she arrived in Enchantment and, to Eryn, it was the most uncanny hours she had ever spent. The fog was already rolling up from the valleys. The cool mountain air and the moisture from the cold Allegheny River brought the fog in rapidly, as it did the night before.

She was disappointed with herself for bowing down to Mr. Uriah Prescot's peculiar power. Why try to figure out the man! Fog crept through Enchantment and she wished she hadn't told him she would leave tonight. As she walked across town she decided it would be better to leave the inn, but the fog—She couldn't leave in the fog! She would talk to Emmet tomorrow then she would understand. Everything would be okay tomorrow.

As she approached Sweet Nicole's Tea Room, she read the sign that bragged *"A Victorian Tea Room,"* and advertised Tea Sandwiches, Imported Teas and Coffee, Scones with a dollop of Devon Cream, and delicious Tea Sandwiches!. She could hear the tinkle of the chime as customers came and went. What did it all mean? How could she come to the realization of what she read, what she dreamed? She couldn't understand what her visions meant, maybe she never would. But she knew that tomorrow she would leave this town, this beautiful town that made her so confused.

Continuing toward the inn she knew one thing was certainly clear. It was those eyes, his eyes, his amber eyes that searched her soul from somewhere, and for some unknown reason. It made no difference to her that Emmet warned her of danger. Not if it meant finding the reason why those same eyes haunted her for twenty years. Was he a part of her past…the past she knew nothing about?

Chapter 4

She came upon the main entrance of the inn and stood a moment, hoping the owner wouldn't be at the desk. When she went inside she searched her purse for her entry card. Feeling it on the bottom she climbed the stairs. Half way up she turned to take one last look at the inn. It was carefully decorated in a country theme with a touch of the nineteenth century. She had such a strong feeling for the place but knew not why. Strange how she felt at home here, not wanting to go this night. From the dining room came the familiar voice of the inn's owner along with what sounded like the girl who brought the gift the night before.

Eryn was angry at him for being so rude to Emmet. He was a sweet old man and if she thought about it long enough, she'd march in there and make a scene! Knowing she wouldn't do that in the man's own inn, she turned and continued to her room.

Upon opening her door she immediately noticed the rosebud lying on her pillow. She walked over and picked it up, inhaled its sweet fragrance, opened the door, and dropped it. Roses were her favorite, but not when they came from that knave! Feeling proud, she grabbed her suitcase. Recklessly she folded and packed her clothes and the few personal belongings she brought with her. In the middle of wrapping the cord around her dryer, she lit a candle and inhaled its rosy scent. What is it with this man and roses? she wondered.

It sounded like someone fell against her door, then someone pounded on it. She looked through the peep-hole and wasn't happy to see Uriah Prescot, the knave himself, standing there, or leaning there.

"Ms. Matheson, er…Sterling, I want to apologize. Open the door, I know you're in there, I saw you come in." His laughter rang through her ears, and with a sing-song attitude, he said, "I'll use my card and let myself in if you don't!"

He wouldn't dare! She heard him scraping something against the door, knowing he would do exactly what he said. Eryn didn't want to give him the chance so she jerked the door open, closing it back nearly knocking him over as he stepped in. "Say what you have to say from *right* there!" The smell of whiskey reeked from him and he had to hold himself up against the jamb. Suddenly he straightened up and pushed his way inside, closing the door behind him.

He drove her toward the bed but she ducked to the side, nearly out of his reach. He grinned as he took hold of her arm, at the same time removing the wilting rose from his lapel, tossing it on the bed.

"You really should accept my gifts. They just may be appreciated one day," he said, with that smile on his face, not caring that a hiccup slipped out.

"I see no reason to accept anything from you," Eryn said. "I came here to get out of the fog. That's all! And why were you so rude to Mr. McDanil? Why do you suddenly want me involved in your life?"

"Oh, so many questions! But I don't owe you any answers. Giving you a flower doesn't mean I want you involved in my life." He hesitated. "But I do," he said pulling her to him. "By the way…I thought you were leaving."

"I am. I would have been gone by now if you weren't holding yourself up in my way—now let me go."

"Please, don't leave tonight," he said, suddenly sounding as sober as a nun. "The fog is already thick. I'm sorry you thought I wanted you to leave tonight." He took her hands in his. "I don't want you to leave…ever."

There went his eyes again, boring straight into hers, invisibly touching, shaking her soul!

He took her hand, gently pressing his lips against her fingers, his amber stare hypnotic. All of a sudden he didn't seem like a stranger to her, but he was, and she was unsure of his intention. He moved closer forcing her back against the dresser.

The candlelight casts monstrous shadows on the wall, making them look like lovers not strangers. Uriah looked in her wary eyes, trying, hoping to read something in them. Damn, Eryn, don't you know me! he thought. It's me! It's me! He wanted to take her in his arms, God, he wanted to love her, but he released his hold, backing away. He had too much to drink and it was hard for him to control himself. "I owe you an apology, that's why I came here." In truth, he meant what he said. "I'm sorry for this behavior, and my behavior in the old man's store." He slipped his hands in his front pockets, then reconsidered, and grasped her shoulders. "You don't understand." Uriah released her again, nervously lifting his hair away from his neck. "Stay and have dinner on the house tonight. Please." As quickly as he came in, he went out.

Eryn was so confused she didn't know what to do. Something about his eyes in the candlelight. Oh, he's familiar to me, she thought. I know him from somewhere, I do. She couldn't admit it to herself that she felt a warmth, *no*, a fever spread over her when he was close. She sat on the bed, trying to sort it out. Visions, familiar faces, a man that sees the future. Eryn thought about all those things, but what roused her curiosity most were the eyes she kept picturing in her head. What about the rear-view mirror image? she thought. What about the dreams? What about…what about….

She walked to the window, pulling back the curtain. The sun had set and the fog was as thick as he said. She would stay. While pacing around the room she lit a few more candles, then sat down. Oh, no! She didn't remember to get herself a book at the bookstore. There was no choice but to finish *Hot Hotel Nights!*

* * *

The dining room was warm and inviting. Nights cool off quickly in the mountains and the small fire in the fireplace crackled. It wasn't crowded for a Sunday evening, but everyone might still be in church. She probably just missed the dinner rush. Eryn knew she had to get out of her room because there was enough tears the night before, and she couldn't face the long night sitting up there alone. A corner table allowed her to see the entrance. Being able to face the door was nearly always her choice. This time she was glad because she saw Hanah Grace come in. She stood, beckoning the old woman over.

"I'm surprised to see you here, Ms. Grace."

"I was hoping to speak with you my dear, Eryn," said Hanah. "I spoke with Emmet and he told me about your meeting."

"Yes, he's very likeable and he told me he's known you forever."

"He told me about that Mr. Prescot," she whispered. "I told you to watch out for him. You take Emmet's advice to heart now. Don't stay here tonight, dearest."

"I don't know what made him burst in and behave the way he did. He's a difficult man to understand," said Eryn. "I was so angry with him, then he came over and told me to stay out of it. Now he asked me not to leave in this fog." Eryn shook her head, still confused.

Hanah patted Eryn's hand, telling her she understood her feelings, then said, "Tell me about yourself. I see sadness in your eyes. What makes you so sad?"

Eryn watched her, wondering if she should reveal her personal life but as she thought, she had an uncanny feeling that she needed to talk to Hanah. Eryn began, "You're right about the sadness. I thought I kept it hidden well, but since I arrived in this town, strange things have been happening. Things I can't explain or understand. Like I told you earlier, I stopped here last night because of the fog. I never did like the fog and I've never seen it like it was last night."

"Typical in the mountains, dear," she said, sipping her tea as she listened.

"It was ten months ago when my husband, Taylor, disappeared. I have no clue as to where or why." Eryn could feel a lump rising in her throat and didn't want to cry. "One day he was here, then he was gone. No one seems to know what happened. His files remain untouched in his laboratory. I don't even know what he was working on."

Eryn began to sob and Hanah moved closer, hugging her. "Here, dear, take this hankie and dry those tears. Don't say anymore. I was in love when I was a young girl and I lost him. I understand completely." Eryn looked at Hanah and hoped she wouldn't be alone when she was her age.

The same boy who took the luggage earlier brought their chicken dinner and Hanah encouraged Eryn to eat something. He smiled at Eryn as he poured both ladies more tea. It was a friendly smile. He was about the same age as her girls. His hair was nearly black, needing a good trim. It hung long in the front, covering his eyes, which showed crystal blue when he swept his hair back. He was about six feet tall, give or take a few inches, with a stocky kind of build. A summer tan still remained. Eryn noticed he had a large scar on the top of his right hand.

When he left, she looked up, seeing Uriah standing in the foyer looking through the doorway at her. His hair was loose and combed behind his ears, falling past his shoulders to the middle of his back. Seeing him standing like that brought familiar feelings back to her. She couldn't place the feeling or the reason she trembled. All she knew at this very moment was she sure liked the look of him.

That sly, ominous smile was on his face; he stood with arms folded, one hand stroking his mustache as if in deep thought. The light reflected off a ring on his finger, a ring that looked too familiar, but she couldn't be sure from this distance. He was wearing a loose pair of Levi jeans, a light blue cotton pullover shirt, and a gray leather vest. The smell of leather, still lingering on her memory from the short episode that just took place in her room.

When he realized her gaze was upon him he turned and left. Eryn suddenly couldn't wait to leave Enchantment, the town that had drawn her in. Her gloomy emotions were as crestfallen as the hidden sun on a cloudy day. Finally, she had to tell Hanah she wanted to go to her room. The meals were put on her bill. She wouldn't accept his offer of dinner on the house.

Before she reached the first step Mr. Prescot slipped from behind the door, cautiously took her arm and turned her toward him. "I'm sorry you're so sad," he said, sincerely. His touch still lingered on her skin after he was gone. She stood with her head down, then raised her eyes to look at Ms. Grace standing in the doorway. Hanah walked over and took Eryn's hand, noticing the compassionate look on his face as he walked by her. A look out of character for Uriah Prescot.

* * *

Eryn was tossing and turning, thinking the sound she heard was in her dream, but reality struck and she knew the sirens were real. She jumped out of bed with a sick feeling, running to the window. The rescue truck raced past her, people were running down the street. She unlocked her window and raised it so she could look to where they ran. A scream ripped from her throat when she saw where they went!

She threw on her clothes and ran out to where the fire was burning. All that was left to the front of the book store was its name hanging on a broken post. She ran through the crowd to the front where people were crying. One young girl told another that Mr. McDanil was such a sweet man, it was too bad about what happened. Eryn grabbed the girl, asking her what happened to Emmet, and where they took him. The girl told Eryn that it didn't look good and he was on his way to the hospital. "The rescue truck left about ten minutes ago," said the girl.

She tried to get near the charred building, but the police wouldn't let her. A policeman turned to get a boy away and Eryn stepped forward, viewing something on the ground. She walked closer, bending down to pick it up when no one was looking. It was familiar to her, knowing a few hours earlier she held it in her hands. As she turned it over she read, *True Stories*, on the charred cover. Most of the book was gone. She hugged the water soaked cover close to her, watching her future wash away with the dirty black water. Turning to go she glimpsed a man ducking behind the building next door. Albeit, she didn't care about the lanky man she recognized, only about Emmet. She asked a policeman for directions to the hospital, planning to check on her friend, herself. As she ran down the street she silently said a prayer for the rickety old man that knew her future.

* * *

Eryn paced as she waited for an answer. No one wanted to tell her anything because she wasn't a relative but, somehow, she managed to convince a nurse she was a very close friend of Emmet's. She promised to try to find out his condition. As Eryn waited she reminisced over meeting with him, feeling like she had known him for a long time.

Eryn wondered what he meant when he told her the answer was in his back room. She brought out the partial book from under her jacket, wondering where the rest of it was. Then she remembered seeing Uriah Prescot. Why was he there? Why did Emmet tell me to leave the inn and what did he mean, he knew the end of the story? So confusing, she thought. It also said she would be with the wrong man. That part scared her. Chills caused her whole body to shudder. A man that looked much too young to be a doctor appeared in front of her, startling her out of her thoughts.

"Mrs. Sterling, I'm Dr. Lincoln. Nurse Abcott told me you would like some information on Mr. McDanil."

"Yes, Dr. Lincoln, how is he? Will he be okay? Please tell me."

"It's against our policy to tell non-family members about the diagnosis and prognosis of our patients."

"I know, but Emmet is a close friend. Please pretend I'm a relative, can't you just once?" Just then Hanah Grace came in and Dr. Lincoln went to her immediately.

"Hanah, I'm sorry to have called you at such a late hour, but I knew you'd want to be here," said the doctor.

"You did the right thing, C.J.." She hugged him, the concern showing on her face. Reaching out for Eryn's hand, the three of them sat down together. The same nurse brought some coffee. The two women stared at each other while the doctor told them that Emmet was still in a coma. Telling them his hand had been badly burned trying to rescue his books, and a burning beam hit him on the head. His vital signs were fair and they hoped he would come out of his coma within forty-eight hours. Dr. Lincoln told the women the first two days would be critical, but as long as his vital signs held he had a good chance.

44

"Well, ladies, I have to get back to my patient." Before he left he turned to Eryn, telling her he was sorry for holding back information.

"I understand, and thank you, Doctor."

She and Hanah remained in the waiting room for two more hours. Unfortunately, there had been no change in Emmet's condition. The doctor insisted they leave and return in the morning. He walked them to the elevator and out to the parking lot. Once in the car, Hanah convinced Eryn to grab some clothes and spend the night at her house.

Chapter 5

The fog had lifted and most of the trip to Hanah's house was clear. There were occasional patches, but it wasn't as hazardous as the night before. The near full moon peeked out now and then to light the way. When Eryn pulled into the driveway she was amazed that Hanah lived in a grand home, proudly built in the mid-nineteenth century. It was about three miles outside of Enchantment.

The housekeeper waved from the veranda, glad to see Hanah back home. She was in her sixties and it was obvious she was fond of her employer. Eryn's eyes lit up when Hanah briefly showed her the main floor of the house, eventually leading her up the elegant stairway to one of the guest rooms.

"My room is two down from here," Hanah pointed to the right, "if you should need anything, dear." She raised her hand to her mouth to cover a sleepy yawn. "The bathroom is across from you. Switch the electric heater on if you're in there very long. Do you need anything?"

She looked down at her clothes, mentioning that she forgot to grab her nightshirt. Eryn looked at her watch. It was nearly one-thirty.

"We'll get you something to sleep in, dear, and if there's nothing else, I'll take this old body and say good-night."

Just then Mrs. Hendric came in with a nightgown for Eryn.

"It looks like a perfect fit, doesn't it, Rachael," said Hanah. It was light blue with a scoop neck and cap sleeves. The silk was pure and old, not the new washable silk that Eryn owned. Eryn thanked the women. Hanah hugged her good-night and left for bed.

She undressed, slipping the gown over her head feeling it slip easily over her toned body. The lace at the bottom brushed the floor, flaring out in the back. It reminded her of something she had seen in some old, fashion catalogs.

The hazy moon went behind a cloud leaving the night black. A branch scraped across the window pane, startling her. She shrugged it off, guiltlessly admiring herself in the mirror. A perfect fit, she thought. She sat down at the dressing table, brushing out her hair. In her mind she saw a reflection of Uriah Prescot. He was smiling at her, standing in a field of daisies, but he looked younger.

A clang against the window caused her to jump. As she leaned over the window seat to look outside, her gown slipped from her shoulder, and before the moon went behind another cloud, she thought there was a movement near a tree in the backyard. When the moon reappeared she looked to the same spot, but saw nothing. Was there a musky fragrance riding on the air, maybe a hint of spice, too?

Her thoughts went back to Emmet and his parting words about the answers. She took the afghan off the wing-backed chair, wrapping it around herself. After opening the door she admired the glow of oil lamps softly burning in the hallway, then she reconsidered and went to bed. Hanah was probably asleep now anyway. She climbed into the high, large bed that Rachael had turned down earlier. The smell of it was serene and pure. It was comfortable and the comforter was soft and soothing. She might need the warmth tonight. An autumn chill was in the air.

She finally drifted off to sleep. In her dreams she had visions of a man who once loved her wholeheartedly. Eryn moaned in her sleep, unaware that her body still responded to the body that belonged to eyes that were still looking at her from within her dreams. She turned over, waking momentarily, reaching for the empty pillow beside her. She hugged it tightly, imagining two arms around her, holding her like they used to. She imagined the man she used to love, but when those eyes opened they weren't the sky blue eyes of her husband....

* * *

Eryn woke to the sound of a phone ringing in the distance. The sun was shining in through the bedroom window. The leaves were crimson on the maple tree outside. She smelled the aroma of strong coffee, needing a cup to chase the tiredness away. Proof of her fitful night showed in her eyes.

Albeit, that hopeful feeling was upon her again. For the past few months she thought she was adjusting well to being without Taylor. Sure, she wanted to miss him, but too many times his violent side entered her peaceful surroundings, and she didn't miss him so much. The feeling of hope quickly wilted. The past two nights in Enchantment had gotten to Eryn's emotions. Today she would take her leave.

She dragged herself out of bed, and washed. Removing her dress from its hanger she slipped it over her head. The loose neckline rested on the edge of her shoulders, and she tied the silk tie to secure it where it lay. The hemline fell to the middle of her calf; she had only worn longer dresses since Taylor left. He liked them short on her, stating she had the legs to wear them above her knees. She didn't have to impress anyone but herself, anymore.

Hanah was having coffee in the dining room. As she poured coffee for Eryn she told her that C.J. called and there was no change in Emmet. Eryn sipped her lukewarm coffee and ate a cheese Danish that Rachael served on a crystal serving tray. By the rich taste, she could tell the pastry was homemade.

"I can't stay any longer," said Eryn, sadly.

"I understand, dear. It's best you go."

"I don't want to. I don't want to run out on Emmet. Will you keep me informed, Hanah?"

"You know I will. You're welcome back at any time."

"I need to come back when Emmet gets better. You know I have to talk to him."

Eryn said good-bye to Hanah and Rachael, promising to keep in touch. She felt a sadness upon leaving the house but knew she had to get back to her comfortable, safe surroundings. The place she didn't have to worry about seeing things that confused her, or of seeing a man with golden eyes who called her by another name.

* * *

She enjoyed the drive back to Enchantment. The river was low in some areas, the shore, dark and muddy. Clouds hung low in the sky and the mountain tops projected themselves above the cloud layer. The maple, oak, birch and poplar trees were colorful with the hues of autumn.

Suddenly an ominous feeling overwhelmed her when she pulled into the parking lot of the Enchanted Inn, making her all the more anxious to get home. As she went up the stairs Uriah Prescot met her, and before she reached the top he blocked her way.

"Let me pass, Mr. Prescot, I'm checking out."

A placid smile curved his lips as he continued to seduce her with his stare. "Call me, Uriah," he said, as his gaze raked over her. "We should be past last names."

Was it a fever breaking out on her body again? Shaking that feeling aside, she tried to push past him, but he didn't budge. What was it about him? There she was, out of control of her own feelings. Defiantly she met his gaze with a threatening stare. Although he hesitated, he let her pass and she hurried the rest of the way, digging for her worthless entry card. As she inserted it in the slot she reached for the door knob, and before she knew it Uriah was behind her, ushering her into the room. He held her and his lips went immediately to hers.

"You didn't come back last night." He squeezed her tighter. "I was waiting for you, afraid you left me."

"I saw you at the fire last night," said Eryn, trying to push him away. "Why did you run off in such a hurry?"

"I had nothing to do with that fire," he said, still staring into her eyes.

"Oh! First you manhandled Emmet in his shop then got brusque with me! I still don't know why."

He whispered softly to her. "There's a time for you to know, Eryn, but not right now," His fingers easily wrapped around her arms and he pulled her close. As he did, the bow came untied allowing her dress to fall from her shoulders. She struggled to turn away from him but bumped her face against the high-boy chest. He watched her, as if wondering what to do next.

Quickly, he made up his mind and the lusty look in his eyes told her what it was. She backed away from him coming to a stop at the edge of the bed. She sat there upon it because there was no where else to go. He kneeled in front of her, tenderly caressing her hand while he looked into her eyes. Then he briefly kissed her lips.

My, God, they were warm! Oh, God, hers were willing! The taste of his kisses reminded her of someone—someone she had known with amber-hued eyes.

What ever was he doing to her? His fingers fumbled with the knot at the top of her dress, but it was caught in the gathering. Warm hands touched her skin.

When she realized what he was about to do she thought to stop him, but he slid the hem of her dress up to her thighs and drew her near, mumbling, "Eryn, you don't understand, Eryn girl, I need you," with his soft breath against her ear, tickling like a feather duster. His fingers gently wrapped around the back of her neck, drawing her hair into his fist.

She tried to squirm out of his clutches, but when he breathed the words in her ear his voice was soft, his touch wasn't new. Again, he pressed his mouth onto hers and she was confused because even though he meant to subdue her, something about it felt right.

"Uriah, no...no, you can't do this." Why were her words soft instead of convincing? Funny she didn't even believe herself.

His hands randomly roamed her body, his lips never tired of touching her. Gently they brushed across her neck, her ear, her cheek, as hungry as a bear after its winter sleep. Without realizing it she lifted her fingers to feel the silkiness of his hair, it felt so familiar. Strong but gentle hands coaxed her down onto the mattress while slowly he lowered himself onto her, and she, almost delirious with the feel of him. It was all she could do to prevent herself from crying out that, yes, she understood and, yes, she needed him too! Where was the logic? Why couldn't she pull herself away from this...this stranger with familiar eyes—familiar everything!

Tenderly he kissed her, causing the blood to surge through her veins like it never did before. For a moment, it was like a dream. For a moment, it was familiar, and for a moment she felt like she knew this wonderful man who was about to capture what no man but her dream lover had known. Her heart was wildly beating in her chest, her breaths rapid and deep.

Without removing his lips from the pulse in her neck, he whispered, "Eryn Matheson, you don't remember me. Please, girl, let me help you remember." Looking into her eyes he traced her lips, tenderly stroking her bruised chin with the pad of his fingertip.

Unaware of it until then, she found herself holding his other hand, her fingers entwined with his. She shook her head back and forth trying to bring herself to reality. "No! My name is Eryn Sterling. I'm not who you think I am."

"Oh, but you are." He touched her chin, turning her face toward his. "You are exactly who I think you are. You've returned to me, returned to us. I waited so long for you to return." He licked his parched lips. "It's been a long time, Eryn…too long."

The bristly tips of his mustache tickled her cheek as he whispered, "Your husband is gone, let me take his place. It should have been me. You loved me once, don't you remember?"

"No, no, I'm married to Taylor Sterling! Please let me go."

"I'm not here to hurt you, Eryn, only to love you." He pressed his body against hers and with his moistened lips he kissed her neck, her ear. Only seconds later his lips found hers again, and this time they were both lost in a fiery, drawn out, remarkable kiss.

The taste of him was familiar and his touch, she felt before. The heat between them intensified as he continued to kiss her. When he raised his head to look in her scared, confused eyes he released her, delicately touching her face, "I love only you, sweet Eryn, I always have, always will."

"This is wrong, please don't do this, Uriah."

"I see we're finally on a first name basis!"

"Let me up," she whispered, practically lost in his gaze.

"Nay, sweet Eryn," he said, as he leaned forward to kiss her again. "You have what I want…what I've needed and no one could give me but you."

"I'll scream—"

"Only when we share our love will you scream, Madam, but I'm sure you'll want no one to hear."

Her resistance was failing, and she couldn't make any sense out of the feelings she had for this man. Did she lose all her morals? Did her mind somehow escape her? His eyes held a look she couldn't read. She had to make him stop now, for she could no longer trust herself. Her hands went to his shoulders, pushing, but there was no give in his weight.

Deep down he knew he wouldn't go any farther if she didn't want him to. "I'm sorry." He removed his fingers and she relaxed, watching his eyes for an answer. Suddenly the door burst open and Uriah was pulled off of her.

The young waiter assumed the worse, pulling Uriah to the floor. Uriah started to swing at him but sat down on the floor instead; he didn't fight back. Cole Dawes grabbed the phone and dialed 911 as Eryn ran into the bathroom, feeling totally humiliated. Before she closed the door she heard Cole say, "You won't get away with it this time."

She heard Uriah's familiar laugh, as he said, "The door comes out of your salary, kid."

Before long a policeman knocked on the door and Eryn opened it.

"Can I come in and talk to you, Ma'am?"

Eryn opened the door and let him in. Before she closed it she saw an officer handcuffing Uriah. She felt gut-wrenching pain over the sight.

"I have to ask, Ma'am. Were you raped?"

"No," said Eryn. She sat on the vanity seat holding back the tears. "I...I, the boy stopped...no." Even as she said the words to the officer she felt ashamed and guilty because she knew it wouldn't have been forced.

"Do you want to call anyone?" asked the officer, as he examined the bruise on her chin.

"No. I just want to get my things and go home."

"We need you to come to the station and give us your statement. I'm sorry."

Eryn began to weep, but somehow contained her body's tremble. "I think I would like to call someone after all. Do you know Hanah Grace?"

"Everyone knows Miss Grace. I can call her for you."

"Thank you. Is he gone yet?"

The officer looked out the door, reassuring Eryn that she could come out. He asked someone to bring ice for her chin which had taken on a nasty purple-blue color.

What seemed like forever finally brought Hanah to her room. "I don't know if he would have hurt me."

But she *did* know he *wouldn't* hurt her and her guilt overwhelmed her. How could she tell everyone she nearly went along with him, that he excited her more than any man ever had. No, she had to leave things as they were. Later she could dismiss the charges against him. Maybe she could call from home and they would let him go. She would figure it out later, right now she only wanted to be as far away from him as she could. She wanted to go home.

"He'll be taken care of. You don't need to worry about him anymore," said Hanah. She asked the officer when they should go to the station. Since there was no assault, there was no need for evidence to be taken. Eryn appeared to be okay, except for the mark on her chin. Hanah told the officer she would have Dr. Lincoln take a look at her. Eryn went to the bathroom, filling the tub with hot water.

Afterward, she sat at the dressing table, brushing out her hair. The purple on her chin had begun to swell. Why was she strangely drawn to him? She cradled her head in her hands, sobbing again.

Nothing like this ever happened to her. Taylor was the only man she had ever known, except in her dreams, and her memories of love were nearly ruined in an instant—and she nearly allowed it. She took a minute and bowed her head to thank God for bringing the episode to an end. But she couldn't forget the remorse she felt so she said another prayer, if only to ease her own guilt.

"Please, Lord, forgive me for the lie I'm about to inflict upon this man."

* * *

Dr. Lincoln was waiting for them when they arrived, putting his arm around Eryn when he saw her. He treated a few cases in the past, but the attacker was never caught. It made him wonder if Mr. Prescot might be the man they were looking for. X-rays were ordered to see if her jaw had become dislocated. "What did he hit you with?"

"He didn't hit me!" She noticed the questioning look on his face. "I did that all by myself. When I turned away I ran into the chest beside my bed."

"Well, in a way he did it then."

"Yes, I suppose he did," she mumbled.

The results were all negative and he told her to keep a cold pack on her jaw. "The bruise will heal in a couple weeks. In the meantime I'll have a report sent to the police department, stating my findings."

"I can't thank you enough, Doctor. How is Emmet?" asked Eryn.

"I praise you, Mrs. Sterling, for thinking of the old man, especially after what you just went through." He looked up from his chart. "There's still no change. I'm sorry, I know that's not what you want to hear."

Eryn sat back and relaxed for a few minutes. She took a deep breath, inhaling the antiseptic smell.

"I want to see you again in a few days."

"I'm going home today, I have to get home. I'll see my doctor there if you think I should."

"I would like him or her to check you to make sure everything is coming along okay."

Eryn agreed, but before she left she again asked him to take extra good care of Emmet McDanil.

* * *

Cole had already given his statement and left the station. Eryn wanted to see him. The deputy told Eryn they had enough information on Uriah to charge him with assault. He also told Eryn, Uriah could pay his own bail and get out. Eryn didn't feel any better after they left the station. That little lie hung over her like a storm cloud.

When they pulled up, Cole was sitting on his porch in jeans and a T-shirt. He looked younger than he did in his work uniform. When Eryn walked up to him she felt embarrassed. He seemed to notice, trying to put her at ease.

"Cole, I came to say thank you for what you did. Why did you tell him he wouldn't get away with it this time?"

"Well, let's just say…I've seen him in action before. He had a little ordeal with another woman a while back. I shouldn't have kept quiet then."

"You've made it up by rescuing me." The lie continues, she thought. "I guess you're out of a job now."

"I'm kind of glad to be out of there. I really never got along with Uriah. He's usually an okay guy and would do anything for you. Most people don't know that part of him, but we just didn't get along."

Eryn sat next to him, taking his hand, looking into his clear, boyish eyes. "Thank you, again."

He blushed a little, shrugging his shoulders. "It was nothing, Mrs. Sterling."

She got up to leave, asking him what he would do without a job.

"I have a bit of carpentry behind me. I think I'll help Mr. McDanil rebuild his book store when he gets out of the hospital. That old guy's always been nice to me."

"We need to say a prayer for him. Cole, if there's ever anything I can do, please call me. I have to leave for home today," she said, as she wrote down her phone number and address.

"I'll be fine. I can go to school full time now. It'll be faster this way." He picked a hang nail on his finger, glancing at Eryn from the corner of his eye. "Did you say your daughter is up at the university?"

"Yes, maybe you'll run into her someday." Eryn smiled to herself, remembering what he said when he picked up their luggage. "Thank you, again," she said, taking her leave. When she got to the end of the walk she turned to wave good-bye.

"See ya in court," he yelled to her.

As she looked to the sky it looked like it might rain.

"Do you know anything about what Emmet told me?" Eryn asked as she drove Hanna home. "Did you know about his grandfather?"

"I have heard stories about him. I never thought they were true. When I was a child, I used to hear people speak of a man that could make predictions. I have talked to Emmet about him," continued Hanah.

"Do you believe them?"

"Yes. Yes, I believe I do, dear."

"Emmet told me I would be happy again. He said he read the end of the story. That part of the book is gone now." Eryn threw her hands in the air. "What *is* the end of the story?"

Hanah reached over and patted her hand. "If he told you that, then I would believe him. When he wakes up, you'll know everything. Uriah Prescot can't be a threat to you, dear. Don't be afraid of him."

Eryn was afraid. Afraid the only thing he threatened was her emotions—and her body! She summoned her composure and helped Hanah to her door. "I hate to leave now but I do have to. You're a wonderful person and I'm glad I met you."

"It was meant to be, dearest. You were meant to arrive in Enchantment. I wish it could have been different for you," Hanah said, lovingly.

Chapter 6

The trip home was long and Eryn thought about Uriah all the way, knowing she would never return to Enchantment for court. Hopefully, she could clear this whole mess up with a simple phone call. She still wanted to return when Emmet came out of his coma. Unfortunately, that might not be any time soon and she hoped to find some answers before long, or forget about the whole confusing thing. She kept remembering Uriah knew her husband was gone. How could he know that? In all logic, there was no way for him to even know Taylor, but she thought about how familiar Uriah looked—and felt.

Maybe I have seen him at Taylor's lab, she thought. But how does that explain how I know his touch? She tried to ignore the fact that she had a warm feeling just thinking about him. Something about the man with blond hair had a pull on her and she couldn't understand it. He called her by a different name—said she loved him before—said he loved her. He had love confused with something else.

The eerie visions she had were put aside somewhere in the deep spaces of her being. She would decide how to deal with them later. She could only do *one* thing at a time. Her name was Eryn Sterling, not Super-Wonderwoman!

Avis' pick-up was in the driveway when she pulled in. Eryn was glad she was there. Sitting in the car for a moment she glanced at her rear-view mirror, thinking about the visions she had seen. Maybe she would forget all that nonsense and concentrate on her life alone. Emmet was an old man. Maybe he was a little senile. What he told her couldn't be real. His grandfather was probably a kook. Maybe Emmet was too.

Avis came running out and seemed very excited. "Mom, are you okay? You were gone longer then I thought you would be." She reached in the car for Eryn's suitcase. "What's been going on? Did Alyce get settled in? Mom, what happened to your face?"

"Goodness, girl, let me get out of the car. I have so many things to tell you, I don't know if you'll understand half of it." Grabbing her luggage from Avis, she continued. "Yes, Alyce is moved in, but we need to get more of her things to her. She will have room in the apartment, it's large. I'll explain the bruise later."

That evening, Eryn was in her bedroom doing lesson plans, and Avis came in and sat beside her. "Mom, I miss Alyce already. I know it's going to be lonely for you, too. Will you be okay?"

Eryn fluffed the pillow, patting it, indicating for Avis to lie down beside her. "Let's talk, baby." Eryn touched her daughter's smooth hair. "Your hair is so light. I wonder if mine was this light when I was young. It's soft and shiny and so straight. I like the way it's cut. The short bob makes it bouncy."

"Thanks, Mom. I need something easy to take care of with everything I do. Do you know I sky-dived last week-end?" Her eyes sparkled as she spoke. "I didn't tell you until after I did it. I know you. You don't need anything else to worry about."

"I guess you're right about that," agreed Eryn. "Was it fun?"

"Wow, it was great! The peace and tranquility of being up there floating was wonderful. More fun then trying to climb Danali last year."

"You've always been the adventurer," said Eryn.

"You've always been the worrier!" said Avis, smiling at her mother.

"How long are you staying, baby?"

"Just a couple of days." She hesitated. "I was thinking about moving back home, Mom."

"Avis, I can manage living by myself. I don't want to, but I can do it."

"I'm sorry, but I want you to be happy again. I miss Daddy, too, but we can live without him. He didn't seem to care about us."

Eryn hugged her daughter and they both did their best not to cry. Avis reached up, softly stroking the discoloration. Eryn knew she had to explain the bruise.

"I was going to wait until tomorrow to tell you and Beth at the same time. Some strange things happened when we were in Enchantment—"

"Enchantment! What the heck is that?"

"It's the town we stayed in. It was so foggy we had to stop for the night. I stayed there the night after I dropped Alyce off. Made some friends there, too." Eryn told her about Hanah Grace and Emmet McDanil, and she told her about the visions. She didn't tell her about the…attack. She wanted to wait until she could tell Beth, until she could decide what to tell Beth, the truth or continue the lie. They talked a little longer and Avis went to bed.

The room was dark and she snuggled down beneath her own fresh smelling covers. She tossed a long time then sat up and lit a candle on her night table. She leaned back on her pillow, hugging the other one to her breasts. Looking around the room she saw Taylor in everything. She saw the candlelight flicker on the walls and thought of the many nights of love in the bed that she no longer shared. Then she remembered the times of anger, too. She looked at his picture on her dresser, the light reflecting in his eyes. Before she knew it she was there turning the frame face down. Back in bed she thought of the visions again. Wondering why she would see eyes the color of amber when she was married to a man with eyes the color of steel, and just as cold. The candle burned through the restless night. Her own bed felt good, but there were too many jumbled thoughts in her head. Her dreams soon turned to nightmares.

The bedroom was the same and Taylor was loving her, but the touch was not soft on her skin. She saw her own fingers betray her as they ran through blond strands. The chime was hanging in a corner and it was blowing around profusely, almost as if a storm were brewing. Taylor was there with his dark hair blowing in the breeze, and Uriah— yes—Uriah was hugging and caressing her as he took her away from where Taylor waited. Emmet was lying on the floor with a charred beam across his head. Taylor was pleading with her to come back...to come back and get him. From around a corner came a blonde woman, whispering Taylor's name. He turned when she reached her hand out to him, and she was with child. Uriah pulled Eryn through the doorway to where candlelight glowed brightly, and the room had a carpet the color of teal. Uriah gently lifted her dress over her head and she smiled into his golden eyes.

A crash suddenly woke her. She jumped out of bed to pick up her candelabra. The wind howled outside. Branches were beating against the window. She walked over and sat on the chair beside the window. There was an eerie darkness. The wind eased, as if being told to hush. She leaned her head against the cool pane after raising it an inch. The air was cool and damp, but she smelled a familiar scent. It was a scent she couldn't remember, but she knew it.

Pain was gradually returning, pain in her heart, pain in her empty soul. She had a longing...to be held by a man. Slowly, she walked back to bed, quickly turning, feeling spied upon. No one was there, but when she sat back on her bed the wind gusted again. You'll be happy again, she thought. The crazy old man's words were clear in her mind. At that moment, she thought she would never be happy.

Her body finally relaxed, able to rest again. Through her dream she felt the silkiness of his long hair falling through her fingers. A soft moan unknowingly escaped her lips. Eyes...eyes she dreamed of before were very close above hers, and lips whispered, I love you.

Her world of dreams caused sleep to be light and the strong breeze blew the curtains away from their resting place at the side of the window. She opened her eyes at the sound of the wind, but the darkness was blinding. Then the dim lunar light allowed a glimpse of the window sill, and if she would have looked again she would have seen the window was lifted a little more than it was when she raised it.

Her dreams returned. This time the nightmare didn't come. This time the hair she touched was dark and the touch was the touch of smooth skin, the familiar touch that her body responded to. But although her body responded to it for many years, something was missing.

* * *

As Eryn carried coffee into Avis and Beth she tried to decide how she would tell her story. She kept making excuses to leave the room. Not yet ready for them to know, but she knew she had to do it now. She sat down across from them and sipped a steamy cup of coffee, wishing she could burn the words from her tongue. She began, "You know, Avis, I didn't tell you the truth about this bruise."

"What do you mean? Why did you lie to me? What happened?"

Beth sat her cup down, knowing by the look on Eryn's face that something was terribly wrong. "Eryn, what is it, what's happened?"

Avis' impatience began to get the best of her. "Mom! What?"

"Well, first of all, I'm okay," Eryn said, as she hesitated. "I told you last night, Avis, that we stopped in Enchantment because of the fog." Eryn bit the soft flesh on her bottom lip, knowing there was only one way to say it. "The owner of the inn attacked me." That's not really a lie, she thought, he did attack my senses.

"What!" Beth and Avis screamed in unison. Beth took Eryn's hand.

"From the very first, there was something about him I didn't like. The way he looked at me and the things he said."

"Where was my sister?"

"I already took her to school. I kept my room, I told you, so I could stay there that night. I wanted to look around the town and visit an old book store." She stood up and paced in front of them. "Well, I met the owner of the book store and from then on my life has changed. He told me some things that were unbelievable but somehow, I think I believe him. I met a wonderful woman named Hanah Grace. She was a great help."

Eryn relived the incident as she spoke. "I was going back to my room to leave. He followed me up the stairs and followed me in when I opened the door. The waiter, a young man named Cole Dawes, came in just in time." Eryn was shaking, hoping they couldn't see the farce as she remembered it. "He knew things about me."

"Did the police arrest him," asked Beth.

"Yes, I have to go to court, but I don't want to see him again."

"You have to, Mom. He can't get away with this."

"The strange thing is…I think he knows something about Taylor." She looked at them with questioning eyes. "I can't ignore that."

"How could Taylor know him?"

"That's what I asked myself. He looked familiar to me, but I can't recall ever meeting him. Strange things began happening when we arrived in Enchantment."

"Right, Mom, tell Beth about the visions."

"Visions? What ever are you talking about?"

"I know it sounds odd but, Beth, I did see some visions. I know you two find this amusing. I still can't believe it. I had a feeling, a closeness to something when I was there." She described the vision she had of the town. "This is all so hard to tell you." She looked at the questioning look on their faces. "I know you think I'm going insane. Maybe I am. You had to be there." She poured more coffee and picked up a bagel spread with cream cheese and strawberry jam. "I have to tell you about the people I met…."

Chapter 7

The next day, Glynn's Restaurant wasn't crowded. "I"ll have the usual," Eryn told the waitress, as she and Beth had dinner.

"Thanks for canceling the so-called date, Beth. I couldn't take trying to impress a stranger tonight.

"Yes, I understand. But you really need to start seeing people."

"This isn't the time, besides I'm still a married woman."

"Well, in name only…"

"Would you mind spending the night at my house tonight, I don't want to be alone," said Eryn, changing the subject.

"Of course I wouldn't mind. I love pajama parties! I'll call Travis and tell him not to expect me." She carefully applied her lipstick, before continuing. "Ever since his dad died he seems to cling to me more. I hope he finds someone to share his life with."

"He will. Your step-son has always had a secret crush on Avis, you know."

"You're kidding! How come I never knew that?"

"Because you were too wrapped up in his father to notice when he was always at my house."

"Oh," said Beth, blushing. "I do miss William. At least he left me a rich widow and I do get along with his son. What else could a woman want, besides someone warm in her bed at night."

"At least you've accepted being without him. I have a hard time accepting loneliness."

"You should be glad as far as I'm concerned," she said, her eyebrows pinched together.

"Beth, don't start on that again.... Should we order dessert?"

"Yeah. How about something chocolate!"

Eryn wished she had bought the truffles for her dear chocolate-crazed friend.

* * *

The street was empty while Eryn waited in the car in front of Beth's modern suburban home. Beth was lucky, Eryn thought. She handled William's passing very well. At least she showed it on the outside.

"Was Travis home?" asked Eryn, when Beth returned with her overnight bag.

"No, but I left him a note. He's twenty-six years old, Eryn, don't worry about the guy. He can take care of himself."

"Very funny. I'm not worried about him. It's just the Mother in me," she said, while she drove down the tree lined street.

Eryn put Beth's things in the spare bedroom and watched television for a while before going to bed. Tonight she would relax better with someone in the house. Her self-assuredness seemed to have slipped away.

Beth stayed up, going over a manuscript she had requested, but couldn't concentrate on. She thought back to the time that she met Eryn. She was wandering around with nowhere to go, having no idea where or who she was. Her age was about seventeen and to this day, twenty years later, no one claimed her. They became closer than sisters and Beth, being three years older, took her under her wing.

Beth checked the locks on the doors and went to bed. While lying there she thought about her best friend again. To think that an innocent trip could have ruined her life. It scared her. She lost her husband, too, but it was a marriage of convenience. It was different with Eryn and Taylor. At first their love was strong and healthy, and Eryn wasn't the whole person that she used to be since Taylor turned abusive toward her. Yes,

Beth was glad he was gone, there's no denying that. So would Eryn when she allowed herself to admit it.

Instantly, Beth recalled a conversation she had with Taylor. He once told her he had the best, most unusual present for Eryn. Saying it was something he had been working on for a while. Beth didn't know why she remembered it now. She opened the door unable to contain her revelation. She didn't wait for Eryn to tell her to enter, she did anyway— "Eryn, I just remembered something Taylor told me! He said he had a special present for you."

She looked up from her book. "What, leaving me?"

"No—"

"He always brought me presents. That's not so unusual."

"Get this, he said there was a man in *Pennsylvania* that dealt in old classics that no one else had. He wouldn't tell me anything else."

"What are you saying?" she questioned, while dropping the pen. "Try to remember."

"There's nothing else," she said, shrugging her shoulders, "that's all he told me. Didn't he ever mention a trip to Pennsylvania?"

"No. This is getting more bizarre by the minute. I feel like I'm going to wake up from a ludicrous dream." Eryn got out of bed and went into the bathroom, pulling on sweat pants and a sweatshirt. "Come on. We're going to the basement to go through some of his files." On the way down the stairs, she said, "Taylor keeps his files in excellent order. If I know what to look for, it should be easy to find. I'll start by looking under the travel file."

After two hours of searching, Eryn said, "There's nothing here. I'll have to check his office and computer."

"Take time off tomorrow. I'll go with you," said Beth. "Two of us can cover more, faster."

"You're right. I'll have to make arrangements to get in. I'll do that in the morning. It's late and I'm tired," said Eryn, when she headed for bed. "Good night."

Beth picked up some of the loose papers that were left on the floor. When she did a photograph of Taylor slipped out. He sat at his desk with a wide grin on his face. He wasn't alone in the photo, and Beth had never seen the blonde woman that sat on his lap with her arm around his neck. She tucked it inside her shirt pocket and decided to wait until the right time to show it to Eryn, so she could explain it. I've never seen Taylor as much as smile at another woman, she thought. That is until he made a pass at me, the jerk. Who is that woman?

* * *

They were having coffee in the breakfast nook when the phone rang. Beth saw Eryn's face glow with happiness, but then a look of sadness crawled into the corner of her eyes. She hung up and looked at Beth while wiping away a tear. Beth took her a tissue, leading her to the table, waiting until she was ready to talk about it.

"That was Hanah, from Enchantment. Emmet came out of the coma. He's going to be okay."

"Eryn, that's wonderful, but something else is wrong, isn't it?"

"He's going to be okay, but Hanah said he has amnesia." Eryn was glad for the old man, although she was feeling a little selfish at the same time. "I'll never find out what he was going to tell me. He has the answers I need!" She practically screamed the words, even stomping her foot. "I believe him, I really do, but this is so hard to deal with. First, Taylor disappears, then I end up in some town, seeing things. I meet two people that hold the key to my future, and maybe my past." Eryn wiped her eyes with the shredded tissue. "Then I nearly get ravished by someone with beautiful amber eyes. How much of this can I take, Beth? The light inside of me is slowly burning out."

"Eryn, stop pacing and listen to me! I know you've been through a lot. And I know you're feeling overwhelmed with grief over Taylor." Beth put her hands on Eryn's shoulders. "You can get through this. I'm here with you all the way, you know that. We'll take it one step at a time, but face it, you can do better. One day you will."

With furrows wrinkled in her forehead she looked at Beth, not liking what she had just suggested. Eryn shook it off. "Well, thank you anyway for heading me in the right direction...again." Eryn got her presence of mind back and planned the day.

* * *

It was hard to go inside the office at first. She'd been too upset to talk to any of his associates much. This was only the second time she visited since he left. She sat in his leather chair, feeling the impression formed by his own body; worn areas showed many years of use. She ran her fingers over the smooth polished surface of the desk. The office was left untouched. Taylor could walk in tomorrow and pick up where he left off.

Memories flowed into her mind as she pictured late nights together. Nights that left everlasting memories, she thought, as she rubbed her wrist that had been badly bruised in that office. She flipped on the computer. The menu blinked onto the screen and she looked it over. A little more than half-way down she saw, ERYN. She entered it, and right before her eyes she read about a trip to Pennsylvania. She called Beth in and they both read the words. It was a trip Eryn didn't know about. "He stayed at the Enchanted Inn." He must have met Uriah, but she wondered how Uriah would make the connection between them. They scrolled the information and suddenly the initials caught her eye. They were E.M.—"Emmet McDanil." Next to the initials was the name of the book store.

"Taylor was there. Why didn't Emmet tell me?"

"Maybe he didn't make the connection," said Beth.

"But he did. He called me Mrs. Sterling from the beginning. I didn't tell him my marital status. I only gave him my name. If he knows, then Hanah knows. They're the best of friends."

"Okay, what have we figured out here?" asked Beth.

"We know that Taylor was there," said Eryn. "He knew Emmet, and probably met Uriah Prescot, too."

"We don't know for sure that he actually went. Maybe he had this scheduled, but disappeared before he had the chance to go."

They turned off the computer and Eryn was flipping through the Rolodex on the desk. On a hunch she went to the M's, and sure enough, Emmet McDanil was there too. It was the address on Main Street, the book store. The card said that he specialized in classic books and he would guarantee to find almost any book a person would want. "I have been trying to find a special book for awhile," Eryn said.

Trying to ignore the face that appeared in her mind, she went to the P's. Nothing there. Almost in a trance, she looked in the E's. There it was! She read aloud—"Enchanted Inn, room 216. He *was* there. That was also my room." Eryn looked up at Beth, saying, "I have to go back."

"You just returned. Do you think you should put yourself through this again?"

"I have to."

Beth put her hand on Eryn's shoulder. "I know you do. Please, let me come with you."

"I have to call the sub line. I have to update my lesson plans." She wrung her hands as she walked the length of the room. "I'll call you if I need you there."

"No, you shouldn't go alone," demanded Beth. "I insist. When do we leave?"

"I want to leave tomorrow. I'll call Hanah tonight. I have to see Emmet."

"I have to admit, I was getting worried about you, but this is starting to make sense."

Eryn picked up the phone, holding it for a moment. She glanced at Beth as she walked out of Taylor's office. She dialed Pennsylvania information and asked for the Enchantment Sheriff Department. It was time to put an end to the lie.

* * *

After dropping Beth off at her house, Eryn thought she was being followed, but the truck sped past her. Her heart sank when she glimpsed the out of state license plate. It went by too fast for her to notice the driver. Coincidence, she thought, just coincidence. She tried to put the pieces they found, together. Eryn was wondering if Uriah had something to do with the disappearance of Taylor, but she couldn't come up with a motive. Of course she didn't know every single thing Taylor did, nor did he of her, but she always knew about his trips and his meetings with other engineers. He talked at length about his work, and she didn't remember any mention of Enchantment or Uriah Prescot.

The unusual gift he meant to buy her. That would be the only reason he kept it all a secret. Her thoughts went back to Emmet. He said he knew the end of the story. Taylor told Beth about a man who did unusual things. She recalled the story Emmet told about his grandfather and the book he wrote. That was unusual! Now the book was missing. She had a portion of it and nothing else. "And why did Uriah ask me if I remembered him?" I think the man must be a lunatic, she thought. "Well, another night of not knowing. I can't wait until I get this figured out." Thinking about the long night alone she knew she had to get back to her usual routine or she would probably lose control.

Before Beth left for her office she noticed a message on her machine. She became frightened when she heard a man's voice with some kind of accent, say, "I'll be seeing you soon, sweet Eryn." She wondered what that was about, why someone left a message for Eryn at her house. She thought about it a moment then dialed Eryn's number. No answer. "Come on, Eryn, pick up, it's me," she said, when her message came on.

"Beth, he was here. Uriah was here!"

"Are you okay?"

"I'm okay."

"Are you sure he's not in the house now?"

"No. I haven't had a chance to check all the rooms."

"Get out of there now! I'll call the police. Go on, drop the phone and leave. Now!"

"Okay! I'm going to the gas station down the street."

Beth listened until she heard the door close and Eryn's car start. Before she hung up the phone she heard another door close and the receiver was hung up.

Eryn was already at the gas station, and Beth saw that she was quite shaken. They could see her house from the parking lot and two police cars were there. Eryn was trembling as she sat staring into space.

The officers came out empty handed so Beth and Eryn drove to her house and a detective talked to her. At first she was feeling safe and glad for her decision to go back to Enchantment. Now she was frightened again and unsure. As soon as she had entered her room she knew he had been there. She walked to her bedroom to get her luggage and saw it immediately. A white rosebud was lying on her pillow, and a candle was burning on the table next to her bed. When the phone rang she was afraid to answer it until she heard Beth's voice on the machine.

Eryn couldn't understand why he was released so soon, she only made the call an hour ago. He must have paid his bail. More questions that would have to go unanswered. She was getting used to it. Now she was more determined to make the trip. Uriah wasn't going to get in her way of looking for Taylor, no matter what he tried. With beads of sweat forming on her forehead she thought of the night before when she felt like she was being watched.

* * *

After the longest night of her life Eryn asked Beth if she was ready. It wasn't possible for Travis to go with the two women so they left alone. All along, Beth kept her eyes on her rear-view mirror, and once she even pulled into a gas station because a car seemed to lag behind for too long. It was the idea of knowing Uriah was on the street, and could be anywhere that made them fearful.

As they went on, Eryn worried for her best friend. The thought occurred to her that she could be putting Beth's life in danger. Even as Eryn thought, though, she knew for sure he wouldn't hurt either of them. He already had the chance to hurt her, and he didn't.

When they stopped for breakfast neither of them had much of an appetite so they ordered coffee to go. They no sooner got in the car when Beth immediately locked the doors, looking around. "By the way, what does this Uriah Prescot guy look like?"

Eryn sucked in her breath as she pictured him in her mind. Oh, yes, he was attractive, handsome, bone *gorgeous*, if a man could be called that, but she said, "Oh, he's nice-looking, I guess. Tall, if you like men that way."

Beth couldn't help but look over at Eryn when she contemplated his description. She noticed the tiny curve of Eryn's mouth, even though she tried to hide it.

Right now it was a good idea not to think about the man that caused the earth to tremble just by a touch. No, Eryn couldn't let herself think those things about that man. But there was something about that man…something she couldn't grasp. "I don't think I'll ever forget him," Eryn said. "What's wrong?"

When you were in the restroom some guy was at the phone giving me some strange looks. I tried not to look at him, but I wanted to be able to remember him. When he smiled it looked like his mouth kind of curled to the side, but when he ran his tongue over his lips, I stopped looking. Why do guys like to do that? It's disgusting. Something about his eyes, they were nice, kind of golden brown…different. You didn't tell me he was so good looking."

She didn't have to say another word. Eryn knew right away that he was following her. "It was him," Eryn said, staring off into the distance. "Okay, we have to decide what to do. You can bet he already knows what he's going to do." Good looks or no good looks, it was obvious he was after her, and she was afraid, although something deep down told her, don't be fearful.

Beth reached in her purse, pulling out a canister of spray. "This is all we have for protection and if he gets close enough, I'm using it!"

"Where did you get that?" Eryn laughed. "Are you sure it works?"

"I'm not sure of anything, but when Travis gave it to me he made me try it out and it definitely sprays. We'll just have to trust it."

"Oh, yeah, and if that doesn't work you always have your Tai Chi." Eryn laughed again.

They almost had to joke with each other to take their mind off their problems. Eryn saw Beth check her mirror again.

"I'm not going to let him make me afraid. He's the one that did wrong, not me. I have to find the connection between him and Taylor and if I have to face him, I will. That might be the only way I'll ever know."

"When we get to Enchantment, maybe Hanah can be more helpful. I know she's your friend, but maybe she was holding something back. Maybe she was trying to protect you from something," said Beth.

"I've been thinking about that. I doubt that she knows very much but I know Emmet does." Eryn watched the side mirror. "I think Taylor found out about his books and he went to find the one I wanted. It's my fault. If I wasn't so persistent about my collection, maybe Taylor would be here."

"Stop that right now! Maybe he went for another reason, did you ever think of that?" Beth asked. "Eryn, was Taylor always a faithful husband?"

"Why would you ask me a question like that?" Eryn stared straight ahead, hiding the tears about to fall from her eyes. "No. No! He cheated on me once. I never told you."

"Are you sure?"

"Do you think I wouldn't be sure about something like that? He begged me to forgive him and swore he would never do it again, you know, the typical, cheat on your wife line."

"Do you know who she was?"

"I never want to know."

"It's not your fault that he came here, either. He used to love you, would do anything for you, back in the old days when he was nice. Even if he did cheat—once. By the way, when did this happen?"

"About five years ago. He's been faithful since," she said with shaky words.

"You keep believing that," said Beth. "The date on the picture was only eleven months ago," she mumbled under her breath.

"What did you say?"

"Oh, nothin', hon, just talking to myself."

* * *

After several hours of driving they were quiet and in their own thoughts, but Beth broke the silence. "Why do you think he stopped following us, if that was him?"

"I can only guess it's because he already knows where we're going."

"That doesn't make me feel any better. I wish Travis could have come with us. I would feel better with a man along."

"We don't need your *Hero* behind the *Wheel*. We can handle this. We need to be prepared for anything, that's all."

"Great!" said Beth.

"I'll protect you and you protect me. Like we've always done."

Suddenly Eryn spoke. You know, Beth, sometimes I am glad he's gone."

"Eryn, you know it hurt me all those years to see you in pain. Your life with him was nearly perfect, or so I thought. I was as devastated as you when he didn't come home that night."

"Thanks for crying with me for all those days and nights. If not for you and the girls, I might have given up." It remained in the back of her mind that Taylor may have cheated on her yet again. Obviously, something made him leave, maybe for good this time.

"Do you think he'll ever come back, Beth?"

"It doesn't matter what I think, Eryn, he's gone now. I know you're in some kind of denial about his abuse against you. I probably shouldn't even say this, but if it takes a man like, say, Uriah Prescot to make you accept it, so be it!"

"Oh, whose side are you on?"

"You're a changed woman now, hon. Leaning on yourself now more than ever." Beth reached over, touching her hand. "I don't care if you get mad at me, but I'm glad Taylor Sterling is gone, and he could stay away forever as far as I'm concerned." She glanced at her best friend. "I really do care if you're mad at me, though. I didn't mean that."

Chapter 8

Eryn was uncomfortable about the fog, and it was a sure thing on an autumn night in the mountains. She remembered the sunset on her last visit a few days before, but this one was one of the most beautiful she had ever seen. Maybe God dipped a brush into his palette, haphazardly splattering it across the sky. Scattering the peach and crimson hues, making up the colors of the setting sun. The horizon glowed in copper, fused with the azure sky. From the highway the blackened trees were silhouetted against the skyline. Within a few blinks of the eye the blended colors faded, and all too quickly were gone, ebbing into an eerie, purple dusk. They were nearly there and Eryn prayed for a clear night.

Their trip was coming to an end and Eryn enjoyed all that she saw. The highway signs sped by and mile markers stood as if hitch-hiking on the shoulder of the road. Autumn was everywhere. Crops were drying into crispy, golden brown straw, ready for harvesting. Some farmers had already turned over their fields and the smell of fresh, black dirt was in the air. Corn stalks sternly stood guard over the farmers who planted them, waiting to have their yield picked so they could come to rest for a season.

"Is this where we turn?" Beth asked, when she read the sign.

"Yes, we're almost there. It looks like we beat the fog tonight."

They drove down the steep hill, coming to a crawl when they eased behind a tractor-trailer doing the posted, twenty miles per hour. As they rounded the bend, Enchantment appeared with all its charm. They slowly drove past the charred book store, and saw that someone had begun clearing away most of the rubble. A lump grew in her throat as she pictured the man who owned it, knowing she still waited to know what he knew, and the waiting was defeating her. She said a silent prayer for him, knowing she would see him the next day.

A short way down Main Street was the Enchanted Inn. She asked Beth to pull into the parking lot. Beth started to ask why, but she sat quietly as she watched her friend tilt the mirror. As Eryn held her breath, she glanced up and saw nothing unusual. Yes, the park was there as was the fountain, but it was just as it was supposed to be. There was no gazebo, no drab colors on the buildings, and the only eyes she saw were her own. Without saying a word Beth started the engine and put the car in reverse. Her look of understanding was clear.

They drove the three miles to Hanah's house. When they arrived, the grounds were flooded with light. "I feel like I'm going home," said Eryn. "You'll like Hanah."

"Let's find out if she really knows more than she's been telling you," reminded Beth.

"I trust her. So will you after you meet her."

As soon as they drove up the long drive, Hanah and Rachael came out to meet them. Eryn's first words to her were to inquire about Emmet. She learned his physical condition was improving each day, but he still had no memory of who he was or what his life was about.

The four women had dinner in the dining room and Hanah told them that Cole began working on the book store. The fire was still under investigation, but Cole had the approval to begin. The fire department had gathered the evidence they needed.

Hanah didn't know Uriah was released. Since his arrest she learned about the attempt on the other woman and Cole was the one who prevented it. Uriah had convinced him that the woman had made advances toward him. Cole admitted to her he was young and naive, and at the time, swayed by Uriah's conniving experience. The odd part about it was the other woman resembled Eryn. She never pressed charges or reported it. She left as soon as Cole arrived.

75

Beth told Hanah she was sure Uriah was in the diner on their way to Enchantment. Hanah walked over and checked her alarm system. "This is on and we can all feel secure. It's hooked up to the police station and believe me, girls, I have friends on the force. They'll be here immediately!" At the cabinet across the room she pulled the brass knob, reached in and to everyone's surprise, pulled out a pearl handled revolver. "A lady can't be safe enough these days. Even in our wonderful town, things do happen."

The ringing of the phone broke the mood and since Eryn was sitting next to it, Hanah indicated she should answer it. "Grace residence," she said, ready to hand the receiver to Hanah. Beth watched Eryn's expression change. The tan on her face had become ashen and her hand trembled.

"...I've been waiting for you to get here, my sweet Eryn. What took you so—"

She slammed the phone down and walked to the window. Beth looked at Hanah and Rachael. Hanah shook her head.

"I can't stay here, Hanah. I'm putting you in danger."

"You're just as safe here as anywhere. I'm not afraid of that man. I've been through a lot worse in my seventy-five years, my dear."

* * *

The last time Eryn slept in Hanah's guest room she dreamed of Taylor. She had more dreams of him in the last week than in the last ten months. She snuggled down, not wanting to think about Uriah's phone call, contemplating what he said about her following him from somewhere. What did he mean by that? The floor was creaking in the room next door and she knew Beth was restless too.

In the dark wee hours of the morning Eryn found herself wide awake. As she watched, moonlight bathed the room in an eerie light. Sleep would not come. The hooting of an owl sounded in the distance, and through the slightly raised window was the acidic smell of decaying leaves.

All the changes that took place in her once contented life unnerved her. She used to believe her life would end if anything happened to her husband. After a while she was so intimidated by him that she felt like she was nothing. She might have broken if not for Beth. But she was a different person now, independent, strong, not dependent on anyone, anymore. It would be another long night. Releasing the taunt stretch to her limbs, she inhaled deeply, sniffing the distant spicy scent in the air.

Outside, the breeze vibrated the branches, while inside, lazy shadows waltzed on the walls. A cloud moved over the moon making the shadows disappear. Once the room became somber she crawled beneath the covers once more. When sleep is forced isn't it almost always impossible? Enough tossing and turning! With eyes red and swollen, she turned on the dim light, looking in the night table drawer for something to write with. With a sudden intensity her fingers found paper and a pen and she began to write, or scribble words and symbols she knew nothing about.

Writing usually gave her comfort, but when she looked at the unintelligible markings she had no idea what it meant. Five rectangular shapes, hanging from some sort of base. Something similar to the chime she kept dreaming about. "Oh, well, one more mystery to add to my life."

Somewhere, deep within her subconscious mind she felt a loneliness trying to rest along side her soul. Eyes, amber brown, all too familiar, came into view and they held a look of worry, of concern. Feeling guilty over visualizing those eyes, she envisioned eyes of blue.

Without control, or the ability to gain control, another so called vision formed itself in her psyche. Before long a face formed around the eyes and the dimple in the chin stood out as the mouth turned upward, smiling. A familiar smile.

In her muse, Taylor was speaking, but his eyes looked to the right, his smile wide. It wasn't Eryn that brought about that smile; he wasn't looking at Eryn at all, but at a light-haired woman. That reflection vanished, but another began playing a role in her unconscious mind....

A chill brought goose bumps to her arms and her hair stood on end. "Please come to me," a voice called to her. For no reason, the image vanished, and Eryn, finding she had dropped the pen, saw words scribbled on the paper, the same words that repeated themselves in her mind. Please come to me, *please come to me.* ...

Gasping sounds were heard; she hardly realized the tightness in her chest, not even hearing the thudding of her own heart pounding. The chill was gone, cold sweat oozed from her pores. Her hair was wet, sticking to her neck. Startled, she came out of whatever realm she had fallen into. Something took place that she couldn't explain. Her palms were wet with sweat, and she reread what she must have written. She wanted to get up and go, no, run to the book store! The back of the book store where the answers could be! But the darkness, and the fear kept her from it. There would be no answers this night. She hugged the tablet to her chest close to her heart, closed her burning eyes, and slept....

He was across the field with the plow. She walked through the grass, knowing she would meet him this day. Long, blond hair, damp with perspiration, was blowing in the wind. His young muscles flexed; his body was golden brown. With all the innocence of a young girl, Eryn saw herself walking toward him. Amber eyes, wide and self-assured, raked over her body as she came near, and she melted at his gaze. The young man picked up a handful of hay and threw it at her.

Eryn turned in her sleep and if anyone watched they would see the sensuous smile. She moaned and sighed, and the smile of a once young girl turned to the enjoyment of a woman. Her body squirmed, the moans continuing as she felt hands on her. The touch was not so smooth, but familiar. Another vision intermingled with her confused dreams...

The creek was clear as the young, red-haired girl splashed in the water. Out of the dense forest, a young man swung out on a swing made of rope, landing behind her. Her eyes danced with no streaks of green when she saw him. He lifted her out of the water, his heart swiftly beating against her. She leaned down and kissed his lips. Beneath the water two bodies disappeared and when they came up for air their lips were still together. They walked out of the water, hand in hand, the wet chemise clinging to her soft, youthful body. He threw his shirt over the bushes and she sat on the shore, shivering even though it was mid-summer. The sun was setting, glistening golden on the creek water. His eyes glistening, golden as the sun, as he straddled her and lay her down beneath him. His eyes were ablaze with lust and she arched toward him. He licked his lips in anticipation while she reached for him, pulling him down, pressing her lips softly against his. The sun dipped below the horizon and in the velvet-purple twilight, a young lass became a woman and a lad became a man.

Eryn suddenly awoke, consciously aware of the dreariness. She rubbed her eyes, thinking that Beth or Hanah tip-toed in and turned off her light. Sleep came again leading her once again to the creek bank cuddled in the strong arms of her blond beguiler. She tossed, feeling herself kicking from under the covers, trying to be free of the quilt.

The dream came to an end, but as much as she had wanted sleep earlier, she now wanted to wake up. It was the touch…his touch and it stroked her thigh as gently as a feather. She tossed some more, turned and squirmed, then jumped up with a squelched scream on her lips.

The moonlight was casting shadows that made her ill-at-ease. Was the door slowly closing? She glanced at the ticking clock, knowing it would be daylight soon. Something left her feeling unsettled. Something didn't feel right. She sat up against the head-board, reaching for the pillow, hugging it against her breasts. She rocked herself to sleep with the yearning of her dream, and the touch, forgotten.

* * *

Beth knocked and walked in looking showered and refreshed. She was carrying a pot of coffee on a silver serving tray. Cream spilled from the top of the shiny creamer, and artificial sugar packets were in the matching sugar bowl. Eryn's eyes were still swollen, her hair twisted and knotted. A wonderful nutty aroma was emitted from the liquid in the china cups.

"Boy, you look like you had a rough night," said Beth.

"I think it was one of the worst I ever had. How was your night?"

"It was hard to get to sleep, you know how it is in a strange bed. I woke up once, but it was okay," said Beth.

"I'm going to the hospital to see Emmet this morning. I want you to come, too." Eryn thought about her vision last night and glanced at the notebook on the table. She wasn't quite ready to explain what she had written.

After her shower she went to her suitcase and reached for her hair dryer, and inside, under her lace panties, was a card with an iridescent image of a rose. She pressed her teeth against her bottom lip. "How did this happen?" She looked to the door. "My, God, I didn't imagine it...."

* * *

The hospital floors were so shiny they looked wet. Eryn's nose twitched from the odor of disinfectant. The feeling of sadness overtook her as she stepped from the elevator. A few more steps and she would see Emmet. "What will I say to him?" asked Eryn, as she pulled Beth to a stop. "I'm a stranger to him."

Dr. Lincoln came out of his office, recognizing Eryn, giving Beth a quick, interested glance.

"May I talk to you, Doctor?" asked Eryn.

"Of course. It's nice of you to come, but I thought you were going home?" He spoke to Eryn, but his eyes were on Beth.

"I did, but now I'm back." She introduced them and wondered if she would get her questions answered since he and Beth were mesmerized by each other. Beth extended her hand, narrowing her eyes as she smiled and said hello.

As the doctor put his arm around Eryn's shoulder he took one finger and touched the light bruise on her jaw.

He led them into his office and sat next to Eryn. "You want to know about Emmet. He's going to be okay. Since he came out of the coma he's been recovering nicely. He still has a headache, but…"

"Hanah's kept me informed. She told me he has amnesia."

"He can remember things that have happened since, but he can't remember what happened before the blow to his head. We call it anterograde amnesia. Eryn, he probably won't remember you."

"I understand. Is there anything I should or shouldn't say or do?"

"Be yourself. Sometimes a familiar face or object can strike a recall in amnesia patients," said Dr. Lincoln.

Eryn thought about what the doctor said. She wondered what she could use that might be familiar. The image of the charred book came to her, and she wished she would have remembered it. She picked up a book from his desk, "May I borrow this for a few minutes?"

"But why—" He had a look of recognition and nodded his head. She knew what the book should look like and in the gift shop she found what she needed.

The room was dark when she and Beth walked in. They saw an old man with his head wrapped in a bandage, lying on his side staring at the wall. Eryn set the blue carnations on his bed side table. He looked at Beth, but he eyed Eryn across the room. He sat up and continued to watch her.

"Please open the curtains, my dear," asked Emmet, with his familiar south-eastern drawl.

Light drenched the room and the sun was shining bright in Eryn's eyes. Emmet pointed his shaky finger at her, looking at the book she held in the crook of her arm. "What is it about your book? I know something about it." He scratched his head and pounded his bandaged hand on the bed. "I can't bring it to mind. Who are you, Missy?"

Eryn walked close to the bed, letting the title of the book show under her arm. "I'm Eryn Sterling. I met you at the book store a few days ago." She tried to keep her words steady. "Emmet, do you remember me?"

"You look kinda familiar." He hesitated and looked searchingly at her but shook his head, uncertain of her.

Her shoulders dropped and her breathing came more steady as she rubbed the book edge with her thumb.

Emmet took the carnations, closed his eyes and inhaled their fragrance in a long, deep breath. "Beautiful, beautiful. I remember this smell."

"Emmet, does anything seem at all familiar to you? This is very important to me."

"I'm sorry, Mrs. Sterling," Emmet said, as he dropped his head down. "I want to remember. Tell me how I know ya and why an old man is so important." He patted the side of the bed, asking her to sit. Eryn went to his side, wondering why he called her Mrs., she didn't say. She told Emmet all the details of how they met. She explained about the book and how he told her he knew the end of the story.

"My grandfather wrote that book," he said. "I don't know how I know that." He thought for a few more moments. "Continue."

Emmet was getting sleepy and the nurse asked them to come back later. "He needs his rest now, ladies," she said.

"Will you please call Hanah Grace's house if he remembers anything?"

"I certainly will. We have Hanah's number in our files. We would probably be fired if we didn't keep her informed of Mr. McDanil's progress." The nurse walked by Eryn and whispered, "We love them both."

Chapter 9

Eryn walked through a cleared area toward the back part of the building untouched by fire. Boards were nailed across the scorched door. Cole came up behind her, touching her shoulder. She jumped at the touch but smiled when she turned around.

"I'm glad to see you again, Mrs. Sterling. I know Mr. Prescot paid bail, and I've been worried for you. Why are you here? Aren't you afraid?"

"It's good to see you again, Cole. No, I'm not afraid."

Beth came up to them, mainly out of curiosity. Eryn introduced them, but Beth said she knew the young man must have been Cole.

"Can I get inside?" Eryn asked him, getting straight to the point. "I do need to look for something."

"We'll talk about it. My treat, where would you like to go?" asked Cole.

* * *

He held the door at Sweet Nicole's and the ladies led him to a table near the back. The first thing Eryn looked for was the crystal chime, and she heard its tinkle as the door closed. Even after she sat down she continued to look at it. It was in her dream, but she saw it somewhere else. She ordered the house tea and excused herself to get a closer look. Finally, it came to her. The picture in her room at the inn. The chime was hanging in the gazebo. But the picture was of the park in the 1800's. It was almost the same image she had envisioned. The crystal looked like it had been shattered then glued in many places.

Eryn joined them at the table and asked the waitress if she knew where the chime came from.

"It's been hanging there for as long as I can remember," she said, "even when I was a little girl. There's a legend behind it. The owner of this tea room knows of it."

"Oh, please send her over! I need to know about it."

"Sure." She called someone named Lesley from the kitchen, who brought their order out with her.

Eryn introduced herself, going directly to her question.

"Well, I do know a little, at least what I've heard," said Lesley. "They say that back about a hundred years or so, a young farmer about twenty miles north of here was betrothed to a beautiful young lady. One day she just disappeared...vanished, leaving him a broken man. Before she left him, he took great pains to make the crystal pieces—one for her, one for him, and three more for the children they planned to have."

"How romantic," said Beth.

"Go on, Lesley," begged Eryn.

"The townspeople built a finely crafted gazebo in the park right down this very street. This young man hung it there because that's where they were going to be married. It was supposed to be some kind of good luck sign or something. Seems like it wasn't so good after all."

"How do you know about this story...this legend?" asked Cole.

"I looked around the museum and saw a picture there, it looked like the very same chime hanging in here. The curator told me."

"What was the picture of?" asked Eryn.

"It's really strange, but it was the gazebo in the park. I wanted to bid on it to hang in here, but someone beat me out of it."

Eryn bit her lip, almost afraid to ask. "Who was it that ended up getting it, Lesley?"

"It was Uriah Prescot. He owns the Enchanted Inn. I have no idea why he wanted it, or what he ever did with it."

Cole and Eryn exchanged glances.

Eryn must have turned pale because Beth put her hand upon her arm, asking if she was feeling okay.

"I'm...I'm fine."

"I really need to get back to work now. I hope the information was helpful. Are you writing a book or something?"

Optimistically, Beth looked at Eryn, since she always wanted to write a book. "Sounds like a good idea!"

Lesley started to walk away, but Eryn caught her arm. "Does this legend have an ending to it?"

"I'm not really sure. Some say the woman returned twenty years later with a husband. Others say the young man disappeared a short time after his love left him. You know how these stories go. If any of it was true, it's probably stretched all out of shape by now."

"Thank you so much."

"Why are you back here, Mrs. Sterling?" asked Cole.

"Please, call me Eryn. I don't feel like Mrs. Sterling any more. Uriah Prescot has already been to my house, and he knows we're here anyway. He called Ms. Grace's house last night. That's where we're staying." Eryn sipped her tea as she watched Beth eat a Scone spread with Devon cream and jam. "Cole, how long did you work at the inn?" Eryn was trying to fit misshaped pieces of the puzzle together. When he told her he worked there about three years, she continued. "I need you to think real hard." She reached into her wallet and handed him a picture of Taylor. "Have you see him there? He's my husband. He's been missing for ten months."

Cole examined the photo, hesitating. "He looks familiar. I'm sorry...I don't think so."

"I found information at home leading me back here."

"Are you sure?" Beth asked him.

Cole looked to the floor. "Yeah, 'um, I'm sure."

Eryn couldn't get her mind off the chime. Even though it was a beautiful sunny day shivers still flurried over her. She had a throbbing in her temples, recalling what she heard, imagined the night before. *Please come to me.* What does it mean? "Can I get in the book store? I *need* to get in there."

Cole paused then nodded his head. "But not now. When it gets dark. I have permission to clean up, not let anyone in."

* * *

They didn't tell Hanah where they were going, but said they wouldn't be long. When they were nearly out of the driveway, she beckoned to them. "The hospital just called. Emmet wants to see you! Something about remembering something. He wants to see you now."

"Are you coming with us?" Eryn asked.

"No, he wants to see you," she said, wringing her hands. "Please call me, dear, when you know something. Be careful."

"We have one quick stop to make on the way."

Cole was waiting outside Sweet Nicole's. They parked the car and he met them in front of the book store. He pried some boards off so Eryn could push the door open, giving her a lantern before entering. "The windows are all boarded up, no one can see the light through them."

She told them to wait outside, that she had to do it alone. They didn't know what she had to do, but they allowed her privacy.

The room was damp and she could still smell leather mingled with the smell of smoke. She didn't know what she was looking for, but felt she would know when she found it. She thumbed through a few books. Before realizing it she was flipping through an old photo album. There in front of her was a photograph similar to the one hanging in her room at the inn. There were pictures of a stable with blacksmithing tools; a man was pounding a piece of metal on an anvil. Another picture showed a man dangling something from his hand. That one drew her attention. Upon a closer look she was sure it was the chime. The aged photo made it nearly impossible to see his face.

Each turn of the page sent a chill through Eryn. It was as if she had seen it all before. In place of the tea room was a cafe. Standing outside it was a man and a woman. "My God! It looked exactly like the couple in my dream." The photo was in fair condition and she could see it clear. The man…the man was familiar!

She looked up from the book, holding the light out to look around.

Bare spots lined the walls where pictures recently hung. A frightening creak silenced her momentarily, but a cat meowed outside so she continued to turn the pages of worn photographs, when one in particular caught her eye. It was in near excellent condition. Lowering the lantern, she saw it clearer. The man owned broad shoulders and long, thin legs. His light colored hair hung over those shoulders. When she looked at the background she saw the Enchanted Inn, but it wasn't an inn, it was only a house.

Hair on her arms stood out, a chill ran the length of her spine. She looked through the desk drawers, finding a magnifying glass. Her hand trembled as she looked at the enlargement of the man. There was no doubt, the man was Uriah Prescot. How? How could it be possible? The photo had to be a hundred years old. She snatched the photo from the album and looked up from her excitement, oblivious to what happened.

She was in a house...a beautifully decorated house with nineteenth century furniture. A richly upholstered, overstuffed sofa and chair was cozily situated near the hearth. There was a round parlor table crafted with black leather on the top, and a worn photo album sat upon it. Fresh flowers sat in a vase on a table beside the sofa. Who put them there? She picked up a newspaper and read the date—October 12, 1882.

Near the door was a dimly lit kerosene lamp. Drawn to the doorway she slowly touched the door handle, and exited. The streets were dirt, she could smell it. Lamplight's, the same as the ones that lined the streets of Enchantment, were softly glowing. A few carriages sped by her on the carriageway. By all rights, her state of mind should have been full of disbelief, but one glance at the photo showed it clear and new.

A couple walked by and she was wearing a long, tan dress with a ruffled petticoat, and a large brown bonnet. The man wore a gray suit with a matching vest, and on his head was a felt hat with a black narrow brim. He tipped it at Eryn when they walked by, snickering when they had passed. With her own faded jeans she wondered what they must have thought. Finally, stepping out she noticed the large beautiful house that was attached to the book store. In fact, the book store was actually the turret addition of the house as it stood now.

Eryn held her breath, trying to prevent the smile from forming, but she was so jubilant she could barely gain her composure. In a matter of seconds she was taken from disbelief to reality. She knew! She knew that in some way, she had crossed through time. Is this what the voice meant? But the face that matched the voice belonged to Uriah. He asked if she followed him, if she remembered him. She didn't remember anything before the age of around seventeen. Maybe Emmet knew. Maybe that's what he wanted to tell her! And maybe now he would tell her the end of the story.

Before turning to go she stood on the walk, spellbound. She was afraid to venture any farther, this time. There would be more times, she knew that. Tonight, the stars were glimmering in the evening sky. Moonlight was gradually rising in the east. The smell of smoked meat filled the pure air, and a whip poor will sang for its mate in the eventide.

Tranquil! A feeling of tranquility floated over her from her head to her toes, from the inside to the outside. There was no other word to describe it. Tranquil!

The photograph was nearly crinkled from the tight clench she had upon it, actually afraid for it to end, but hoping it would.

She turned to walk inside and a breeze blew her hair across her face. Reaching for the door she stepped inside, but the lantern blew out, causing her to fumble around trying to find her way. What sounded like a deep sigh stopped her in mid-step. Moonlight filtered in through the opened door, casting shadows on the wall. Through the dimmed light something in the corner looked like the figure of a man, a man with broad shoulders. She sucked in her breath, then caught a glimpse of the lantern before another cloud appeared. Haphazardly, she reached for it, searching in her pocket for a match. Two were left and from somewhere a light breeze blew the first out. She struck the last one, thankfully accomplishing her feat, and the lantern glowed.

Quickly swinging around, no one was there. As quickly and nonchalantly as the first time, the same thing happened again, but this time she found herself back in the old man's book store, unscathed in the process. The crinkled photo went back where it rested for who knows how long, and she closed the album. Kneeling low to slip beneath the planks, she blew out the lantern, closed her eyes and stepped out.

Standing upright in the cool night air, feeling the wet dew, smelling the dampness, told her she was back to normal, whatever that was. The fog had come in so rapidly, so thick, that it moistened her skin like a spray. Her eyes didn't open until she heard Cole's voice.

Stuttering was all that came out of her mouth as she tried to speak. "You won't believe this! I went through some kind of time warp. I was in this very same town, but it was 1882, I saw a newspaper! I was in the past. I was in another time!"

Cole and Beth threw a sidelong glance toward each other.

"We have to get to the hospital. Emmet must have remembered what he wanted to tell me!" They both continued to stare at Eryn as she proceeded to lose control of herself. "Let's go!"

"I'll meet you there," said Cole. "I'm curious now, I have to understand so I can help you, Eryn."

"Okay, but let's go now," she said, already on her way. She yelled over her shoulder, "By the way, Cole, is there another door to the book store?"

"Yeah, but it's boarded shut like the front," he said, standing with his hands in his pockets. "It's off the alley, why?"

"Will you see if it's still boarded, please?" Eryn's voice was shaky.

"Is something wrong? It was okay this afternoon, but I'll check."

"Thank you," said Eryn, trying to force a smile.

While the women left for their car, Cole checked the alley, noticing the boards lying on the ground and a pry bar close by. "No wonder she was worried," he said. "Someone's been in there." He took the pry bar and leaned over to pick up a board. The sound behind him came so suddenly he never had a chance to look up. Someone grabbed him from behind. He was led inside the book store and made to sit on the floor in front of one of the beams.

Uriah tied the rope loosely around his hands and bound him to the beam. "I have to convince her, Cole."

"Why don't you just leave her alone."

"There are things you know nothing about, kid, so don't interfere." At the door he stopped. "You might want to head toward the hospital when you get loose."

* * *

No street lights lined the dark highway that followed the Allegheny River. Traffic was light after the local people settled in their homes for the night. Eryn noticed the jutting of the car as she accelerated, thinking little of it. When it got worse, even Ms. Mercedes Benz, take-it-to-the-dealer Beth, asked what was wrong with the engine.

"It might be bad gasoline," said Eryn. "That's what I get for saving a buck. I'll stop at the service station ahead and get it checked."

"Is there one out here? It doesn't look like there's much out here at all," Beth said, squirming in her seat.

"I know there's one ahead near the hospital." Peering closer to the windshield, she said, mainly to herself. "Why is it always so foggy here?"

"I'm glad we're nearly there," said Beth. "I don't like these dark roads." She looked out the rear window seeing only blackness except for a lone car far behind them. "You're right, the fog does come in fast here."

Eryn explained how bad the fog was the night she and Alyce came to Enchantment the first time.

"It would be easy to go off the hillside without the white lines for a guide," said Beth.

As Eryn heard the words, the idea of going over the hillside struck something familiar in her and she felt a sudden sadness. A moment later Eryn said, "Well, we aren't going over the side...we aren't going anywhere." She pulled to the shoulder, coasting to a stop. "Great!"

"How far to that station?"

"About three miles, straight *up* that hill."

Beth reached into her bag, taking out her cell phone. Unfortunately, no service. She turned it off, putting it back in her bag. "A lot of good that does us."

They sat trying to decide if they should stay in the car or get out and walk. Beth wanted to stay, Eryn wanted to leave. "We'll flip a coin," said Eryn. Whatever the decision was, they knew they would stay or go together. Bright fog lights appeared directly behind them, the reflection, resplendent in her mirror.

"Good," said Beth. "Maybe it's a good-looking state cop. I bet his phone works!"

Eryn saw his silhouette as Beth was opening her door. She grabbed her arm. "No! Lock it!"

"Eryn, don't be silly. We need help."

Eryn stretched over her, grabbed the door and slammed it closed. "It's him!"

There was no time to react because Eryn's door was snatched open, and a large hand reached in and held her arm, pulling out the key.

"Let go of her, you monster!" Beth tugged at his arm.

His glazed eyes and strong breath gave away his excessive use of alcohol. Beth jumped out, running, kicking at him like a champion kick boxer. With one movement he grasped her wrists. Using his body to pin Eryn against the car he picked Beth up and sat her on the front seat. "Don't worry, if I know Cole Dawes, he'll be along here shortly. Just stay right where you are." He pushed down the lock and slammed the door. With a scheming look on his face he looked at Eryn with the lopsided grin she remembered. "Now you know the secret. We can go back. That's where we're from, Eryn, don't you know it yet?" He took her by the arm, leading her to his truck.

"I'm not going anywhere with you."

"You have to give me a chance. You have to let me prove this thing to you..."

"I won't go with you."

"I need to do this, Eryn. Get in," he insisted as he hoisted her up.

Rain was beginning to fall. He pulled out, racing past Eryn's stalled car as she looked back with fear. At the first side road he stopped and turned the lights off. Rain pelted against the windshield. He touched her face, turning her toward him. His lips pressed against her cheek, at the same time grasping a handful of hair into his fist. He inhaled its smell as he nuzzled his face into it. "I missed you," he moaned, fervently. Fingers, warm and gentle caressed her neck, unbuttoning two buttons, letting his lips travel to where his fingers led. She squirmed, trying to push at him as he continued to hold her. With his face so close to hers, he moved in to taste her lips. To him they were so sweet, so sensual. Her hair dropped from between his fingers and he looked directly in her eyes.

It all happened so fast Eryn was still in shock, not yet able to analyze what just took place. That touch she dreamed about was now upon her flesh, the tingle confused with fear.

"If you stayed you would have found him, your *not* so precious Taylor. He's there, you know."

She started to speak, but he pressed his lips against hers again. Somehow she sought and found his hair, heedlessly jerking his head back when she pulled it. When she let go he took off his belt and attempted to wrap it around her wrists.

"No, please don't," she begged.

"You can't hurt me anymore, sweet Eryn. I can do any thing I want, and believe me girl, I do want." With a condescending look he slowly licked his bottom lip. Reaching for her hands, he held them both in his. His lips softly kissed her, his tongue barely pressing against her teeth.

The smell and taste of alcohol overwhelmed her. She wanted to get away from him, but at the same time, something told her not to be afraid. As if something told him to stop, he sat back and looked ahead, contemplating what to do next.

With his attention momentarily away from her, she reached over and grabbed the door handle, leaping out the door, running as fast as she could. The hard rain drops hit against her face. The fog was thick, hiding any sign of refuge. Low branches scratched her face, and behind her she heard leaves rustling as they were crushed beneath his weight. The sound of breathing came closer and before she knew it she tripped, falling to the muddy ground. Exactly her kind of luck! Her forehead hit a log and she thought, hoped she would lose consciousness, for it would be better than being with him. He eased her unto her back, right away seeing the cut on her forehead.

"No!" she screamed, as rain fell in her face. "Let me go."

His hair, already drenched, dripped in her face. Sadly, he spoke. "I've waited too long for you. Why do you have to make this such a challenge, Eryn?" He knelt down beside her, his arms holding her tightly, and he sighed, whispering, "Eryn, I have to do this…have to help you remember—remember us."

Her head throbbed. Rain washed the blood from her forehead down the side of her face. Obviously she wasn't going to pass out. She wanted to think, to outsmart him. "Uriah, what happened to my husband?" she asked, hoping to distract him from going any farther, but she also *needed* an answer.

"Never mind him. You'll forget him…in time. Why don't you try to remember me? Listen to me…and to your heart."

"Tell me if he's okay, please," Eryn begged, oblivious to his words. She didn't want to cry, but tears rolled down her face, mixing with the blood and rain.

"He's okay." He tried to wipe the tears away with a familiar gentleness. "Why can't you forget him? He's not worried about you, he's off playing with someone else. Let me help you forget him," he said, before he brushed his lips across her forehead. This time his mood became sensitive, smoothing her hair back, examining the cut on her head. "Eryn, I *need* you, I need you back in my life. Since he brought your picture out to show me, I've been insane. I hoped you'd find a way back here, back to where you belong—back to me!"

"You are insane. I'm his wife, and I want to go home."

"You should have been my wife."

"You're crazy!" The wet dirt was soaking into Eryn's clothes and she was shaking from the cold.

Uriah finally helped her up. "Come on, we don't need to discuss our fate out here in the rain storm." He led her back the way she came until they reached the truck. He turned, facing her. "You finally returned, Eryn. I don't want you to leave again until you can remember what you left behind. Please, try to understand that's why I do what I do. Please, say you'll come with me willingly." He dropped his head, and she swore the wetness in his eyes was not from the rain. "The pain was too great when you left me."

His eyes looked sad when he spoke to her and for no reason she felt a lump in her throat. That look brought back something—something she had seen before, and it was hard to swallow, both the lump and the fact. "I must be crazy myself. I'll come with you, but only because I need to know what's happening to me."

He lifted her up to the running board of the truck, holding her head down so she didn't hit the roof. "Try to remember, Eryn. Can't you remember?" He kept repeating the words and as funny as it seemed, she *almost* could have believed him.

He climbed in on his side and fastened the seat belt around her. There was a clean cloth in the first aid kit and he dabbed at the cut on her head. "It's not too bad. You're still very beautiful, Eryn." He put the truck in gear, spinning around back unto the paved road. "I don't like seeing bruises on you. I hope it doesn't hurt," he said, as he gently touched her chin. "They thought I did it to you, back at the jail. You shouldn't have tried to escape me, look at your forehead now. You must stop running away from me, girl."

Eryn glared over at him, noticing his crooked smile in the glow of the dash lights. "You were probably proud to have them think you put marks on me. In a way, you did put them there."

He laughed loudly then looked over at her and stopped the truck. "You remember how those marks got there, and I would never do that to you. I might have marked you with love, though, if that bus boy didn't walk in. You used to like it. Is that what you're afraid of, Eryn? Can't you admit that you felt something?"

There were all kinds of things she wanted to say to him, scream at him, but she still didn't trust him. Knowing she was at his mercy, she kept them to herself.

"Don't worry, Mrs. Eryn Sterling. I'm confident I can claim you back before long."

"I'm only going with you because I need to know, need to know why I have these feelings." And these crazy visions, she thought, to herself.

He drove recklessly up and down the hills, around curves, passing other traffic along the way, nearly hitting a tractor trailer head on; it was so foggy. Eryn's muscles remained tense, and she was sure her heart would stop beating on the spot. He drove like that for about an hour then pulled onto a dirt road. She watched as he shifted into four-wheel drive, surmounting the steep, rutted road. They climbed up and turned onto another road, not much more then an overgrown path.

Chapter 10

The cold rain drizzled outside as Cole tried to wriggle out of the bindings. Tugging at the knot only made it worse. "Dammit! When I catch up with him I just might kill him! Son-of-a-...Damn, damn, damn!"

It was difficult, but he managed to stand, sliding the rope up along the wood. If he tugged at it, the beam would fall, but then again it may take part of the ceiling down with it. He would be of no help to anyone if that happened. Finally, as he rubbed the rope against a fragment in the beam he felt it loosen. Within a few more minutes he was free.

The fog was thick, much whiter than usual. Headlights bounced off the mist, making it hard to see. Not many feet ahead there was a car pulled off the road with hazard lights flashing, and as he sped by he slammed on his brakes, recognizing it as Eryn's. Beth was opening the door when he ran up to the car.

"Where's Eryn? Good God, what happened?"

"He...Uriah took her!" she answered, "I'm glad you're here." They could be anywhere by now, Cole, we have to find them!"

"Come with me," he said, helping her out. "We have to go to the sheriff, we can't do this alone."

"What good are they going to be, they let him out, didn't they?"

"Yeah, they released him," answered Cole, opening the door to his truck. "But we still can't do this alone."

95

"Well, we have to find her, God only knows what he's going to do! Is he deranged or what?"

The ride back was treacherous. The fog slowed them down and Cole didn't want to be slowed. When they entered the sheriff's station, Deputy Franklin questioned them. Beth was nearly hysterical as she explained every detail of what happened. The sheriff put every deputy on patrol. They proceeded to set up a road block, unable to do anything until their prey made the next move.

Beth contacted Alyce telling her to stay where she was, there was nothing she could do. She called Travis to inform him in case Avis called. The last call was to Hanah Grace.

Knowing they had to see Emmet they left for the hospital immediately after the report was taken. They barged into the nurses station, paying no attention to the late hour. However, they were told he was sleeping and he couldn't be disturbed.

"Shame on them for even considering it!" they were told. Beth made a scene until they let her talk to Dr. Lincoln. Upon hearing the situation, he immediately escorted them to his room.

"I've met you before haven't I?" asked Emmet. He looked at them, smiling in recognition.

"Yes, Mr. McDanil. I was here today with Eryn." Beth looked at the doctor and he motioned for her to continue. "Uriah Prescot has taken Eryn. He just *took* her!" She waited for his reaction. "Why did you need to see her this evening? Did you remember something? We need your help."

"I wanted to tell her I remembered something about her, but I don't think it can help now." Emmet closed his eyes trying to remember more. "I see her outside my store trying to make me tell her something." He slapped his hands down on the bed, bandage and all. "I was holding a book in my old arms, telling the pretty little thing to come back."

"What did you have to tell her, Mr. McDanil? Please try to remember."

"I do nothing but try to remember! This old mind is in a tizzy," Emmet cried. He shook his finger at Cole. "I can tell you that...that Mr. Prescot...I remember something about that man, but the memory ain't clear… You gotta find her." He drifted off as if thinking. "Tell me again why that pretty thing came to Enchantment?"

"She was taking her daughter to school…." Beth told him about Taylor's disappearance and the visions Eryn had. "It's the strangest thing. She came out of your book store tonight, saying—" Beth looked over at Cole. "…said she saw this town in its past. Does that make sense or mean anything at all to you? We didn't understand her." She hung her head, looking at the floor. "I don't think we can believe her."

Cole spoke up after listening to what they both had to say. "Emmet, do you think it would help if you went back to your book store?" Cole glanced over at the doctor who started to object, but Emmet put his hand up to stop him. "I'm good enough now, C.J.. I see no reason why I can't go. It's 'bout time you let me outta here anyway."

"I'll consider it, but not until morning. It's too cold and damp to be running around out there now."

"Tomorrow might be too late!" objected Emmet.

"Tomorrow!" He looked at Cole and Beth, saying, "You two need to leave. Mr. McDanil needs his rest now. I'll let him go with you in the morning. Come by about ten o'clock, he'll be ready."

During the time they were in the hospital, the fog had lifted and the sky was jet black with a collection of glittering stars. They were both sleepy. "Are you staying with Ms. Grace?" Cole asked Beth on their way to his pick-up.

"Yes, she invited me to, but I don't feel right being there without Eryn. I barely know the woman."

"She's a nice lady. She wouldn't ask if she didn't want you there. Besides, Eryn's car won't be fixed until who knows when. You may as well stay at her place."

"You're a nice young man. Thank you for helping us."

"I'm in deep now. I've been unsure of Uriah since I saw him with that woman."

"When did that happen?" asked Beth.

"About three months ago. You know, she looked a lot like Eryn."

"It's almost like he was waiting for her. Eryn said he looked familiar, but she never could place him." Beth took out the picture of Taylor with the woman on his knee.

Cole glanced over at it, pulling the truck to a sudden halt. "Let me see that picture!"

She handed it to him and he turned on the interior light. "I've seen them together, here. That's Eryn's husband, isn't it? Who's the woman?"

"I was hoping you could tell me."

"They stayed at the Enchanted Inn about nine or ten months ago."

Beth looked over at him, wide eyed. "That's when he disappeared. I found this picture when Eryn and I were looking through Taylor's things. I didn't show it to her. She told me he cheated on her once about five years ago, but the date on this picture is dated eleven months ago. Imagine that!"

"Well, now maybe you know why he left."

"But how does Uriah Prescot fit in the picture?" she asked.

Cole flipped on his turn signal, heading toward Hanah's. "I know they didn't get along very well when he was here. In fact, they had a fight. That's where Uriah got the scar on his jaw."

"He deserves it," she said, folding her arms stubbornly in front of her.

"Before you get all excited, I should tell you he didn't lose. He holds a black belt in some form of martial arts. I don't know why he didn't kill or maim me when I grabbed him. He could have."

"There's something strange about that man. It's eerie the way he chases after Eryn, isn't it? He told her he knows where Taylor is. That's the main reason she came back. He even called her by another name. When I met Eryn she didn't have a past. I wonder if Uriah knew her before."

"She didn't have a past?" asked Cole. "Ah, what's that supposed to mean?"

"No. Kind of like Emmet, I guess. We posted flyers and the police put her picture in the paper nationwide, but no one ever identified her, so I kept her."

"Beth, I saw a picture of Eryn. It was the one she had in her wallet today, the one with her husband. In the picture I saw, the half with Taylor was ripped off. I couldn't tell her because I knew he was here with someone else."

"Where did you see it, Cole?"

"When I barged in on Uriah with the other woman, it was lying on the floor. You know, when I think back to it now, I'm not sure he was harming that woman. Maybe he was right when he said she came on to him."

"We at least know Taylor was here, but where is he now?"

As they rambled on they reflected on what Eryn said about traveling to the past. Cole passed a car on one of the few passing lanes along the mountain highway. Neither one of them believed her, but they were afraid not to. What was one more strange happening in this whole confusing mess.

The remainder of the ride to Hanah's was quiet. Dr. Lincoln's handsome face appeared to Beth, causing a hidden smile. She remembered how he towered over her when she stood beside him. His body looked quite solid and his grip was strong when he shook her hand. Brown, wavy hair was cut short, squared off in the back above his collar. The gray, plastic framed glasses fit his face perfectly and his hazel eyes sparkled.

She remembered how he looked in his expensive pleated pants, walking ahead of her. Even with his white doctors coat she knew his shoulders were broad and his arms long. Blushing, she quelled a sudden urge to be held in those long arms. She wondered how much younger he was than her; it didn't really matter. His left ring finger was bare. Now that mattered! she thought with a smile.

When Cole pulled up at Hanah's he told Beth he would pick her up about nine in the morning. She bid him farewell then met Hanah at the door.

After eating a sandwich prepared by Rachael, Hanah and Beth went to the sitting room to relax and talk of their concerns.

"Miss Grace, I need to ask you something," said Beth. "What's so unusual about Emmet and his book store?"

"What do you mean, dear?" Hanah stood across from her, pouring some hot cocoa. "Anything could have happened to you, leaving you alone like that," she made a clicking sound, the tongue against the teeth kind.

"I'm a skeptical person, Miss. Grace. Do you know anything?"

After a short hesitation she spoke in a tone no different than asking Beth to pick up something from the corner store. "I know that she probably did see Enchantment in its former time. Eryn didn't imagine that."

"I don't understand," she said, almost in a question. "That's not possible."

"It is in the back of Emmet's book store." Hanah didn't know if she should say any more.

"But how? I'm *not* convinced of this. And who else knows, actually believes this?"

"I don't know, exactly. Emmet knew. It had something to do with his grandfather. If Emmet never gets his memory back the secret will be lost."

"Well, let's say this bizarre notion could be true. Does Uriah know?"

"Yes, dear, he knows. You won't believe this one either, and I can't say I blame you. It's a right good thing you're sitting down, dear." She hesitated. "Uriah is from that time, Beth, and Taylor is living in the days of the past, as well."

Beth stood. "Wait a minute, if Uriah is from Eryn's past, then...then—I don't understand..." she said, sitting again.

Hanah's whimsical smile proved Beth's theory. Her best friend is a...a time traveler...? "I'm... I'm puzzled. Wow! No wonder no one claimed her." All she could do was look to the floor and continue shaking her head.

"It's okay, dear, she's still your best friend."

"Does that blonde woman have anything to do with this."

"I don't know much about her, dear, except Taylor *is* with a woman. Emmet told me he thought Taylor might've deceived him with the motive he used to go there. Said he wanted the perfect gift for his wife. It's sinful, but Emmet took a lot of money from him."

"Hanah, you talk about this like these people just went to another town over the hill. Do you realize what you said? You're talking about going back in time here."

"I know, dear." Hanah took her hand. "Why do you automatically think it can't be?"

"Well, no one ever heard of *real* time traveling. Miss. Grace, that's only something people fantasize about. People write about it all the time, it's fiction. It's only fiction." The look on Hanah's face didn't change. "My God, you must know that." Beth couldn't accept what she was just told. No way in hell that could be possible. Sure, the past is then and the present is now, but that's exactly what it is. Then and now! Not a combination, not equal to, or the same as. Separate, different, not together!

"Dear, Beth, how can I convince you this thing is true." Hanah stood, looking out into the dark night. "Eryn is your best friend. You should accept this." She turned toward Beth. "Have you ever seen the wind?"

Beth stood up, holding the ice bag against her temple. A headache was coming on. "No. You can't see the wind."

"My point exactly. You can't see the wind, but you know it's there."

Beth Van Tine was speechless.

At that precise moment a soft draft of wind brushed a twig against the very window Hanah stood at. Beth scrunched her nose, wrinkling the smooth skin between her eyes.

Speechless!

Gently she shook her head, but the more insane she wanted it to be, she couldn't help but actually think about it as being a reality. After all, Eryn wasn't the kind of person that made up stories. *She* certainly was convinced. Beth brought her thoughts back to reality. "Are you sure? I mean… I mean, you're sure you didn't hear something wrong?"

"My hearing is especially good for a woman my age, dear."

"Then it was all planned. Taylor knew exactly what he was doing, he's not missing or in trouble. I hate that man even more now! So this was all about escaping with his little tramp. When did it all go wrong?" She sat down then got right back up, pacing this time. "That doesn't change what has already happened to Eryn, though. I'm so worried about her with that man. I keep remembering how he grabbed her through the door when he jerked it open."

"I'm not crazy about the man much, but I saw the way he looked at her a few times, and as much as I hate to say, I think he loves her in his own odd way. I don't think he's going to hurt her," said Hanah.

"Then why did he try to rape her, Miss Grace?"

"Try to…" She was silent for a moment remembering the farce Eryn kept up. "Eryn didn't tell you the truth?"

"What are you talking about, what truth?" Her head was throbbing by now.

"Eryn called the sheriff, telling him Uriah didn't attack her. She called the day before you came here. He already paid his bail at the preliminary hearing, so as soon as Eryn came back she was going to sign the papers and drop the charges."

"I wonder why she didn't tell me." For some ungodly reason Beth had a good feeling involving Eryn. She never would have felt that way about her with that man yesterday, but she had a feeling, and her feelings usually turned out right. Outside, the wind gusted and a lonely train whistle sounded in the darkness. Beth knew there would be no sleep tonight. As she sipped her drink, the chocolate was sweet on her tongue, and she thought of her friend. Maybe this man was the one that should have claimed her twenty years ago. Maybe this is who Eryn has longed for.

Right now, Beth was warm and safe, but still fearing for the woman she knew so well. Eryn wouldn't have dropped the charges if Uriah had attacked her. She closed her eyes, picturing what happened on the highway. From the light of the high beams she saw the fiery gaze in his wild amber eyes, knowing the eyes were familiar. I've seen eyes like that somewhere else, she thought. Putting that aside, a smile came to her lips and her thoughts went to Dr. Lincoln. That good-looking, young, and single, Doctor Lincoln.

Chapter 11

The bumpy road caused them both to be knocked around in the truck cab. Eryn's head throbbed. Her thoughts were of Beth, worrying about her on the roadside. Why is all this happening? she wondered. Am I really awake or is this a nightmare I can't wake from? She lay her head back against the seat, and glanced over at Uriah.

He sat there in silence.

She had to find a way to get through to him. "Tell me where my husband is."

He gave a smirky little laugh, but didn't answer.

She asked again.

Nothing.

The ruts were deep with mud and the truck labored to continue up the hill. Before long he stopped and turned off the lights. "If you give this a chance, you'll learn about yourself."

"I'm here for that reason, and that reason alone."

"Oh, it might be fun in the process, but I suggest you don't try to run off. I can think of things I'd rather do besides chase you through the woods."

He started to leave again into the foggy night, but she had to ask more questions. "Wait! You have to tell me what's going on." Okay, she *was* getting out of control. The raise of his eyebrow and his cockeyed smile reminded her of that. "Okay, I'll settle down, but tell me what you're going to do."

He put the truck in gear. "I'm going to make you remember me—then I'm going to marry you." He looked over his shoulder, checking for traffic. "We were engaged once, remember? I don't remember us breaking that off. I waited a long time for you to get here." Glancing at her, he continued, "You didn't know that did you?"

"But I don't know you. *How* do you know me?"

"I've known you forever, sweet Eryn. You've know me just as long. Somehow that blackguard you're married to learned of Emmet's outlandish little secret. When he first came here he offered to pay a lot of money to take you to 1882, but little did he know, you've already been there."

"How is that possible? And how did I get there tonight? Where did I get to tonight? *Tell* me!"

"Your friend, the old man, didn't know what he had. He should have kept quiet about his family secret."

"But how can someone go to the past and back to the present again? It can't be!"

"It was a secret his grandfather found out about. Well, he made the mistake of writing about it in that book of his. He could see things that would happen. Too many people started knowing."

"Did he see what happens to you, Uriah? Did he see you go to prison for abduction?"

"Of course, he knows everything, he knows that we live happily ever after, forever and always—And you agreed to come with me, so you can't say I abducted you."

When he said those words, *forever and always*, something in her memory recalled a man, a light haired man, and damn if it wasn't the same man sitting next to her. She chased that thought right away. "What choice did I have? Are you saying you wouldn't make me come?"

"This is how it goes… No I probably would make you come anyway, because you need to know the truth. But you'll see. After we satisfy our yearnings for each other, you can't resist me anymore, like before, and you fall in love with me all over again. Off we go into the proverbial sunset, as they say." He laughed so hard he nearly drove off the road.

Eryn wanted to clobber him, but definitely not anger him. Instead she tried to ask where he was taking her.

"You'll find out soon enough, but I'm not sure I want to wait anymore." With that he stopped the truck and unhooked her seat belt. He moved next to her, de-tangling her hair with his fingers. "I want you to be with me again," he whispered in her ear, "it's the right thing."

"Are you a crazy man? How can I be with you *again*, I don't remember ever being with you *before*. " She tried to ignore his fleeting touch and the jittery chills that went with it. The scent of him was alluring, spicy, all male, and she wished he'd leave her alone, for when she inhaled it, more memories flooded her thoughts. His nearness frightened her, consciously hoping it wouldn't come to this, and now she was trembling. He kissed her face, the bump hurting when his lips were near it. When she turned her face toward him she felt his needy body press against her. While his hand ever so gently caressed her, she cried.

"Don't cry, Eryn, I won't hurt you," he whispered.

"Then don't do this," she whispered back through sobs. "Uriah, that part of the story won't come true." She held her breath, afraid to say what was on her mind. "Emmet told me I would be happy again. He said he read the end of the story."

"And you will be, sweet Eryn, if you give us a chance." Uriah continued to hold her, his words, low, soft in her ear. Obviously becoming aroused, apparent by the deep sighs and rapid breaths across her neck. She couldn't admit that his touch caused her body temperature to be a few degrees higher than the normal 98.6.

"Taylor is the only one who will ever make me happy. Since he's been gone the light inside of me has burned out. Do what you will, but I will never love you." Her body went limp in his arms. Nothing mattered to her. He could do what he had to do, and she promised herself she wouldn't enjoy it too much.

"Taylor Sterling will never make you happy, only I can. Don't fool yourself any longer, Eryn." He tilted her face upward, meeting her glare. "The light can't burn out if it's never been lit. I'm the only person that can ever light it." He undid a button, stroking the smooth silk of her blouse. Warm fingers reached to the back, skillfully unhooking the contraption called a bra.

How talented! she thought. He can unhook it right through the material. Oh, what a man! Eryn was seething inside, trembling inside, confused inside. He better not snag the silk!

His breathing quickened. This should have been the time to be afraid, but instead, visions of another time entered her memory. A light haired man was making love to her in another time, another place. Eryn wanted to hold the vision there in her memory, explore it, but it became clouded when thoughts of Taylor appeared. Giving up the other image she closed her tired eyes for a moment, thinking of him.

If, indeed, her sanity was intact, she felt the side zipper on her pants go down and a warm hand caressing her belly. With his hands moving to her hips he adeptly lay her body down, lifted off his shirt, positioning it under her head. Rain pounded on her metal jail and water rippled down the windshield. Strong gusts of wind overwhelmed the truck and loud cracks of thunder rumbled in their ears. He took a blanket from behind the seat, recklessly covering them. It was the blue eyes of her husband she summoned, but all she could see when lightning flashed was the amber ones above her face. Her pants were being removed from her waist, his gentle fingers exploring her softness. All she could remember was looking into his lustful orbs, when he stopped to look at her, saying, "I love you...I love you..."

Sleepily, she remained idle in his arms, imagining his blond hair wasn't blond at all, but dark. The hands with callous could be imagined smooth, if she tried. Eyes looking in her eyes, saying I love you, were not amber, but blue, they really could be if she pretended hard enough. But the body about to love her wasn't unfamiliar at all. It felt like a body that she knew well. With her eyes closed tears found their way through her thick lashes and rolled down her cheeks. The body could be familiar, she could imagine it. Yes, she could, if she tried real hard....

* * *

The sound of birds singing their melodies were trying to bring her out of slumber. Her body ached from sleeping in the cramped position in the truck cab, and she was cold. Remembering the episode of the past night, her eyes sprung open wide. Uriah was at the steering wheel smiling at her, stroking his mustache as if nothing was out of the ordinary. He poured a cup of coffee from the thermos, and handed it to her. She should have been afraid of him, but the feeling wasn't of fear. She didn't know what it was. Hesitantly, she reached out of the blanket, noticing she was fully dressed, except for the few buttons he undid last night. She leaned into the door, trying to stretch, hoping to hide her confused thoughts. Despite his stare, she couldn't look at him, embarrassed about the prior night.

"What's wrong, sweet Eryn? You act like I've already violated you. Maybe I should have while you were *sleeping*." Uriah touched her chin, gently stroking it with his thumb. "Don't make a habit out of falling asleep on me, girl. You should be glad I'm a gentleman." He watched her for a moment, then released her. "I have to take a walk. Do I have to restrain you before I leave?"

Eryn shook her head, looking away. A dream…it was a dream! One that she'd had many times, but this time the touch was real. But he was still a stranger and suddenly she shook with elation, more than elation, to know the assault didn't happen. Luck was with her this time, but it was too soon to be lucky because Uriah still had his insane idea. Was there a way out of this?

Now that she knew a part of the story she had to help Taylor. No wonder he disappeared without a trace. He's supposedly somewhere that's unbelievable! Without her help he wouldn't have a chance. If Emmet never remembers, he may be stuck in the past forever.

She thought about what happened when she ran out of the book store. Was it the photo she picked up? The photo of Uriah? How on earth did she go through? She didn't know how she went through or how she returned. How would she do it again? That was the question of the hour. Suddenly, a terrible idea entered her mind. If anything happened to the store he would be lost forever. Oh, she had to get

Uriah to take her back! And she wondered if that was why it was burned.

The stale coffee was lukewarm, but it still warmed her. The morning was cold, damp, and faintly foggy. She wondered if Uriah had slept or stayed awake guarding her all night. How did she fall into such a deep sleep? Under the circumstances, she thought she would never sleep.

When he got back in he poured himself a cup of coffee, brushed his hair, and fumbled with the radio. Eryn recalled the words he spoke to her earlier. He said he waited for her. What did he mean by that? Sure, she was warned to watch out for him. Things kept getting more confusing. Now she was beginning to have faith in that old book that Emmet cherished. If only she could have convinced Emmet to tell her what he knew. This could have been avoided! She found it hard to believe what she had read, but why would someone believe something so outrageous. It wasn't something that sounded credible. No, not at all.

Her hair was matted with dried mud. On her forehead she found a bump with a deep cut, and blood clotted around it. Her clothes were stiff with caked on clay. Trying to run her fingers through her hair was useless.

"There's a creek over the hill if you want the mud rinsed out. This truck isn't going anywhere until I dig it out. The water will be as cold as ice, though."

Needing to stretch and relieve herself, she took him up on his offer. Oh, a squat in the woods! Didn't she love that idea. He took her by the hand, helping her out the driver's door. Inept at climbing over gear shifts, she bumped her knee on the four-wheel drive shifter knob. Then upon standing she was lightheaded. After a few steps she was sick to her stomach, sure she would vomit. Not steady on her feet, and hating it, she leaned on Uriah for support. His body felt as strong as it looked. The hill was hard to climb down; not even sure she wanted to continue, but when she heard the creek water splashing she looked forward to the cool water on her head.

He helped her kneel down while she threw water on her face. Uriah soaked a rag and cleaned her cut. The water was freezing cold but felt terrific on her aching head.

"You need to get this mud from your hair. Lean over, I'll try to rinse it out." He cupped his hands, competently pouring water over her long, tangled tresses, feeling her shudder as the water chilled her. Eventually, she pushed his hand away, leaning forward. "I can do it faster if I dunk my whole head in," she said, with teeth chattering. After doing so, she wrung out the ends, holding them on top of her head as she rinsed the mud from her knees.

Uriah was sitting on a large rock by the bank watching her every move. Wondering what to do about getting her clothes dried, she wouldn't ask him. Instead, she walked out a few feet and submerged her whole body in the frigid creek. At least the mud and clay were gone. Even with his eyes scanning each move she made, she removed her pants—a difficult task beneath the water. She could use the blanket for protection when she got back in the truck. Whether he liked it or not!

While Uriah sat on the bank with a self-satisfying grin on his face he pointed to the east. Turning her eyes to where he pointed she watched the golden sun rise above the horizon. Oh, good! What excitement would this day bring?

In the distance she saw a stream of smoke rising from a chimney with something that looked like a windmill standing directly behind it. He walked out to where she was, taking hold of her wrist, pulling her with one hand. The current was running fast and although it became shallow she lost her balance on a slippery rock, but Uriah caught her before she fell. Was that supposed to make him gallant? she thought. Hah! While holding her, his fingers arrogantly pressed against her breast. She didn't want to see the way his tongue moistened his lips, so she looked away from his craving gesture.

Jerking herself away she lost her balance, falling directly on her derriere, using a few choice expletives in the process. That time he let her fall, but he watched her get up by herself. She looked up at him, seeing the cunning corners of his mouth curve upward as she stood. Let him enjoy the look of my wet, silk blouse as it clings to my cold erect breasts, I don't care! "I don't *care!*" she said, shouting at him, as he sat so smug on the shore. She tried to ignore his gaze, still shivering, still cold, still erect. Her sarcasm turned to worry, abruptly thinking about later. Albeit, she didn't have much of a chance with him. He didn't plan to let her go any time soon and she didn't relish the idea of being with him for one more minute, not one more second!

At the truck he gave her the blanket, then waited outside while she stripped off the wet blouse and wrapped in it; she had no choice, in fact, because the clothes were freezing on her. It seemed the high mountains get a lot colder than her flat, near sea level city.

The truck's heater was on, but she continued to shiver even though the warmth was blowing on her. To top it all off wool always pricked her soft skin and this blanket was no exception. So what was one more inconvenience! Her life was over as she knew it, over…since she met the crazy man with amber eyes. Well, very nice amber eyes at least!

After their trek down the hillside he bent over and took a key from under a stone. The exterior of the cabin was made of logs, rustic. It looked old, yet, it looked new too. When he opened the door, Eryn was impressed. Almost like the door opened into another century, like when she went through the book store, or whatever she went through. It was a large open room. Near the center was a wrought iron stairway with thick oak steps leading to a loft. A large brick fireplace was against the west wall.

The furniture was nineteenth century. Eryn considered herself an expert in the furniture business because she studied that era intently. Uriah must have liked a little of everything because he chose an eclectic style, whether on purpose or by accident. A parlor table sat in the center of the room, adorned with a tapestry draper; a chess game was set up, ready for a quick Checkmate, if she played. One dozen white roses were creatively arranged in a tall crystal pitcher. In the corner near the fireplace was a doll carriage. Inside was a doll baby made of bisque and burlap, with large, clear blue eyes.

After Eryn got over the surprise of the Victorian interior, she went to the fireplace to add more seasoned logs. She looked around for matches, finding them in a decorative tin can near the hearth. Uriah watched as she crumbled newspaper, packing it around the logs. Before long, flames were shooting upward, the heat warming her face. He went to the loft to change into dry clothes.

Once she was satisfied with the fire she sat on the floor, soaking up the heat. Her short lived calm quickly faded when he called her to come up stairs.

What nerve! she thought. Imagine him—thinking he can coax a snake right out of its hole! She didn't move from her spot on the floor. It wasn't going to be easy for him. If he wanted to have his way with her he would have to fight for it! Besides, her dizziness returned and she couldn't attempt the steps. Hearing his voice up there, she glanced at the pile of wood and reached over to pick one up, but his foot came down on the log just before she grabbed it. "What are you, some kind of Ninja, transporting yourself around like that!"

"Yeah! Remember that," he chortled. "I'm not giving you a chance to ruin us again, Eryn. Not until I can make you understand. There's no need to try anything with me because I will surely win." He reached for her hand, and lifted her to a standing position. "I asked you to come up with me."

"Why?" Her eyes casts flames of fury at him, however, the more trouble she gave him the more he seemed to enjoy it. Well, he's going to have to fight me for it anyway, she thought again. "No," she said defiantly, and the green in her aqua eyes dominated the blue.

Uriah was in her face in an instant. "It's not like you to say no and mean it." He pulled her against him, thinking he would love to rip the blanket from her, but she had it wrapped around her too tightly. It wouldn't be to his advantage to threaten her anyway. That's not what this was about. Trying to control his emotions, and thoughts, he took the end of the blanket and pulled it up around her shoulders. So be it! He lifted her hair, gently nuzzling the back of her neck.

Peace would not come easy for him this day, for a painful screech came as she took the heel of her boot and scraped it along his shin bone. Eryn tried to wiggle away from him but, damn, if she didn't get twisted in the blanket, losing her balance. Together they tumbled to the sofa. Exactly what she needed!

His anger heightened but he contained it, taking her hands in his, actually enjoying the predicament she put herself in. "Eryn, I'm sorry I have to keep you here," he said, glad to be holding her. "When are you going to learn not to defy me?" He squeezed her tight against him, concealing his face in her still wet hair.

"You can't hurt me," she whispered. "It's been done before. Uriah, I want to leave. You can't make me do what I will never do." Although she took the chance of angering him again she said it anyway. "You can't keep us apart."

He looked in her eyes, his with a look of sorrow and shock. The only words he heard were of her being hurt before. "He hit you?" he asked, as he pounded his fist into the cushion.

She turned away from his stare not having to speak to answer him, for he saw the reply on her face.

"Damn! Don't you know he's the one keeping you apart, not me!" He raised up, trying to ignore her body beneath him, intentionally allowing his gaze to lock on her turquoise eyes. He noticed the green flecks danced when she was angry, like before. "Eryn, if you only…" His head dropped, resting upon her chest. Without another word he stood up and raced out the door, helping it slam behind him.

* * *

In the loft there was a flannel shirt hanging on a hanger, and she shook it incase there were any spiders hiding in it. Sitting on the bed she buttoned the shirt. It was a brass tester bed, harboring a dark blue canopy. The bedroom was done as beautifully as the downstairs, but today she was in no mood to enjoy it.

The walls were of the natural log the cabin was built from. A walnut armoire with large double doors sat against one wall. On the south wall was a wide arched window trimmed with blue and green stained glass in a triangular design.

At the end of the room was a tall bachelor's chest, typically, with a round mirror and a wooden box on top. Two antique picture frames sat on the chest. One with a red haired girl; Eryn could have looked like that when she was young. Ironically, it looked like the girl in the picture in Emmet's book store. The other frame was of Uriah. He was easy to recognize sitting with the same girl. The peaceful look on their faces showed how happy they were. Next to the window was a cheval dressing mirror. A scrolled oak rail ran the length of the loft.

Eryn saw a brush on the dressing table and went to the mirror to brush her hair. It was so tangled she pulled knotted strands out. A stranger looked back at her in the mirror. Her eyes were red and swollen and mascara was smudged beneath them. When she fell in the forest hitting the log, it caused an egg size bump on her forehead. A nasty purple-blue shadowed it. The gash looked about an inch long, and deep. The soreness was still there, her head still throbbing. How could he think he loved her, looking as terrible as she did now.

She still felt dizzy upon standing and the nausea returned. Lying on the bed she stretched then rolled to her side, bending her knees until the nausea passed.

Thinking of the previous night in the truck she hated the reality of it, it was too real. Something about his movements and his touch was familiar to her. She grew tired of denying it. It was true, the look in his eyes along with the sound of his voice, brought something to the surface, something that she couldn't, wouldn't explain to herself.

She heard him come back in, definitely not wanting to be on the bed when he saw her, but she was lightheaded, unable to get up. Thinking about it took too long, for he was up the steps and in the room in less than a twinkling.

"Are you okay, you don't look good?" he said as he sat on the side of the bed.

"My head is spinning and I'm nauseated," she said, hoping to dissuade him from anything he might have on his mind.

He propped another pillow behind her, parting and smoothing out her hair with his fingers. "You might have a concussion, lie still for awhile." He left the room, fidgeting through things in the kitchen. The light on the wall flickered as he screwed in a fuse and the refrigerator kicked on. Water splashed in the sink, roaring as it ran down the drain.

Still sickened, nausea churned around deep in the pit of her stomach, rising in her throat. Uriah came back up, turning off the light, and pulling the shade down over the window. He returned with a wet cloth and laid it across her forehead. It felt good even if she did shiver from the chill of it.

"Let me make you more comfortable." He took the blanket off the rack and gently lay it over her, tucking it around her sides. Little things like that seemed familiar, too. If she had been in her right mind she would have been alarmed when he lay next to her, his hand on her shoulder, stroking her hair. But as it was, she felt so badly she didn't even care that he was there.

Soon, he got back up. She listened as he closed the dead bolt across the back door. Fighting sleep as long as she could it finally overcame her. On a good day, Eryn Sterling could control her thinking, but there was no way for her to control the visions that went on as she slept.

Hands were caressing her and warm lips brushed her ear. The breath on her skin was sweet. Kisses covered her face and she wrapped her arms around the broad shoulders. His lips covered hers, his tongue hot; she accepted it, and liked it. Her fingers played with the golden hair at the nape of his neck. His skin was hot under her hand as her fingers traveled over his body; his hips were so tight! She trembled with delight as her body longed for the love she so badly waited for. The hardness of his body pressed against her until she could wait no longer.

The pleasure that was promised was delivered as the two lovers moved together as one.

Surely, and slowly aroused by the sounds of nature, she was coming out of her semi-sleep. Sparrows chirped and a coyote's howl was close by. Outside, the wind cried with a lonely sound. Rain tapped against the windows, sounding like hail stones against a tin roof. Eryn moaned and unbeknownst to herself, softly whispered a name. She lay there a few moments, yawning and stretching. The heat from another body was next to her and she slowly opened her eyes, suddenly focusing in on where she was. Ever so slowly she turned her face toward the sound and her nightmare once again was real. Knowing she was sleeping with next to nothing on, she didn't want him to awaken while she was still there next to him. Slowly, she sat up, and as she stepped off he took hold of her wrist.

"Where do ya think you're going?"

She saw that he didn't have a shirt on, afraid of what else he didn't have on.

He threw the covers back—all too soon seeing what he *did* have on, which was a pair of green, silk boxer shorts. She quickly turned her head, not wanting to see they were made for his body to wear.

"Do you realize whose name you call out in your sleep? If you miss your deceiving husband so much, why is it you call the name of this man?" He threw his legs over the side of the bed. "It hurts me deep inside when you won't give me a chance." He kneeled down on his knees separating her legs, moving close to her. "I need you...I need your body beside mine. It's been too long without you." He leaned toward her, putting his arms around her, gently drawing her head to his chest.

She thought it better not to say anything. If he wanted to take her right then, he could. With his muscles flexing the way they were she had no chance against his strength, and little clothes to get in the way. Before that thought left her mind, without warning he stood up and put on his jeans, tossing her a pair on his way down the steps.

She ran after him. "Uriah, please take me to Taylor."

"I'll never take you to him. He doesn't want you there!"

She looked at him closely for the first time. His amber eyes held the look of pain. The familiarity kept coming back, but she couldn't pull it from her memory. God knows she really wanted to. Thinking it over first, she said it, knowing she had to play by his rules. "If you let me see that he's safe, I'll reconsider my relationship with you. I know for some ungodly reason you think you love me, but I need to know he's okay."

"Why should I trust you?" He struck a match to light the burner and put a pot of coffee on the stove. "You don't even understand that Taylor doesn't want to be a part of your life anymore."

"Uriah, I do mean it." She grasped the railing. "And you can trust me because I've given you no reason not to."

He turned on her quickly. "It doesn't matter whether you mean it or not. I'm deciding things from now on. You don't need to know if he's okay. He doesn't deserve your loyalty." He was getting angrier, moving closer to the steps. "He doesn't want to come back, and you, sweet Eryn, can't go after him."

"Why did you do this to us?" Tears, having a will of their own, would fall soon.

Uriah walked over to the steps, grabbing the rail with both hands. "*You* did this! I loved you in those days of yesterday. You left me, and when I was offered the way through I left, too, looking for *you*. I ran away looking for *you*. I tried to find *you!*" He paced the floor beneath her. "Now we're both here, this is meant to be for us." He sat at the table, dropping his head into his hands. She looked down at him from the loft, trying to comprehend what he said. "It couldn't have been me. It couldn't be me," she repeated in a whisper, trying to choke down the lump.

"It is you. When I saw your picture in his wallet I knew it was you. I thought you found your way back to Enchantment—to me." Sitting steady, he continued, "Think, Eryn. You can remember if you *think* hard enough."

Slowly, she went down the steps and sat on the sofa. True, there was no reality to it, but she felt so drawn to Enchantment. The visions, the photographs, the chime. The chime! She remembered what Lesley told her. The man, his betrothed left him. Oh, my God! thought Eryn. Was it Uriah? No. No! "It's all too unbelievable," she mumbled to herself.

"What's unbelievable?" he asked, sweeping his fingers through his hair, lifting it off his back and letting it fall again.

When he did that the whole of her insides lurched. What was that feeling tumbling around? Watching him do it again actually numbed her soul for some reason unbeknownst to her. After regaining her poise she tried to think of what they were talking about. WHEW! If he knew he did that to her, she'd be in big trouble. Getting her mind back on the subject took some doing. "Wh...what did you say?"

"You're the one who said something was unbelievable. What is?"

"This! This whole thing," she said.

"Eryn, that other woman a few months ago, I know you heard about her. I thought it was you. I wasn't trying to assault her. That's not who I am. She looked so much like you that when she came on to me, I let myself believe it was you, I wanted it to be you. And by the way, thanks for letting them think I was attacking you. I could've went to prison."

"What's the difference, you're going for holding me here anyway."

"Then I might as well have my way with you, too."

"But that's not who you are, right!! She slammed the words into his ears.

Silence filled the room while they tried to out stare each other. Inwardly, Eryn allowed herself to be terrified, but outside she put up her wall. "I called the sheriff and told him I was dropping the charges, but you were already out."

"Thank you."

"I didn't do it for you." Silently she thought about the guilt and shame she felt for allowing the lie to continue as long as it did.

Uriah remembered the incident in room 216. He still felt the fervor. The touch of her fingers still lingered on his skin, the passion burning in her eyes. Maybe she won't admit it to herself, he thought, but her body *already* admitted it to me. He dropped the subject.

"Eryn, you don't have him to love anymore, you might as well love me." He smiled with that twist on his lips, as if it was a natural thing to say.

"This is all so hard for me to believe. If I hadn't been in the book store and gone through, as you say, I wouldn't believe any of this." She sat down in a chair across from him, feeling the need to be blunt. "It wasn't me, it's not me. I'm sorry for your loss, Uriah, and I'm flattered, but I would know if I was in love with you." She thought to the time twenty years ago, her first memory. It was true that she had no memory of her prior life, but what Uriah said was preposterous.

Annoyance ruled his actions as he grabbed her by the shoulders. "You are her! I don't care what you say or think...you are her." Eryn shook her head over and over again, but he kept drilling her. "Don't you remember the park we walked in? Don't you remember the gazebo we sat in, our first kiss was there. That's why I put you in that room at the inn. Didn't you see the picture, didn't you remember, girl?"

Yes, she saw it—*No,* she didn't remember! She tried to pry his hands off her shoulders, but his grip only tightened.

He looked deeply into her eyes, whispering, "Maybe it's me you long for, not him. Stop fighting me and give into it. Give us a chance."

"Even if it was me, it doesn't change the way things are now. I've been with him for nineteen years. We're a family."

"You were a family. Your marriage with him is over, his choice, not mine." Uriah dropped his hands from her shoulders and stepped back.

Eryn sat down on the floor in front of the fire, her back to him.

"You're lying," she said calmly. "It won't work, I know you're lying." Restless and irritated, she got up and poured herself a cup of coffee. "I need some aspirin," she mumbled to herself, rubbing her temples. The injury to her head pained, and she hurt all over.

Uriah went to a cabinet, opened a bottle of aspirin and set two in the palm of her hand. "Can't you accept your fate?"

If he was trying to manipulate her, it wouldn't work. He was trying to convince her he was right so she'd care for him. Well, that wouldn't work, either. Pondering on the situation at hand, she didn't know if he would try to get intimate again. He wanted her...she knew that, but each time he got close to it he would leave. She didn't think he would have stopped back at the inn—couldn't believe he stopped in the truck. Would she have stopped him, herself? No one was here to rescue her, that was for sure. She couldn't even depend on herself. Where he was concerned, her will was weak. Who would protect her from her damn self?

"I have to go get the truck," Uriah said. "Come with me or I'll have to restrain you until I get back."

"You don't have to, I won't leave." Building trust was a start. "You can trust me," she said, eyes lowered to the floor.

"These woods are wild around here with coyotes and black bear. A bob cat was spotted around here not long ago."

"I won't leave," Eryn said.

He handed her a cotton throw from the sofa. "Take off the shirt," he ordered.

"Why?"

"Isn't it obvious? Just take it off and give it to me."

He turned his back while she did as he ordered. Eryn threw it at him, defiantly standing in front of him, wrapped in a cotton throw with her arms crossed against her. He took it along with her boots and headed up the hill toward the stuck truck.

"Hmm," she said, pacing around the cabin. After repeating a few more hmm's, she said, aloud, "Keeping me here will be as hard as getting cookie dough back it the tube." At the window she watched him trudge up the muddy hill. He'll see! He'll see, she thought, as she searched the room....

Chapter 12

Beth didn't look like the type that wanted to ride in a truck used for construction, or whatever, so Cole borrowed a car and arrived promptly at nine. One look at Beth told him she had a sleepless night. Driving to the hospital seemed longer than usual. The trees were nearly in full color and beautiful. The eastern sky was iridescent blue, the clouds, high and windswept. Sun reflected off car bumpers on the road making a blinding light. In the distant west the sky was dark and stormy.

Emmet and Dr. Lincoln were waiting in the lobby, and he looked better than he did the night before; so did Emmet. His silver hair had been trimmed and neatly combed. A bruise was still on his forehead and the stitches had only a small bandage covering them. After being wheeled to the car, Dr. Lincoln insisted on putting a walker in the trunk, telling Cole to make sure he used it. The orders were to have Emmet back in two hours. He told them that seeing something as familiar as his book store might trigger his memory.

Dr. Lincoln stood with the nurse as they drove away. "Uriah Prescot has quite a reputation, but honestly I don't think he can be accused of rape."

"You've treated several rape cases lately, and you know the rapist has never been caught."

"Yes, I worry about her being at his mercy, *if* he is the guilty one. I hope

I don't have to see her as a patient when he's done with her. *If* he's the one."

"Yes, me too. On a more positive note, Doctor, did you notice how ravishing Ms. Beth Van Tine looked this morning?"

He couldn't hide the smile that brightened his face. "Um, yes, Nurse Abcott, I noticed thank you."

* * *

Emmet sat forward when they came in view of Main Street. His expression showed that he was trying to remember. "It's right up here, I know it is." When they were near the tea room he knew exactly where it was. He hadn't seen it since the fire and they didn't know what his first reaction would be.

"Have you remembered anything else, Mr. McDanil?" asked Beth.

"I remember somethin', but it don't mean nothin' to me. Maybe it'll help this old brain when I go inside. I'm thinking 'bout a book I need to find. I don't know which one, but I'll rightly know when I find it."

They pulled up in front and Cole went around to help Emmet. He got the walker out, but Emmet kicked it aside.

"I don't need that thing."

"But…"

"Never mind the doctor. That man worries too much." Emmet pointed to a two-by-four lying in the rubble. "Bring me that piece of wood. That should hold an old man up." He looked at his lifelong place of business. "Oh my, it's almost gone."

"The rear part is fine, Mr. McDanil," said Beth. "Eryn was here last night," she hesitated, sadness creeping into her voice, "…before Uriah took her. She was looking through a photo album and she found a picture of you, and a man that looked like Mr. Prescot."

Emmet stood straight and tall, looking at the entrance. "You did a good job of cleaning up, boy. …I suppose we better go in."

Cole went ahead and lit the lantern. He held it up to look around the place. Emmet and Beth came in and he walked every inch of his store. He sat in his leather chair, inhaling the smell of it. The putrid smell of smoke still lingered in the air. "I'm at home here. It looks different, but I can remember this." He struggled to get up and went to the desk. On top was a photo album. He haphazardly turned the pages, lingering here and there, examining each picture.

He scanned an old photo of Enchantment, the way it looked a hundred years ago. "This one's familiar to me." He held it to the light, then listened. "Do you hear the sound of the chimes in the wind?" He looked around to see if they heard, but they were not there. He looked at his surroundings and saw that, in fact, he was the one who wasn't there. The room—his back room—was transformed to the way it looked when he was a boy. He walked through the door to the outside. He turned, seeing his grandfather's house. Memories flooded his thoughts, and suddenly it was all clear to him. Suddenly, he knew his quest.

He knew that he wanted to tell Eryn about her man called Taylor. That he wasn't all he seemed to be. Was he wrong about being afraid of Uriah? Maybe Taylor was the one that was the danger. Was she with the wrong man from the beginning? He couldn't find the book so he couldn't be sure, he hadn't read it in so long. His eighty-eight year old mind forgot things sometimes. He knew she would be happy again, but he wasn't sure who she was supposed to be with. The book never lied in all his life of having it. It got him through a lot of tough times. Maybe it wasn't fair, but it helped him, and now if Eryn made the right choice, it would help her. Where was the book?

The night Uriah came into the store so angry, he must have been afraid Emmet would tell her about Taylor. Emmet wrung his hands. To think this all could have been different if he had reread the story and been able to tell Eryn. Instead he confused her all the more.

Emmet McDanil was like a new man! He hurried though the park and around the gazebo, needing to rebuke the demon. He had to get to Taylor. Emmet had to know which man was the right one for Eryn. He had to help because it was his fault Eryn was in the predicament she was now in.

The man's dark hair hung in his eyes as he forged the steel. Sweat dripped from his brow and his dark hair hung in wet strands, clinging to his neck. Muscles bulged in his arms as he pounded the hot steel against the anvil. His apron was barely tied around his chest. Sweat glistened on his back as his body moved in tune to the clang. Damp hair curled in ringlets and poked out around the apron. His boots were nearly to his knees and fit as tight as his breeches. Large sun-browned forearms were nearly covered with leather gloves. When the old man went in, eyes of steel looked up at him.

He quickly closed the barn door and put the steel down to cool. "Mr. McDanil, what in God's name are you doing here?"

"I came to tell ya yer wife's here in Enchantment. She found the Portal and stepped right through. She's a lookin' for ya."

Before Emmet could finish, a woman walked into the stable carrying a cold drink, and she was heavy with child. She walked to Taylor, putting her arms around his neck, dripping some of the cold liquid down his back. He tried to get free of her hold but she laughed, squeezing tighter, then she saw he had a visitor and she released him.

Emmet quickly determined that he had been deceived. He always suspected it, but the amount of money he was paid caused him to keep his mouth shut and ignore it. But then Eryn, sweet Eryn, had to come into town and he couldn't let her be hurt. It all started with the foggy night his granddad wrote about. The fog, and the lonely woman with eyes he wouldn't forget. He gave Taylor a look of disgust, turned and walked away.

Taylor chased after him. "Old man, you *can't* tell her about me, you can't tell her I'm here."

"She already knows and if I have anything to do 'bout it ya will not hurt that pretty little thing. If I have to, I'll destroy the Portal and ya won't be goin' back." He looked toward the woman. "What you're doing is wrong." Emmet jerked his old arm away and stormed out. "Wrong, I say."

Taylor grabbed the woman, drawing her into his arms, hugging her a little too tightly. He watched Emmet close the door. "You stupid old man," he mumbled, "I already tried to beat you to it, but the damn thing didn't burn down."

He hurried down the street to his grandfather's beautiful, strange house. Once inside he closed the old album. Turning around he saw Beth and Cole waiting for an explanation. He smiled at them, relieved, because he now knew Eryn was with the man she should have been with. He explained all he thought necessary. They felt a little better knowing that Eryn wasn't actually with some rapist-murderer. But Emmet was an old man and maybe things weren't as they seemed. His mind was old and he didn't always remember everything.

Chapter 13

Eryn could see him on the ridge. It was plain to see the truck wasn't going anywhere for awhile. She looked around, finding a pair of green rubber boots under the stairway. She went upstairs to search for clothes. Half way up she stopped and thought about gaining his trust. Forget it, she thought, I can't wait. She found a ragged, faded jean jacket and the jeans he threw her earlier. Out the window she could still see him on the hilltop trying to dig the tire out. She laced the boot and tied it as tight as she could get it. Her small foot slipped in and out of the boot no matter how she tried to lace it. They were sloppy big, but she had to try. Uriah was hooking the winch up to a tree and he didn't look happy.

He glanced down toward the cabin then continued with his work. Eryn searched the drawers for a key to the side door, smiling when she found it, wasting no time getting out. She ran down the trail that led to a clearing, and then into the trees. The clearing went easy, but the undergrowth and the low trees made it hard to go through, especially with the oversized boots.

The sound of the winch whined and she knew he was still busy working. It was bow-hunting season, and she hoped to find a hunter that could take her out of this beautiful prison. She trudged on with the boots slipping nearly off with each step, and when she stepped in mud she had to pull the boot out or her foot would slip out of it. It must have been about a half mile, then it was quiet, and she hoped she didn't hear the whine of the machine because she was too far away, not because he was finished.

She came to a road that was only there for fire emergencies, and stopped to catch her breath. The woods were quiet except for the occasional caw of a crow. The fruity aroma of smoke cured meat filled the air, reminding her she was hungry. Her head was spinning, the nausea, again churning in her stomach. After a short rest she darted across the road. Looking to her right, she choked on her own fear, for she saw the gray pick-up racing toward her. "No!" She ran as fast as she could, her boot sticking in the mud, but she didn't take time to pull it out. Instead, she slipped them off both feet and ran on without them. A large bushy pine tree was ahead and she ran for its cover. The door slammed and branches broke under his angry steps. She ducked behind the tree, not quick enough!

Hi seized her, trying to catch her before she fell to the ground. "Trust! You said I could trust you!"

She screamed as the weight of their fall pushed them into the mud. He took both her hands in one large one, cradling her head with the other. "You said you wouldn't do it! You said you wouldn't leave!" He drew her head toward him, staring into her scared, disoriented eyes. "Damn, Eryn, listen to me!" He released her hand, holding her close against him.

He hadn't caught her soon enough! When they fell she hit her head on the ground, and she heard his voice, she saw the look in his eyes, but all she could do was mumble nonsense to her nemesis before darkness passed in front of her eyes.

* * *

Uriah looked at the woman on his bed. She was beautiful, even full of mud. Dropping his head into his hands he sat forward in the chair. What was this force that made him need her so badly? He loved her deeply, couldn't help himself for sure. The thought of someone else having her was enough to destroy him. For twenty years it destroyed him, plus a few more. He waited, worried, wondered about her.

He wrung out the cloth in the basin and gently patted her face. He felt sympathy for her, and disgust for himself knowing he was keeping her against her will now, well sort of. She winced when he touched her, but the beautiful Eryn remained asleep. Her feet were scraped and he cleansed the wounds. He took off the torn coat, throwing it on the floor. "What was she thinking running around out there? She could have run into a desperate hunter." An inner voice told him that she might be safer, even with a desperate hunter.

The jeans were caked with mud, her lace panties, ripped and muddy. He slid them off and tossed them aside. Dirt and sweat streaked her neck, settling between her faded tan breasts. He moaned in anguish as he looked at her. The water was tinged red; he changed it and continued to wash her body. Her muscles were taunt, her belly flat with a few stretch marks. He kissed them. "Marks from bearing children that should have been mine," he whispered. Closing his eyes for only a moment, he repeated words that would forever be etched on his soul…

"Uriah, boy of my youth, man of my life. I am your woman, no longer a child. It is with you that I will forever be. I want to be young with you, old with you, forever with you. I want to be the mother of your children. I love you, Uriah, boy of my youth, man of my life."

He lingered over the words he often remembered. Words said to him, meant for him, taken away from him. Why had this terrible thing happened to them?

Jerking his thoughts back to the woman on his bed, he watched her, leaning forward, kissing one cheek then the other. Continuing his task, he turned her, lathering the scented soap over her back, hips, and thighs. Gently he turned her over and washed her limbs up to her inner thigh. Waiting… His fingers quivered wanting to seek the womanhood hiding within the soft folds of her lonely body, squeezing her thigh to keep his hand still. He needed her like a diabetic needed insulin. She was his life, his insulin. How could he stand it? It wouldn't be the same if he took her against her will but, God, he might! He thought if he could make love to her she would remember. Remember the way they used to love when they were young. She loved it when he loved her, and if he could just be patient…she would again.

He didn't want to, but he ripped an old sheet and loosely tied her hands to the brass headboard. She looked helpless lying there with her eyes closed and wetness deep within her lashes, and hands bound. He bent forward and softly kissed her lips.

"I'm so sorry, sweet Eryn," he whispered. It was a dreadful thing making her stay against her will. The cut on her forehead broke open and oozed blood once again. He butterflied the wound closed with tape strips.

Uriah felt horrid shame at what he did, but deep inside, no matter what shame he felt, he knew he would do it again if it meant keeping her. He studied her again, leaving her unclothed, and couldn't resist the urge to crawl on top of her and take her...but he did resist, pulling the comforter over her. Seeing her with her wrists bound left him feeling like a warden not a lover. A rock-hard lump rose in his throat, and it would probably be there for a long time.

The ground was wet and the decaying leaves were slippery. Running... running from something—Eryn knew she had to get away. Run some more...keep going, a voice told her. No...get up...get up, Eryn...make yourself get up! The sound of twigs cracking was getting closer behind her...he was on top of her...Screaming! Screaming! Screaming at her!

"No!" Eryn woke herself up with her own scream. She tried to sit up, realizing her hands were tied to the bed. Her head pounded and her anger only made it worse. She didn't get away! All she remembered was running from the cabin. Then she saw his truck and heard him yelling...yelling at her. Dizziness was all she felt before everything went black.

Her squirming caused the comforter to slip from her shoulders, revealing her nakedness. Be still, she told herself. Seeing Uriah come up the stairs wasn't what she wanted to see. What she wanted to see was the sheriff hauling him away in handcuffs, but she knew that wasn't going to happen. She slid down farther under the blanket so she would be covered when he did return. Her head ached.

The smell of ham reminded her she hadn't eaten in a day. Sounds of a spatula scraping against an iron skillet drifted upstairs. She wondered where he got the food. Eggs, firmly tapped, were cracked and whipped to a creamy yellow with a fork; she could picture it as she heard his movements. The cabin was filled with the smell of potatoes frying.

Eryn saw that the cloth used to tie her hands was loose enough to slip her hands out, but she left them tied. Her lips were dry and her tongue felt a burning cut inside her mouth. She vowed to get out of there, away from Uriah. That feeling of foreboding suddenly returned as she heard his boot on the bottom step. With her eyes closed, feigning sleep, she thought she better not say anything to him- because she had nothing nice to say, and she didn't want to see what he was like when he was in a real rage.

She opened her eyes when he approached with a tray filled with sliced browned ham, fluffy scrambled eggs with diced green pepper, and butter soaked toast, cut in half. Thinly sliced potatoes were fried brown and flecks of black pepper topped them. A clear square dish held strawberry preserves. There was a stoneware sugar and creamer nestled in the corner of the tray, and two mugs of steamy black coffee were filled to the brim. A single, white rose adorned the tray in a cut glass bud vase.

He set it down on the bed and removed a knife from a sheath at his side. He cut through the cloth and it snapped apart. Eryn wriggled her wrists in circular motions, rubbing them, making it look worse than it actually was. He unfolded a napkin, laying it over her chest, then picked up a fork, scooping up a bit of scrambled egg, attempting to feed it to her. With her hand she brushed it away and the fork sailed across the room.

"No, I will not let you feed me like a baby." She glared directly into his eyes and never had a look of loathing like she now did. "And give me some clothes to put on! I'm no beast for you to cage."

He laughed at her but went downstairs and returned with a package. He put it on the bed, indicating she should open it. When she unwrapped it she found a rayon dress in a mixture of lace and velvet, with a long floral skirt. The sleeves were long. It was V-necked and buttoned to the waist. The color was teal and ivory. A shoe box contained a pair of cream-colored slippers with satin ribbon laces. She liked the colors and styles very much, but Uriah would never know it.

She slid the tray to the side. I get nothing to wear underneath, she thought. Thinking he was leaving, she waited, but he only moved to the railing, standing against it, watching. What's the difference, she thought.

He already stripped me anyway. She let the comforter slip, holding it enough to barely cover her breasts. She took pleasure in watching his disturbed stare. Let him suffer! He looked uncomfortable as he straightened, shifting his weight to the other foot. But he continued to stare anyway.

Pulling the dress over her head she stepped out of bed and it slowly fell from her shoulders, flowing down over her body. He came toward her and she backed into the table. From his pocket he pulled out a necklace. It was a heart locket pendant: gold with a small gold tassel hanging beneath it. Surrounding the heart was an array of intricately designed tiny hearts. When she reached out to take it he circled her, brushed her hair to one side, and hooked the clasp.

With his hands on her shoulders he led her to the mirror next to the window. The length of the chain allowed the heart to rest on her chest with the tassel hanging between her breasts. She only noticed it after she saw that he noticed it. Uriah took the brush and began to brush her hair. She reached for it; their hands touching, causing a warm river of tingles to run down her spine. Eryn pulled away and he went back to eat. Through the mirror she could see him. As she brushed, she watched him without his knowing.

Most of the tangles fell out and she pulled the ends over her shoulder, brushing gently until it shone. When she glanced at him, the way he looked at that moment brought the familiar feeling back to her. Could he be right...? Could he be?

"Eryn, this is getting cold, come over here and eat," he said, before heading back downstairs.

When she looked out the window she saw the great beauty of where they were. The sky was as blue as she had ever seen it. Sun was shining brightly and the wet dewy grass glistened. For as far as she could see there were forested mountain tops peaking through the mist; she counted seven ridges in the east. Again, she thought about what he said. Could he be telling the truth? It did look familiar to her. She raised the window, smelling the crispness of the autumn morn. She watched a hawk as it drifted on a current of air until before long it soared downward in search of a meal. Her stomach grumbled. She carried the tray to a table by the window, sitting there with her breakfast as she looked out at the day. Actually, he turned out to be a fine chef. It was delicious! Would she tell him? Oh, it was doubtful. The coffee had cooled and after the cream lightened it, she drank of its creaminess.

He returned with the pot of coffee, refilling her cup. As she reached for the cream he rested his hand over hers. "I'm sorry." His hand remained—their eyes met—and their gaze locked, but this time the daggers didn't jab at each other. A beam of sunlight reflected off his eyes and there seemed a sense of urgency about them. He leaned toward her, "Eryn…" She looked away, afraid of what he would say.

"Am I so abominable to you? Let me have a chance to prove myself."

"You proved that you are insolent," she said, staring at him.

"But I don't have to be. Be with me, sweet Eryn, that's all I ask."

"Look at me Uriah Prescot. I'm bruised and cut, my head is sore. You can't manipulate me this way. Taylor tried, too. If what you say about the past is true, how did you treat me then? Did you abuse me? Did you want to find me again so you could hurt me? How, Uriah…how did you treat me?"

"Eryn, I'm not the abuser here." He got up with a start and went to her. "I loved you, that's all I did. I loved you with my whole being, with everything I ever did, with everything that was possible."

"Then why did I leave you? Why?" For the first time Eryn thought about the possibility of it being factual. She did have visions of Enchantment, visions of enchantment with him, too. He did rouse something in her. But the feelings she had since she first saw him were of fear. She looked at the floor, chewing on her bottom lip. She thought of the many times through the past years she woke after dreaming of a man, a man with blond hair. She saw eyes in her dreams, amber eyes. His eyes. "When I first saw you I thought you were someone I met before."

Uriah raised an eyebrow at her sudden honesty. He stood quiet not wanting to break her concentration.

"I felt fearful of you from the beginning, why is that?"

"I don't know, Eryn, and I don't know why you left me, either. I've been waiting twenty years for that answer." He stacked the dishes on the tray and carried it down.

She looked outside again, then walked to the dressing mirror. This mirror is from another century, she thought. It's like everything else around here, old and beautiful. Through it she glimpsed the image of herself. The bruise was nearly black on her forehead, causing a light blue shadowing around her eye. The cut would scab over and heal. He took good care of it. It seemed like a habit she didn't like, seeing bruises on her face. It had been roughly a year since she observed a mark on herself.

The color of the dress she wore made her eyes a soft blue-green, like the color of a tropical pool. Her pupils were enlarged and the whites showed streaks of red.

As she looked at her image she saw tears form in the corner of her eyes. They spilled out, running down her face. So much had happened lately. Wouldn't she remember if she had loved him? But when she thought about the years of yearnings she had for someone she dreamed about, she knew she had to at least consider what he said. She always felt like she cheated Taylor when she woke from a dream about a man she didn't know. Was Uriah that man? Oh, it scared her to even think about it.

Chapter 14

It was wonderfully warm and the perfect autumn day. Uriah persuaded Eryn to take a hike through the forest. He went to his truck and pulled the seat forward, taking out a box. He lay it on the table and to Eryn's surprise, unwrapped a revolver. He loaded six bullets into the chamber.

"This is a Cimmarron.357 magnum. It's a replica of my 1875 Remington and will protect us from any kind of animal we may encounter." He closed the chamber and clicked it shut, checking the sights while holding it over his forearm, pointing it directly over Eryn's head. "You might want to grab that old jacket. It's cooler in the forest, but you already know that—don't you?" He overused that smirky smile again.

Sure, she would go along with him. Maybe enjoy their little hike at the same time. She would even pretend to be complacent, but would make a mental note of each step they took.

* * *

The grass was wet even though the sun burned brightly. Her boots were dried by the fire the night before. The leather felt tight on her swollen feet and the scrapes on the bottom hurt. The meadow must have been cut once since spring because the field grass was about a foot tall, and someone cut a path leading into the woods. A gentle breeze was blowing from the north. Once they entered the trees the temperature seemed about ten degrees cooler and the breeze was even calmer.

They were on a constant downhill grade when the wooded area opened up to an apple orchard and a natural spring. The canopy from the trees offered shade with an occasional ray of sun seeping through. Some of the ancient apple trees stood majestic over the newer, younger ones. It reminded her of she and Uriah. Old and new. He was from an old time and she, a new time.

Uriah explained that there was once a farm house where the cabin stood and the farmer, his great-great grandfather, owned the once fertile land for as far as they could see. They walked the perimeter of the land to the southwest until it led to the Allegheny National Forest. Heading south again, the sun warmed their faces. Slowly and carefully they went down a steep incline, finding yet another natural flowing spring. Dozens of deer tracks surrounded the small puddle formed by the constant flow.

"Eryn, look at this!"

She knelt down to see what he was so excited about.

"This is a black bear paw print. See the impressions of its padded toes? You can even see the claws in this print." He looked up at her to examine her reaction. "You thought I was lying to you—I wasn't. The male bears around here can weigh over six hundred pounds. Not something you or I want to run up against."

"Why don't you just take out your big *gun* and *shoot* it?" she said, turning her back to him.

Pretending he didn't hear, he cupped his hands and drank from the cool spring water, smiling at her sarcasm. As feisty as ever, he thought. At least she spoke to him. "That's good water, pure and natural, no additives, just like it used to be. Remember?"

He stomped the mud off his boots and they continued. The climb up hill was harder. Eryn was glad she changed into the jeans and flannel shirt. Uriah was being an overly protective gentleman, and if she tripped on a small stump or tree root he was there to steady her. She didn't want his help, but he was there anyway.

Suddenly he grabbed her, pulling her down to a kneeling position, putting his hand over her mouth. She twisted, startled at his reaction, but silently watched as two hunters plodded past them a few hundred yards from their path. They were laughing and yelling obscenities at each other. Their bows were dangling toward the ground and the arrows were on their back in a quiver. It seemed they wouldn't be prepared to shoot anything. She squirmed a little more indicating that Uriah was holding her too tight. He didn't release his hand until they were well out of range.

"Why did you do that, you rogue?" she said, pulling herself away from him. "Leave your hands off me!"

"The *rogue* just walked past us. Do you actually think you'd be safer at their hand?" She tried to wriggle away, but he held her wrists. "If you scream, I might shoot them, it's that simple. Their life is in your hands."

Eryn shook her hands free of him. "What kind of man are you?"

"One that loves you," he said, as he raised his finger to his lips, blowing her a kiss. "I'm just protecting you, Eryn."

Turning away she thought that he could be despicable when he wanted to be.

"Those men are on private property and shouldn't be. Don't think they're all out here to hunt deer, Eryn, some are hunting two legged animals. You know what I mean?" He reached out and brushed her cheek with his knuckles. "You're naive about life here."

"Is there anyone else around here?" she asked, nonchalantly, hoping for a real answer.

"Not for miles and miles," he said, as he smiled. "By the way, sweet Eryn, no one knows I have this place. It's been in my family for many years. Remember? There's a different name on the deed, just for my protection. No one knows we're here."

She rubbed her temples with her fingers, snapping at him. "No, I don't remember, and I wish you'd stop asking me if I remember. I don't remember anything! Can we continue now?"

After walking for about an hour the path led them back to the orchard. Birds were whistling in the stillness. It was a completely different world here for sure. A place of peace, but for Eryn, it was a prison, and it was turning her into a number one bitch!

"Can we stop for a minute?" she asked.

"Anything you want, Eryn." He picked an apple from a low hanging branch, polishing it until it was shiny and delicious looking. He tossed it to her, telling her it would be the best she ever tasted.

She bit off a piece, savoring the cool tartness. It was very good and she wondered what type it was. It wasn't a kind she ever bought at her local supermarket. The magnificence of the area drew her attention away from him. The branches of the aged, oak trees were ashy brown, but their leaves were brilliantly colored with golden yellow leaves, while some were crinkled, ready to fall to the ground. The oaks were old and large. Two of them side by side had trunks five feet across. Spruces and Hemlocks grew rampant in the forest, the green of their boughs balancing the color.

Peacefulness overcame Eryn as the quiet encompassed her. It seemed familiar and serene. In the distance was a quick, rat a tat, tat, rat a tat, tat, like a fast hammering, but she realized it was a woodpecker looking for insects.

She squinted at the sky while looking through the trees, feeling as though she were moving, staring straight up, watching the billowy clouds ease through the quiet blue. She might have lost her balance if not for the tree stump she sat on. Looking at Uriah with his flannel shirt, tight blue jeans, and work boots, she thought he fit in here. Under different circumstances she would have been pleased to be in these surroundings with a man that looked like him.

They continued on their hike, each step bringing more beauty then a city girl could imagine. Many leaves were crushed on the ground, but the trees that still held their leaves stood tall and beautiful, the sunlight heightening their color. In the near distance she saw an enormous gray stone boulder, and it was nearly the size of a dump truck. Uriah took her hand, leading her around it. He pointed to a carving. When she looked closely she saw their names engraved in it with the date of July 3, 1881.

Uriah stood back, watching her, but saw no reaction. She didn't remember how important it was for them to put their names on that rock. She can't remember why we did it, he thought. She doesn't know she's seen this forest a hundred times.

They came upon a sound like a clackety clack, clackety clack, thump, thump, and Uriah explained that it was a pump for an oil well. "This one runs on electricity, but in the beginning they siphoned right off the gas within the well for their power. Oil was first drilled near here in 1859, by a man named Edwin L. Drake. Everyone thought he was crazy just like you think I am, but he was right, and so am I."

Eryn read enough history books and did research on the nineteenth century. She also knew the university she took her daughter to was in the same town where oil was first successfully drilled in the United States. Her grumbling stomach interrupted her, reminding her it was lunch time.

When they chose a spot and settled down to eat, the afternoon temperature had warmed. "I don't know where or when you get this food, but it does taste good," said Eryn, as she ate a piece of cold chicken.

"That's easy, sweet Eryn. I had it packed in a large cooler in the bed of my truck," he said, reaching for his thermos. "I'm always prepared, you know. Don't ever be surprised at what I do." He twisted the cap off a bottle of soda. "I've been through a lot, and experience has taught me most of what I need to know to survive. I'm capable of taking care of us, have no worry." He handed the bottle to her.

Pushing it away, she rebutted. "I don't want you to take care of me. I have a life, I have a family. Uriah, I have a husband."

"You had a husband." He stood up and leaned against an old pine tree, gliding his revolver out of its holster strapped to his thigh. He held it out, took aim and pulled the hammer back. The piercing crack echoed through the mountains, and in less than a second a bright red and yellow apple splattered on the ground near a dying tree. He pulled the hammer back again, squeezed the trigger, and the crack penetrated Eryn's ears until she had to cover them. The whoosh of the bullet went straightforward above her head.

"I told you before that Taylor Sterling is gone." He looked her square in the eye, a nerve twitching in his jaw. She didn't know how to read him. He showed no sign of lying.

The gun easily dropped back into the leather holster. When he saw the scared look on her face, he swallowed a lump in his throat. He leaned over, picking up a twig to hide his look of concern. With his pocket knife he shaved the twig, needle thin and used it to pick his teeth.

Ignoring the soda, Eryn poured herself more of the hot coffee and propped her knees up to put her arms around them. There was a new chill in the air. With both hands wrapped around the mug she smelled and sipped the hot brew. She wanted to believe with all her heart that he was lying. "What about the visions I have, Uriah? Did I tell you about that? Taylor is alive, you can't fool me."

"Believe what you will, but is it really Taylor in your vision?" With that he walked off a few yards then turned around and came back to where she sat.

When he returned he set his pistol next to Eryn. "Pick it up." She stared at the weapon, hesitated a moment, then reached for it. As soon as her fingers touched the smooth walnut stock his large hand wrapped around hers. She stood up with him behind her, and he bent his knees to be at her height.

"Pull the hammer back and slowly raise it straight out in front of you, using both hands to steady it; now bend your elbow just a little. Don't leave your arm stiff or the recoil will hurt you."

She did as he instructed.

"Aim by looking down the barrel, lining up your sights. See the little nub on the end of the barrel? It needs to be right in the center of the cut out V right here." He pointed as he instructed. "Now gently squeeze the trigger."

She followed his directions, and with him still bracing her, she squeezed the trigger, the recoil jerking her arm upward. Ouch! It hurt anyway! The bullet ended up somewhere, obviously not on the target, but at least she knew how to aim if she had to. He remained there behind her, the warmth of his body prickling her nerve endings. His arms were still around her too. He took the gun and strapped it in its place as he leaned against her. Letting him linger there, she had the sudden urge to rest her head against his chest. But before that notion went any farther, she stopped herself from thinking that his feel was pleasant, by moving away.

"Do you want to tell me about those visions?" His personality changed quite quickly and she never knew how to take him.

"When I arrived in town the first night, I was sitting in my car, and I thought I saw Enchantment as it looked in the past."

"What did you see?"

"I saw the park."

A smile spread across his face, a self-satisfied smile!

"...Then I saw a pair of eyes looking back at me in my mirror."

"Oh? Were they your own?!"

"They were blue eyes!" She lied.

"Okay, think what you will about him, Eryn. But believe me, he doesn't think about you."

"You're insufferable. How could I ever care about you like you say I did? You had to be like this before. I can't believe you suddenly got this way."

"Love can do a lot for a man, my love. Losing a love can do a lot to a man. I've been hurting for a long time." He walked over to her, taking her up by the arm. "I'll not be hurt again, girl." He gently pressed his lips against hers. "I only want my lips to hurt from kissing you too much, sweet Eryn." They stood there together, only inches between them, looking into each others eyes. Then he took her hand and put her arm around his shoulder. "Leave it there." He took the other arm, putting it on his waist. "The hunters are returning. We need to convince them we want to be alone," he said through the crooked smile on his face. "Remember—their life—your hands?"

She could do nothing but cooperate with him. She endured his tender, passionate kisses, but dug her nails into his shoulder for spite while his hands willfully explored her body.

"Well, well, what do we have here?" heckled one of the hunters as they came upon them.

Uriah released her enough to speak. "If you don't mind, the lady and I want to be alone. We don't want any *strangers* bothering us. Know what I mean?"

Eryn thought she saw Uriah nod to the older of the two men.

"Sure mister, we know," said the older man. "But you got a nice lookin' woman there, and it's been a while since we seen someone like her. She's not one you'd...care to share is she now?" He winked at Uriah.

Eryn's eyes grew as large as a Frisbee when she heard his comment, suddenly fearful of what Uriah warned her about earlier.

"You men are on private property, you need to get the hell out of here." Uriah stood back enough to show he had a weapon and wouldn't back down. "Landowners around here don't appreciate anyone on their land, especially when they're hunting illegally on posted land, so when you go, we can finish what we were doing so we can get the hell out of here, too. That way no one gets caught trespassing."

He sounded convincing to her.

"And I don't appreciate your attitude toward this woman here, so be on your way."

"Well, just thought I'd ask, in case she was someone you…barely knew. Know what I mean?" said the older of the two. The younger one stripped Eryn with his eyes, watching as Uriah's hands possessively held her.

"Yeah, I know what you mean, man, all in fun right, guys?"

"Right. We'll be seeing ya. Take her easy now."

They walked off laughing, almost hysterically, and the younger one glanced over his shoulder, winking at Eryn. She felt Uriah's hand clench tightly when he saw what the man did. She pulled herself out of his arms when they were out of sight.

Oh, well, he enjoyed the feel of her while it lasted.

Eryn suddenly lost interest in the beauty that surrounded her.

"I told you all hunters here weren't hunting for four legged animals."

Before he let her sit back down he brought her to him, kissing her lips one more time, then released her. "Pour me some of that coffee, will you?"

She was glad he had asked her that because it gave her a chance to get away from him again. He sat across from her and devoured a ham and cheese sandwich. She nibbled at a half of one, not liking the way the cheese melted into the bread from the heat of the sun. Sandwiches weren't her favorite food, especially one that sat around hours before she could eat it.

She sat down again, this time on the soft grass. Hugging her knees she tried to chase the chill away, thinking that the short time she was in his arms, it made her warmer, inside and outside. Watching him while he was stretched out on his side, she realized he was taller than she thought; he definitely wasn't that lanky. In fact, with his sleeves rolled up she could see muscles flexed as he leaned on an elbow, supporting his upper body. His shirt fit tight against his chest, and he was fairly muscular and strong looking.

He was looking off at something, in his own thoughts, and Eryn gave into the uncontrollable urge to keep looking at him. His blond hair was soft and thick, hanging straight down to the middle of his back. She rather liked it that way—a lot. Yes, he was a handsome man. Beth would call him sexy, yes, definitely sexy. He appeared to look different to her now. He had a rugged look about him. A look she didn't notice the night she first saw him. His expensive clothes gave him a different personality. Which one is the real Uriah Prescot? she wondered.

She fought off the urge to reach over and put her fingers through his tawny hair. Immediately she shook that thought from her mind. Her inner being couldn't explain why she wanted to touch him. Fingers that grasped his coffee mug were large, much larger than Taylor's, much warmer, and much gentler. His staring off into the forest gave her a chance to bring new emotions out from within her. Her lips still felt the pressure from his passionate, coerced kiss. It didn't feel bad, she thought, a little embarrassed and angry at herself. Indeed, it felt very good!

When she looked up she found his amber eyes boring into hers, almost as if he just read her mind. She tried to hide a soft, near smile, suddenly afraid of herself. Afraid that all the strangeness of the past week had caught up to her. Deep inside, the fear churned as she felt afraid. Yes! Afraid that what he spoke was true. True that it was he that she yearned for, not Taylor.

Undeniable emotions were spilling out from somewhere. She tried to picture his so-called attack on her, but all she could see was the dream when he was lovingly holding her, pleading for her to love him. Thoughts and images of that sort were unwanted and she betrayed herself. Her eyes closed to prevent the hot, stinging tears from falling. He couldn't know she thought these things. Any excuse would allow him to force himself upon her. While picturing the heated episode, again she wondered if she would have the strength to defy her own double-crossing emotions. Heat rose to her face, and she could feel the blush overwhelm her. Afraid to look at him she searched for something in the pack…anything, not to look at him now.

But he knew, somehow, he knew.

He took hold of her hand, her eyes lifting to meet his fiery gaze. He leaned toward her, and her eyes closed. She allowed his lips to touch hers, his tongue to softly separate them. His hand held her at the nape of the neck while his other brushed her hair away from her face. She released the fight in her, her hand finding his smooth hair, her mouth willingly responding to him. The kiss was long and passionate, explorative and caring. No hands caressed her body and he didn't press himself against her. It was two people and one kiss. One kiss that greatly warmed that little section of the forest.

Oh, my God! Eryn knew she never should have let it happen. Her fear was fulfilled, she allowed it and yes…yes, she felt recognition. She jumped up and he was immediately beside her.

"You felt something, Eryn, admit it, girl."

"No, no! Leave me alone, stop doing this to me." She ran away from him not knowing where she was going. Strong hands caught her and gently took her shoulders, turning her around to meet his gaze.

"You can't tell me you didn't feel it. Let yourself go, let the memories escape from where they're held captive."

"I… I imagined you were my husband," she lied. "I wanted to believe it was him I was kissing."

"You know better then that, and so do I! Something just happened between us back there. You might deny it to yourself, but you can't lie to me. I kissed you too many times in the past. Yes, Eryn, the literal past! I know the love you can offer, and I felt it then. It's still burning inside you, girl."

She stood shivering from the cold while reading anguish on his face. Oh, she knew it alright, knew it was still burning. But how could she put it out? She wasn't allowed to burn for someone else.

For some reason the sadness he showed caught her off guard and she too felt his agony, his pain. She let him lead her back to where they picnicked. Together they packed up the food and he lifted the pack onto his back. He gave her his jacket, and she gladly accepted it. Words didn't come between them on the way back.

In the clearing they spotted the cabin and Eryn picked up her pace. It would be hard to get away. Hard to escape the dense forest. She had more reason to leave now. She had a life with Taylor and maybe that life wasn't over for sure. Maybe Taylor was home waiting for her to return, yeah, maybe he was waiting and wondering. Sure, the chance of him waiting for her would be like finding potato chips in a Pringle's can. Even if Uriah was right, there was a reason she left him. She didn't care if she never learned why, if it was true.

The two hunters were the only people she had seen in days. There had to be more hunters out there somewhere. She would rather take her chance with a total stranger because she knew at any time, Uriah could become a raving lunatic and drag her off to a past life, and she would never see Taylor, never see Alyce or Avis.

Chapter 15

The next several days were spent sitting by the fire and browsing through magazines. The rain pelted against the log building and at times it turned to sleet. When the wind increased, it forced the temperature down and the rain couldn't help but freeze. The evening dusk came early and the nights were long. When morning came it was hard to awaken because of the dreariness.

It was true, she had plenty of food, the cabin was wonderfully warm, she was dry and he didn't inflict any pain upon her. Albeit, she was his prisoner, but she somehow felt healthier, probably due to the daily walks and fresh air. She had all the comforts of home, except it wasn't home. Often, Eryn's thoughts were of the ones she was snatched from. She thought back to that night. Was it really only a short time ago? It felt like a lifetime in her beautiful prison with a warden that was a Dr. Jeckle and Mr. Hyde.

Reflections of the book store fell upon her mind and she purposely made herself remember what she saw when she passed through the Portal. Uriah told her she would have found him if she stayed. Where could he have been? What could he be doing? She thought over each vision she had, looking for a sign, but all she could see was the man that held her captive. And his damn golden eyes! Each detail was gone over again and again, but to no avail. She didn't tell Uriah about the voice in her head: the one that begged her to *please come*... Afraid it wasn't Taylor's voice. Knew it wasn't. Following the instructions, she did what the voice said. She went to find someone and found the old photo...of Uriah.

Offhandedly, she flipped through a magazine so he wouldn't know where her thoughts took her. Once she looked over, seeing him slouched in the chair with his leg casually thrown over the arm. He was peering at her with his eyes narrowed in that sexy way of his, in his own thoughts. He smiled a caring smile, causing her to avoid his eyes. After the incident in the woods she couldn't trust herself to get lost in his gaze.

"Are you really concentrating on that article or plotting your escape?" He laughed, but was so serious.

"I tried that once and I didn't get very far. I'm your prisoner here, I'm not going anywhere."

"Eryn, I've been your prisoner for too long. Only you can parole me. I can't wait forever." He sat forward in his chair. "You've sentenced me to a life in prison."

Prison, you want prison! She thought. "Okay! You're released from loving me. You don't have to love me anymore. You're a free man, now can we both go home?"

He jumped from his chair and snatched the magazine from her hand. "Do you think I can turn my emotions and love on and off at your damn request? I'm afraid it goes a bit deeper then that, sweet Eryn. I can't, won't allow my emotions that."

"Nor will I," said Eryn, preparing herself for an outburst that didn't come. Instead he went to the fire and angrily threw some logs in. Sparks scattered outside of the fireplace and Uriah quickly brushed his pants off, jumping back. Eryn pretended not to see, but to herself, she smiled at his rampage.

He went to the cupboard and poured a tall glass, half full of whiskey, twice. "I'm going to chop more firewood. Why don't you find something to eat around here. I'll be hungry when I come in." With that he stormed out and slammed the door.

To overcome her anger she went to find something to cook. She would cook it all if she had to; knowing he had to go to the market soon, she would wait for her chance.

It grew quiet outside, no more thump of the wood falling from the chop of the ax. After she sliced potatoes, she scattered them in the skillet to brown. She looked out the window just as he was resting on his ax handle. When she pulled the curtain back he glanced her way. His chest was faded-tan brown and sweating, hair sopping wet and clinging to his face. Even from the distance she could see the amber flecks dance in his eyes, and whether she wanted to or not, she thought of their kiss in the forest.

He turned away from her and she let herself think about him. I gave into him like it was something I had always done, she thought. It seemed so natural. She watched him through the window, hating to let herself know she was beginning to get used to the look of him.

When he brought the ax up, his pectoral muscles strained and extruded, something she hadn't paid attention to before. His biceps were bulging under the stress of the ax, and his abdominal muscles looked rippled like a mackerel sky. His tight black jeans shamelessly hugged his hips, outlining his strong calf muscles, enhancing the length of his legs. Feelings of betrayal crept over her again, but were ignored. This time she wanted to remember, she had to know if he spoke the truth, or was he a crazy man.

She stirred the potatoes then placed herself at the window. He pounded the wedge deep into the log and swung the mighty ax with all his strength. Eryn let her eyes close, and listened… Thump! Crack! Thud! Thump…crack…thud…

The field in the background was green and filled with wild daisies and buttercups. A washed out red barn stood lonely except for the outhouse behind it. Pine trees were small and planted in a neat row along the front and side of the yard. Mountains in the east were standing above the foggy mist. The back acreage dipped downward into a deep valley and trees grew tall above the slope of the land. The grass in the meadow was turning a rich kelly green while a fat, bright breasted robin struggled to pull a worm from the earth. A sound rang out, thump…crack…thud… A stocky built, tall young man was bent over stacking wood. His arms gleamed with sweat as the spring sun beat down on him. His shoulders were turning pink at the top, and light hair hung long and wet beneath the bandanna he wore around his head. The man straightened up to stretch, and slowly turned. Straight, white teeth appeared against his sunned face. His lips curved in recognition of the girl approaching. The sun cast light off his enchanting amber orbs as an auburn haired young woman with turquoise eyes handed him a cool drink. He bent over, grabbed a bunch of daisies and handed them to her.

Eryn opened her eyes and had to sit at the table. There was no denying it, Uriah was telling the truth all along. Why didn't she remember? Could she have been born again into this generation as the same person without a memory of it? Did something happen to her when she accidently found the rift in time. Something that didn't happen to him? Suddenly her heart beat erratically as she tried to chase the thought right away. She thought of Taylor. Maybe Uriah was right, maybe he did leave on purpose. Eryn didn't know what to do. It hurt her to think of the agony Uriah had gone through, needing and loving her as he did, and she, not even remembering him.

Confusion ran throughout her brain. She did have a relationship with Uriah, she once loved him. It was true. It must have been special for him to hurt so badly for so many years, and still he hurt. Not remembering the details was the best thing for her. She could already feel the torment of being torn between the two, one from the past and one from the present. How ironic that the present returned to the past and the past is now presently here. She was somewhere in the middle.

Uriah entered and saw her at the table as the potatoes burned in the skillet. When she looked up at him, he saw her long lashes separated with tears and the wet streaks down her cheeks.

Choking down a lump, he looked at her, suddenly realizing what he was doing to her. Her beautiful eyes held the look of a sad beagle puppy. He had to admit, it was all because of him. He kneeled, "Eryn, let me hold you, please let me comfort you."

Her elbow was leaning on the table, her head leaning on her hand; she reached out to him, but remained silent. He took her hand in his, bringing it to his lips and gently, ever so gently, kissed her fingers. The smell of raw potatoes lingered on her skin and he tasted the dried starch. Uriah stood, reaching down for her other hand, pulling her to him. Her eyes wouldn't meet his until he took her chin and lifted her face. She finally squeezed her eyes shut not wanting to look for fear of exposing her revelation. She let him hold her as she lay her head against his chest. Smoothing her hair, he hugged her but not too tightly. She took a deep breath, inhaling his maleness, along with a slight scent of spice that still remained on his skin.

"What is it, Eryn? Have you remembered something? Tell me what makes you cry, girl?"

Had the time for honesty finally come? She didn't know what to do or say. Words still couldn't be found to bare her feelings.

"I'm sorry for all this, Eryn. I've been selfish and cruel and you should hate me. It would have been better if you escaped me. I'll take you back to your family." As soon as he said those words a heart-wrenching pain overtook him, and he held her, and held her…. That he couldn't really take her back yet was a fact, and he knew it.

She shuddered as a vision of them appeared to her again. They were younger and he was holding her like he was now; she was crying. Outside, through the door she saw the trees were all in their same places, but now they were sixty feet taller. In her vision he was begging her not to leave. Here, now, she felt the same pain she felt then. Agony overwhelmed her as she remembered how she told him good-bye. She saw a young girl, herself, walking away from a young man, him. He was standing alone, arms at his sides, and when she forced herself to look back, two…three…four…bright, white daisies slipped from his fingers and she saw, as the sun fell on his face, the flecks of gold in the eyes, which showed tears.

"Uriah," she said, as she leaned back, but not far enough for him to release her, "I've seen some things…. More visions have appeared to me."

Compassion filled his eyes. "Tell me, Eryn. Tell me what you need to tell me."

"They were of us, of this place, of…daisies."

He wrapped his arms around her, bending over, burying his face in the hair lying on her shoulder. She lifted her arms and wrapped them around his waist. Her emotions overcame her and she wasn't ready for them. Her body shook and tears rolled from her eyes, unable to be contained.

Uriah's chest became wet from her crying and she tried to understand why she wept.

"Why did I tell you good-bye? There's so much I can't understand. How did I leave the past and why didn't I go back? How did I get to the present...? How did you?"

"You never gave me a reason why it was over between us, but I knew you still loved me, and I could never accept your leaving."

"But how does someone pass through time?" Eryn wriggled out of his arms and went to the door to observe the area. Now she knew why she seemed at peace with the surroundings. Somewhere in her sub-conscious mind it was secure to her. She turned back to Uriah, awaiting his answer.

He led her to the sofa and sat beside her. "There's some kind of Portal, a dimensional entryway. I read about it in that book of Emmet's." He stood and paced across the room two times, then sat back beside her. "Someone showed you the way, Eryn. I couldn't exist, everything reminded me of you. You didn't come back, you disappeared, vanished." Taking her hands, he looked in her eyes. "I was so torn that I had to get to you. Eryn, it doesn't make sense at all. It just is!"

"Is that the only way? Through the book store?"

"Yes. ...I don't know."

"Do you think there's another way to go through the Portal?"

"I don't know. I can't tell you any more." She felt he held back some of the details, and she didn't know if it was because he wanted to, or if he really didn't know.

"Why can't you tell me any more? We have to start trusting each other."

"Why, sweet Eryn? Where are we going? We were over, remember? Why should I trust you?" He stood, looking down at her. "I know you want Taylor back."

"I need to understand what happened. I need to know everything about my...my past, I need to know about us." She bit on her lip, and touched his hand. "This is hard to comprehend, can't you see that?"

"Of course, I see it. I had to go through it too. It wasn't easy for me to understand, either, and I had to deal with losing you."

"And I had to deal with losing Taylor." She didn't mean to hurt him, but she thought a moment, unable to control a fit of anger. "You're the one that took him away, you're the cause of my losing him!"

"Wait a minute. I had nothing to do with him disappearing through the Portal. He paid a lot of money to get through there. I told you he didn't go alone. Will you listen to me, girl?"

"How did you know I wouldn't return to you? Why didn't you stay where you belonged?"

His temper began to show. "Why didn't you, Eryn? It was months after our parting that I went through."

"Yes, but you knew how to get back but you didn't."

"I had no reason to, but I went back many times to see if you returned. Did you mean good-bye, sweet Eryn, should I have stayed there?"

"I don't know," she answered, looking away.

"Now we're together again. We can't waste this opportunity."

"Did you have to get rid of Taylor to gain this opportunity?"

Uriah had about as much of her questions as he could take. She was making up excuses, would do anything to avoid admitting the truth to herself. He got up and paced the floor, throwing the potatoes in the trash. The raccoons will eat good tonight, he thought. He poured two large splashes of whiskey and downed it, then tipped the bottle to finish it off.

"Why didn't you come to find me after you learned I was his wife?"

"In case you hadn't noticed, girl, this is a big country. I hoped one day you would search for Taylor, and somehow stumble into Enchantment. And you did."

"You had no right to ruin four lives."

"Damn it, girl, for the last fricking time, I didn't have anything to do with ruining your life! Instead of trying to find fault with me, try seeing him for the scoundrel he is. He left you. He left you. Accept that!"

She didn't know how to react to what he said, so she held her head in her hands, shaking her head no, no.

"And you, sweet Eryn, had no damn right ruining our future." His words were slurred. "I wasn't mean to you, I didn't abuse you like you think I did, that was Taylor's M.O.. All I ever did was love you. We had something special, you have to feel something. You still owe us a future, Eryn, and we will have it," he demanded. He was beside her so quickly she didn't have time to react. His fingers clenched her arms, holding tight. He kissed her so hard her head tilted back, stretching her neck and throat. The taste of whiskey sickened her.

"Stop it, get away!" She pushed him but he subdued her. He forced her backward onto the sofa and his body fell upon hers. When he pressed his lips against hers she tried to fight it, at first, but suddenly… the taste of him wasn't disgusting. The feel of him came back to her, and even though she wished to be away from him, her lips reacted to his. A quick image of them together came into her memory, but vanished when she heard a thud on the back porch, bringing her back to sanity. "Uriah, don't do this, please," she whispered.

He didn't hear and was bent on having his way, if only for the satisfaction of getting even, and because his loins ached and he couldn't wait any longer for her to accept. The alcohol controlled him now and he could do what he wanted. She needed it as much as he did, he could feel it in her submission to him. Besides, he was in charge here…she was his prisoner and she would like it.

She had on the same tight jeans and for the moment he gave up the struggle to get them off. It gave her more time to think, but she was losing ground. He grasped her hand, entwining his fingers in hers. "Stop opposing me, Eryn, you know this is right."

"No, not like this. Please stop," she said, each time he released his lips from her mouth.

"Plead all you want, Eryn, but soon you'll plead for me not to stop, like in the past. Remember?"

She used all her strength and her muscles grew weak under the strain. "Uriah, think about what you're doing. Please give me time to accept you." But all the time she objected, her fingers ran through his silk-like strands, and then she knew, knew it had to be…

"No, no more time to accept anything but what we once had together."

And he felt her surrender…

"You can't win…my love…this way," she whispered, as she pulled him closer to her.

With him nuzzling her neck, the familiar tremors shook her body.

When his lips found their way to the hard peaks of her breasts, he suckled right through her flannel shirt, sending her neglected appetite to the limit.

"Can you understand, Eryn? Can you know how much I love you?" He straightened her body out on the sofa, surmounting her. The look in his misty eyes when he stared, excited her and she closed her eyes. She relaxed. Once again she heard the sound and this time Uriah looked to where it came from—

"Are you sure your woman wants to be alone with you now, mister?" said the younger hunter they met in the woods as he stood inside the doorway.

Still beneath him, Uriah felt her suck in her breath. He glanced at the box where he kept his gun, knowing he didn't have a chance to grab for it. Not with all the liquor he drank.

"Let the little lady up."

Uriah didn't budge as he shook his head trying to clear it. Damn whiskey, he thought.

"Guess I'll be getting her myself." He came near to them, and when Uriah turned to grab him he kicked Uriah in the stomach with his boot, jerking Eryn up from under him as she screamed.

Before she knew it he held her hands, pulling a greasy scarf from his pocket, tying it around her wrists. Her eyes showed a look of fear that Uriah had never seen before. He leaped for him, but the man grabbed a log by the fireside and swung it, hitting his mark as Uriah's limp body crumpled to the brick hearth. The hunter laughed so hard the pack of cigarettes rolled up in his sleeve, fell from his loose T-shirt. He pushed her toward the door and she looked back at Uriah, terrified she would never see him again.

Once outside he lifted her up into the Jeep, leaving his hands on her hips, grinning. "Soon you'll be glad to be rid of him, little lady," he said in a bad John Wayne imitation.

The Jeep splashed down the badly washed out road. He grabbed her wrists by the grungy scarf and laughed as he let them drop. When she looked over at him he winked with his bloodshot eyes, and her stomach turned. She was still in a flurry over her episode with Uriah and she tried to get control of herself. He had a large scar on his forehead and when he noticed hers he reached out to touch it, but she knocked his hand away.

"You two looked all lovey-dovey out there in the woods, what happened?" he asked. "You looked like ya couldn't make up your mind back there."

Eryn hoped to gain some sympathy from him. "He threatened to shoot you if I screamed."

"Well, well, I guess you spared our sorry lives, huh, little lady."

"Will you take this off my wrists?"

He reached over and rubbed her thigh. "Why would I wanna do that?"

Suddenly the brutal truth sank in and she started planning what she would do, knowing she would rather die than be at the mercy of this wild creature. She tried to sound naive and dense. "Thanks for rescuing me. What's your name?"

"Just call me Dalton, little lady, it's a name you're gonna grow to love."

"Are we going to the police?"

"The police don't wanna see me. Little lady, you got this all wrong. You came to our rescue. My brother sure will be proud to see what I brought us."

Eryn sat, hoping the man would think she was stupid. This is Uriah's fault, too, she thought, thinking of him lying in his own blood. The whiskey probably took his pain away. But her eyes filled with tears when she wondered if he was dead.

The Wrangler bounced and rocked along the muddy road that wasn't large enough for two vehicles to pass. He turned onto a narrower path. Rain was falling hard. She rested her hands on her lap. He kept reaching over and touching her; she couldn't get any closer to the door.

She glanced down at the handle and without thinking she pulled it and rolled out. When she tried to stand she fell down from the sharp stabbing pain in her ankle. Crawling wasn't fast enough because soon he was grabbing her, her face close to the mud.

"You sure are a fighter, little lady. I like fighters." He pulled her head back and she smelled sweet alcohol and stale cigarettes on his breath. He turned her onto her back, trying to kiss her mouth, but she came up with her knee to his groin, and he screeched in pain. Bending over he lifted her to her feet, pulling her back to his Jeep. He sat her inside while he hooked the seat belt around her hips. She watched him stumble to his side while he still grimaced in pain. And she was glad!

When he sat down he still held himself, looking at her with a hateful glance.

Oh, no! What did I do now? she asked, silently praying for a quick death.

"My brothers at the camp, but don't worry, I won't take ya in fron'a him. I like my privacy, ya know, I ain't giving no lessons to him." He put the Jeep in gear then scowled at her. "I've been kicked before and I can recover real fast. He can have what's left of ya," he threatened, as he sped off.

He carried her inside and sat her on a chair at the table. The other hunter stood with his mouth agape. "Look what I brought us, Chase."

"Lord, what did ya do, boy? Where's Uriah?"

"He ain't coming. He's laying on the floor bleedin'."

"You gotta take her back, boy. This is a mistake. He's gonna come looking for you."

Dalton tipped a cheap bottle of wine and drank what was left. "Nope. Can't drink and drive, big brother!"

He was nearly as tall as Uriah but very thin. His camouflage pants were greasy and his green T-shirt was too large. He had sideburns, a prickly looking face, and his brown hair was unkempt. Grease was under his fingernails, and a cheap watch was on his arm. He was about thirty-years old.

Dalton took out a thin bladed knife and slowly cut through the knotted scarf. He sat on a chair in front of her, seemingly savoring each saw of the blade. As soon as it was nearly cut through she pulled until it snapped, and the blade slipped, putting a deep gash on her left wrist. She tried to push him away, but he grabbed her jaw. Her blood dripped on the floor.

Chase grabbed a thin dish towel and wrapped it around her injury. Blood soaked through until he pulled it tight, then held her arm upward. Dalton pushed him away, removing wet strands of hair from her face, reaching to the top button on her shirt. Chase tried to talk some sense into his brother, but he was deaf to him.

"You must truly be a fight'r, little lady. I saw ya weren't happy with him, unless that's the way ya like it." Dalton undid the second button and hesitated on the third. "Let's see what ya be hiding," he said, as he pulled her shirt open, trying to peek inside.

"Dalton, you gotta let her go," said Chase again, but his eyes followed to her half open shirt. He took her arm, holding it upright, applying pressure to it before Dalton knocked him away.

"Shut up, Chase."

She lifted her knee, but he tightened his thighs against her, eliminating the chance of her kicking him again. The pain in her wrist was excruciating, and it was a struggle to keep her shirt together.

Still sitting in front of her, he went for the next button. "Is that the only way Prescot can get himself a lady? He should do like I do...just take what he wants! But I guess that's what he was trying ta do. Too bad for him, cause now it looks like I get it instead. Hah!" He laughed, and the alcohol reeked in Eryn's face.

Chase tried to examine her wrist and he kept begging his brother to stop and take her back, but Dalton jumped up and hit him in the head with the wine bottle. He fell to the floor, passed out. "Now, no audience. Didn't want ta share ya anyway."

Her heart sank to the floor along with her last prayer. He carried her, chair and all, to a dingy back bedroom. The foul, musty smell nearly made her sick. Twin beds were side by side with room for nothing but a kitchen chair between them. A curtain was all that separated the two rooms; he pulled it closed, telling Eryn to get on the bed and lie down.

She wouldn't move!

The next thing she knew, she was sitting on the bed with his hands on her shoulders. It was her defiance that led her and she kept trying to get back up, but he held her firmly.

He unsnapped his pants, putting his knife down on the chair. When he leaned over to untie his boots she grabbed it and nearly succeeded in sticking it through his stomach, but she nicked his thigh instead. He pushed her against the rickety headboard, taking the knife from her. "Ya crazy woman, why'd ya go and do that?" He ripped a piece of the sheet and wrapped it securely around his leg, stopping the flow of blood.

With that secured he knelt on the bed. Eryn prayed for a miracle as

Dalton's hands pushed her down. With the weight of his skinny body, he forced his lips on her. With what she thought would be her last prayer, a loud crack rang out. When he jumped up, a shot knocked him back on the bed. Eryn rolled over to avoid him falling on her.

Uriah scooped her into his arms. As they went through the cabin, Chase was coming to. The two men stared at each other and Eryn saw a terrible rage simmering in Uriah. He carried her to the truck, wrapping a blanket around her. They sped down the bumpy path and turned back onto the road toward their cabin.

"Uriah, how did you find me?" Her teeth chattered as she sobbed.

"I followed his tracks in the mud. The rap on the head wasn't as bad as it looked. How bad are you hurt, Eryn?"

"My ankle is sprained, I can't walk on it. My wrist is cut... I don't know how bad, but it's bleeding a lot!"

"How did you get so muddy?"

"I jumped out of his Jeep."

"You could've killed yourself, girl."

"I didn't care."

He raised an eyebrow, glancing at her and she knew he wanted to ask.

"No, he didn't, Uriah." She saw his expression mellow.

"I'll kill him, Eryn. Did the other one hurt you?"

"He tried to get him to leave me alone and take me back to you, but his brother knocked him out with a bottle. Uriah, he knew your name."

Uriah pulled her over to him so he could put his arm around her. He stopped the truck, not caring to hide the mist in his own eyes. "Eryn, I'm so sorry, I promise never to let you be hurt again.... I'm so sorry." He clung to her, letting her cry. She reached over and clutched his arm, needing someone right then. Comforting was needed and Uriah had just saved her life.

Chapter 16

He carried her into the cabin, setting her on the sofa to examine her. Her ankle was already purple and swollen, but his main concern was the laceration on her wrist. Unwrapping the cloth he saw a deep cut that looked like it barely missed an artery. It needed sutures. He rested her elbow on a pillow and told her to hold pressure to it while he retrieved a first-aid kit.

As he helped her to the sink he poured whiskey over her arm to cleanse it, holding her tightly until it quit burning. After he dried it well he lifted her, carrying her to the table where he had spread out a towel. Carefully he pinched the pieces of flesh together and stretched the thin strips of bandage across the wound in place of sutures. When he was satisfied at the way it looked he put sterile gauze over it, wrapping it loosely. Before he raised her injured ankle to the chair across from her, he saw the cut on her lip, and asked through clenched teeth, "Did he hit you?"

"No, I hit the headboard when he pushed me down."

A pain jabbed him in the pit of his stomach and he slammed his fists down on the table, twice. He stared at her, watching the tears well up in the corners of her eyes. He clenched his fists, grabbed her, held her and wanted to cry with her.

Uriah filled the bath and escorted her into the bathroom, leaving until she got in the bubbles. When he returned he kneeled behind her with the sponge, squeezing hot water over her shoulders. "Can you forgive me for what I've done?" He dropped his head to his arm, as it rested along the rim of the bath. "I tried to make you do something you're not ready to do. I was like a crazy man, again." He touched her hair. "I couldn't stand the thought of him tormenting you." Eryn lay in the water with her eyes closed, having nothing to say.

"I realized I was no better than them. I've tormented you too, and I don't know how to show you I'm sorry." He moved to her side, lifting her hand out of the foamy bubbles. "Eryn, I need to convince you that you loved me. We need to be in love again. Will you give me a chance?"

With her head resting on the back of the tub she looked straight in his eyes, locking her gaze onto his. This time she truly saw him for the first time in many, many decades. "I know I loved you once, Uriah. I don't know why it ended for us or why I ended it." Her eyes filled with tears. "Can you tell me anything that might help me remember?" She had to talk to keep from thinking about Dalton.

"I was surprised when you came to me that day, telling me we had to stop seeing each other."

"Tell me about that day," she said, quietly.

"It was early spring, the beginning of April. I remember the field was rampant with wild flowers. I was chopping wood and you came out to me..."

"You bent over and grabbed a bunch of daisies," said Eryn. "I brought you something to drink."

Uriah turned on the hot water to warm her bath. "When did you remember?"

"I didn't really remember. It came to me in a vision, when the potatoes burned. When I saw you chopping the wood, it appeared in my mind, but not in my memory. I saw myself walking away from you, but I don't know why. I really don't know why!" She looked at him, forgetting the fact that he took her away nearly by force. She only saw the love in his eyes, and she wanted to hide the love in hers. "I don't know what to do." She watched the bubbles, first one, than many slowly fade away; they were diminishing like her life as she knew it. "Will you leave while I get out?"

Uriah left the room, throwing her a towel on his way out. She felt better washing the odor from the musty mattress off her body. Uriah returned and carried her to the sofa, then poured her a glass of red wine.

"Thank you, it will help me sleep," she said. "Let me check your head where he hit you?" she asked, bending his head down.

"It needs a bandage."

"It's fine, not bleeding anymore."

"Uriah, is he dead?" she asked.

He looked into her eyes, noticing her teeth pressed against the soft flesh of her bottom lip. "I don't know."

Any feeling of emotion for Dalton escaped Eryn. She didn't know how to feel. She was glad in a way, but the thought of Uriah killing him unsettled her. "Won't his brother go to the police?"

"I don't think so. His brother is the one that abducted you and tried to rape you. He cut you with a knife and assaulted you. No, I don't think he'll go to the police."

"Can you be sure they won't come back? For revenge?"

"I'll check on their camp in the morning. They're probably already gone. Have no fear of them, Eryn."

Uriah had a rush of emotion pass over him as he saw her sitting with nothing but a bath robe on. With her hair wet and combed straight back she looked like he remembered her when she was young. It made him lust for her all the more, and he couldn't allow himself to do that anymore, for he promised. And he meant it!

She didn't remember the intimate times they had when they were together. It was on the same land, and the same trees saw what went on then. The barn still stood, but it was as rickety as their love was now. The farmhouse that Uriah's father built was to belong to them when they married. The house fell in a storm as did their love. If she could only remember why she left, thought Uriah. He loved the rosy glow the hot water left her with, once again feeling the embers scorching him on the inside. Oh, but he burned for her! "Eryn, go put some clothes on."

She stood, letting her good ankle support her as she held the robe tightly around her, but she hesitated. "Uriah, thank you. I don't know what to do from here on, but thank you for saving me." She bit her lip and looked to the floor. "But it was your fault for taking me away anyway."

"And I sincerely apologize for that. I hope one day you will be able to forgive me for not letting you leave yet."

She hobbled to the steps, attempting to ascend them. He lifted her, carrying her upstairs to the chair near the window. Candlelight created a soft glow in the loft, and she felt safe. Why she felt safe with her abductor, she didn't know. But she did feel safe, quite safe.

Uriah pulled a Saratoga trunk from behind a door in the wall. "There's some things in here you might enjoy seeing." He dragged it over to her then went downstairs. "...but they're kind of old," he yelled back.

Through the window she noticed the fog had lifted and in the dark black sky was the soft glow of a yellow moon. It gave a hazy light to the land around her. She leaned on the window sill, sliding the window open, peering out into the moonlight. Surrounding the moon, a myriad of stars twinkled in the ebony sky. She searched the heavens, as she always did for some reason, and, yes, there it was as usual. The seven stars that made up the big dipper, the one constant she could be certain would always be there. As she looked into the night she knew she had seen this same sight before. It was a long, long time ago. The dampness bathed her face, chilling her smooth skin. A coyote howled in an easterly direction in the otherwise noiseless night. She shivered, grasped the robe, and took one more long soulful look before pulling the window closed.

She found at least a half dozen women's dresses. There were petticoats, bonnets, gloves, boots, stockings, chemises, and a cloak with a hood. When she pulled out a black crepe dress she was saddened. A mourning dress, a dress she didn't want to know about. She pulled out a handbag that was made of silk, along with a pair of aqua slippers with ribbon straps that wrapped around the ankles. There were high kid boots and a shorter boot. A magazine caught her attention and when she pulled it out she saw it was called, "Harper's Bazar." She flipped through it, carefully putting it back, thinking she would look at it later. She rummaged through the trunk, more out of curiosity than anything. Her fingers felt the smooth silk before she saw it. When she pulled it out, recognizing it, her fingers let go. It was the same dress she had on in her dream. She chose to wear a silk chemise of ivory then lay the dress across the trunk to admire it, and wonder.

Uriah returned with an ice pack. His eyes slowly scanned the length of her body and rested upon her face. "Come over here and put this on your ankle." He saw the dress spread out on the trunk and smiled. "Do you remember that dress?"

She told him no.

Bending over to extinguish the flame on the candle she caught a reflection in the mirror. She stepped backward when she recognized herself. A blush spread over her face. She saw in a vision, beneath her, a flaxen haired man, and whether it was a vision behind her own eyes or a reflection in the looking glass, the golden flecks sparkled as the candlelight flickered in his eyes.

Without her realizing it, he picked her up and carried her to the bed, the vision lost for now. He put a pillow under her leg and lay the freezing pack on her ankle. It burned until her skin grew accustomed to it, but she felt relief.

"I like your choice." He inhaled the smell of the chemise. "It still smells like you. Innocent."

Ignoring the blush, she said, "I found several sachets tucked inside. I like the fragrance, but I can't place what it is."

"Eryn, why do you collect old books?" he asked, candidly.

"I don't know for sure. I've always been interested in the nineteenth century. I still can't seem to find the very one I lack in my collection. For some reason, it's important to me."

Uriah lifted the lid on the trunk, looking for something, moving things around. He looked up at her as she watched his strange actions. Reaching inside, he didn't take his eyes from her. He went to her while she adjusted the ice bag on her ankle, handing her something wrapped in linen. She reached for it, knowing it was a book. Her eyes went to his as they both held it—the look and the book. Uriah let go of his end and she nearly dropped it from its weight. She slowly unwrapped the cloth. With the book turned on end, she saw the gilded edges and the dark brown binding. The leather was in perfect condition as if it just came off the printing machine. She turned it over, her eyes resting on his gaze. "However did you get this, Uriah? How did you know it was the one I needed?"

"That's why your hus...Taylor came here a year ago."

"I don't understand. Did Taylor tell you which one I wanted?"

"Taylor didn't tell me a damn thing about it! I rescued this from your things, Eryn. It's always been yours, your father and mother gave it to you for your sixteenth birthday." Uriah opened the cover and pointed. "They wrote inside. Emmet would have been able to get one, though. Somehow, your subconscious knew it was always special to you."

"It seems my subconscious always knew more than I allowed myself to know."

All was quiet between them as she lay on the bed, and he sat near the window looking into the darkness. She watched his reflection in the window, liking the way his hair fell off his shoulders when he didn't have it tied back. His face was handsome and his eyes were remarkable. She had seen those eyes many times in her dreams. Her daughter had eyes similar to his. She pictured the vision of them together, entwined in his bed, and warm chills sent hot flashes all over her body.

"We were lovers?" she asked, not looking at him, knowing the answer anyway.

Cautiously, he turned, looking at her in that wanting way of his. "We were more than lovers. I tried to tell you." He went to her, putting his hand on her shoulder, but she leaned away just a little. Gingerly, he struck a match and lit the candle beside the bed. When he tilted her face toward him, she couldn't look in his eyes. In her mind she pictured Taylor and felt heart-wrenching pain creep into her soul, not knowing which man she betrayed.

But she was drawn to him, and the glow of the moon in his eyes proved to be too much for her, leaving her with no choice but to allow his hungering lips to softly touch hers. He sat on the bed, pressing his obsessive body against her, his hand wrapping around the nape of her neck. Fingers tenderly groped at her chemise, his hot palm caressing her back. Finding her hands, he took hold of them, putting them around his neck, feeling only slight protest. She left her arms there, allowing her deceiving fingers to play with the long strands at his nape.

As his tongue searched, darted, tasted with a hunger, tears trickled from her closed eyes. Yes, she wanted to stop him, to run away from him, but a small glowing part of her wanted to know him, wanted to know if he belonged to her before. She wanted to know if she had made a mistake when she passed through the Portal that ended one life, but allowed another to begin. She wanted to know...without even realizing it—she needed to know where she belonged.

With her body being the white flag, her emotions, the surrender, Uriah felt her alluring body respond in the way he needed it to. He removed the ice pack to the floor, then lifted her chemise over her head, the way he did many years ago, then stretched out beside her. Her skin was cool and bathed in the soft rays of moonlight. His loins exploded with expectation as his lips tenderly, lovingly explored her, every bit of her. Eryn felt as though she had drowned in a hot pool of ecstasy when everywhere he touched sizzled like water drops on a hot griddle.

Momentarily, he stopped, watching her face as he slowly moved on top of her, silently wondering why she was letting him continue, but he saw the look of longing on her face. Before she could change her mind he kissed her lips once again. The caress against his taunt muscles was enjoyable, and her touch was warm.

Her lips, full and moist, responded to his as she felt the throbbing, echo through her own body. When her lips grew hot through her own pent up passion she thought of Taylor, but only for a moment. The intense amber eyes looking down at her chased the other image away. The thick, silky hair between her fingers reminded her that he was what she needed, and what he offered was what she craved. It was Uriah's face she saw, his body that she wanted. The caress on her skin was rough, familiar, and the whole essence of him filled her spirit. The part of her that had been neglected for so long, now desired what only her body remembered. She knew...yes, she knew she was being loved by Uriah Prescot, and she knew it was Uriah Prescot that loved her in her dreams for more times than she could count. Who else could do this? Who else would do this? Who else should do this to her? Only him! Her body surprised her as she welcomed him into her sweet warm place, responding to him with a familiar passionate ritual. Before long, her heart, her body, and her soul moved in perfect unison with her lover from a different time.

* * *

Eryn eventually fell off to sleep knowing she was a woman torn between the past and present, torn between Uriah and Taylor, torn between love and hate for herself, and for fate.

Chapter 17

She had been asleep for a short time when Uriah quietly got out of bed. A while after he left the loft she heard his truck start and leave. It would do her no good to run away now. After the experience with Dalton she knew it was hopeless to try to get away. There was nowhere for her to run. And then there was Uriah. What about him now? If the circumstances had been different she might have been able to give her heart to him, but as long as he was responsible for keeping her, she couldn't. Even if they did have some kind of bond in the past, which she now believed, she couldn't pretend that the last nineteen years didn't happen. Even if she did lose herself in the fleeting moment of passion, she couldn't pretend.

She finally had an answer to who she was and where she came from, but somehow, that was no consolation to her. It was more like an impossibility. Something mysterious happened to her when she went through the Portal, but it didn't happen to Uriah. They all would have been better off if he was the one who forgot. But she couldn't help but feel some kind of emotion for him. Emotion! she thought, it was much more than emotion now.

The roar of the engine woke her in the quiet of the night. When Uriah returned she could smell the odor of smoke on his clothes. She pretended to be asleep, but she felt his tender lips kiss her cheek, and heard when he whispered he loved her, telling her sleeping conscience that she would never be alone again. His cool, naked skin was pressed against hers, and with each passing minute it became warmer and warmer until it was so hot she had to separate herself from his touch. It had been a long time since she shared her bed with another body. His every move disturbed her. Eryn told herself that what happened on this night, would never happen again, but right now his arm around her felt too pleasant. Damn, she was angry at her own body for deceiving her! It didn't matter that they were once lovers because she knew they would never be again. Even if her body remembered, but her mind didn't, and even as she said never again, her body smoldered from the memory.

Restlessness kept sleep away, but she dare not move for fear of waking him. The heat from his body felt good next to her as a chill settled into the loft.

Whatever did he think now? He was already so unpredictable. He might think this moment of ecstasy meant she would spend the rest of her life with him. He couldn't be more wrong! He would see! He would see! Unable to lie in bed any longer she slowly sat up, reaching for the chemise she had worn for such a short time. Quickly, but quietly she left his bed.

The moonlight had moved around to the western sky and spiked moonbeams lit the room. She put another log on the fire, scattering the coals around the pit. A crispness was in the air, making its way through the cracks. Eryn wrapped the cotton throw around her, putting water on for a cup of herb tea. She leaned against the stove until the tea kettle released a hiss, removing it immediately hoping not to wake him. A warm bath sounded inviting. No, the running water would spark his curiosity. Right now she wanted to be alone with her thoughts and pity herself just a little.

His scent remained on her, bringing a reflection of them lying together. She sat down on the floor, fluffed two large pillows and leaned back against the chair. The heat of the fire dried her tears as they seeped through her eyelashes. Savoring the warmth of the tea, she closed her eyes. Pillows scattered on the floor weren't as comfortable as the bed, but sleep was imminent, and Eryn finally did just that. The heat of the fire gave her comfort. With the throw wrapped tightly around her she felt secure, at last.

Sometime later, a loud crackling from the fire woke her with a start and she jumped, thinking it was a gun shot. A quick glance toward the door reminded her of what had happened this night, before her interlude with Uriah. She wrapped her arms tightly around one of the pillows, trying to force the sound of his gun from her mind. Finally, after lying awake for a long time a peaceful sleep came to her, but even though her body rested, her mind did not.

It was a dreary night and the crescent moon barely showed itself through the clouds. Eryn was in the front seat of the old car with her head pressed against the arm rest. Taylor was there, his weight upon her. He begged, while he suckled gently on her ear lobe, and she trembled. Somehow, without her knowledge, she felt the tingling in her loins before. Her fear was awakened and fingers were all over her. A constant begging came from his lips, and when the moonlight sneaked out for a few minutes she could see an unimaginable wanting. She told him, no, and he told her that he couldn't wait anymore, he'd wanted her since he first saw her. She tensed in his arms as he reached back and locked the door. Then he pulled off his shirt and tossed it to the floor. The look in his steel blue eyes told her he didn't hear her refusal. She tried not to yield to him, but he forced the love from her, and that night he claimed her as his.

"Eryn, wake up," Uriah said, as he shook her, "You're going to burn up so close to the fire."

She opened her eyes, saddened, but only she knew it was from something no one knew about. The dream left her unsettled. The first time Taylor forced himself on her. Today they would call it date rape, never hearing of the word back then. It was hard to control her breathing, suddenly overwhelmed by her muse. After opening the curtains, she returned to the pillows by the fire.

Daylight was just breaking, the horizon with a purple-black hue. Stars still glowed brightly. Eryn had a hung over feeling…a throbbing, disoriented feeling in her head, almost like being drugged. Sleep didn't come easy for her of late. She stretched out, lacing her fingers behind her head. Uriah made coffee and the smell of it seeped through her nostrils, causing her stomach to grumble.

The water spray in the shower stopped. She panicked, thinking what could have happened last night if Uriah hadn't rescued her. Did she give into him because of gratitude? No, deep inside she knew she needed to remember how, if, he used to love her. He seemed to think her memory would immediately come back if he could make love to her. That's probably a line he used on all his women, she thought, but no matter whose excuse it was, it happened and her heart deluded her because the memory of them together, was clear.

She sipped her coffee, wondering how he took last nights events. He could go to the hunter's camp this morning. Do what he must do before she tried to talk to him. The coffee was acrid, but she relished the warmth as it flowed through her, wakening her from tiredness. The headache was slowly getting better, but she couldn't shake the whirling in her brain. She decided to quit drinking wine from now on.

Uriah poured his coffee, standing at the sink staring at her with a look of satisfaction. "Moonlight becomes you, Eryn."

Unfortunately, she liked the look he had on his face. It reminded her of the way he first looked at her at the Enchanted Inn. The thought of them together roused new feelings. So much for trusting herself. Another chill, whether it be internal or external, shook her whole body.

Uriah noticed, wondering if it was the coolness of the morning, or him. He sauntered over, sitting down in front of her. "About last night…"

"Uriah, you have to go to the hunters's camp, remember?"

He took her hand in his, looking down at the floor. "That's been taken care of already. Don't be concerned about it again."

"But…"

"I said you don't have to be concerned about it. It's over, that's it. We won't talk about it again."

Their eyes met and held, each trying to read something in the others. Eryn was the first to break the trance-like stare. "Uriah, will you take me to the time past?"

He started to object right away, but she put her hand up to silence him. And it did.

"I need to see where my life was. I've lived all these years with no past. For as much as I know, my life began at age seventeen. Can you imagine how I've felt, feeling like no one on this planet wanted to find me. I prayed for the day that my family would claim me."

"I always wanted to find you, I searched for you—but not soon enough," he whispered under his breath.

"But I didn't know that. I felt so helpless and worthless." She was holding back tears. "I thought someone just, just threw me away."

Uriah moved beside her, reaching out, holding her.

"I probably made a big mistake by running away from you. When I ended up in this time period I forgot everything. Can you believe that, Uriah?"

"Yes, Eryn, I believe it because I see all of this isn't familiar to you."

"Why didn't it happen to you? Why didn't you forget anything?"

He paused as he watched her tuck her legs up under her. "I told you before, I read some things that the old man wrote. He did it all the time. He discovered the Portal and perfected his traveling back and forth. Then he would write about what he saw in the future, calling it predictions…but, sweet Eryn, he was always right." He thought about the prediction that one day Eryn would come. "He could've made a fortune if he used his wit."

"Some things are more important than money."

"I know that," he said, savoring her closeness. "Have you remembered anything about us, sweet Eryn?" he asked, as he gently stroked the swelled area of her ankle.

She noticed his knuckles were scraped. "I don't remember anything. I've only had a few visions."

"Have you ever had these visions before? I mean before you came to Enchantment?"

"No, Uriah, I never had visions of us if that's what you mean." She lied to him again, remembering the dreams she had, the constant longing for someone.

He stood up, quickly losing his temper. "That's because Taylor Sterling found you, making you forget about me!"

Eryn jumped up as quickly as Uriah did, facing him. "No, he didn't *make* me forget, I just forgot. I don't know what I would have done without him and Beth. You know Beth, the one you left helpless on the road." Flames were ignited between them again.

"She's fine."

"How do you know?"

"I know."

Eryn sat down and felt a sense of relief over worrying about Beth. For some unknown reason she felt confident with what Uriah said.

The anger passed as quickly as it flared. He sat back down beside her.

"Will you take me back?"

"I can't."

"You can't or won't?" she asked.

"I won't because I don't want you to forget what you already know about me. You're still too depressed."

"What does that have to do with anything? I might remember, too. You said you know everything about it, you can help me do it right."

He waited before he went on. "You ended our relationship a long time ago. What good would it do for you to go back and collect your past?"

"I must have a family. What did they think happened to me?"

Standing, he went to the window, looking through it with a far off look he didn't want her to read.

"Uriah, answer me, please."

Moving back to the sofa, he grasped her hands in his, touching his lips to them. He put his arms around her, hugging her tightly to him. She didn't object, but her mind was racing, waiting for an answer. She tried to ask him again but he held her too tight. Releasing her a little, but remaining close, he saw genuine sorrow covering her beautiful green-blue eyes.

"What is it, Uriah?"

"Eryn," he stammered, as he tried to find the right words. "I hate to be the one to tell you this. It's not pleasant." He watched the expression on her face and it held a question mark. There was nothing for him to do but continue. "Oh, Eryn—" he engulfed her in his arms, close to tears himself. "Your family was killed."

She tried to stand, but he held her at his side. "What do you mean?"

"Your mother and father and little brother were going home from a late church service. The fog was so thick they couldn't see very far ahead of them…"

"Go on."

"Are you sure?"

She nodded.

"They were on the curve along the river when a bear came out of the woods, scaring the horse. It reared. The horse and carriage went over the side." He searched her face, still holding her in his arms. "The wagon rolled over your mother and brother. A neighboring farmer found them early the next morning. Your father was still alive to tell the horrible story, but he died later. Eryn—" He continued to hold her against him as tightly as he could, "I'm sorry to have to tell you this. Sweet Eryn, I'm so sorry."

"I don't know how to feel." Albeit she had no feelings, but that didn't stop the tears from welling up in her eyes. "I can't mourn something I don't remember…" She looked at Uriah. It was the same with him. She couldn't love him if she couldn't remember. "Yet, I still feel a loss." She hesitated, tears rolling down her cheeks. "The mourning dress I found in the trunk, it was for them. You know, I've always hated the fog for as long as I remember. I've been terrified of it, you know that's what brought me to Enchantment."

"Yes. You were depressed, you stayed in that lonely house and wouldn't even see me. I thought that had something to do with you leaving."

A reflection came to Eryn and she pictured the scene of her leaving him. She couldn't identify the feeling at first, but then it came to her. "I had a feeling of such loss in my heart when I went to you, I can remember the sadness. I couldn't take another loss and I was afraid I would lose you, too. God, Uriah! Why did I leave?"

"You weren't thinking right, you were so overwhelmed with grief."

"I was so alone and lost, I feel it in my soul now, my God!" Eryn clenched her head in her hands, looking straight at him. "What did I do?" A look of complete sadness spread across her face as reality hit her. Uriah didn't do anything to make her leave him. She had loved him! She loved him so much. She didn't give herself time to deal with her family's death. As much as she hated to admit it to herself she had to now. Leaving Uriah was a mistake! Then she met Taylor and made a life with him, loved him, and that wasn't wrong. Was it? "I'm so confused, Uriah. I don't remember any of it. Seventeen years of my life has vanished. I'm not even sure I was seventeen." She blew her nose in the tissue. "Was I?"

"You were exactly seventeen, Eryn. But because you don't remember, doesn't mean it didn't happen," said Uriah.

"I have to go back, can't you see it might help me?"

"Tell me, Eryn, will it make a difference if you remember? Will you forget Taylor and his abuse, and continue where we left off? Will you be able to give up this part of your life? Can you give up our past life? This is not only about me or Taylor. It's about your daughters and your life here. You can't have it both ways."

Someone has to lose. It would be her. "I can't answer you. This is the only life I know. But I love my girls, my friend, my work, and yes, I love Taylor. In some morbid way I still care for the man that treats me like a...a punching bag." As she thought, she wasn't sure how much she loved Taylor anymore. When she looked at Uriah, she didn't see fear, didn't see pain, she only saw the soft look in his eyes, and yes, she saw the love there. The love that was only for her.

She had her answer.

Uriah kneeled in front of her. "My poor, sweet, Eryn, you're still lost. It was so good with us. I want you to remember, but I can't risk taking you back."

"Don't forget I did go back on my own and nothing looked familiar to me, but when I returned, I didn't forget about my life here. I wasn't there long enough, though." This time she took hold of his hands. "I need to see more things, please allow me this."

"I have to think about it, and you should think about what I asked you. I'll let you know when I decide." He stood. "I have work to do outside." With that said he turned to go, but when he reached the door he went back to her, looking deep into her eyes, then kissed her softly on the cheek, "I always have and I always will love you, sweet Eryn." The door slammed behind him.

* * *

Eryn filled the bath with the hottest water she could stand. She lay back in the clear water, sipping her second cup of coffee. A storm cloud hung over her head. More and more pieces came together to fill in the large seventeen year gap. Her parents! Her little brother! Gone. Gone! Now she was close to the chance of bringing it all back to her memory. The chance to go back and find what she lost.

She heard the ax as it sliced through the wood with his mighty force. She knew how his muscles flexed when he chopped wood, and she remembered how they flexed last night. Her eyes closed, the image of them together in her mind. She didn't want to ever think about it again, but she couldn't erase it from her memory. The one thing she wanted to erase, she couldn't. True, she had been willing and responded to Uriah in a way she thought she never would. It was never like that with Taylor. He didn't take time for her, only time for himself, never cuddling and lying together afterward. Uriah pleased her more in one night than Taylor did in nineteen years. After he came back to bed, his arms were around her the whole night long, too. And for sure, she did enjoy it; it was familiar, and once she really did love him.

She scrubbed her skin with the scented soap, working it to a thick white lather. She let some of the water out the drain, filling it with steamy hot water again. It was relaxing and she wasn't ready to get out. With her legs stretched out as far as the bath would allow she rested her head on the high sloping back, lifting her hair until it hung over the back. Once again she thought of the previous night, still remembering his touch on her everywhere, and she closed her eyes. Maybe, she would let herself think about it for a moment. One little moment wouldn't hurt.

* * *

While she dried her hair it dawned on her that he left in the night. When he returned he smelled of smoke. Then she went over their conversation about checking on the hunters. They must have been gone, or were they? He became defensive when she asked about them. She decided she didn't want to know.

She had to think about the question he asked her. Could she choose Uriah over Taylor? Could she? How could she forget Uriah now that she knew about him? Leaving the world where her daughters, her flesh and blood, lived was surely out of the question. But she loved Uriah once, they were going to be married. What she had with Taylor, she also had with Uriah, but better, or so she was told. Uriah—the man out of her past. Her past... she had none!

Chapter 18

After Cole took Emmet back to the hospital he and Beth pulled into the drive and were surprised to see Alyce come out with Hanah. She borrowed a friend's car and came to Enchantment even after Beth begged her not to. Beth smiled, hugging the young woman that resembled her best friend.

"I couldn't stay away, Beth, don't be angry with me."

"I knew you'd come anyway. Were you able to contact Avis?"

"She'll be here in the morning, she's flying in. Do you have any news about my mother?"

"No, baby, I'm sorry there's nothing to report."

Hanah ushered everyone inside and served coffee in the sitting room. She asked them all to stay for dinner and they accepted, even Cole.

"How is Emmet, Cole?' asked Hanah.

He and Beth looked at each other and Beth nodded to him. "He's tired now, but Miss Grace, his memory has returned!"

"Oh my! That's wonderful news. How did it come about, what made him remember?"

"The book store," said Beth. "Remember what we talked about earlier, about the blonde deception? You were right."

Beth wanted to tell Alyce that her father was alive, but decided not to say anything to the girls about him. It was too confusing and unbelievable.

She also wanted to tell her, her mother would be safe, but she thought it better not to say anything about that either, for fear of going into too much detail she would never understand. Besides, Beth wasn't sure she believed all she heard, anyway. How could something so abnormal be true? Beth knew the only thing she could do was offer all the encouragement she could, and in a nonchalant way, lead the girls in the direction of thinking that Eryn would be okay.

Alyce sat next to Beth on the settee. "Do you think my mother is okay?"

"Yes, I believe she is, Alyce. This man doesn't want to hurt your mother. She can take pretty good care of herself."

"Why did he take her anyway?"

"He knew her from the past, always loving her. It seems he has something to prove and when he does, I think he'll bring her back."

"When we stayed at the inn that night she had bad feelings about him, but I laughed at her. I never would let her go back there if I thought she wasn't safe. I thought he was just flirting with her."

"When her mind is made up she does what she wants," said Beth, "you know that."

"I feel so helpless. Isn't there anything we can do?" asked Alyce.

"No, we can only wait," said Beth, as she exchanged glances with Cole.

After dinner Alyce helped Hanah clean up. When she and Hanah returned to the sitting room Beth and Cole stopped talking immediately. Alyce felt as though she was intruding.

"Cole, why don't you take Alyce into town and get her one of our famous waffle ice cream cones?" said Hanah.

"Would you like to?" he asked her.

"Yes, I would, thank you. I have to do something besides sit and wait."

"The carrot cake ice cream is the best," said Hanah, as she winked at Alyce when she flipped the outside lights on.

After they left, Hanah sat with Beth. "Is Emmet really okay, my dear?"

"He'll be fine, Ms. Grace. He remembered everything after he spent some time in the...uh, book store."

"I've been so worried about him," said Hanah. "I used to be in love with him, you know. I doubt I will ever get completely over him."

"I can see that. Now we just have to concentrate on finding Eryn and praying she'll be safe. At least this Uriah Prescot loves her and if he loves her, he probably won't hurt her, right, Ms. Grace?"

"I hope we're right about all of this, Beth. I hope we're right, dear."

That night the three women stayed up late, talking, and putting a five-thousand piece puzzle together, trying to keep their minds off the one person that brought them all together. Who would know a short time ago that the paths of these complete strangers would cross. And who would know that somewhere through a thing called a Portal, a distant time in a different dimension, continued.

* * *

In the morning, Cole picked up Alyce to take her to get Avis. She was flying into a small airport outside of Enchantment. She and Cole had a lot in common and got along well. Cole would be going to the same university when the next semester began and they would probably see a lot of each other. They were headed toward the same engineering goal. Cole knew he had a secret attraction to Alyce the moment he saw her come into the inn. He never thought she would be sitting next to him in his own vehicle.

They stood outside the terminal at the airport. Alyce pointed out the plane that had to be her sister. "No one makes an entrance like my sister. You'll like her, she's one of a kind."

"I like you," said Cole. When she flashed a smile his way he saw the same sparks in her eyes as he saw in her mothers, and he saw something else that was familiar, but he couldn't think what it was. "Are you identical twins?"

"No, definitely not, and we're nothing alike, as you will soon find out."

Avis waved to them as she approached. "Any word yet, Al?" she asked before any introductions could be made.

"No one has heard anything."

"I'll find them…and when I do he'll be sorry he messed with the Sterling family!"

"You don't know who you're dealing with," said Cole.

"And who are you...?"

"Avis, this is Cole Dawes. He saved Mother from that man."

"Well, how come she's gone now if he saved her?"

"Avis!"

"I'm sorry, I'm so worried about Mom." She reached out, taking his hand to shake it. "Why did she come back here anyway?"

"It's a long story. We'll tell you on the way to Hanah's house."

"Okay, but I have to make arrangements for my plane. I'll be a few minutes," she said, as she left for the hanger.

"I told you we were nothing alike." Alyce smiled her sweet smile at Cole.

"You're right about that."

They walked to the truck to wait. "Who does she take after? You look a lot like your mother, but your eyes are a combination of hers and your sisters. They're real nice to look at."

"Avis must take after Mother's side of the family. Everyone says that. I enjoy looking like my mother. She's beautiful, vibrant, and self-assured. And thank you."

"Sure," said Cole, as his eyes lit up. "Eryn is beautiful. I said you look like her."

Alyce wasn't one to blush, but this man brought heat to her cheeks, and she knew her color was scarlet.

When Avis returned she wondered why they were staying at a strangers. "Doesn't this, Hanah Grace, mind a bunch of strangers staying at her house?"

"Well," she looked at Cole, "she hasn't up until you," laughed Alyce.

Cole had to look the other way so he didn't burst into laughter.

"Thanks a lot," she said, as she popped her gum. "So...what's with you two? You didn't tell me you had a new guy."

"Avis?" asked Alyce.

"What?"

"Will you shut up."

Cole looked at Alyce's eyes through the rear view mirror, knowing he liked her a little more than he liked anyone else, ever, and he smiled.

Alyce told her sister everything that had happened. That she was sure

Beth knew more than she was telling, but couldn't get her to open up. Cole sat quietly, wanting to calm their fears, but he knew it would be too hard for them to understand.

He would leave it up to Uriah to find a way. If anyone could help right now, it had to be him. He had to convince Eryn. He listened to the beautiful young lady next to him and as he did, he knew she couldn't be entirely happy until her mother was found, suddenly realizing he wanted to make this woman happy.

Chapter 19

After her bath Eryn went up to the loft and decided to try on the aqua-colored dress. At first she circled it as it solemnly lay draped across the bed. It roused a feeling of gladness in her but she knew not why. Sitting on the vanity seat, Eryn couldn't make herself put on the dress. Meandering her way over she stood above it, debating.

Finally, she could go as far as holding it in front of her, strolling over to the mirror, admiring it. With one hand she gathered her hair, twisting it around her hand holding it high on her head. Putting the dress down she pinned her hair with a large clasp she found in the armoire, wondering if it once belonged to her. Her damp hair chose not to be unruly, the dried ends falling softly around her face.

Again, she held the dress against her slight form, knowing it would fit. She began to hum a melody, and for the life of her couldn't recall what it was. An eerie tiredness came over her. At the moment there was nothing better to do, so yielding to it, she lay down on the bed, clenching the dress, drifting off to sleep—

She sat at the small square table and as she looked over the menu she hummed a tune. It was at the café, and as the sleeping woman looked into her own dream she noticed something was missing from a corner near the door. The young red-haired girl's eyes followed a young man walking in front of the window. The door opened and the girl smiled. In front of her was a tiny, black velvet pouch. Eyes coyly looked up as the man sat across from her, taking her hand, kissing her fingers. He opened a small green velvet pouch, and inside was a gold band with black etching. She opened the pouch that sat in front of her; a matching band was snuggled inside. From his inside pocket he took out a piece of velvet, unrolling it. Inside was five rectangular shaped pieces of crystal. He showed her the engraved letters on two of them. One was his name and the other one was hers. They joined hands, the man holding her fingers to his lips, and while he lovingly gazed into her eyes the golden flecks shimmered in his.

The ticking of the clock was the first sound Eryn heard upon waking. All else was quiet. The silk dress was still in her hand; she released it but it was creased from her tight hold. Dust particles coruscated through the air as they plummeted through the rays of sunlight. The stained glass that surrounded the top of the arched window allowed colored light to dance on the polished, wood floor.

She needed the extra sleep and her eyes were clear now. From where she lay on the bed she could see the billowy cumulus clouds scattered throughout the cornflower blue sky. She wondered where Uriah was, almost expecting to see him looking over her, as he did many times when she pretended to be asleep. The clock struck eleven times.

She slipped on a black jersey shirt that hung far below her hips, then donned the jeans she washed the day before. They smelled like the fresh mountain air, feeling stiff at first, but fitting her nicely. That autumn chill was definitely in the air, landing a shiver right on top of her. The clear sky looked like a summer sky but, still, something about it said autumn. This time of year was deceiving, fooling one into thinking it would stay warm, but when the sun rested for the night in the mountains, an early frost could cover everything in an instant.

The back door slammed. Uriah ran up the steps, abruptly coming to a halt when he saw Eryn, as if he were searching for her. Those chestnut hued tresses were wild and wavy, half out of the clasp. Uriah actually liked the look of her, all casual like that. His stretched-out shirt didn't look bad either. "Black looks good on you, Eryn." For some reason he had a look of relief on his face, but it didn't last once his eyes fell on the crumpled dress. It was pain that marred his handsome features then.

She fumbled at the hair clasp trying to undo it, but her hair was tangled in it. "Will you help get this out?" she asked.

"Anything you ask, sweet Eryn."

After he finally untangled it he took the brush and brushed her hair. He smelled the sweet fragrance of it and with eyes closed, he tilted his head back, inhaling, remembering. There was something he loved about the way the red highlights bounced in the light. As he stood behind he put both arms around her, holding her close to him.

She wanted to pull away, but his arms felt like a ball of security, knitted into her soul. She rested her head back against his chest, wanting to think of someone else, someone with eyes of blue, but his face didn't appear to her. His face was tucked away, the iron wall of memory slammed against it. Uriah's moans were all she heard. Moans when he ran his hands down her sides, groans when he ran his hands over her hips, and sighs when he ran his fingers across her belly. She took his hands in hers before they reached the taunt tips of her breasts, wanting to stop him, but hoping it didn't. Albeit, his hands were bound in hers, but his lips continued their job of kissing her cheek, tickling her ear, and brushing against the sensitive hollow in her throat.

"Eryn—I need you so much," he whispered. "Last night was over too soon. Let us do it better this time."

Better? There was a better? She thought it was the best it could be already. But she wiped that thought from her mind immediately!

His breath was warm, moist in her ear, and she felt an arousal that she didn't want to feel, that she wanted to feel, didn't want to feel. Damn! If she could just make up her mind. There must be a way for her to distract him without him realizing that's what she was doing. "Uriah, I'm hungry. Let's go make something to eat." The growling of her stomach came at the perfect time.

"Let us satisfy our hunger right here." He turned her to face him, that sensual look in his sensitive eyes. How would she get out of this? Why in hell would she want to? The "good" conscience won!

When she started to leave he took hold of her arm, mercifully staring into her eyes. Towering above her he gently wrapped his fingers around the nape of her neck and with his other hand, tipped her face upward toward him.

"I want you…right now, right here. I'm hungry too, sweet Eryn." With that said he kissed her lips ever so tenderly, not releasing her except for an occasional breath. It was hard, impossible, to ignore his lips covering her mouth, sucking gently on her bottom lip, tracing the top of her mouth with his tongue. All that exploring allowed him to lay claim, owning her lips, her emotions, her soul, and *he* knew it.

And so did she!

Eryn quickly became lost in his lust, losing the battle of trying to keep her emotions in line. Trying to keep her body from melting right there on the floor. I can't, won't respond again, it's not fair, she thought, hoping she could do it. Pulling out of his grasp, hopelessly out of breath, she said, "Uriah, we have to talk."

Unfortunately for her, he was oblivious to her words.

"Stop!"

"I can't!"

He didn't release her. All that was released was the heat of his very own body penetrating her thick clothes. His lips, warm as they may be, caused her to feel heated all over, barely in control of her breathing. Her hands wanted, needed to touch him, but she was afraid. She'd be happy when she learned what she was afraid of. "You promised you wouldn't do this again, please stop."

"I promised I wouldn't force you, hurt you."

"Well, you are hurting me!" Having to reject him hurt more than any attack could.

"Oh, Eryn, this has got to hurt more than giving in to me… It's only you, only me. Nothing else exist except us." Pulling her even closer, he whispered, "This is our world again, we've found each other. Sweet Eryn, I love you, we need each other."

She couldn't take much more of his begging words, she would break if she didn't get out of his strong, warm arms. "No, not right now." If he thought there was a chance of loving her later maybe he would go away and leave his tender, loving lips off her.

As suddenly as he held her, he let her go. "What do you want to talk about? You already know what I want to talk about." He traced her lips with his finger, the wanting, lustful look remaining in his eyes.

She never knew a man's feelings to show in his eyes as Uriah Prescot's did. Something good in her inner being, soared.

Eryn moved away from him and walked directly to the stairs, hiding from him the steady beat of her excited heart. "Who built this log house?"

"I did," said Uriah. "Why?"

"Who decorated it?"

"I did. Why?"

"I love everything about it," she said, looking at him with an erratic smile before hurrying down.

Uriah sat on the bed, holding his head in his hands, trying to quiet his body before he faced her again, for the look of her inflamed him and he had to keep in control. He knew she would like the place and its decor, he did it completely for her and no one else. Gradually, the pace of his racing pulse slowed down. Slowly, his heart went back to its normal beat. The perspiration evaporated from his chest, back, everywhere perspiration could be. His legs got their strength back and he could once again see her, only to have his body enticed one more time at the very sight of her.

She actually was hungry as she went to the refrigerator. It was stocked with more food. "Where's this food coming from? You can't have all this in the back of your truck, Uriah," she said when he stepped off the step.

"I went shopping."

"You left me here while you went shopping? Did I sleep that long? Will you take me with you the next time?"

"I don't know. That's another thing for me to think about," he said, a wry twist on his lips.

"And I need some clothes, I want *my* clothes."

"What's wrong with the clothes in the trunk? You used to love those clothes."

"This is not *1882,* and I'm not that person anymore. You seem to keep forgetting that. Don't you?"

"You *are* that person, Eryn, you're the one that keeps forgetting." His voice mellowed and he looked at the floor. "You are her."

Eryn wanted to go to him, but she wanted to run from him, too. What am I supposed to do? she wondered. Suddenly she wasn't hungry anymore. The gorgeous, summer like day drew her outside to the porch where she sat on the rattan sofa. It was beautiful though chilly, apparent by the chill bumps creeping over her skin. In the distant east she counted the seven mountain ridges. The gold and red foliage was brilliant. Where is this going to end?

Uriah came out, handing her a dish of sliced apples and small squares of cheese. He went back inside, returning with a mug of tea, with cream, the way she liked it. She only gazed at him in amazement. He sat next to her. She felt his stare. "I like your hair down and loose."

And I like yours down and loose, more! she thought.

"You didn't wear it like this before." He held a thick handful to his nostrils. "Only when you came to my bed did you wear it straight like this."

Oh, but he's a bold one! Feeling the heat rise to her face she turned the other way. "Not many women wore their hair down straight, Uriah. That wasn't proper for a lady."

They were both quiet for a time, each in their own thoughts. No rebuttal from him.

"It's beautiful here isn't it, Eryn?"

"Yes, it's very beautiful. I could live here always." She didn't realize what she said until the words escaped her own lips. Hoping he hadn't paid attention she tried to change the subject. "Have you thought about taking me out of here, shopping, breakfast… The past?"

He touched her chin, turning her to look toward him, softly kissing her lips. "I want you to live here always." He released her and stood on the step. "We're stocked up on food for awhile. There's plenty of time," Uriah answered.

She knew he would say no more.

Chapter 20

"I need to take a walk," said Eryn. Uriah looked down the long path that led to the road. "No, not by yourself."

"Okay then, follow me if you will." She tightened the lace in her pigskin boot, but left the lace on her injured ankle loose, and walked down the grassy drive to the path that led to the road. She turned, looking back at the cabin, conveniently shielded behind the shrubs and low boughs of the hemlocks and spruces. Uriah always kept his pick-up in the barn. Even if someone did happen to drive down the road and, by chance, see the cabin it would look like no one was there. With the grass kept fairly long it looked like someone visited occasionally. Uriah wanted to keep it that way.

The road wasn't well traveled and the ruts were deep. She left, walking to the south. A short time ago she ran through these woods trying to escape. She looked at the tree line, wondering how Uriah knew which way she went, when she didn't know which way she was going. Good thing he did find her. It could be Dalton that now kept her. For sure, it wouldn't be pleasant. Leave it to fate—sometimes it works to your advantage—sometimes it doesn't.

Bending over she traced some wild turkey tracks in the muddy road. It led into the forest from the other end of Uriah's property. She looked at the ragged road she ran across, remembering the fear when she saw his truck bouncing after her. The mere thought of it brought a shudder. At least they seemed to be at some kind of understanding or misunderstanding now. Exactly what it was wasn't clear yet.

Uriah wasn't too far back. Before he followed he strapped on his pistol. The tree line was about one-thousand feet in. However, she didn't think she wanted to walk in the forest just then. She waited for Uriah to catch up. "How did you know where to look for me when I ran off that first day?"

"Logic," he answered.

"Where are we?" asked Eryn, not expecting an answer.

"Now," he said, tapping her on the nose, "would you know if I told you?"

"No, but I would like to know anyway."

"We're in the Northwestern part of Pennsylvania."

"I knew that much. That's not what I asked you."

"Be satisfied knowing that much, sweet Eryn."

She hung her head toward the ground. "You can trust me, Uriah." And she was sincere. "Why would you build out here practically in the wilderness?"

"Because it is the wilderness. I wanted seclusion. This is where my roots are, it's what I'm used to. When you left, my heart went to." His voice quivered. Eryn thought his eyes were misty, finding a mass of emotion forming in her own throat. What was this feeling she felt for him?

She reached out, touching his unshaven face. It was the first time she really touched him, except, well, during intimacy. "Uriah, I am sorry for what has happened to you, but I can't feel what you feel."

He took her hand and pressed his lips to her fingers, squeezing his eyes closed, whispering, "You can feel this if you try."

The whole inside of her felt something, seeing the expression on his attractive face, feeling his breath on her skin. A reflection of the last dream of her in the café appeared to her and he noticed the tenseness.

"What is it, Eryn, what's wrong?"

She pulled her hand from his, trying to remember more, but it slipped away. "Is it cooling off?"

"The sun went behind a cloud. It'll come back out. Come here," he said, as he pulled her closer to him, hugging her, "I'll warm you."

She didn't resist him.

They walked for two miles. There were no other houses, hunting camps or cars. We are definitely away from everything, she thought. But where does he get the food? On the way back she decided to walk in the other direction tomorrow. The direction Dalton took her.

Before they reached the path that led to the drive, the clouds darkened and rolled in quickly.

"A storm's building. The wind's whipping up from the north." Uriah shivered as he commented on the change in the weather. Eryn looked at the sky, hugging herself to ward off the sudden chill.

"I'll get some oil out of the barn to fill our lamps. We'll need them if the power goes out, it happens all the time. How 'bout carrying in some firewood? We'll need a good fire tonight." He winked at Eryn then left for the oil.

She picked up three good-sized logs and stacked them on the porch, making one more trip before hauling them inside. A partially burned log was in the middle of the fireplace and she stacked some kindling wood around and beneath it. She ripped up a brown paper bag, threw in the strips and lit it.

The wind blew the door open and Uriah was right behind it. He looked reckless with his hair blown all over his head, covering most of his face. She ran over to close it. It had begun to rain. The sky was dark gray, the fluffy clouds swept away by the wind. A fog was already lingering in the valley.

Uriah brought in a battery operated radio and the fuel for the lamps. As he filled the third one the lights flickered and a crack of thunder startled them both. "You're not afraid of storms anymore?" he asked.

"I'm not afraid of them, but I don't love them. Was I afraid before?"

"Oh yes, sweet Eryn, you certainly were."

"Well, I'm glad I forgot that."

"Don't be glad." He put his hands on her shoulders. "Please, don't be glad you forgot. I want you to remember everything. I want you to remember how you looked at life, how you looked at butterflies and rainbows, and me," he whispered.

"I still like those things. And white roses and daisies."

A firebolt of lightning flashed through the loft window and a terrifying clap of thunder followed. The lights went out.

"Where's the damn matches?"

"I have them." Eryn handed the box to him as the firelight fell on his eyes and the reflection created a twinkle. She liked that twinkle, liked it a lot.

Concealing his stare, he enjoyed the sight of her slender silhouette with the firelight behind her. Closing his eyes for just a moment, he remembered a time that firelight excited her. Indeed, it excited her a lot.

The blazing fire and lightning streaks gave them nearly all the light they needed, but he kept a lantern dimly lit in a far corner.

"How about one of my famous Prescot salads for dinner?"

"Okay, I'll help," said Eryn, as she put water on the gas stove for tea.

"Cut the core out of this lettuce while I chop this wicked onion. Oh, you don't like onions, do you?" smiled Uriah.

"You don't *cut* out the core! Hold it with the core down and SLAM it on the counter. See, it comes right out." She smiled, tossing it in the trash. "No, I don't like onions, you're right again." Together they prepared their meal. Eryn even managed a smile now and then, but when she caught herself enjoying the moment she looked away, dreading the coming night. Firelight was all she needed, something about firelight....

* * *

After dinner she took the opportunity to straighten up the cabin since there was nothing else to do. Uriah kept watching her, smiling in that way of his, but now she didn't hate it...so much, and that frightened her.

An uneasy feeling lingered and she couldn't figure out why. Maybe because once upon a time storms frightened her, and her subconscious knew. There goes that sub-conscious-knowing-thing again. Since the well had an electric pump she did everything she could without using water. "How long does it take to get power restored?"

"A week is about the longest I remember, but you never know out here. It depends on where the line is down." Uriah reached for her hand.

"Why don't you sit down, there's nothing more for you to do. I'll have room service come in tomorrow."

"Very funny!" she said, as she smiled.

He liked when she smiled and he surely didn't see it often enough.

She turned to walk away, but he took hold of her wrist.

"What did you want to talk about this morning or was that an excuse to get away from me?"

If there had been more light he would see the surprised look on her face. He seemed to know her every thought.

"Are you planning on keeping me against my will forever?"

"Will you ever willfully stay? And I thought you agreed to stay with me."

"Will you tell me the truth about my husband?"

"What truth?"

"He is alive, isn't he?"

Standing tall with his hands in his pockets he turned away from her. He was glad she still had doubt. He needed more time to convince her that she could love him once again.

"Uriah?"

"I won't answer," he said, awkwardly swinging around to face her. "If I say he's dead, you'll hate me. If I say he's alive, you'll try to get to him. Although I said I'd let you go, I can't."

"You'd rather have me stay and hate you?" she asked.

"You can hate me now, but when you remember, you'll love me again."

"Can you be sure I will ever remember. It might never happen."

"The old man got his mem…" Uriah let the words slip out of his mouth without meaning to.

"What? What did you say, what old man?"

Uriah brushed it off with a wave of his hand. "Your memory might come back ten minutes from now, if you let it. You're having visions of us and won't admit it."

"I don't understand you. You've lived without me for twenty years. Why can't you just continue without me?"

He went over and knelt down in front of her. "Yes, I existed without you and I hated each day alone. I can't pretend that you're not here now."

"The woman you loved is not here. You're fooling yourself and making yourself miserable. You can't keep me a prisoner."

"I can and I will if I have to, and you're the one that's fooling yourself, not me."

"Do you have any idea what will happen to you when you're caught? You'll be a prisoner then." She tenderly bit on her lip, looking down at the floor. "I don't want you to go to jail." I really don't, she thought to herself.

"No kidding! That's why I bailed myself out when I did. I didn't rape you, and I wasn't taking the blame to make some crooked sheriff look good. They came down hard on me trying to blame me for being the serial rapist the whole damn sheriff's department can't catch."

"You were like a crazy man, at first."

"Yeah! And what were you, Eryn?"

Oh, she was charged up now! "Kidnaping is a new charge!" And maybe murder, she thought again to herself. "When they catch you, you'll be put away for a long time!"

He moved within inches of her face. "They won't catch me. I didn't kidnap you! You agreed to come. We'll leave this time period if I even think they're close, until you can remember."

"Then let's go anyway." Eryn's demeanor mellowed, thinking she found the moment she waited for.

"Don't worry, my sweet Eryn. If I have to take you there to get us away, you won't connect with Taylor Sterling." He pointed his finger at her. "Get it in your head, he doesn't want to unite with you."

"What does that mean?" she asked. "Uriah, what do you mean? Why do you keep saying that?"

He walked over and banked the fire with no plans of answering her. With the oil lamp in his hand he walked to the stairway, reaching out to her. "It's time for bed."

"I'm not coming up," she said, defiantly.

He continued up the steps, put the lamp on the chest and came back down. In an instant she was lifted in his brawny arms. "It's time for bed," he said on his way up.

The oil lamp was dimly lit. Anywhere else it would have been romantic

190

looking. Uriah dropped her on the edge of the bed. He examined the bandage on her wrist, unwrapped it and saw that it looked better. His concern showed in his deep amber eyes, knowing it must hurt her. When she looked up at him, she read his look correctly.

"Disrobe, sweet Eryn." Uriah wasn't the least bit shy, and the steadfast look lingering on his face was meant to be threatening.

"No, I won't!"

"Yes, sweet Eryn, you will. This is going to happen," he said, as he unbuttoned his own shirt. "I've longed for you all this day and you, my dear, will have to stop denying it yourself."

Eryn scooted up to the brass headboard, attempting to brace herself against his evident charge. All the while he kept his eyes on her as he stepped out of his pants, leaving them where they lay. Their eyes met, holding for what could have been eternity. The desire there was irrefutable—his obvious, hers—elusive. He crawled toward her on the bed knowing her drawn up knees wouldn't stop him, and the way she protectively hugged them wouldn't be a match for him.

With one jerk her legs were pulled out from her hold. She didn't wrestle him when he straddled her. He covered her with his warm eager body, and while leaning on his elbows he peered into her eyes. "Can't you pretend once and set yourself free from your torment? I see it in your eyes, Eryn, I hear it in your voice, and I feel it when I touch you. You feel something for me." He traced her lips with the pad of his finger. "Let go, please. Last night was only the beginning. Let it go, girl."

His closeness astonished her; her pulse sped up when he looked at her with his beautiful gold eyes. Why did she have to dream about them for twenty-years? No rebuttal left her lips. It mystified her the way he knew what she thought. She didn't know she exposed herself to him so well. I'm my own betrayer!

"Say something, Eryn." He shook her slightly to get her attention.

"You promised," she whispered, her eyes teary.

The top button came undone and then the second as the raging wind howled, lightning flashed, thunder boomed, and tears hid behind closed lashes.

When the fifth button was undone and the shirt pulled apart he leaned down, lost in kissing her neck, her chest, her breasts… He tugged at the snap on her jeans. "Damn jeans, women weren't meant to wear these things," he said. "But they sure look good on you, girl."

"They aren't supposed to be taken off by someone else," she whispered.

"I gave you the option," he retaliated.

The storm raged on outside. Eryn felt like she was swept away in a whirlwind, twirling, swirling! Her emotions were gyrating, caught in the same storm not knowing where they would land. Her captor needed, wanted her, it was no secret. He loved her, but he couldn't get beyond his lust to respect her.

She didn't fight him when he removed her jeans, straddling her body once again. The silk cloth that he wore was cool against her skin. He pressed his palms onto hers, capturing her fingers in his. She knew it was useless to resist him, for his desire strengthened him, and weakened her. All it took was his warm, moist lips on her skin. All it took was a moment to absorb everything he told her. It didn't take even a minute before she knew he had been right. She wouldn't admit that she could feel something. He was right, too, that lovemaking would help her remember. The vision of their naked bodies lying together came to her again. Don't think of it! she tried to tell herself, but the vision remained, and with the vision came the reality of her breathing as it grew deeper and quicker.

Uriah's body was warm, his skin smooth as he moved above her. With the constant flashes of light hypnotizing her she felt like another person in another place. She tried to wriggle her hands free from his, but he squeezed her fingers, avoiding any release. "Uriah, please don't do this. Please?" She wouldn't look at him and as she begged him not to, her body begged her to let him, especially since she knew what his body could do to hers.

"Yes! Yes, I need you, sweet Eryn."

"Uriah, please don't," she said, avoiding her own feelings.

He raised up on his elbows, looking into her damp eyes. She saw his eyes looked wet, too. "Do you really want me to stop? Won't you give yourself a chance?"

Her eyes closed and she turned away from his gaze. Her heart was beating strongly in her chest, the flutter strong against his flesh. It bewildered her! Ah, she could easily give in. Oh, she wanted to! The human smell of him enticed her, the honeyed taste of his lips encouraged her, and the whole man of him excited her. She admitted it! She had no choice but to admit it. But no… She wouldn't let herself go.

He raised himself off of her and with a fingertip he touched her chin, turning her to look at him. He tried to understand the look of her, but read a blank. Softly he kissed her quivering lips long and zealously. "I love you and because I do, I'll wait until you're willing." He looked long into her eyes, hoping she would encourage him, but she did not.

He left her there alone in his bed.

She was holding her breath, swallowing hard as she tried to get back to normal. The whirlwind calmed down and stopped spinning. She landed. Is it really where she wanted to be though? she silently and shamefully asked herself.

The pounding of the rain kept her awake or was it the pounding in her chest? Uriah was downstairs and she heard the faint sound of music on his portable. She could grow used to his warmth at night. No wonder he was in such a quandary about what to expect from her, she was confused herself. "Taylor, wherever you are, I'm sorry," she whispered, while falling off to sleep.

She saw a man coming toward her and he had different colored eyes. One was clear, steel blue and the other was a desirous amber. His hair was dark but when the wind blew through it, blond streaks showed through. The man was young looking, but as he came closer, lines of age appeared at his eyes. He smiled and a dimple was in his chin with a jagged scar running through it. When he waved, a gold band shone from the sunshine and it was etched in black. A black cloud appeared and a bolt of lightning came from the sky spinning and twirling, encircling him until he was lost in it.

A loud crack startled her and she screamed as she woke. Uriah was there looking out the large window. "It's okay. The old dead oak tree came down. The one we planted when we were betrothed." He had been watching her sleep and somehow she took comfort in that.

The memory of her dream came back to her and she remembered the gold band. It brought a reflection of a dream she had before. The first time she dreamed of herself in that dress, it was Taylor she sat with looking so happy. Or was it? She tried hard to remember, and as she pictured it she knew she didn't actually see his face. She assumed it was him because of the ring. She did have it specially made, but had it been for Taylor? Had she seen the ring before? "Uriah?"

"What is it?" he asked, turning to face her in the dark.

"Did we ever have wedding rings made?"

"Why do you ask?"

"I had dreams, in them I saw wedding rings."

He went to the chest of drawers and rummaged through the middle drawer. He opened then snapped closed a box, then tossed it to her. She felt the bed where it fell. Looking for her shirt, she felt around. Uriah stood at the bedside holding it out to her, turning his back after a flash allowed him a look of her nakedness. He wished it didn't pain him so greatly. She went to the window, and with the light streaked sky she saw the dark velvet. It looked worn. She held her breath as she opened it, knowing inside was a gold band. When she opened it she saw it was etched in black.

"This is Taylor's wedding band! I designed it for him!"

Uriah was by her side, slipping it on the third finger of his left hand, and it fit. "No. You designed it for me. There's an engraving inside."

She had to sit on the window ledge to steady herself. She envisioned the dream of them showing each other their rings. It wasn't Taylor I sat with, she suddenly remembered! I had that look on my face, that look of being in love. With Uriah! She looked over at him, her eyes filling with tears. It was for this man, this stranger by her side. Her heart was breaking and it beat rapidly within. A part of her remembered him while a part of her knew another man, and she hurt for both of them.

It was Taylor that captured her heart two decades ago and her life was with him. He was her life... Then there was this man. Did he have to come into her would and turn it upside down, tell her things she didn't want to know. Life was just fine without her knowing. It was just fine. For a while.

He took the ring off and slid it between its velvety folds where it rested alone for many years. He tossed it into the drawer and headed downstairs. Before he stepped down he turned and looked in her direction. "Eryn, if you ever want to remember anything about us, remember you chose me first."

Chapter 21

The wind continued to howl through the night and the temperature dropped. Sleet tapped on the window and the lightning and thunder ceased. Eryn, shivering from the chill, lay on the bed unable to return to sleep. She thought of her family, wondering if Alyce could study, was Avis up to another dangerous adventure, did Taylor yearn for her?

She wondered what Uriah was thinking about as she went to sit at the window. Yes, she felt sorry for him. He couldn't help how he felt and acted toward her. She tried to understand, she did, but wasn't sure she could feel what he felt. He was right. Did she want to remember? That would be too complicated. It's better that she didn't know what it was like to share his life, to share his dreams and, yes, to share the memory of his bed. I've got to leave, she thought, and all the while she felt a knot tighten in the pit of her stomach, and a lump lay heavy in her throat as she collapsed on the bed and finally slept.

* * *

Sound was extinct and the quiet could be heard. No birds chirped, the wind was still, and the trees shed nearly all their leaves overnight. It was damp in the cabin. A darkness hung in the cozy, beautiful loft bedroom. There were no shadows, for the sunshine was tucked behind a fluffy cloud high in the sky above the dark clouds that loomed in this little corner of the country. No sun would brighten this morning.

The smell of apple wood drifted to the top of the loft and the dampness seemed to diminish as if the fire had recently been stoked. Uriah quietly climbed the steps and lit the lop-sided white candle that smelled like vanilla. He caught his reflection in the mirror, noticing how different he looked, the way he looked before Eryn left him. Happy and whole. Was it really twenty years ago? Twenty years plus a century? His hair had darkened from the flaxen blond it used to be and he inherited the crows peak hairline from his father. Small lines outlined his golden shaped eyes, but his dark brown lashes were still long. Darkness shadowed his usually, clean-shaven face. He glimpsed the jagged scar and grimaced as he remembered the pain from it, and the man who put it there. He thought he looked taller, noticing he now stood straighter, with his shoulders back, not slouched forward. The dark circles beneath his eyes proved he had long sleepless nights.

Tonight, in the beginning he wanted to keep and eye on the storm, but he relaxed when it eased up and the first snow began to fall. He thought of Eryn as the night went on. The burning in his loins wouldn't let him sleep, either away from her or next to her. It would torment him either way.

He turned to watch her sleep, her tousled hair recklessly spread out on the pillow. As she faced the other way he noticed the mole beneath her chin. Her long black lashes fanned out over her sleeping eyes. What do you see in your dreams, sweet Eryn? A slight scab still remained on her forehead. She still had the purple shirt on and the comforter was pulled up to her waist, but the shirt was open, and a smooth, faded tan breast was partially exposed to his gaze. She was weakening, he thought, she wants to remember but is afraid. A leg was half out of the cover and a toe wiggled as if to shoo a fly away. Her arm was lying across her abdomen. That much of her skin had remained tan except for a light circle on the third finger of her left hand. She recently removed her wedding ring, he thought. On the other hand she wore a diamond ring with two garnet stones surrounding it.

While she lay there, he watched her chest rise and fall with each breath.

He so wanted to touch her. The woman called his heart right out of his body, for it belonged to her.

Slowly, something called to him and he made his way to the bedside. The loft was dark except for the dim candlelight. He felt sinister, but he reached down and smoothed her hair. Gently, he pulled the shirt to cover her nakedness even though he wanted to remove it. He covered her bare leg and saw the tiny red nick on her shin bone from his dull razor. She stretched her legs. It would be so easy to have his way with her. There once was a time that she crept in on him, removing her clothes, lustfully, having her way with him. But those days are gone, she doesn't remember, won't remember, he thought.

The hair stood up on his forearms, nerves prickling the back of his neck as he resisted the urge to just take her. "I love her, I won't hurt her," he whispered. Uriah knew it would be heaven if he could crawl in next to her and feel her warmth against him, like it used to be, but the woman had become his hell. Softly he kissed her forehead, almost certain he saw a smile.

* * *

Eryn woke to the sounds of dripping, melting snow slapping against the soggy ground. She thought the storm had diminished when the thunder and lightning stopped. She didn't expect to see an early snow. A lot of things happened to her lately that she didn't expect. Why should the weather be any different. She quickly dressed. When she slipped on the jeans she remembered what Uriah said the night before. She decided she would wear them every day if she had to.

He was asleep on the sofa so she put the cotton throw over him. She did it without even thinking. It seemed the natural thing to do. For a moment she watched him, feeling a tingle tumble around inside of her. She knew why she had once loved him. He could be sensitive when he wanted to be. He was strong, he was smart, and he gained much experience through his years, and with everything he had inside him, he loved her.

She watched as he stretched his long legs out until they hung over the end of the sofa. Tossing his head to the side it sounded like he spoke her name. His hair nearly covered his face, and she loved the way it looked. Her eyes fell to the scar on his jaw. To think that her husband was the one to put it there. Uriah defended her even before she was here. He was more handsome than any man she laid her eyes on. What more could a woman want? If only she could feel love for him. If only....

She grabbed the old, big rubber boots from the hearth, wondering when he had salvaged them from the woods. They brought memories. She was already making memories with Uriah and she didn't want that. The jacket was on the hook and she grabbed it along with a cup of coffee and went outside. Before leaving she couldn't help but turn and take another look at him.

It was snow, although it was wet and mushy. Clumps of it hung ponderously on the pine boughs. They nearly dropped to the ground with the weight of the few inches of slush. Water soaked the ground and left it slippery with mud, causing her feet to sink and slip. Mud splashed on the back of her legs as she walked through the trees toward the orchard. The thick dark rain clouds released a slushy rain, turning to heavy wet snow flakes that melted when they hit the ground.

Walking through the forest was peaceful, but she wondered who could be there. She sat on a stump and held her head in her hands. It would be easy to leave now, just go up the hill and down to the fire road, then...then where? Inside she felt lonesome, like a longing of some sort. The feeling was for Uriah, the need for Uriah. He was what she needed. It could no longer be denied. She knew it was true and almost wholly believed that Taylor was forever gone from her. He was gone a long time ago, she knew...but she had to be sure. While looking around she didn't feel safe, hadn't felt safe since Dalton. Suddenly, the wind whipped up and the ground became slightly covered with snow, and mud lay in the watery tracks. What an ugly sight snow and mud made!

Uriah would probably be looking for her. With the big rubber boots, cold hands and ears she followed her tracks back. She half expected to see his clenched fingers grab her from behind a tree, but she didn't care. This game was getting tiring. She would either have to give in or demand he take her back. As of yet, she didn't know which it would be.

As she got nearer to the cabin she didn't see any tracks but her own. Was he still asleep? After doing the best she could to stomp off the mud she went inside and set the boots by the fire, putting another log on. While she stood and rubbed her hands together, Uriah woke, sitting up rapidly.

"Where have you been?" he asked, seeing her red cheeks.

"Walking in the orchard."

"I didn't hear you leave."

"Obviously, or you would have been right behind me." She actually smiled.

"Of course I would," he said, winking at her.

"Yes, of course you would."

"We're going for a ride today. Get ready."

"Are we going shopping?" she asked.

"No, only a ride."

Eryn ran a hot bath and noticed a tin container filled with bath salts. As she dumped in a small handful the smell of lavender brought an image of a woman she didn't know. The woman resembled her, but her hair was fiery red and she somehow knew she smelled like lavender. She shook off the dark feeling and pinned her hair up so she could hurry through her bath. She was excited about leaving this place that could have been wonderful. The place she couldn't escape from.

The truck was warming up and the exhaust fumes drifted inside. She was tired of wearing the same old clothes and his beat up old jacket. Now she had to wear his gloves and knit cap. She got in beside him anxious to be gone from her prison.

Uriah sat with both hands on the wheel, staring ahead.

"Well, what are we waiting for?" she asked.

"You're not going to like this," he said, while reaching into his pocket. "I have to blindfold you until we get on a few miles."

"That's not necessary!"

"It is," he said.

"I'll stay here then and forget the ride."

"No, we're going. Now slide over here."

She squinted her eyes at him but did as he demanded. He slipped the bandanna over her eyes and pulled the knot. "Now, scoot down in the seat."

"This is ridiculous!"

"It is necessary."

All she could do was think about her predicament as they drove ahead in blackness. She didn't know where they were so how could it matter what she saw. Even as she thought about the blindfold, it made her kind of excited. That one she would never figure out!

After a short time she felt the smoothness of the paved road and he pulled to the roadside and untied the knot. His eyes looked a deep amber, nearly brown as he looked at her. "I'm sorry, Eryn. Try to understand that I did it to protect you."

"You should look the word up in a dictionary so you know what it means," said Eryn. "Protecting is quite the opposite of what you're doing to me! I think you're only protecting yourself."

"See it how ever you will."

* * *

"This is a state park, now," Uriah said, as they finally pulled into a blacktop parking lot. "We'll follow that path and when we get to the end you'll be amazed at what you see."

"Nothing amazes me anymore," she said under her breath. "I've already seen all the woods I want to see."

"But not from this vantage point," Uriah said.

Eryn saw only one car in the parking lot and a couple was sitting on a picnic table engrossed in each other. Maybe they'll recognize us if they just turn around and look up, she thought.

Uriah wrapped his hand around hers, tugging until she had no choice but to follow.

"If we see anyone out here you can't speak to them. Do you understand?"

"Yes, I understand...warden."

"There's no need to be sarcastic, Eryn."

It was nearly noon and the snow was gone. The sun came out after all and the clouds, fluffy and white, were whisked through the sapphire blue sky. They walked a few hundred yards through the trees.

"Get ready to see how I made my living for a few months, Eryn. How I would have taken care of you." Excitement could be heard in Uriah's voice as they got closer to what he wanted Eryn to see. "You used to come here with your little brother and watch us work." He watched for her reaction. "But you were always afraid for me."

She looked into space for a time and Uriah saw the squint of her eyes, the grooves in her forehead, hoping she wanted to remember. She knew he watched her so she tried to think of something else, but as her mind tried to race past the question of what he had talked about, she had an image of something being built, something large. Unexpectedly, her palms became sweaty, beads of sweat trickled down between her breasts, and she felt an overwhelming fear creep over her. She pulled off the knit cap, her hair falling around her shoulders as she shook it out. He told her to put the cap back on, but she refused.

Between the trees Eryn saw a structure that spanned nearly a half mile over the valley connecting mountain top to mountain top. "You helped build that?" Eryn gasped.

"Me and about forty other men."

"No wonder I was afraid for you!"

As she and Uriah walked out of the trees Eryn's eyes widened, and she stood frozen. The iron railroad viaduct stood near 300 feet high and far, far below were nothing but trees. The backdrop looked like an artist's easel with crimson, orange, green, rust and gold. The colors of autumn stood out.

Uriah went ahead of her, jumping on the track and Eryn stepped up after him. She walked out about ten feet, until the track stretched out beyond the ground. There, she was unable to take another step. Side rails about three feet high were along each side. There was a small walkway on each side, but in the center she saw right between the railroad tie, straight down.

"Come on, Eryn," said Uriah, taking her hand. "We can walk across then hike the path back up. We need the exercise, let's go."

"I can't!" Eryn refused to budge one step. She didn't care if Uriah threatened her. "Uriah, I'm afraid of heights. I can't walk across that."

"You weren't before."

"I don't care." She backed up moving slowly until she was on solid ground again. "No, I can't walk across."

"When did you get this fear of heights?" He looked at her with a questioning frown.

"I don't know, I think ever since I remember. I know I'm not walking across there."

"Okay, okay, I won't make you." With that Uriah jumped up on the rail and stretched his arms straight out for balance.

"Uriah!" Eryn threw her hands to her mouth to squelch her scream. "Get down, please!"

"We built this old thing to last. Trains hauled lumber and coal across this valley for eighteen years before they had to rebuild it in 1900 to accommodate heavier trains."

His jovial attitude changed and he looked off in the distance. We had some good men working on it. Many of them were my friends."

"Please come down now. You're not twenty years old any more you know."

He jumped down, but as he did his foot slipped, falling between the railroad ties and Eryn screamed again. She knew it surprised him as much as it did her. When he lifted his foot out they both smiled.

"That was close," said Uriah.

"Can we go back to the truck now?"

She turned and looked back when they reached the trees. She didn't know why it made her feel so frightened. It must be because Uriah used to hang around on ropes, securing the girders three hundred feet in the air. But how do I know that? she wondered.

When they were almost to the parking lot they stopped to read about the bridge's history. There were three pictures, each depicting a different phase of building, and yes, men were working from ropes, dangling in air. Uriah called her over, pointing, "This little dot of a man is me." He pointed to another that showed a crowd of people waiting for a ride across the valley. "This was my friend. He didn't get to complete the job."

Eryn studied the picture hoping to recall something. "I probably knew some of these men."

"You knew most of the ones I knew." They looked at one another and shared a feeling of sadness. Eryn looked at a picture but it was so old, faces were not clear. She moved to another picture. In it, off to the side, just about where she and Uriah had stepped up to the track, she saw a young girl about seventeen standing with a little boy. Uriah moved beside her.

"Yes, Eryn, I think it's you and Joseph."

She surveyed the picture, but it was like seeing it for the first time. There was no recollection, no vision, no memory. "Do you have any photographs of me, of my family?"

"Yes, at the inn I do."

They walked a few hundred feet and down some wooden steps to a large deck that was recently built as an overlook to the viaduct. They walked out to the rail and Eryn couldn't release her grip. The wooden deck was built atop a boulder about thirty-feet long. It was nearly flat on the top, continuing about twelve feet past the deck rail. Uriah took her hand and led her to the side overlooking the edge of the rock. He pointed. When she looked in the direction indicated, she read the words, *Uriah loves Eryn.* It was nearly washed away with age, and it could barely be read. She looked at him, biting her lip, wanting to say something.

Uriah backed her into the corner and moved in as close as he could get. "You look beautiful. Your torrid blue eyes show bright against your red cheeks. Are you cold, sweet Eryn?"

Before she could answer he took her by the shoulders and kissed her quickly on the lips. He didn't move away. Staring into each others eyes he felt passion, she felt confusion. She felt his body heat and he felt her tension. The closeness unsettled her, it excited him. He sat down on a step on the deck, pulling her to his lap. The vast park was empty of people, as if they were the only two alive. He put her arm around his neck and wrapped both of his arms around her waist. She struggled to get up, but his arms held her firmly. "Sit still."

"Please, let me up, Uriah," she said, while looking in his eyes.

"I'm not going to hurt you," he whispered, relaxing his head against her chest. "This place brings back memories, girl. I need to feel you near me."

"You keep forgetting, I'm a married woman."

Quickly, his expression changed. "You're wrong...I can't forget you have another man's name. I can't forget he was the one holding and loving you all the years I waited for you…"

"You have to forget," she interrupted.

"You have to forget, sweet Eryn. He's forgotten you." Looking up he said, "You've forgotten the wrong man."

"We can't keep doing this over and over. You will never stop me from getting to my husband!" She wished she hadn't said it.

Uriah let his arms slip from around her waist and she jumped up. He did too, and gripped her shoulders, pulling her close to him, his lips hard on her mouth. Her squirming made him fight even more as he ran his tongue against gritted teeth. She let her body relax because she remembered that he liked a struggle. But then his lips became soft, his tongue gently tickling the inside of her lips, and without realizing it her heart softened to him. His pursuit became more intent, and he kissed her like it was his goal in life to do so.

Behind her eyes she saw a vision of a little boy with red hair hiding behind a tree, laughing at them. Uriah's fingers tenderly caressed her breast and he pressed his body against her. "We were so perfect together, sweet Eryn," he moaned against her ear.

His hands captured her rounded hips, pulling her close to him until she could feel the man of him respond. His lips warmed where he touched—her eyes, her ears, her lips.

Her fingers could no longer hold themselves back! They grasped his neck, feeling for the familiar long hair down his back. It slipped free from the clasp that held it, the silkiness familiar and exciting to her touch. In her mind, she saw this man with blond hair, long and loose. She remembered how it fell in her face, tickling her nose as he gently and vehemently moved above her. She remembered his touch and the fleeting moments they shared in ecstasy.

No, please…she begged, for she didn't want to remember. She argued with herself. Taylor, she must set her mind on Taylor! But while Eryn tried to think of the man that deceived her, her lips betrayed her as they searched for the warm, moist mouth that was in her presence. Small, slender fingers cheated her as they wrapped themselves around the shoulders that were in her reach, and her body deceived her as it pressed itself tight against the man that was strong and new in her memory. She responded to Uriah with every bit of her essence. She remembered!

With her arms entwined around his neck she held him as tightly as her newly born strength would allow, afraid he would get away. She remembered! Their lips, sensitive to the need couldn't be drawn apart. Passion grew. She remembered! Each body was as before, in perfect accord with the other...

"Excuse me." A man's voice from out of nowhere startled the two lovers out from whatever realm they had drifted into.

"I'm Ranger Meyers, the fall tour train will be stopping here anytime. How 'bout taking this to your car."

"Sure," said Uriah. He spun Eryn around and pointed her to the truck. "No problem at all. Thanks, Mr. Meyers," Uriah said, without looking at the man. "Keep going," he said to Eryn. He looked back and the ranger was looking after them rubbing his chin with his gloved hand. He fumbled for his keys, glancing at Eryn, his blood still flowing hot.

"What's your hurry?" Eryn asked, as he nearly pushed her into the truck.

"It won't be long before he recognizes us. Damn posters are up everywhere."

After they left the park, but before they turned onto the main road, Uriah turned to Eryn. She smiled at him. He had no words, only one of the sexiest smiles she had ever seen, and she adored it. He leaned over, softly kissing her, and she welcomed it, kissing him back with all the passion she had buried for so long.

She remembered!

Chapter 22

All the way back her thoughts were of the two of them. She remembered some of the things they shared, and all the while that feeling of love drifted over her like a warm wave, but still confusion raked across her emotions. Visions of them filled her mind. The creek, together in it, the meadow—walking hand in hand, the loft…loving in it, and planting crops in the field. They shared so many things it bombarded her all at once.

Uriah took the back roads home, concern showing on his face. What if they did get stopped? What could she say now? She couldn't let them take him. Suddenly, wholeheartedly, she loved him! Glancing over at him she had the urge to wrap her arms around him and pull him close. And she did. She wanted to be with the man called Uriah Prescot. Once, she thought he was the most handsome man in the world. Now with the years past, she looked at him, knowing he was still handsome.

"Uriah, I have to go back and pick up the pieces. Can you understand that?"

He pulled the truck to the side of the road. While looking into her aqua eyes he saw a look, different from what he saw before. The look was real this time, he knew for sure. The green flecks flickered when she smiled, and only on occasion did the green appear when she was happy. "I understand, Eryn. I know you need to go back." He hesitated, gripping the steering wheel. "We'll go back. If it'll help you, we'll go back."

"Do you mean it? When can we go?"

"I don't know yet, sweet Eryn. Soon."

He pulled back onto the road, still worried. Eryn leaned back against the head rest, watching him. He's taking me back, she thought, but a dark cloud materialized overhead, and her smile faded, leaving a feeling of apprehension.

She read a look of fear on his face and she touched his arm. They clenched hands. She needed to be near him. He turned off onto a gravel road that climbed a steep hill, stopping half way up. After setting the parking brake he got two sodas from the cooler in the back.

"Why are we stopped?" she asked when he got in and popped the caps.

He set the bottles on the floor and reached for her. She willingly went into his arms. Their lips touched and nothing else mattered. For Uriah, it was a sense of completion, his search was over. To Eryn it was the answer she searched for, for the past twenty years. Her search was over, too.

"Is this why we stopped?"

Uriah hesitated before he looked at her and she read sadness on his face. "Eryn, it kills me to say what I have to say." He looked at her with shame. "Eryn, I've tried to protect you."

"What do you mean?"

"I've tried to protect you from the truth."

"What truth?" Her fingers smoothed his hair back behind his ears. "What are you saying?"

"You won't want to believe me but I swear, I'm not lying to you." He reached out to touch her face, but she leaned away, not knowing what to expect. Grasping her arms he pulled her close, not releasing her for anything. His heart was beating faster, his pulse racing, and she felt it. He looked in her eyes, lost in their radiance. With both hands on her face he leaned forward and kissed her. She loved the way his full lips felt as they tenderly pressed against hers. At this moment she didn't care what he told her. It had been too long since she felt the arousal from his warm love, at least too long since she let herself admit to it. For a moment she forgot about Taylor, forgot she was another man's wife. Her strength had grown weak in his embrace. She knew the young love they shared, and she knew it would be enhanced with time.

When he released her she was breathless, and he knew it. He so wanted to feel her respond and she finally remembered. How could he tell her the truth and break her heart? His stomach tightened, his heart beat a little faster because he knew what he regained might soon end. Beads of sweat rolled down his back and his palms were wet. She'll think I'm the rogue she called me earlier, he thought, and maybe I am.

She took a deep breath, smiled, and her white teeth glistened in the light of the setting sun. "Now can you tell me what is so important?"

His eyes lost their sparkle. "Eryn..." He fondled her fingers nervously kissing them. "Eryn...Taylor has a new life there. He has a new woman and a child on the way, he has no room for you anymore." He expected a rebuttal and prepared himself for a struggle, but she showed no reaction. The green specks in her blue eyes dominated.

"Eryn, it doesn't matter, I will love you forever. Please, say something to me." His heart was breaking.

Looking at him, now with antagonism, the darkness appeared on her face. "What! WHAT! How can you do this to me? Is this another one of your deceptions?" Her nostrils flared and she pulled her hand away from him. "How far will you go to get me to accept you, to love you, to get me to willingly go to your bed?"

Slowly, he raised his eyes to her. "It's the truth. I know this and so does the old man, Emmet. He knows the end of the story and so do I. Remember what it said, Eryn."

"You're not telling me the truth, Uriah. Emmet lies in a hospital bed with no memory. He tried to warn me...they all did. If I listened I would be safe at home, alone but safe." Her eyes filled with tears. "I was beginning to have trust in you, then you deceive me like this. Plainly, I began to feel this love for you. I could love you and forget him if you just didn't continue to tell me these lies!" She tried to get out her door. Thankfully, he parked so close to a tree she couldn't open it far enough.

"Let me out of here!" she screamed at him. "Let me go! Damn, let me go!" Eryn pounded the seat with her fists, at the same time knocking her head against the head rest. She was more than angry at Uriah. Angry with herself for nearly giving in to him! He almost persuaded her this time. What a manipulator! she thought. Her body was willing! Her lips accepted his! Her fingers wanted to touch him! She almost betrayed herself again. Was it a part of his plan? Let him keep me forever, she thought. I'll die before I ever let him close. She looked at him and through clenched teeth said, "I'll leave you if I have a chance." The green in her eyes exploded. "I don't care what you do with me. I went back by myself and I *will* get a chance to go again. You can't watch me constantly…I *will* get away from you."

"Think what you will now, but know that I don't lie about this. You'll see, Eryn, I'm not deceiving you. I love you." He reached over to put her seat belt around her and she glared at him as if he were poison. His face nearly touched hers while he hooked the belt, and even though she seethed, his nearness created a trembling.

"Shouldn't you put your scarf around my eyes? You surely don't want me to see where we are!"

He threw it out the window and sped back onto the road.

* * *

It was nearly dark when they got back. The ride was silent. As soon as the truck stopped Eryn opened the door and disappeared into the darkness. He raced his truck to the edge of the meadow. Fishing through the glove compartment he found his flashlight and was after her. He stopped, intently listening to the night. Leaves rustled in the light breeze, whip poor wills sang and a hound bayed, but he heard no other sound except his own breathing. Think man, think! Which way would she go this time? But he sensed she went the way that was familiar to her. Uriah was glad the power was still out because he saw a car go down the road, something he never sees, not even during hunting season. Please, dear God, don't let them see her, he silently begged.

He heard a twig crack in the distance, but didn't move. It could be a small animal…it could be her. The wind shifted direction and he got a whiff of the lavender bath salts she used earlier. His hunting instincts came to him and he smelled the air, listening.…

He slowed down his own breathing, closed his eyes and concentrated. To the right of him another twig snapped in the cool air. He still didn't move. Slowly, he reached to his hip and felt the hard steel. It was there if he needed it, and ready. He stealthily moved through the forest. The crescent moon let loose just enough light for him to reach out and grab her around the waist. She screamed a quick, shrill scream and soon saw it was Uriah. She was both relieved and angry.

He released his hold on her and she let out a long, slow breath. "Don't try this again, Eryn, please," he whispered close to her ear. "These woods don't grow only trees, you know."

Feeling like a prisoner again, she said, expressionless, "Can we go to the cabin now?"

He pointed with the light in the north direction. She came to a halt when they got to the brown, muddy creek and he watched her shoulders tremble. "I can't go on right now, Uriah. I don't care if you drag me."

"Drag you? I won't drag you," he said, touching her hair, curling a soft wave around his finger. "I won't hurt you." Still wanting her so much, he kept himself in check, standing an arms length behind her. Her silhouette in the clear night excited him. His body never had a chance to cool down, his loins still begging for her love. The creek held a memory he cherished, and it was emotionally difficult to be standing there with her.

She wouldn't turn and look at him. She couldn't, for her eyes would give her away. Eryn didn't know what she ran from. Was it because her body still craved his or because of his lying tongue, but she knew he wasn't lying. She put her hands to her face and dropped to her knees on the damp ground. "...I don't need Taylor anymore. I'm sorry."

Uriah moved in front of her, staring down. "Eryn, please trust me. I'm not telling you anything you don't already know in your heart. I wouldn't hurt you like that."

"...but how do you know this?"

"I know. Remember, I met him at my inn?"

"I have to find out for myself if what you say is true." She glimpsed the vision of Taylor with the blonde woman. "You have to understand. You keep me here with you, yet, you expect me to believe and trust you. Come on, even you can see it makes no sense."

He crouched in front of her. "I couldn't let you go once I found you. You are my light, Eryn. I had to keep you until you could remember; I knew you would, eventually."

"But you took me away from everything. How could you do that?"

"Because I love you more than you love yourself, girl. I was selfish, I admit that. But, sweet Eryn, can you deny this love you have for me? Can you—now that you know?"

Her knees were hurting, dew soaking through her jeans. Thinking about what he said, she reached out and touched his face. His hair was still hanging loose and she touched the cool smoothness of it, all the while trying to reason with herself. The smell of his cologne filled her nostrils; she remembered it now. No, she couldn't deny his love, not now. She wanted his love…she wanted to love him…she wanted to be with him again. But the shield raised, reminding her she belonged to someone else. On top of everything else, she couldn't help but wonder. Would Taylor hurt her again? Would he? Yes, he would, was her answer to herself. Yes, she wanted to be free of Taylor Sterling. In truth, she did want to be free of him.

Uriah stood, reaching for her hand. She accepted it, feeling a tingle even from a nonchalant touch. "Let us get out of these woods. Little animal eyes watch us," he said. He reached for her other hand, but instead he sat beside her. He looked at the black sky. "There are a manifold of stars there, Eryn. The sky is spectacular tonight. That one," he pointed to the bright planet of Venus, "is what you are to me. Of all the others that are beautiful…that one is the brightest and most ravishing of all—you are my light. You were when you were seventeen, a woman child, and you are when you are thirty-seven, a grown woman."

He held her hand to his lips and kissed each finger, not removing his eyes from hers, then went back and slowly and ever so gently kissed them again. Those same familiar yearnings of old went through her loins, causing her aching womanhood to long for what he wanted to give. Somewhere deep inside her spirit the embers smoldered and the flames spread. Love was ignited once again. In the dim moonlight she could see his magnetic eyes, hear the moaning as she saw the want there…the need there, and she remembered how it used to be. He was the man who taught her. He was her first. He was her love. And now she knew that she loved him, really loved him.

Her legs were weak, trembling. "This was our place, wasn't it, Uriah?" Her pulse quickened and her heart pounded. He knew it too. She leaned over and eagerly coaxed his lips until hers covered his mouth completely. There was no need for him to thrust his tongue, her mouth waited for it to tease. Lips were soft and direct. They knew where they were going and they found the way.

Finally, love had come home!

She grasped his hair, lacing her fingers through its thickness as he lay her down on the grassy shore. She was the one who took control with her passionate wanting lips, gently kissing him, her tongue barely touching his. She felt the coarse hair of his mustache against her lip, her cheek brushing against his whisker-laden face. Her titillating fingers ripped at his buttons, pulling his shirt open, nuzzling the soft wispy hairs on his chest. Virtually out of control she kissed her way back, finding the throbbing pulse in his throat, gently pressing onto it, and tasting the sweat on his neck. She raised her seductive eyes to his, wanting, needing to look upon his face.

When he saw the blue-green orbs filled with need he could hold out no longer. "Sweet Eryn, I love you. I can wait for you no more." With that he encompassed her with his whole self. Her throat, her shoulders, her breasts felt the heat of him. Her belly, her hips, her waiting womanhood longed for him.

Uriah was a man in love, in all ways lusting for the woman he found. "Our love was born in this very place, do you remember?" His breath came more rapidly as he whispered this in her ear, and his words rose in circles around them in the frosty air.

"Oh, Uriah, I remember. Can you ever forgive me for destroying us? My God, I'm sorry!" They groped at each other, finding their way easily in the dark of night. He knew nothing could stop this love from finally bonding, but it was then that she put her hands on his shoulders to halt him.

"Wait!"

"Eryn, don't do this to me, don't do this to us. Don't stop us this time, we need each other," he moaned, breathlessly.

She smiled the sultry smile he remembered. "Go get the blanket." He started to leave, but she caught his arm, holding him back. "I remember, Uriah, and, I love you, I love you so much." His eyes smiled, and he hugged her tightly, hoping the words he heard were real and not some apparition telling him lies.

There was no fear in her as she leaned against an old bare tree, staring at the ebony sky, absorbed in a peacefulness she hadn't known for some time. The clearness of the night allowed her to see the Milky Way easily. The vast amount of stars made it difficult, but she did what she usually did whenever she looked at the stars. She searched for the big dipper, and oh yes, it was there.

He spread the blanket on the ground and Eryn kneeled down. Uriah kneeled in front of her and gently lay her on the soft down quilt. Fiery lips found each other in the dark. His hands freely roved her body, arousing them both. He unbuttoned her buttons slowly this time, kissing her where each button opened, setting her skin aflame. The whisper in her ear remarked about her wearing the same tight pants. Intentionally, she wriggled from his grasp, stood up and undid the button. He slid his hands over her thighs, hugging, pressing himself against her, all the while inhaling the scent of her, recalling memories in the process.

If not for the hooting of an owl and the crisp night air the man and the woman would have thought they were having a dream, a dream they both shared for so many lonely years. She undid the zipper and he lay back on his elbows, enjoying what he could see in the shadows. He saw the white panties as the zipper slowly went down, knowing they were lace. He remembered, in their time, she would not have had such under-things. She was a girl woman when she left and had not learned about such things. One thing he liked about the present was she was bolder, and he smiled. She was more experienced, he thought, and he frowned. He should have been the one to teach her through these years, not Taylor, he didn't deserve her, deceiving her like he did.

Eryn slowly pushed the jeans down, seductively lifting one leg out at a time, kicking them at him. Instantly, his mouth curved into a smile. She kneeled and looked up at the starry night, slipping the shirt from her shoulders. He went to her and with a flick of the front-closure, her bra hung loose on her arms and he peeled it off, inhaling her scent of lavender on it.

Albeit, she stood naked and all the stars twinkled, enjoying the sight as much as Uriah. He removed his clothes and pulled her down on his hard muscular body, wrapping the blanket around them. Lifting her hair he gently smoothed it away from her face. He drew her to him, meeting her warm, inviting lips, enjoying her sensual, enchanting body. The night was cold and a fog enveloped them, but their bodies were hot and wet with sweat and mist. Their lovemaking was strong and hard, yet, tender and caring, too. They became one, and as their bodies moved together, a love that was more than a century old was reunited.

* * *

Afterwards, satisfaction crept through the two bodies that lie entwined and dreaming. The blanket shielded them from the frosty dew and the misty fog. The planet Venus, shined brighter than any other light in the dark blackness of the heaven. Nightmares didn't rule their sleep this night, and their only movement was to cling tighter to the love that had begun again.

Chapter 23

The water in the creek splashed onto the shore. A Downy woodpecker was propped up on its short, stiff tail feather and his chisel-like beak drilled holes in the bark above them. The black and white plumage and red head patch proved it was a male. The stately apple tree dropped apples, making a gentle thud as they hit the ground. The sky was gray-blue with the golden sunrise penetrating the trees. A new day had begun.

Uriah lay still as he gazed at Eryn, still asleep. Her chest rose with each breath and his shirt barely covered her. The ground was like a sponge and the downy blanket was soaked through. Air was empty and the forest, noiseless except for the call of the killdeer, whistling its own name. She slept with a peaceful look, not like he was accustomed to seeing lately. Her simmering rage was over. She remembers us, he thought.

She mumbled something that was unintelligible and smiled in her sleep and it made Uriah smile. "Sweet Eryn, I love your being," he whispered, as he gently touched his lips to her cheek. Her eyes fluttered, but she didn't awaken. Watching her sleep caused him to hunger for her. He missed her for so long. His prayers were answered, his dream came true—fate prevailed! She was there in his arms, there in his life, back in the fullness of his heart, not tucked away in a corner. She was beautiful. Time had taken care of her. Maybe something changed them when they entered the Portal because they both kept their look of youth.

Her eyelashes fluttered and she smiled without opening her eyes. He stroked her arm with a sense of urgency. The love gushed from his soul. Don't let her think this a mistake, dear God, he thought. She felt him beside her, submissive to his touch. A shiver moved her closer to him, encouraging him to stretch out next to her. "Are you ready for a fire?" he taunted her. Another curve and her teeth gleamed between her lips.

"I mean in the fireplace in our cabin."

"Yes, Uriah," she sighed. "I'm ready for a fire. Any fire you want to build."

That he smiled at her brazenness proved he liked it. He kissed her shoulder and possessively embraced her. "Let us go back now," he said, without making a move to leave.

She found her wrinkled shirt and shook it out before putting it on. Her jeans were soaked under the blanket. Uriah finished snapping his jeans and picked up the remainder of their scattered clothes. They both looked through the trees when they heard a branch snap.

* * *

She immediately filled the bath while Uriah made a fire. The water, full of lavender, drew her in. Things looked different now. The sight of everything was enjoyed. She noticed the antique, tortoise shell hair combs that she didn't pay attention to before. The border around the ceiling was stenciled in a rose pattern—now she appreciated the look of it. This place, this beautiful place was no longer her prison. Amazingly, finally, she didn't feel the loss for Taylor that she had for so long, and she didn't feel the tension with Uriah. A smile appeared at the thought of him. But a dark shadow hung in the gallows of her psyche when she thought of what she did to him. No love could be as strong as his. He waited forever to ultimately find love again.

He knocked on the door, bringing her a mug of coffee. "For you, sweet Eryn." He sat on the wicker arm chair and watched her relax in the flowery-fragranced water. Only once did he have to splash water at her before she invited him to join her. When he stripped his clothes he sat down behind her, stretching his legs out around her thighs. She leaned back against him and enjoyed the feel of his wet, warm skin. "Eryn?" Uriah had a serious sound to his voice. "What happens now?"

"I don't want to deal with that yet. I want to enjoy us right now, okay? We have a lot of time to make up."

He stroked her face, running his finger from her chin to her navel, pulling her against him in the water. "Okay."

Afterward he took a pewter pitcher from the vanity and poured water over her tangled hair. Eryn stood up and he wrapped a fluffy towel around her. She tucked the edge in above her breasts and he painstakingly combed out her hair. "This is how it used to be. You practically lived here with me." Then she took the comb and gently untangled his long silken strands, and he couldn't have enjoyed it more.

She turned him to face her, pressing her body against him. He lost his balance and nearly slipped back into the cooled water.

"Did you build here on this same property, hoping I would return?"

"Everything I did for the last twenty-years was for you, hoping you would soon come back. I knew you would some day…but not when."

She didn't seem to hear him. "Uriah, sweet Uriah," she smiled at the way his phrase sounded coming from her lips.

"Yes, *sweet* Eryn?"

"I do have to find Taylor…"

"But, Eryn…"

"No, not to leave you—not ever again. But we have to allow him to come back to his own time. He has a life here, too. He has a family. His daughters need to know he is okay, and I have to explain."

Uriah looked at the floor and picked at the skin on his finger. "You still don't believe me. He doesn't want to come back." Her questioning eyes led him to continue. "You asked me how I knew for sure. When he came to my inn he was not alone."

"Was she blonde?"

With saddened eyes he looked to her. "How did you know?"

"I had a dream or a vision when I was home." She told him about the dream of him, Taylor and Emmet…and the blonde.

* * *

Sitting at the table eating oatmeal and toast with strawberry jam, they talked. "Uriah, I know now that I love you." Her blue eyes were soft as they looked in his. "I love you deeper than I thought possible, but, Uriah, would you have forced yourself on me?"

He went to her side and buried his head in her lap, ashamed. "I'm sorry for all the sorrow I inflicted on you." He raised up, touching her jaw that was free from the bruise, and he touched the scar that lingered on her forehead. "I was crazy in pain for you. My heart ached, I couldn't think, for rage blinded me. I wanted you to remember so badly, but you didn't. I was afraid I would hurt you. I want to believe I wouldn't take you against your will, but like I said, I was blinded. Deep inside my soul, I asked myself that same question, and to be honest with you—I don't know. I wanted you so bad, girl."

"I'm so sorry for what I did to us. I still don't remember the other part of my life—my parents, my little brother. Did he have red hair?"

"Yes, so did you when you were younger." He felt her damp hair. "It's quite dark now, but there's still red streaks when the sun captures it. I like it."

"When we were back at the viaduct, I saw a vision of a little boy laughing at us from behind a tree."

"We tried to get at each other every chance we could."

When he said those words, Eryn smiled.

"Sometimes Joseph caught us kissing, and laughed."

"I don't want to remember them, Uriah. If the pain was so great for me then I don't want to know."

He raised her to stand in front of him, his height overshadowing her. He surrounded her with his arms as he held her. Leaning over, he rested his head atop hers, smoothing her hair. Eryn felt secure wrapped up in him, and she loved his tallness—the complete feel of him.

"I have to put the truck in the barn. I'll be right back," he said. letting her go after a few moments.

Upstairs, Eryn looked at herself in the mirror. Something was different about her. The frown was gone and a look of hope was on her face. Her eyes were bright and they sparkled with love.

There was a rumble in the distance and it was getting closer; she ran to the window. It was hard to know what direction it came from because it echoed off the mountain tops. Finally, she saw, not far above the trees in the east, a small plane. It looked to be searching for something. For me! she thought.

She stepped back away from the window, but before she did she saw the shadow of smoke billowing out of the chimney. Her hands clasped as she prayed that they didn't land, not now. Where was Uriah? She took the steps, two at a time and looked out the kitchen window. He was nowhere to be seen…no wait, she saw him inside the barn. The door was ajar and he was looking through a slight crack. His truck was inside, out of sight.

A plane circled above. The barn door creaked closed and the chestnut haired woman stood back away from the windows. The sound of the engine faded into the distance.

"Uriah!" Eryn called as she ran to the barn. She opened the door, finding herself being pulled in by large hands while he stood behind her, holding her.

"You could have been rescued but you stayed inside," he said as he clung to Eryn.

She looked back at him. "I don't want to be rescued."

"Thank you, Eryn," he said, as he continued to squeeze her against him.

She turned to face him, standing on her tip toes, reaching up to kiss his lips. "I won't leave you."

* * *

The candle burned on the dresser and the night was cool. The sky was ebony and filled with stars while the Milky Way stretched out across the vast blackness. One star out of all of them shone brighter than all the rest.

Eryn buttoned the back of the dress as far as she could reach. She swept her hair up like it was in her vision, and her eyes sparkled in the candlelight. She took one last look at herself and was pleased. In front of her was the image of the girl in her vision. Except for a few lines around her eyes she looked the same. She was ready. He would be pleased.

Before she went down the steps, she stopped. A smile appeared on her lips. She walked to the chest of drawers, opening the middle one, and under Uriah's white socks was the black velvet box. She slowly opened it and pictured Taylor, but she immediately shook him out of her mind. "I made this for Uriah, first," she whispered. She slipped it over her finger. It was much too large so she put it over her thumb and bent it towards her palm to hold it there. She lifted the hem of her dress and walked down.

A delicious aroma overwhelmed the room with a combination of apple wood from the fire and vanilla candles. The drapes were tightly drawn and candlelight flooded the rooms. The table was spread with a lace tablecloth and his Staffordshire china was carefully set. Uriah stood at the marble topped cupboard, pouring two glasses of rich, red wine. He turned as she stepped from the last step. With raised eyebrows he said, "You're beautiful, sweet Eryn." He handed her the red liquid.

"Mmm...so are you my handsome abductor." She smiled as her eyes slowly absorbed every inch of him.

Uriah wore black, loose fitting denim jeans and a light aqua silk shirt. A dark teal cravat was tucked in at the neck. His black leather boots were lusterless at the end of his lean legs. His hair was combed straight, loose behind his ears, the ends straight against his back. Eryn noticed his face was clean-shaven and his dark mustache was trimmed. His long brown eyelashes were thick, surrounding his cat-like, aureate eyes. Standing with arms folded, his lips turned upward into a crooked smile that Eryn now took pleasure in. As she walked across the room he could see her firm silhouette through the gossamer fabric.

She turned and looked at him, pleased. What a handsome piece of work to look at, she thought. "You wear my favorite color, sir."

"I know, madam."

"How?"

"I explored your home when I...visited last. I learned a lot about my...girl woman."

"The room you put me in at your inn was decorated in my favorite colors, too."

"Coincidence—my decorator did that, but…" he hesitated, "your husband mentioned that his wife would like the room."

Eryn's eyes dropped to the floor then back to Uriah. "He talked about me when he was with someone else?"

"Only when I pried information out of him. And she was visiting the boutiques, most of the time." He pulled out her chair and she sat down. He sat across from her, taking her hand in his.

"How did you make the connection, Uriah? How did you know I was his wife?"

"When he got his credit card from his wallet your picture slipped out with it. I asked to see more. He actually had one of your wedding day." His eyes darkened. "You didn't wait very long did you?" Their eyes flashed at each other across the table. He blinked, sorry for his sarcasm. "I knew it was you, Eryn."

"But Cole said Taylor was bragging about me."

Uriah looked irritated. "He came in on the middle of the conversation. Cole overheard me asking why he was with someone else when he had a gorgeous wife at home. He tried to convince me this woman was a business partner so he bragged about what a wonderful marriage he had, to throw me off track, I think. Cole only heard that part."

"So Cole misunderstood everything that was said?"

"He must have. Your husband deceived the kid but not me. Eryn, do you really think that kid could have pulled me away from you if I didn't let him?"

Eryn eyed him up and down, finding delight in what she looked at. "I wondered how that happened."

"I hold a black belt in the Martial Arts. I could have killed him if I'd wanted to. I'm glad he brought me back to my senses." The look in his eyes said he couldn't have felt worse about it. Their eyes met, locking, and the warmth spread over them. With their gaze still embraced, Eryn slipped the ring from her thumb and put it in his palm. "Read the inscription to me."

He leaned over and touched her chin, kissing her long and gently. He read: "My Uriah—Forever and Always."

Her eyes misted and she dabbed at them with her napkin,

noticing the candles had burned down and the room took on a romantic glow.

"I've fixed this wonderful dinner for us, but I am only hungry for you, sweet Eryn. Can you negotiate the stairs with me? I have had more wine than you. A lot I think!" He refilled her glass and stood, then moved behind her, nuzzling her neck. "Come to my bed," his raspy voice whispered.

Nothing else need be said. Eryn stood and he leaned on her, and she led him to the stairs. He stumbled on the first step. She giggled, but he managed the others on his own. She felt a tingling wash over her, just as anxious as him to reach the top. He held out his hand to assist her up the last step, bowing, sweeping his arm toward the bed.

She started removing the extra pillows. He took one and brushed her across the head with it. She looked over at him watching that twisted, sly smile spread across his face. Eryn couldn't help herself. She picked up another pillow from the chair and threw it at him, then smiled. Before they knew it they were whacking each other with pillows and laughing insanely, until she grabbed his pillow away from him. He waited, still holding her with his gaze, then went to her, immediately kissing her. "You're luscious, woman," he said with a leering grin.

That seductive look of his excited her so much. She sat on the bed and slid up to the pillow, watching him unbutton the first two buttons. Impatiently he pulled the shirt over his head, tossing it to the floor. She crawled to the edge of the bed, reaching for him, running her fingers over his bulging muscles. Her hands ran over his shoulders, down over his taunt biceps and she gently raked her nails over his skin.

His fingers struggled to undo the tiny buttons on her dress. Finally, the last one was undone and he felt her bare back beneath. He sighed as he untied the sash and loosened her dress at the waist. When he lifted it over her head she nonchalantly covered her nakedness with her arms.

"Don't hide yourself from me," he said, removing her hands. "I want to look at you." He leisurely caressed her breasts with his hands, his mouth, feeling her erratic heart beat against the flesh of his lips. Taking her chin between his fingers he lifted her face to his, admiring the heated stare he saw in her eyes. She lay on the bed, reaching out to him.

"I desire you, every part of me desires every part of you, sweet Eryn," he said, crawling on top of her. "You tempt me by being alive."

Beneath him, she stroked his firm body, kissing his face, his throat, anywhere she could touch. Her fingers reached for his hair, entwining it around her fingers as it tumbled around her face. Lost in a deep, dynamic kiss neither was in a hurry to fulfil their passion. Eryn's pulse was quick, her body on the edge of ecstasy. Their lips parted only long enough to rest their eyes upon each other, infatuated by the fervent stares.

"Uriah, if you hadn't taken me I would have never known about you, about us." She kissed his lips again. "What a terrible thing to think of."

"I would've come sooner if I could find you."

Kissing her the way he was kissing her, nuzzling her neck in that tender way of his, the familiar whisper in her ear all caused her blood to sizzle.

"Your body ravishes me, woman. You were made for me, your body, for mine. I can never love you enough!"

"Nor I you…"

In the heat of passion he eased onto his back, pulling her to him, arching his body to meet hers. She traced his lips with her finger then kissed him hard while he responded with erratic quivers. "You, madam, are more intoxicating then the wine," he said as he rolled over, crawling again on top of her. "I love you," he whispered.

"As I do you, my knight." Eryn's alluring body took him to inconceivable heights with each movement, but when she spoke to him with the words of possessiveness, he could no longer put off the consummation of their unity, driving deeper, thrusting fully, letting the fusion of their love be satiated, now and forever.

* * *

Finally! Eventually! After a while, the flame died down, the fire turned to embers and the embers glowed until they became ashes, and the ashes rested until they would be rekindled with, but a spark.

Chapter 24

"This is very good roast beef. You are a master in the culinary arts," Eryn said, as she and Uriah sat side by side in bed.

"I've had to do for myself for a long time. There's been no one since you. I had to be able to take care of my inn, too, so I had to know these things."

"I saw you with the girl outside my door at the inn."

"There's been no one real my sweet, jealous Eryn," he said tapping her on the nose.

"Oh, I see."

"Oh, you see, huh?"

"Yeah," she smiled, "I see."

After they finished their meal, they both knew they had to talk and make plans if their life together was going to be.

"I have to turn myself in. There's no other way."

"But I can explain that you didn't kidnap me. Did you, Uriah? It seems like forever ago."

"Yes, in reality I did. You know you didn't really go with me willingly, even if I want to believe you did. I have to acknowledge the fact that I did wrong by stealing you away against your will."

"But I did agree to come. I could've put up a fight…if I really didn't want to. Uriah, you stole away my heart, that's all. They have to listen to me, they can't charge you unless I file a complaint." She looked at him with her own sly smile. "The only complaint I have is…you didn't do it soon enough." A light blush rose to her cheeks as she heard herself speak.

"I doubt that will help my case. Your friend is an eye witness. I sure didn't want to bring her."

"Oh? I remember she told me you were flirting with her in the diner," she said, with a raised eyebrow.

"Sure I was, I admit it." He liked her jealous attitude. "I did it because you would know it was me." He licked his lips as if to remind her.

She once loathed the expression but now it enticed her. "It worked because if Beth was a little quicker she would have sprayed you with her canister of gas."

"I'm glad she wasn't then! I also subdued your young rescuer and tied him up. He'll press charges for certain."

"I can talk to them all. I can't let them take you away from me now." She held his hands, and took his fingers to her lips, kissing them.

"We have to deal with Taylor Sterling," he said.

The mention of his name brought a lump to Eryn's throat. A very short time ago she cried a million tears over him, had sleepless nights over him, yearned for him. Now it was like they were both different people. For years, she pretended he was the same man she married but sometime, a while ago, she noticed the changes in him, denying it to herself. His love for her had died and it was the best thing that ever happened to her. Eryn looked at Uriah with sadness. "What about my daughters? How can I tell them their father is stuck in 1882 with a woman carrying his child. How do I tell them about you?"

"They're adults, they'll understand. By the way, they're beautiful girls. They sure are close in age, you didn't wait very long for that, either."

"Uriah! They're twins. Why do you keep saying things like that? Taylor took care of me, it doesn't matter how soon we got married or how soon we had children."

"Twins, huh. I have twins in my family, too. The one that was with you here in Enchantment looks like you. What's her name, Alyce, isn't it? The other one looks neither like you nor Taylor." Her names's, Avis…or something like that, isn't it?   Eryn nodded yes, surprised he knew both

226

their names. There was silence but Uriah spoke momentarily. "The old man has already told Beth and Cole Dawes where he is. Maybe they told the girls."

"What? How? How do you know this?"

"I've been following things."

"How do you know what my daughter, Avis, looks like?"

He hesitated before he spoke trying to come up with a quick answer. "I saw her picture in your bedroom, and in Taylor's wallet."

"Did Emmet really get his memory back?"

"Yes."

"I'm glad. Uriah?" She bit her lip and lowered her eyes to the floor, then asked, "What is the end of the story?"

"You're living it, woman. *I* am the end of your story."

"...But why was Emmet so afraid for me?"

"He's an old man, Eryn. He mixed the story up a little, he was confused. I'm not your enemy."

"He said you were dangerous."

"I am." The sly smile spread across his lips.

"That you are, sir." Her stare floated upon the deep amber pool of gold in his eyes, and her look was of such sincere love. "You're dangerous for me to love because I can't stop." She seized him in her arms. "God, I love you, Uriah." She clung to him as if her life depended on it. Leaning back, she smiled, still watching him. Her eyes scanned his face. "Tell me about this scar," she said, outlining it with her finger.

"You know don't you?"

"Yes, but I want to hear it from you."

He tried to read her face. "Taylor...he knew I was on to him. He paid Emmet a lot of money to get him through the Portal. He caught me off guard. It seems I've been lax in my martial arts practice."

"Emmet worked with him?" She felt betrayed. "You mean he deceived me, too?"

"No, no, he was deceived. Taylor convinced him he needed to experience the trip before he took you into it. Emmet didn't know he planned to stay there. He told him the blonde was his partner. She's his partner all right."

"How did Taylor find out about it? It's not exactly what people go around telling... Is it?"

"No, Eryn. A year ago Taylor came here looking for the book you looked for. Emmet thought he would do right by him and let him in on the secret because he was so interested in the past. Taylor kept in contact with him, befriending him. Phone records should prove that."

"He disappeared about ten months ago. When did he go through the Portal, do you know?"

"About a few weeks before you came," said Uriah.

"Where was he all these months?" she said, more to herself then to him.

"I don't know, I didn't ask him. I didn't know he wasn't with you all that time."

"Why the fire, Uriah? Why did you do it?"

"My sweet, sweet Eryn, you want to believe I'm the bad guy, don't you? I didn't set the fire." He faced her, resting his hand on her knee. "Shortly after, the old man went through the Portal and told Taylor he had to come back, he couldn't stay there. It was innocent. He was so naive he didn't figure it out about the other woman. He still hasn't as far as I know."

"Oh, Uriah, this is crazy. Why did he burn it?"

"I don't even want to tell you."

"Tell me. I have to know everything," she said, as she leaned back, hugging the pillow.

The only way to say it was just to say it. "He didn't want you to follow. He couldn't take the chance of you ever following him to Enchantment. Maybe he read the book, who knows."

"Well, it didn't work. I went through anyway. Damn, I could have caught him."

"Then what, Eryn? He could have kept you there. It was risky for you to go, you shouldn't have. That's why I was there to protect you."

"You were?" Eryn thought back to the lantern blowing out in the book store. "You were protecting me? Uriah...I love you." She cuddled close to him. "He really wants to stay there?"

"Yes."

"Well, I still have to face him. I have to let him know he didn't get away with this. He owes me too, Uriah. He didn't only walk out on me, he left his girls and didn't care about what happened to them."

"I know, Eryn. I said I would take you back and I will. We'll see him together."

"Does he know I come from the past? Or that you do?"

"I don't think so—but the old guy does. And he doesn't like me, but he did like Taylor. He might have told him."

"I so want to visit my own time. I want to see how it was, Uriah. I've read so many books about that era I feel like I know it but…"

"You don't want Taylor to be there?"

"Right. You will take me back and show Enchantment to me?"

He hugged her close to him. "I will, sweet Eryn."

She relished the feel of his warmth next to her and was satisfied that she knew everything. And she did remember a lot about Uriah. "What was my whole name?"

Uriah played with her hair as it tickled his chest. "It was Eryn Rae Matheson, soon to be Eryn Rae Prescot. If you didn't know your name how come you're called Eryn, now? What about when you saw it engraved in the rock and on the tree?"

"No, I really didn't, at least I didn't know I did. When Beth found me she thought I looked like an Irish lass. She asked me my name, and I just said, Eryn. I didn't know if that was my name or not, it just came out that way."

"Remind me to thank her for taking care of you for me. You are an Irish lass by the way. Your mother was Irish."

"Wait until I explain this all to Beth. We better take her a lot of chocolate when we see her."

"I can get her chocolate like she's never tasted before," said Uriah. He got out of bed and went downstairs. When he returned he brought Eryn another glass of wine. "Here drink this, Sweet Eryn." He lay down beside her without removing his jeans. "Sleep well, my sweet, sweet Eryn," he whispered as she closed her eyes. "Sleep well."

* * *

The woods were dark, moonlight casting shadows throughout the trees, displaying an eerie appearance. The sound of a fist against a chin was the only sound.

"Damn you Chase, I told you to take your crazy brother the hell away from here. I should have killed him…and you! If I hadn't got there when I did you'd be standing at his grave right now. I'm not done with him yet!"

"Aw come on. I didn't know he was going to snatch her away from you. I tried to get him to take her back."

"A lot of good that did when you were knocked out cold on the floor." Uriah grabbed him by the shirt. "I better not see his repulsive face around here, do you understand? Do you?"

"I understand, Uriah, calm yourself down, I took care of him," he said, as he rubbed his chin. "You burned that damn camp real good there, you know."

"How much do I owe you for the groceries?"

"Fifty-nine dollars and seventy-five cents."

"Did you get her clothes?" asked Uriah.

"Yeah, man. It wasn't easy. Her car's locked up in the pound."

"Thanks. Here's an extra hundred for your trouble. I don't have to tell you to continue to keep quiet about this, do I?"

"Don't worry 'bout me, Uriah," he said taking the money. "You did me a pretty good favor awhile ago. Her car's ruined, you know. How much sand did you put in there?"

"Enough." He smiled that crooked grin.

"Things are heating up pretty good in town. Somethin's going on."

"What do you mean, Chase?", he asked, putting his wallet back in his pocket.

"Well, there's been a lot of meetings going on in the sheriff's office. That red-haired spitfire and the old man have been going in and out a lot. That young one, too…what's his name?"

"Cole Dawes," answered Uriah. "It might not be long before I turn myself in anyway. It's the only way we can ever have a real life together."

"You'll be breaking Glorie's heart, man. Is Eryn the one?"

"She's the only one. Why don't you give Glorie to yourself," he said, with a laugh.

"That's an idea."

"I have another favor to ask of you."

"Anything, man, ask away."

"I need to go to my inn and pick up some things. I need you to keep an eye on Eryn. To *protect* her, man." Uriah took him by the neck. "Protect her, not hurt her…no brother, no friends, got it?"

"I got it, man. You know you can trust me. I owe you my life."

"C'mon then. Where's your truck, I'll need it."

"My Jeep's about a half mile from here. It's in a safe place." He pointed off to the south. "You know where it'll be."

"She should be asleep a few hours. She drank wine. It always makes her sleep, but sometimes she still wakes up. I'll be back before that. Give her this note if she wakes before I get back."

"Everything'll be fine," said Chase.

"You don't have to even look at her. She's asleep in the loft. I only ask that you keep the outside out and the inside in. Got it?"

"Yeah, I'll take good care of her."

"She doesn't need taking care of, I do that! Just protect her." He stared at him long and hard. "Give me your keys." As Uriah went out, he stepped back inside and gave a warning look. "I love that woman, Chase. I trust she'll be safe."

"She will be. Not to worry, man."

Uriah was gone about twenty minutes and Chase thought about the woman upstairs. He remembered the quick glimpse of her body when his brother played with her. He had seen the same woman in town, before Uriah stole her, and he admired her from afar. He thought she was a good looking woman then and decided to follow her, until he saw Uriah enter the book store a while after she did. He waited outside and watched her go back to the inn, knowing he didn't have a chance with her if Uriah Prescot already saw her; he would surely try to claim her as his own. Chase knew that he pined for a woman from the past and this one fit her description all too well, so all he could do was stand back and watch. Now this same woman was in an induced sleep upstairs with only him downstairs. He walked to the first step and felt drawn to climb the rest of the way.

Slowly he peeked over the rail at the sleeping woman. He looked back at the door and knew if the man had returned and found him even this close he would be sorry, but the woman looked beautiful as she lay dreaming.

He stepped closer to the bed and saw the dark hair nearly covering her face. He couldn't resist the urge to move it away so he could look at her. She turned, mumbling a few words and he thought he heard Uriah's name. He continued to stare at her and without realizing it she opened her eyes, but in her drugged state she couldn't comprehend what she saw. He backed away watching her toss and turn a little, and the coverlet fell off her shoulders. She had on a t-shirt that must have been his. He sat down in the arm chair and watched. Out the window he saw the near fullness of the moon.

His brother came close to losing his life this time. Any normal man knew better then to mess with Uriah, for he wasn't a normal man. He worried that his brother would not heed the warning and forget this beauty of a woman. He still talked of her and how close he came to owning what she had, and the scar still remained on his thigh to remember her by. He still wanted more to remember. Dalton was crazy for even thinking about it. Uriah let him live for some reason, only he knew.

The comely woman turned again in her sleep and he thought she looked at him, but he couldn't be sure, for his eyes were scanning the rest of her body. Chase couldn't sit and watch any longer. He went to the side of the bed, pulled the cover over her shoulders then went downstairs.

* * *

A state trooper drove behind Uriah for five miles on the interstate. He set the cruise and obeyed the laws. Finally the trooper pulled over a speeding car. He parked the Jeep a block away. The festival was nearly over and many people were still celebrating.

The inn was secluded and only a dim light burned inside in the hallway. It looked lonely among the other buildings. He missed it. He inserted his key and shut off the alarm. His gun was stuck in his belt. Quietly he stole up the stairs to room 216. He rummaged through the dresser and glanced at the Daguerreotype photograph of the park. He missed his own time, too. He lived in the present Enchantment for twenty years and fit in like everybody else, but was a loner and lonely. He would have died if he stayed on his farm without Eryn. When he thought of her he mellowed. The woman of his dreams is in his life again, forever. He dropped the thought and collected his items. He'd been gone for about an hour and he worried for her, but knew he could trust Chase.

Back on the street the townspeople were dancing in the road to a band contest. He pulled his baseball cap over his eyes and continued on. A group of four people came toward him. The tall, thin woman with fiery red hair bumped his shoulder, almost knocking the box from his hands as they passed. She stopped and looked back, as did he. Their eyes met and she saw something familiar. Uriah turned, ducking into the shadows, and when he looked back he saw she still watched after him.

He parked Chase's Wrangler in the same place and gathered his belongings. Standing in the shadows he watched his cabin before he entered. Everything looked safe and quiet. He saw the oil lamp's soft glow upstairs where his love slept in a coaxed sleep. He thought of their lovemaking. Eryn was gentle, naive, like she used to be but she knew exactly what to do. Uriah cringed when he thought of Taylor. I should hit him again for no reason other then being with her, he thought. But if he hadn't been, maybe Eryn wouldn't have fended so well for herself. I still hate him for being with her all these years. His blood boiled when he thought of her with him but that would never happen again, and now his blood would boil in a different way.

After he walked part way back with Chase his insides were already tingling, waiting to get up to Eryn. He blew out the lamp after taking a long look at her while she slept. Stripping his clothes off, he crawled next to her warmth. Her breathing was deep and even. "God, I love her," he said aloud, snuggling as close as he could get. He caressed her lithe, sleeping body, feeling her movements as she wriggled to get comfortable. He stroked her sweet smelling hair as it slovenly lay over her breasts. Barely aroused from sleep, she reached her hand over Uriah's arm, but it slipped down between them, resting at his thigh. Her tiredness wouldn't let her go any farther. Desirous of her once again, he put his arm under her neck, drawing her against him, and he slept while Eryn tossed.

The chime was dangling wildly in the turbulent wind. Taylor was trying to take hold of it but his fingers couldn't grasp it. He was standing on the rail of the gazebo. The chime had five crystal, rectangular shapes, two with an inscription she couldn't read. The last one that hung at the bottom had a large letter inscribed on it. The trim was copper and the rounded top held each piece of crystal.

His dark hair was whipping around his face, his shirt wide open. Wind blew the soft ringlets of chest hair close to his perspiring body. His fingers searched for the hook that held the chime. His third finger, bare of a wedding ring. Eryn saw herself walking toward him, wearing only Uriah's silk shirt. The cravat was holding her hair back, and she barely felt the wind. As she climbed the first step he turned his steel-blue eyes to her and they were emotionless. Tears were in the corner of her eyes, but didn't fall. She could read part of the inscription now. It was her name. It was made for her. The steel eyes raked over her as he finally won the struggle with the high gusts and the hook. His face was distorted with a disgusted look as he held the chime out to her, then…let go, and it shattered onto the ground.

A crash woke them both as a tree hit the steel barn roof. Uriah held her close. "I have a terrible headache," Eryn mumbled, rubbing her temples in a circular motion.

"Do you want some aspirin?"

"Please."

She lay with her head back after gulping the pills. "Why do I always get a headache when I drink wine? I feel so groggy and my stomach is upset." She reached to her temples again. "I had a nightmare."

"Eryn, sorry I gave you the wine, that's why you have the headache. Tell me about your nightmare."

"I can't think right now. Wait till my headache goes away and my head clears," she mumbled, "then I can tell you about it."

Uriah tucked the cover beneath her chin and caressed her body again. She felt his need against her, arousing a need in her. "What time is it?" Her words were slurred.

"Three-thirty," he whispered, breathing heavily.

She turned to her side, putting her arm around his neck. The desire heightened in both of them, but there was no time for caresses or kisses or words. The animalistic need in two lovers overpowered anything in between and he quickly and passionately took her with all the love he could muster.

His need had to be met quickly because he loved her for so long and too much time was lost. *She* needed to be taken quickly and fully because she felt the pain of her dream and the rejection from the blue eyes hurt her; she needed to feel secure. She loved Uriah now, and with his arms still holding her, she felt more protected than she ever felt.

Chapter 25

Dawn climbed out of the night, leaving the horizon a misty gray, not yet bright. Uriah awoke before Eryn and he moved to the side of the bed to watch her dream. Admiration flowed from his soul, and he knew he was more in love with her than anyone had a right to be. His life began when she walked in the door of the Enchanted Inn. My life is whole because of her, he thought.

With his chin resting on his hands he leaned on the bed, listening to her breathe. She would feel better when she woke. The headache would be gone, her head clear. He purposely gave her more wine than she needed because he wanted her to sleep. It always made her sleep. Chase was the only choice he had to keep his secret, but Uriah didn't approve of the way he handled his brother. I still owe Dalton for the way he treated her, for touching her! he thought. His teeth were clenched and his fingers constricted into a tight fist when he pictured him with his hands on her. No, he wasn't through with him yet. He had to shake the image out of his mind, for if he dwelled on it the man would be dead. Kissing her cheek before he left, she still slept peacefully.

After his shower Uriah wrapped the towel around his waist and combed his wet hair straight back, tying it with a leather thong. He checked his mustache and decided not to shave. "I guess this scar is here to stay," he mumbled to himself as he traced it with his finger. If Taylor hadn't caught him off guard he wouldn't have the scar, but Uriah got the best of him and he wouldn't forget it. He smiled at the thought of him lying on the ground at his feet. *I'll do the next one for Eryn.* He grinned at himself in the mirror. The crooked grin…the Prescot trait. "Life is bright again," he whispered to his own image.

He looked at her quiescent figure, knowing he couldn't get enough of her and he wanted to love her, yet again as he dressed in front of her sleeping form. Today they would decide what to do. He had to acknowledge his fate for what he did.

The middle drawer held his socks and he smiled, resting his eyes on the black ring box. It is as it was yesterday. Uriah sat near the bed and pulled on his socks then stood at the large arched window to greet the morn. The nebulous mist was blue and rising from the valley in an undetermined pattern. The valley to the south had cleared and from where he stood, high above the tree tops and fields, about a half mile away, he saw the conglomeration of sheriff's cars.

"Damn!" He didn't seem surprised. "Eryn, put some clothes on, girl…they've found us."

Her eyes opened, unsure of what she heard. "Wh…what did you say?"

He turned toward her, apparent that his eyes had lost their sparkle. "They found us."

"No! No, Uriah!" She ran to the window with only the sheet to cover her, squinting her eyes to see. She was in a panic. "Uriah—let's go! Get the truck and let's go!" He stood in front of her while she screamed. "Go get your damn truck!" she wailed, as she pounded him on the chest.

Hesitantly, he took her fists in his hands, holding them while she cried, but she broke free of him and pulled on the dress he bought her. Although he pretended to be valiant, he wanted to take her, grab her hand, run, flee the castle he loved so much! He was suddenly saddened at what was about to happen.

"Uriah, I'm dressed, please go get your truck and let us leave."

"Then what, sweet Eryn? To go where, girl?" He drew her to him and she clung, like an ivy vine clings to a brick wall, not wanting to ever let go. Uriah pried her arms from around his neck. "We have to go, but first…" He put his mouth on hers and pressed hard against her, feeling her quiver while he tasted the salt of her tears. In her ear was the murmur of the voice she knew so well, whispering that he loved her.

Her arms clung to his neck as she stretched to find his lips, and for the moment he was lost in the feel of her nakedness beneath the dress.

"Eryn, you have to listen to me." He clutched her to him, nuzzling his face into the crook of her neck, needing, wanting to remain with her forever. "This place is yours, now. It's in your name, too."

"No," she cried, pulling him closer against her. "I want you here in it with me."

"I will be, girl, I will be, only not right now."

"No…"

"Listen to me, sweet Eryn." His eyes were sad, nearly damp with tears. "Last night while you slept I brought you things you need to see. Please go through it all, and…don't leave me again," he pleaded, pulling her against him.

"Never again!" Her dispirited eyes were full with tears, her long lashes, wet and parted. Two hearts were breaking, agony stabbing their emotions like broken shards.

"The things are in the sideboard downstairs in a box. It's information you wanted." He held her a while longer. "We have to go downstairs and wait for them."

"No…"

"We have to…" He enveloped her a last time before he led her to the stairs, knowing if there was any chance of escape, he would take her and go.

"I can straighten it out with them, Uriah." Alarm sounded within her as she suddenly remembered Dalton. "If you did something terrible to Dalton, please don't tell them. They'll never know. His brother can't say anything."

"Sweet Eryn, I'm no murderer. He was taken care of, but I'm no murderer; we'll talk about it later. He shouldn't have *touched* you!"

She stroked the stubble on his face, "Its okay—I'm okay."

Motors revving, repetitious screeching, and doors slamming brought them back to the reality of what was happening. Five sheriff's cars pulled in front of the log cabin and about ten men got out and hid behind their doors.

"The keys to my truck are in the visor if you need them, and maps are in the glove compartment, but please—stay here, don't leave me!" The composure he was always able to maintain somehow escaped him. Stay calm! he pleaded to himself, stay calm.

"I'll be here, Uriah, not to worry, my shining knight," Eryn said through a blur, as she tried to smile for him.

"Come out, Uriah Prescot, we have ten armed deputies here. You don't have a chance to escape." A husky voice, with a long drawl trumpeted through the bull horn.

He headed for the door and Eryn ran after him, taking his hand. Gathering her strength, she said, "We go together."

He grabbed the old jean jacket and wrapped it around her shoulders. "No matter what happens, I love you, sweet Eryn."

They were no sooner out the door when a large deputy hit Uriah in the back with the butt of the rifle while another grabbed Eryn. She tried to get to him, but three deputies threw him to the ground and cuffed him as they held him; he didn't put up a fight.

"Leave him alone, he didn't do anything!" yelled Eryn from across a patrol car. "Don't hurt him!"

They showed no mercy in dragging him to their car, allowing his head to bump the top of the door when they pushed him into the back seat.

"Uriah!" Eryn called, her face wet with tears. He looked at her through the window, blood dripping over one eye. As they drove away he winked and smiled the smile that only he could produce.

* * *

Eryn sat in the same sheriff's station that Uriah was in, but they may as well be a thousand miles apart. Her heart was crushed like chips at the bottom of the bag. The tissue they gave her shredded, falling to the dirty, tiled floor. The ugly, yellowed room was stone cold, but she didn't feel it. Eryn didn't feel, for all but her heart was numb.

She sat with her head buried in her folded arms at the table. It did no good to cry, they wouldn't listen to her anyway.

"Mom..." Avis softly called to Eryn as she opened the door. "Mom?"

Eryn looked at her daughter and Avis ran to her mother's arms, crying like a baby. "Mom, it'll be okay. You're safe now, he can't get you again."

"Avis, you don't understand."

"What has he done to you, Mom?" Avis stood, wide-eyed. "How bad has he hurt you?" She kneeled down and rested her head on her mother's lap.

Eryn smoothed her silky hair, so missing the feel of it. "He hasn't hurt me, Avis." Eryn looked to the floor, pressing her teeth against her lip, then she looked up with a smile. "He loved me."

"What are you saying this for?"

"I love him, baby. It's a very long story and I will tell it to everyone, but right now I have to try to see him."

"Why would you want to see that monster?"

"You're listening to me, but you aren't hearing me. I'm in love with that man." Eryn reached for her hand. "You've got to try and understand what I say, Avis."

"Yeah, right, Mom. In three weeks you've fallen in love with a wild man who abducts you? How do you expect me to believe that?" Avis stood, looking at her mom as if she had lost all her sensible faculties, and her eyes filled with tears. Dumbfounded, she turned around and walked out of the room.

The sheriff came in with a tape recorder and wanted Eryn to tell him exactly what Uriah Prescot did to her.

"He loved me, that's all he did to me."

"Are you saying the man raped you, Mrs. Sterling, and how many times would that have been?"

Hatefully, she looked into his gleaming, satiric eyes. "What did you just ask me?"

"We need to know so we can charge him." He had a leering grin on his face and Eryn thought him disgusting. He reminded her of Dalton. "You'll have to go to the hospital for evidence as soon as we're finished here."

"We *are* finished here! You'll be going to the hospital if you don't let me see him. I refuse to answer any of your questions."

"Now, Mrs. Sterling, I see this is all a shock for you, but the sooner we can deal with this matter the quicker we can get him put away."

"Leave me alone!"

"I think I'll send in your family."

"No."

"No?" he asked.

"I'm not ready to see them yet. I'm ready to see Uriah Prescot."

"Well, Missy, it will be a cold day before you see him anytime soon. That guy sure must have brainwashed you. He fooled us all but we knew we'd get him eventually, thanks to your daughter and the fly-by with her plane."

"Listen to me. He did *not* abduct me."

"You don't have to be afraid of him," said sheriff Tottleman. "He can't hurt you. Did he threaten you if you told us the truth?" There was that sick grin again.

"No!" Eryn stood up and with a quick swipe of her hand the recorder fell to the floor, shattered. "No one is listening to me!"

He stood up to leave. At the door he turned. "Maybe we'll try this in a few more days, Mrs. Sterling. You need to get to that hospital."

Only when she thought things couldn't get worse, a rape counselor came in and sat down beside her. "I'm Tiara and I can help you get through this. I will escort you to the hospital." She took Eryn's hand, compassionately patting it.

Angrily, she shook her hand free. "First of all, I was *not* raped. That jerk of a sheriff had no business assuming I was."

"I'm sorry," said Tiara, "I didn't know. He does kind of come off as a jerk, doesn't he?" Eryn knew she found someone that would listen. She told the story to Tiara then followed her to the dingy room where her family waited.

After everyone hugged her and fallen tears were wiped away, they went to Hanah's house. Emmet was there and he told Eryn about the mistakes he made, interjecting that he hoped it didn't cause much trouble.

Oh, no, not much trouble at all! she thought to herself, but she choked the words out, "No, no trouble at all." Holding nothing back this time, as if it would make a difference now, he told her what he learned about Taylor when he went back through the Portal, including the other woman.

Her mind was only on Uriah. The sheriff wouldn't let her see him, no matter how she insisted. Hanah recommended an attorney and as soon as Emmet finished his story, she called him. The girls thought she had lost her mind but, reluctantly, gave her the benefit of the doubt.

Cole was with them at Hanah's and Eryn asked him if he would take her to see the lawyer.

"Mother, we're going too," insisted Alyce.

"No, you're not. I'm fine and I'm doing this alone."

As Eryn stepped out the door, Beth took her arm. "Eryn, are you really okay? Do you need me to come along?"

She had more to tell, Eryn could read it in her eyes. She hugged her friend, "I was so worried about you. We'll talk when I get back." She hugged her again and it felt good. "Yes, Beth, I am okay, really." She had missed her. "You will never believe the things I know."

"Yes, I will, Eryn. I already do know. I don't quite believe it all, but I do know. I can't wait to talk to you about it." Beth grasped Eryn's shoulders. "What do you want the girls to know? We haven't told them anything."

"It's time to tell them everything. I'll do it when I come back. I hope they'll understand."

"They will, they have to," said Beth.

* * *

Sitting in the lawyer's office, the country decor reminded Eryn of Uriah. He would like the way it looked. Everything was for him since he filled that empty space in her heart. Eryn told the lawyer everything. Everything that happened except for the Portal. He said if Cole and Beth didn't press charges and if she didn't, there should be no reason to hold him. He told her she may have a fine for filing a false attempted rape charge against Uriah. But then again, Uriah probably wouldn't press charges against her, so in the end, they both were even. Eryn felt certain he would be back in her arms this very night!

They went to the jail together, but the sheriff would only allow Mr. Stanley in Uriah's cell. Eryn waited with him. "Why are you making this so difficult?" she asked him. "You could let me in to see him if you wanted to."

"Lady, for three weeks we've had every available man searching for you. We've had dogs and planes and it cost the tax payers a lot of money. Now, I hear you say you were all cozy and warm tucked away in your little log castle in the mountains."

Eryn glared daggers at the man. "That's not exactly how it was. You probably don't know what it's like to love someone, do you, Sheriff Tottleman?" He ignored Eryn for the next few minutes and stuck his head into the papers on his desk.

When Mr. Stanley returned Eryn went to him. "How is he? Have they treated him okay?"

He raised his hands, motioning for her to wait. "Sheriff, that man needs medical attention for that gash on his forehead. I suggest he get it immediately!"

He called in a deputy to take Uriah to the hospital. Eryn went to the phone down the hall and called Dr. Lincoln. She told him they were bringing Uriah over and asked if he could personally see him. "I'll explain later, please Dr. Lincoln." He heard the fear in her voice and agreed. Eryn trusted him.

Eryn and Cole waited in the corridor where the deputy watched the door. Boldly, and in a show-offy way, he held a rifle across his chest. She strutted away from his glare and sat on a chair across from him, trying to ignore his leers. "Cole, he didn't kidnap me…well, he did, but it's not like that now. No one understands."

"I think I do, Eryn. You see, I had it all wrong. Beth showed me a picture of Taylor with a woman on his lap." He waited for her reaction and saw one of no surprise. "That was the woman he was with here recently. I couldn't tell you before. It seems he deceived all of us."

"Yes, all of us," said Eryn. Carefully, she approached the subject. "You mean you know where Uriah and I are from?"

"Yeah, I know. So does your friend. She doesn't quite believe it, though. I think I'm crazy for it, but I do believe it—I think."

"My girls?"

"Beth thought it was better not to tell them anything."

Eryn smiled, knowing that Beth always knew what was best. "I'm glad. However, I do have to tell them."

"Did you ever think of showing them instead? It's not an easy thing to convince someone of."

Dr. Lincoln came out of the guarded room and came to Eryn when he saw her. "He'll be okay, fifteen stitches took care of him. Care to explain now?"

"I don't know where to begin but I can tell you, he is my life." Eryn looked up at him with eyes bright and he saw that love lived there. That was all the explanation he needed.

The door opened and Uriah stood in it with his hands cuffed behind his back. A large white patch was taped above his left eye, his hair loose, and in his face. Blood stains were on his shirt. Their eyes met, causing her to run to him, but as she came within reach the guard stuck the butt of the rifle into her hip. Uriah didn't take kindly to that show of force against his woman so he elbowed him in the ribs, flinging him against the door jamb, then stood there waiting for his reaction. It was as quick as he expected, and he grabbed Uriah, moving him along just as he leaned over to kiss Eryn's lips. Uriah haughtily laughed at him. Dr. Lincoln and Cole took hold of her before she caused any more harm to herself. "Let him put me in jail, I don't care!" she yelled after the guard.

"Calm yourself down, you aren't helping him," said the doctor.

"I can't stand this, it isn't fair."

Cole took her back to the motel where Beth and the girls were staying, knowing there was a lot of explaining to do. She instructed Cole to come back in an hour. They sat at the table and listened while she told her side of the story. Avis had a hard time believing that her mother was in love with another man, and she wouldn't accept that she would suddenly turn her life over to a stranger.

Alyce tried to understand, but it was all too confusing for her. They believed that Uriah was from her past, but not exactly how far back. Beth, being just like her in many ways, understood, but she knew things the girls didn't—the Portal, her friend coming from the past, and her golden eyed devil that chased her through a century.

Eryn told them that she might have an idea where their father was but wanted to be sure, telling them she might be wrong, hoping not to get their hopes up too much. Eryn decided not to tell them the part about the Portal until she and Uriah explored that subject a little further. She sent them all out to get some food, making up the story of needing to be alone for a few minutes.

* * *

The cabin was about twenty miles outside of Enchantment, but the whole area was so secluded it seemed like hundreds of miles away. Cole made sure she got inside before he left. "You're sure you know how to get back to town?" he asked.

"Yes, I know. I wrote the directions down. Please tell everyone not to worry, and that I'm sorry. I have to do this, and don't bring them here. I need to be alone right now."

He went out to the path and looked back at the log cabin, silently praising Uriah for the magnificent job he did building it.

"Tell them I love them," Eryn yelled after him. He waved an acknowledgment as he walked down the path to his truck.

Their cabin didn't look the same. Together they were like two candles that made a single light, but now it was dark and dreary, not sunny and bright. She found the portable radio, longing for some music. She listened to a popular country station and immediately heard a song that sang of love. I won't cry, she thought. She'd done too much of that and she wouldn't do it anymore! All she wanted was some normalcy. She wanted her old self back again. Which old-self would that be? she wondered. Thankfully, this separation wouldn't be forever.

She carried the box from the cupboard and sat it on the floor then started a fire in the fireplace. She saw her suitcase by the steps and wondered how he got it. When she went to it she ran her fingers over the expensive leather. It was good to have something familiar. She opened it and saw everything exactly as she packed it at home. What a difference, she thought. When she packed it she was frightened of what the future held. Now she was still frightened, but she knew the future held Uriah and that was good. It was the past that concerned her now. The thought of

Taylor came to her, finally realizing she accepted his leaving. Uriah made it easy for her. Knowing now she only mourned what they once had. In reality, it died a long time ago. She looked out the window, watching a cloud drift away from the sun. "I'm really okay with it," she said.

She didn't know what she would find in the box, but the first thing brought a smile to her face. Uriah had put a beautiful opalescent, lavender glass bowl in the box and carefully filled it with enough liquid for a tiny white rose bud to float in. How gallant! she thought. Its aroma was strong like a fresh cut flower, yet it was mixed with a musty odor from the old things inside. Next to it was a card: *My sweet Eryn, I write this, my love, to once again tell you that you are my light in the night. I love you. Forever and always—U.P..* She traced his initials with the soft pad of her index finger and leaned the card against the rose bowl on the table.

Inside a large yellow envelope were photos, yellowed and faded with age. The first one was of a couple, the man sitting on a large, handmade tree swing, and a lovely woman standing beside him with her hand on his shoulder. The man had a long, drooping mustache, typical of the era. His hair was thick, parted on the side, dark in its hue. He wore breeches with suspenders and a boxy looking coat with thin stripes woven in. A hat was on his lap. The woman had light eyes and Eryn knew her hair was red. She looked like her. Her hair was long, cascading over one shoulder. She was the woman that reminded her of lavender. Her dress was full with a bustle on the rear and a train that just touched the ground behind her.

In the background was a tall, roughly crafted windmill. The old house had a steeply pitched gable roof. The walls on top looked to be made of timber beams and the bottom was stone. Eryn began to feel all warm inside, allowing her fingers to tenderly outline the two figures. When she was too overwhelmed to imagine any more, she hugged the photo to her breasts, reaching for another. It was of a little boy with freckles like the woman. As she looked closer she saw it was the same boy she envisioned. Joseph, her little brother. Okay, she said she wouldn't cry anymore, but she did when she thought of his early death and the pain it must have caused her father before he died on the river bank. When she thought of these people it was like a rope, squeezing, tightening around her heart, the grief—profound. Her family was gone, it hurt her now, even though she didn't remember them. It was like the sad ending to a movie, albeit, she didn't see the beginning.

Beneath the family photographs was a large photo of herself. She was beautiful, but the photo was in very poor condition with some of the edges broken off. It was in color and someone—Uriah, had to have it colorized sometime in the last twenty years. It was the way he remembered her. Her hair was pulled back, except for some uncontrollable tendrils. She even had freckles on her nose. Her jaw was square and her petite nose was pugged on the tip, as it remains now. Her deep set eyes, the color of turquoise, stood out beneath thin, nicely arched eyebrows. Lips barely curved in a smile.

She wore a mint green lace dress that was draped off her shoulders with two layers of lace ruffles across the bust. Around her neck was a choker that was green lace like the dress, with a brooch in the center. She was truly a young lady right out of the Victorian age.

For an hour she looked at photographs, trying to fit pieces of her life together. She found an elderly couple's picture, thinking it was probably her grandparents. Upside down on the bottom of the box was a photo of Uriah. He was as handsome a boy, as he was a man. His young, cat-shaped eyes were fascinating. As he smiled at something off to the side his lips were turned into a curved grin. Eryn loved the look of him. She once thought Taylor was handsome, but the image of Uriah set her emotions on fire.

She went to the stove to make a cup of decaffeinated tea, hoping Uriah didn't do anything foolish. So badly, she wanted to be with him. She loved him for getting the box of memories for her. By chance, she remembered he said they were at the inn and wondered if he went after them when she slept last night. Wine always made her sleep well, especially when she had too much of it. She shrugged it off, for she trusted him to take care of her. If he thought that was best, then it was.

She took her stiff body outside to stretch and to breathe some fresh air into her lungs. Crows, with their articulate squawking, were calling back and forth to each other from somewhere in the tall trees. She strolled a few hundred feet and looked back. Her cabin? Yesterday it was romantic and picturesque but today it was lonely and sad. Excited to continue, she went back inside and sat with her legs wrapped around the box. Grabbing at whatever was next, she pulled out something that was wrapped in cloth and tied with a strip of leather. Carefully she undid the bow, letting the tie fall to the floor. She quickly unfolded the cloth and there it was, the scorched pages of Emmet's book. She was in awe. Finally, the opportunity she longed for. Did she really want to know the end of the story? It would be so easy to accept Uriah's explanation that, indeed, *he* was the end of her story. She turned the fragile pages even as she thought about it. When she found the right page her shoulders shook from a shiver as she reread the beginning… *She will find trouble when she goes through the Portal…* It would have been trouble if Taylor found her. She never would have believed that then. She continued:

The woman will try to go through the Portal. She must not go alone. There is danger there for her. Her life will be shattered by a man she once trusted, but another will rise out of the past to protect her the rest of her days. His hair will be golden like the fields of wheat and his eyes will sparkle like golden dust. This woman bore two children that exist in the *present*, but were conceived in the *past…*

Eryn's eager eyes stared into the fireplace as she tried to comprehend what she read. *"Two children made in the past,"* she whispered. She looked upward, mouth agape. "Oh, my God!" she said, as she threw her hand to her mouth. "Oh, my God!" She had to go on! The pages were yellowed, old and worn, and the bottom of the page was singed. It was hard to read. The light was dim, but she squinted her eyes to see:

This will be the end of her sadness. A choice must be made for her to stay in the present or return to her own era. She will be happy again when the right decision is made. When she and her defender have made the decision, the Portal must be forgotten forever. It is not to be used again. It is not right to travel to the days that are no more—

Eryn put the book down and took a deep, erratic, breath. *He is* the end of my story and the beginning of my life. *He* is their father. "Their father!" she said, as a smile warmed her face. She thumbed through the pages, reading bits and pieces. If Emmet had told her these things in the beginning she wouldn't have believed him. How could she? It had to happen this way. The predictions of the old man had to be carried out. It's a lot to comprehend. There was a greater force at work and who was she to even question it.

Before she put the things away for the night she rummaged through the contents, finding a red velvet pouch. When she opened it she saw a brooch. The same one as was in her picture. It was definitely old, more than a hundred years. It was shaped like a peacock, its tail spread open. Diamonds, topaz and emeralds set in it.

Tiredness prevailed, and as much as she wanted to examine the other items, her lonesome eyes closed and she collapsed against the fluffy pillow she leaned on. She fell off to sleep inhaling the sweet familiarity of the rose.

This night in the heavens, clouds concealed the shine of the brightest light in the sky. The two empty arms of the woman alone in the cabin, subconsciously reached out to the arms that belonged to the man who stood behind iron bars, looking upward for his light in the sky. And he, too, noticed that the clouds shielded the twinkle. He watched a little longer and only he saw as it peeked itself out through the mist only for a moment, reflecting in his eyes. He smiled. It was still there.

Chapter 26

When Cole picked up Alyce, Avis paced the floor while she ripped him apart. "I can't believe you took her there and left her!"

"Listen, she knows what she's doing and what she wants," said Cole, calmly.

"No, she doesn't, she's in shock or something."

"Something wonderful happened to her, Avis. You better accept that," said Cole.

"How can you see something wonderful in an abduction and maybe a rape."

"Your mother doesn't act like she's been raped, and you know it."

"I know my mother better than you do," said Avis. "That's a bunch of—"

"This time, I know her better than you," he interrupted.

"I'm going to that jail to find out what he did to Mom," she said, looking at Alyce and ignoring Cole.

"You can't see him. They won't even let your mom see him," he said.

"Well, I wonder why…"

"That's enough, you two. Avis settle down. We're not doing anything until we talk to Mother. Cole's right, something did happen to her. You saw the look on her face when she spoke of him."

"She's bewitched by him," said Avis, refusing to believe anything else.

"Cole and I are going out. Don't do anything foolish, Avis," said Alyce, as she grabbed her coat and went out the door.

* * *

Avis drove the three miles to pick Hanah up for dinner at Sweet Nicole's. She couldn't stand another night alone in that motel room. She felt a little better now that she knew her mother was all right, physically. She figured Uriah Prescot must have drugged or hypnotized her. She wasn't acting quite like the mother she had three weeks ago. What does he hold over her? she wondered.

"Hanah, what do you think is going on with my mom?" Avis asked, after she ordered a cold turkey plate.

"I told Beth before that I didn't believe he would hurt her. Obviously he loves her in his own way. Maybe she fell for his attentiveness. It's been awhile since your father left. She's been with only him for three weeks, twenty-four hours a day."

"My mom's not like that. She too sensible, she wouldn't fall for just anybody."

"Avis, maybe your father is out of the picture for good. I don't mean to hurt you, dear, but it has been nearly a year."

"I need to talk to that man, Hanah. Do you think the sheriff will let me?"

"No, I don't think you should. The sheriff is not a pleasant man. Now, my dear, you eat your dinner. You watch out for that sheriff, too."

* * *

"Come on Sheriff Tottleman—Mark, let me in to talk to him." Avis sat on his desk and swung her leg while she hiked her denim skirt up higher on her thigh. Subconsciously, she bit on her bottom lip. "Maybe I can get something from him that you can't." Her eyes penetrated his cold, listless orbs.

"And maybe I can get something from you, young lady." He walked over and leaned over her, running his finger over her shapely thigh. "I get off in an hour."

She glared a hateful gleam straight in his eyes and swiftly lifted her foot until it was very near his manly pride. He suddenly changed his mind and told her he was only kidding with her. Her glare changed back to her sly smile.

"Oh, what the hell. It ain't gonna hurt nothing. Come on, young lady." He pointed the way and smiled as he followed behind watching the innocent sway of her thin hips. When they got to the door Avis followed him through the small corridor of cells as a couple of whistles acknowledged a female presence.

He was stretched out on his back on the narrow bunk with his fingers clasped behind his neck. They intently watched each other through the bars. He knew who she was right away. As she paced the length of his cell he watched her, recognizing her from her picture on Eryn's dresser at home. He was pleased with what he saw. Her blond, bouncy hair was like her personality; he could tell. He sat on the edge of the bunk. "What can I do for you, Miss Sterling?"

She eyed him from head to toe and if he wasn't her mom's attacker, she could have enjoyed his look. "What did you do to my mom? Drug her? Hypnotize her? What?"

"I did no harm to your mother. I wouldn't hurt Eryn," he said, as his gaze drifted away from the girl.

"Well, she's out at your prison right now, doing who knows what. Why would she do that?"

His face broke into a wide grin to think that she was going through her box of old things.

"What are you grinning about? Did you set some kind of trap for her?"

"She's doing what she needs to do. Something you know nothing about, little girl." He seemed to be agitated. "Don't worry about her." He smiled again and she saw his white, straight teeth against his smooth skin, and the crooked smile was familiar to her. No wonder Mom is so entranced by him, she thought.

He walked over to the bars and wrapped his fingers around them, looking closely at Avis, but he could have been looking in a mirror. Her cat-like golden eyes stared back at him, and he smiled at her, as his mind raced to many nights of love, twenty-years ago. "How old are you, Miss Sterling?"

"I'll be twenty-one in January."

"Damn," he said, but in a good way.

"What business is it of yours, anyway?"

"You are a beautiful young girl, Avis. Your sister is, too."

She suddenly became captivated as she looked at his amber eyes. Eyes that looked at her everyday in the mirror.

Her eyes.

He had a pull on her, and she didn't know why, but she liked being drawn to this man.

"Your sister looks like your mother..."

"Yes, everyone says that. When did you see my sister?" She hesitated, for she knew it was when he tried to attack her mother. At least that was the story she was led to believe. Avis bit her lip again and it caused Uriah to grin. Just like her mother.

He reached through the bars and felt the silky ends of her hair. She didn't move away. "Like I said, your sister looks like her mom, but you look like your...father." He stared deep in her eyes and already loved the girl he looked at. Grasping the ends of his own hair between his fingers, it was as silky as hers.

"I'm sorry, but I don't look like my father."

"Yes, yes you do, Avis," he smiled.

"You think you're pretty smug, don't you, Mr. Prescot? I hate you for what you did to my mom, but you'll get what you deserve." She smiled and Uriah noticed that she had a crooked smile, even if it was sly.

"Avis, I know your father; you are just like him." Their eyes met and held.

"Sheriff, I'm ready to leave!" She raised her voice to be heard. "Get me out of here!"

The sheriff returned, taking Avis by the arm, purposely brushing against her breast. As he did so, Uriah gripped the bars until his knuckles turned white as he watched the beautiful woman child, his beautiful daughter, leave.

Avis shook her arm free from the obnoxious sheriff and ran out the door, not realizing she was crying until she reached her car. How could this happen, she thought. How can I be the image of that rogue?

* * *

The hum of the old refrigerator woke Eryn and before she was completely awake she remembered where she was and why. The cabin was cold along with her heart which was desolate. The clock stopped at two-thirty. Time might as well be stopped, she thought. But suddenly Eryn smiled. This was a new day. She looked at her watch. Uriah's preliminary hearing was in three hours. With a lot of luck she knew they could be together this night and forever.

She went to the barn to get the map out of the truck. Could she really find her way to town? The barn door was difficult for her to open, but her strength seemed to have increased in the short time she had been there. As she sat in the truck she glimpsed a shadow pass the shuttered window. "Probably a crow!"

After she went back inside the cabin she turned the lock on the door. She took the county map and looked it over while she drank a cup of coffee. While sitting there, her mind couldn't concentrate on the map. She smiled as she thought about the silk dress and could see the stares of everyone if she wore it to court. Uriah would be pleased, but she knew her family would think she was insane after all. She looked over her own instructions to Enchantment. They would be easier to follow so she put them on the table with the things she would take. She went to the box. They would go through the rest of it together and he could explain the unfamiliar photographs. Taking the brooch out, she also sat it on the table. He would be pleased.

Eryn carried her suitcase to the loft and took out her gray, slim fitting slacks and pink sweater. The gray tweed blazer was wrinkled so she would hang it in the bathroom—the steam would smooth it. When she passed the window she thought she saw something shiny in the distance. She would look with the binoculars after her shower, right now she was in a hurry.

She took the hair dryer and carefully curled the ends of her hair under until it was nearly dry. She sprayed the back and crimped it with her fingers until there was soft waves. It had been a long time since she had her make-up and she applied it ever so carefully until the look was right. "This is me."

She wondered which one Uriah liked best, her in the nineteenth or twentieth century. With the towel tucked around her breasts, they were full and prominent above the top and she liked the way she still looked. Uriah's T-shirt was hanging over the chair in the kitchen so she let the towel drop and pulled it over her head. It nearly hung to her knees. She made her way to the loft to dress, noticing the front door was ajar so she slammed it shut and locked it, thinking she had already done that.

She hurried up to the loft. Excitement was in her step, taking two steps at a time, but just as she reached for the hand rail at the top of the steps a hand reached out, ruthlessly pulling her up.

Shocked at the force, not to mention being scared out of her wits, she screamed. Before she could think she was pushed on the bed, the force nearly knocking the air out of her lungs. Dalton was on top of her, smothering her face with his wet, tobacco smelling, lips.

"We've something to finish, little lady. Seems like we don't even have an audience now, either. Just like I like it. You been tormenting me, little lady, and you didn't even know it…."

* * *

"I told you not to leave her out there, Cole, now where is she?" said Avis, as they sat in the courtroom. Uriah was brought in, in handcuffs, searching the room for Eryn. Beth read a look of fear on his face and couldn't help but notice his eyes.

He looked at Avis and they stared at each other, neither wanting to be the first to look away, then he looked at Alyce. It was then that Beth noticed her best friend's daughters' resembled the man from her past.

Uriah barely heard anything the judge said to him, but his lawyer seemed outraged a few times. He turned to look at Beth as if looking for an answer. She recognized him from the restaurant. Eryn did all right this time, she thought as she eyed his tall, muscular stature, liking what Eryn had found…or had found her. No harm was done, Beth thought. He didn't really hurt her or Cole and he did lock the door after he put her inside the car. He couldn't be all bad.

Uriah was oblivious to what was going on until the deputy removed his hand-cuffs. His lawyer told him he was free, he could go. He heard a deep sigh from Avis. She stood, staring at him. When he looked at the others he noticed the concern on their faces as they searched their watches, looking to the door.

Damn! They don't know where she is either. Fear swept over him; could she have been leading him on…waiting for her chance to escape him like she promised? He couldn't think—couldn't focus….

Beth went toward him and when she saw him up close she knew for sure he was the man she bumped on the street.

"Where's Eryn?" he asked, as he grasped her arms too tightly.

"I don't know. We're worried."

"Something's wrong," he said. Beth admired the man for his concern. Chase unexpectedly went to Uriah and pushed the others out of his way. He told him his brother was crazily obsessed with Eryn and now, he was missing and it seemed that Eryn was too.

"I need someone's car… Now!" he said, half out of his mind. "I have to get to my cabin." Chase had never seen this man so compelled and before he could finish his thought Uriah grabbed him, dragging him to the door.

"Wait!" Avis yelled to him. "I have a better idea."

He stopped and looked back at her.

"Put on your flight jacket, mister."

Avis filed their flight plan and took off in her single engine Cessna 180, barely missing the tree tops. "Quite the adventuresome type aren't you, Miss Sterling."

"Don't tell me you're a worrier, too," she said, as she smiled at him.

He reached out and patted her on the shoulder. "Nope. I love it, now little girl, get this plane flying."

She stared over at him and hesitated before speaking, "Tell me you'll never hit her."

"What?" He saw the seriousness in her amber eyes. With a smile that melted her heart, he said, "Never."

Chapter 27

"Leave me alone! Uriah will be right back." Eryn pounded Dalton on the back, but it was like pounding on a sack of potatoes. It was impossible to twist away from him, for he held her hair in a tight knot.

"Don't try it, little lady. I know his butt sits in jail in Enchantment."

"No, he's out—he'll be here! This time he *will* kill you."

He laughed. "You mean like he did the last time. I don't think so. You and me will be far away before he ever gets here. But I'll possess you and ever'thin you got, and you'll be begging for mercy way b'fore he gets out."

Eryn tried to get his smelly body off her. His clothes were dirty and musty and he smelled of cigar smoke. His face was bruised. He had stitches along his jaw and above his eye. His skin was rough on her smooth skin. He was of slight stature, and maybe it was the extra work she had been doing or the fresh mountain air, but she noticed she gained some strength.

Her mind was spinning so fast, she thought she would fight to her death if she had to. The pistol was in the drawer beside the bed, if only she could get it. Momentarily she relaxed the fight in her, hoping he'd think she was submitting to him. It worked. He released his grip on her hair, relaxing his scrawny body on top of her. She ran her hand down his back and across his hips, hating every disgusting minute of it.

"I knew you couldn't resist me, little lady. That guy probably ain't good as me." He leaned on his left elbow to stroke her cheek and Eryn noticed bruises on his arm.

She was breathing hard and steady, her eyes closed, first picturing it in her mind. Seductively, she brushed his leg to persuade him she was enjoying him. Then with her breath held deeply she exhaled and thrust her knee into his groin with everything she had! He screamed and grabbed himself, doubling over in pain. In a blur she grabbed the knob, moving so fast she surprised herself. Her lean fingers wrapped around the butt of the pistol: she cocked it and aimed. His eyes grew wide.

Albeit, he grimaced in pain but dove at her anyway. Gently, but surely, she squeezed the trigger. The bullet hit its objective. He grabbed his shoulder, and again she cocked the hammer, aiming with both hands on the weapon. Dalton sprung at her, and she fired, but he knocked the barrel away and the bullet shattered the beautiful arched window.

He swung at her and when she dodged his fist he grabbed the gun from her hands. Opening her eyes, looking up she saw the gun barrel pointed inches from her nose. Her pulse quickened, but she wasn't ready to quit yet. Uriah had tried to train her in some self-defense techniques, but she never paid full attention to his instructions. If only she could remember them now. Think Eryn!

Dalton tried to rip the T-shirt off, but she clung tightly to it. With the barrel of the gun he ran it the length of her body, stroking her thighs with a sick smirk on his face. She chewed on her bottom lip and looked to the ceiling, thinking what to do next. The green specks danced in her eyes as he outlined her lips with the gun barrel.

"I can shoot you before or after, little lady, it don't much matter to me. It'll be easier if you just give up and let me do what I'm gonna do. You can't win here, little lady."

His rough, scrubby face was too near hers and she cringed at the things he whispered. No! She would not give up and let him win! No! She would win… Or die!

Dalton continued teasing her with the weapon. She put her hands on his shoulders and smiled at him, a sexy, fake smile. If it worked once, it might work again, she thought. It disgusted her immensely, but she ran her tongue across her lips and stared into his frightening eyes. He smiled back, flashing his yellow stained teeth. Her nightmare was real! He started to stretch out on her; she continued to smile, but when he least expected it she forcefully pulled down on his shoulders, bringing her knee up to his chin with full force! He fell back, the gun slipping from his hand. Blood dripped from his mouth as his teeth bit through his lip.

There was no time to sit around and listen to the expletives that raged from him. Eryn screamed as he lunged for her. Grabbing Uriah's robe she was on the bottom step before he got off the floor. She threw the robe half on herself while she fumbled with the lock on the door. When her fingers finally succeeded, she was out. The robe tied securely she ran toward the barn. Running away was getting to be a habit she didn't like!

The side door slammed behind her as she fought to find the right key. Not quick enough; he grabbed her and they fell to the ground. Although she squirmed away from him, she fell again. Running straight toward her, she instinctively lifted her foot, glad that he ran right into it. She grabbed the keys from the ground. A log lay beside them and she grabbed it, hitting Dalton over the back as he tried to get up. She didn't know she was even on her feet until she felt her legs running!

The ignition key was in the visor and she was able to start the engine. "Uriah, I have to take down your door." And she accelerated. She watched Uriah shift into four-wheel drive enough times to know how. It kicked in and the metal doors flew to each side as she slammed through them. Dalton anticipated her move, jumping on the running board as she sped by him. He reached in the window and turned the steering wheel so Eryn could only go in a circle. It was all she could do to keep her hands on the steering wheel and try to push him away at the same time. She lost the battle when Dalton elbowed her in the head. Her limp body slumped over on the seat. Stretching in, he turned the key off. As he held pressure to his shoulder wound he leaned over next to the truck, in pain. "Man, I never expected her to be like that. She's my kind of woman!" he groaned.

The roar of an engine was heard in all directions as its echo bounced off the ridges. The Cessna flew over the pine trees along side the cabin. With blood dripping from his face and shoulder he shoved the semi-conscious woman to the center of the pick-up seat and sped into the woods.

"She's in trouble, Avis, don't let him get away!"

"You know this territory better than I do, where do you think he'll go?"

"There's a clearing to the south! I saw Chase's Jeep there. Maybe he'll try to get to it."

"Okay, let's go for it," said Avis.

"Damn, I thought I could trust Chase to keep his brother under control. He doesn't want to live any longer," said Uriah. "Nobody takes what's mine. Now he has my woman and my truck."

Avis gave him a strange look out of the corner of her eye. "Your woman and your truck? In that order, huh?"

"You're something else, girl. Now find my woman and truck."

"There!" Avis pointed. "He *is* going to his Jeep. What's wrong with my mom?"

"Can you get any closer?"

"You bet." Avis flew low to the truck, long enough for Uriah to see her lying on the front seat. Avis had to pull up or crash. Uriah looked back, and Dalton stopped and fired two shots at them. "He has my gun, too! He's stuck. He's stuck real good. If we're going to get her this is our chance."

"But how, I can't land here!"

"Girl, where's your sense of adventure? Okay, listen carefully. You're going to circle back and come in at tree top level. Keep your speed just above a stall with full flaps."

"What are we going to do?"

"Land in the trees," said Uriah.

"Okay, we'll just do that, if you say so. Here we go!" She circled as he instructed. Dalton was hooking the winch to a tree.

"You're going to yank back on the stick to pull the nose straight up. The tail will be down." He watched his daughter manipulate the plane with ease. "Okay, now the plane will be in a total stall with no forward movement—no vertical movement."

"Are you sure this is going to work?"

"I'm sure, now when the plane falls backwards into the trees the wings will catch on those two large oaks. Now! Do it…full flaps…easy, little girl…yank it back!" He helped her pull on the yoke. She followed all his directions and the next thing she knew she was looking straight up into the clear blue sky. "We need to figure out a way to get down. Damn, we need a rope."

Avis looked at him and smiled her familiar smile. "I have a rope."

"You have what?"

"With a harness," she laughed. I climb mountains!"

He hugged her. "I love you, little girl." And she liked the feel of him.

They looked up at the plane hanging in the tree and couldn't believe what they saw. "My boss won't be happy about this. I still don't believe it," said Avis. "How did you know this?"

"You might say I'm a little adventuresome, too."

They eased up to where they heard the winch. Shovelfuls of dirt flew as Dalton dug out a tire while the winch hummed. "Wait here," said Avis. Uriah grabbed for her arm, but she was too quick. She proudly strutted to where Dalton worked and unbuttoned a few buttons on her blouse. "Where'd you come from out here all by yourself?" she asked.

He stopped what he was doing, walked past the door to nonchalantly check on Eryn and sauntered over to Avis. Uriah proudly watched with a mindful eye.

"Well, looky here. Never mind where I came from, where'd you come from, little lady?"

"Looks like you ran into some trouble, mister." As she said the words she positioned herself, throwing a round kick to his temple, instantly sending him to the ground. Uriah was at his side before his vision cleared. He wrapped his fingers around his throat, squeezed for a moment, then punched him in the jaw. Within a second, he punched him again in the nose, and when Dalton finally got up again, Uriah positioned himself and used a Karate kick to his head, throwing him to the ground, dazed and sore.

Avis was already in the truck with her mother. "Mom, it's okay— Mom." She wrapped the bath robe snugly around her and held her. Uriah tied Dalton's hands with the leather thong he used for his hair and left him on the ground.

Eryn's eyes fluttered and when she opened them she looked into two pair of amber cat-eyes. Their hair was both mussed with twigs here and there. Avis had a few scratches on her face. Uriah's arms were scratched, his knuckles cut. She reached out and smoothed her daughter's hair. Uriah looked into her eyes, hugging her close to him, not letting go for some time. Avis saw the way they looked at each other and kind of liked how they looked together. She smiled, but wasn't sure why.

Off in the distance Eryn saw what looked like a plane sitting atop two trees. She rubbed her eyes and knew she couldn't have seen that. "Uriah, you're free?"

"I'm free, sweet Eryn."

She looked at two of the people she loved, suddenly overcome with joy. "How is it that you two are together, and how did you get here?" She was still feeling dazed.

Uriah and Avis looked at each other, smiling. "It's a long story," they both said together, their smile the same. Eryn lay her head back expecting her dream to end soon.

When Uriah looked to where he left him, Dalton pulled himself off the ground and ran off into the trees. Uriah left Eryn and Avis, running after him. A short time later, Uriah returned, alone.

Chapter 28

Eryn woke in a crisp, white-sheeted bed, smelling the same antiseptic smell she remembered. Her head throbbed and her vision was blurry. She knew there were flowers in the room by the fragrance. Suddenly she remembered the previous day and pulled the sheet up to her neck, pulling her knees up to her chest. Could it have been true that she really saw her daughter with Uriah? Imagine that!

She looked out the window at the puffed up clouds in the cerulean blue sky, frowning as she reflected back twenty years ago. She guessed her age to be about seventeen when she met Beth. Was it really that long ago? She was walking down a road; it was dark and she remembered the moon rising above the horizon. The clothes she wore were all she owned. She must have looked like a ragamuffin. When Beth stopped her car and stepped out, Eryn thought nothing of her modern appearance with her red-hair and snappy green eyes. She wore tight white shorts and a green halter top. Her hair grew to the middle of her back, curly. She wore sandals that wrapped twice around the ankle.

The look of the future was no surprise to Eryn, for she had no recollection of another time. Beth took Eryn off the street then and there. She thought she must have been in a disastrous situation, but Eryn could not tell her anything. Eryn didn't know her name, where she came from or anything. Eryn remembered, too, that for the next few weeks when she woke up, she would vomit.

A middle-aged man came to take blood and Eryn snapped out of her muse. She was oblivious to what he did as she remembered the sickness those early mornings after she somehow found her way through the Portal.

When the man left, she thought again to the time her life began. Beth talked to a detective and they put her picture in the paper hoping for someone to come forward and identify her. It never happened. Beth's parents provided Eryn with a place to live. They didn't know what kind of education she had, but she seemed intelligent enough, so they helped her get a job with the local elementary school where they taught. She couldn't help but wonder how she got to be three hundred miles from Enchantment. To this day, she couldn't remember.

"Mrs. Sterling?" It was Tiara, the counselor. Another interruption she didn't want. Eryn said hello to her but wasn't in the mood for company. "I just wanted to see how you were. There's a big write-up in the paper. Have you seen it?"

Eryn asked her what it was about and wondered how it concerned her.

"It told of how your daughter and Mr. Prescot flew in and rescued you from that creep. She crash landed in some trees, on purpose." Eryn thought of the plane she *thought* she saw in the trees, and smiled.

As Tiara was about to leave she stepped back inside and became serious. "The sheriff's sure he has the serial rapist, Mrs. Sterling. You're a hero to a lot of women around here," she hesitated, "including me. Bye now."

Eryn certainly didn't feel like a hero, she couldn't even think about Dalton. When she did she shivered and trembled. She wondered how badly she hurt him and what did Uriah do to him after he ran into the forest. She could have killed him, maybe she should have.

She became reminiscent again. This time her thoughts went to her husband. She thought it was love from the moment she saw him, that's why she never told anyone when he forced himself on her many times. Thinking she was carrying his child, they married. Beth looked in the phone book for a last name for her. She took care of her identification and a birth certificate and gave it to her one day with a birthday cake a year after she found her. "Happy Birthday, you're a year old today," Beth told her. Seven and a half months after Beth found her the twins were born and nothing was ever said about their early arrival. She was young, they were twins, everyone said twins arrived early all the time. Eryn always wondered who the girls looked like. She figured it was her side of the family since she had no idea what any of them looked like. Everyone for generations, on Taylor's side, was dark haired and blue eyed.

Beth's entrance disturbed her thoughts, but Eryn was glad to see her friend. In fact, she broke into tears when Beth hugged her. "It's finally over, Eryn. I don't know how this all happened, but you really have answers. I don't know how you walked out on a guy like that though. From what I see that sickness you had those first weeks was a little more than nerves and stress."

"We were practically kids, Beth, but yes, we made them together."

"Oh, my! Do you remember him?" She hesitated. "Do you love him?"

"Yes, I remember a lot about him, and I remember I loved him. That's all I need right now."

"He's gorgeous, you know that."

"He is isn't he," smiled Eryn. She threw the sheet off, hugged her knees and rested her chin on them. "How long do I have to be in here? Look at this gown!"

"I'm not sure. That wonderful Dr. Lincoln should be in soon."

Eryn saw her seductive expression and knew she was interested. Beth had a hard time hiding her feelings.

"Can you believe such a thing exists?" asked Eryn.

"You mean the Portal?"

"Um hmm." Eryn sat starry eyed.

"Do you remember how you found it, Eryn, or anything about leaving your other life?"

"No, but Uriah said I was depressed over losing my parents. I told him good-bye, and he never saw me again until I walked into his inn." Eryn lowered her eyes. "I didn't know I was with child, I don't remember any of it, but I've had visions of some things like Uriah, my mother, my little brother, Joseph. He was a cute little boy with red hair. And, Beth... I really am Irish."

Uriah peeked in the door then went to the bed and took Eryn in his arms, kissing her long and intently, then presented her with a rose bud—

Beth watched the two of them together. She was happy for her friend. As she looked out the window she waited and smiled to herself. Glancing over at them, she noticed he was very handsome, and she saw the gold sparkle in his eyes as he touched Eryn's cheek with his finger. There was a hint of green shimmering in Eryn's eyes as she looked back at him. Beth silently wondered about Taylor. Was he really gone for good? Or was he sitting on the sidelines, waiting.

"How does it feel?" Eryn asked as she lightly touched the bandage above his eye.

"It's nothing. Are you ready to leave, sweet Eryn?"

"Yes, when can I?"

"The doc should be in shortly," said Uriah, as he looked at Beth. "You should be happy." His straight teeth flashed when he smiled at her.

"Maybe!" She smiled back.

"Is there something I don't know, here?" asked Eryn.

Uriah stroked Eryn's thigh. "It seems the doc and your friend here have something going. He still isn't pleased with me, though."

"I'll explain you to him," Eryn said. "Is he your Hero behind the Wheel, Beth?" She never saw Beth blush before, but there is a first time for everything.

Avis came in with a new dress for Eryn, and Alyce and Cole followed, hand in hand. Eryn's eyes widened as she looked up at the pair. "I see Enchantment has been enchanting for someone else."

The girls both hugged her. Uriah and Cole looked uncomfortable being in the same room with each other.

"I think you have a lot to tell us, Mother."

"Yeah, Mom." She looked at Uriah. "Seems like you left some things out of your story. Care to tell us the rest?"

"Well, Mother?"

Eryn looked long at her daughters and saw Alyce had Uriah's nose and the ear lobes were the same, too. This was the first time they were together as a family. "I will." She took Uriah's hand. "We'll tell you everything."

Eryn did her best to explain about Uriah, but she didn't tell them about the Portal through time. Telling them he was from her past wasn't a lie, for he was. The book said she had to decide whether to stay or go. Talking to Uriah first would be the best thing to do. As she looked at him, feeling his hand in hers, she couldn't wait to get him alone. Three weeks passed without being apart from him and she grew to depend on his presence, and right now, his presence excited her.

* * *

Uriah pulled the truck into the barn and didn't ask about the doors. He had them fixed already. The gear shift slipped into first and he released the clutch. The barn was shaded from the sunlight and carefree shadows abounded.

"You did good, Eryn."

Her look was of perplexity.

"The twins," he smiled.

"We did good, Uriah."

"We did, didn't we!"

"I didn't know about them when I left, I'm sure I didn't. I would have stayed if I had known about them." She turned to face him. "I'm sorry, Uriah."

"You also did good fighting off Dalton. You did real good."

"I wouldn't have been so lucky if you hadn't found me. After he knocked me out I have a feeling he would have killed me whenever he finished with me." She hugged him tightly and cried; she didn't want to, but she did. "I got my experience fighting you off." She tried to laugh.

"I'm glad I kept my gun out of your reach."

"I'm glad you taught me how to fire it."

"Me too."

"Let me see what you've learned, sweet Eryn," he said, as he poked at her. Each time she touched his hands he blocked and tapped her on the chin, or nose or cheek. Thinking quickly when he left himself wide open, she reached down toward his most precious part, but it seemed he was

267

very protective of his manhood. She got hold of his hair in the back and refused to let go until he engulfed her in his arms.

"I've had enough fighting. What's the opposite of fighting, Uriah?"

"Lovin', sweet Eryn."

She smiled. "That's what I need from you right now."

He quavered when she spoke words of that nature to him. Once or twice his heart skipped a beat when she moved in his arms. He stared into her eyes until he was close enough to close them before he touched his lips to hers. With only his hands he possessively manipulated her body until she reached her peak of emotion, dissolving in his arms, ready to accept what he offered. He leaned against her, forcing her down on the seat until his head touched the arm rest and the gear shift knob poked him in the hip. "Come with me, Madam, this is too much for me. My own vehicle beats me up."

He took her by the hand and led her into the cabin. Before the door closed against the jamb her dress was over her head in a heap on the floor. Effortlessly she slid the metal button through the button hole and pulled his pants apart until the zipper was down. She stroked his chest, running her yearning fingers around his waist, caressing his hips as she pulled him closer to her. No calm remained as two thumping hearts beat against one another with the same tempestuous cadence.

He reached out and picked her up in his arms, planting his lips firmly on hers, and blindly stumbled to the sofa. She inhaled deeply as he unhooked her bra and slowly stroked her back, her hips, her thighs, lingering on her soft breasts. She gracefully doffed her panties, knowing her unbridled panting was driving him to delirium. Hastily, he stripped his clothes and threw them in a pile on top of hers; wasting no time as he took the hardened peaks into his mouth, leaving them only to explore lower until he found the smoothness of her inner thigh, moving until the soft wispy hairs protecting her waiting warmth, tickled his cheek.

She felt his fiery breath, his hot, moist tongue against the warm, dark, inner parts of her, and her whole body tingled with each breath of air against her skin. She grabbed hold of his hair, pulling, then arching, enjoying each uncontrollable erratic shiver. Before long, she felt his lips against her breasts once more. He raised up and looked into her eyes sending an unknown erotic force flowing intently over her, enticing her to want more. Her lips lightly touched his neck, her nails brushed over his shoulders as desire imprisoned her body, knowing only *he* could release the passion. As his maleness found the way to her woman's pride, she welcomed him while she arched upward to meet the whole extent of him, the tempo of her rhythmic pulse matching his. Nothing existed around her, nothing except the fervor that Uriah caused within her. All she could feel was his body, against, beside, inside hers. Her body quivered with excitement beneath him as her hungry climatic cries were again screamed into the air. She clung to him, holding him as his body shuddered, bringing his own passion to the highest peak, then to a contented climax.

After a while, their desire had ebbed and their bodies were relaxed, still linked with a bond that refused to be broken. Satisfaction was definitely absolute!

Chapter 29

Somewhere hidden in the misty blanket a mourning dove cooed. The bed in the loft was kept warm by the body heat of two lovers that found each other, lived for each other. After their fiery desire had been kindled, even once more before the day was over, they both fell asleep long after the sun reached its zenith. Dreams of a past love were tucked away in the sanctuary of their memories as the woman and man shared the same love induced visions, visions of the life they would share for the rest of their existence....

* * *

"Uriah, which time do you like best?" Eryn asked, as they lay in bed side by side while twilight drenched the horizon.

"I like the conveniences of today, but the calm of yesterday."

"Which Eryn do you like best?" she asked, as she bit her lip.

"You are the same, my sweet Eryn," he answered, as he stroked her hair.

"How can I be, Uriah?"

"You are still innocent, but strong. Your beauty is enhanced, and you are the woman I knew you would grow to be. I told you I loved your youth and—"

"I warn you to watch your words, carefully, sir."

"...and I love your experience."

"What experience might that be?"

"Your experience with life, sweet Eryn, your experience at being a mother...and yes," he nuzzled her neck, "your experience in my bed."

She blushed. "Uriah, I cheated you out of so much. I will never forgive myself for that." She stroked his powerful arm. "I took your children away, how can you forgive me?"

"I can, that's all that's important. I've had many years to get passed the anger, I can understand that this happened to us for a reason. We may never know the reason, but now we are as we were." He held her hands in his. The love she saw in his eyes was real. She thought of the first time she saw him, the first second time, a few weeks ago. The shudder he caused in her, she could now admit to. The chill from his stare told her things she wouldn't allow herself to think about. The heat from his nearness drove her to hide what she felt. Now she knew all those things happened for a reason. He was her first love. *No one* forgets their first love!

She pressed her lips to his fingers. "I will spend the rest of my days making it up to you. My...our daughters will accept you. They're bright and beautiful girls and you'll get through to them—You definitely got to me, Mr. Prescot."

"I only brought out what was already there," said Uriah. He jumped out of bed. "Get dressed, we're going outside. The sky is clear tonight." He patted her on the derriere and started to get dressed.

Before he stepped into his jeans, Eryn took his hand and pulled him close. She found his lips and kissed them softly. "Thank you, Uriah."

He smiled his one and only, famous Prescot smile.

* * *

"The stars *were* beautiful tonight," Eryn told Uriah as they sat on the floor in front of the box of keepsakes. "When did you get this box? You told me it was at your inn."

"It's our inn now, and I want to be with you in that bed, in that room, in our inn."

"When did you get it?" she asked again.

"I went to town the night you drank too much wine."

"You left me alone?"

Uriah hesitated, lowering his eyes to the floor.

"Uriah?"

"I didn't exactly leave you alone, sweet Eryn."

"Then wh…"

"…Chase stayed with you."

"What!" She jumped up, dropping what was on her lap. "Uriah, how could you?"

"He's my friend, has been for twenty years. I trust him."

She stood in front of him. "You weren't there the night Dalton took me. His eyes were all over me just like Dalton's were, he just didn't touch me with his hands."

Putting his arms around her, Uriah tried to comfort her. "Did Chase *let* him touch you?"

"He tried to stop him but…"

"See, Eryn. He wanted to protect you, but his *brother* didn't care what he did to you." His hands went into fists. "I'm still not done with him! He may be in jail for a long time, but I'm not done with him yet." He relaxed his fists. "And besides, I firmly let Chase know he did wrong by not getting you out of there."

Eryn saw the complete look of hate in his eyes and it frightened her. "Let it be. He'll be taken care of."

"Yes, he will be."

"You really trust Chase?"

"Yes, do you think I would leave him here with my sleeping lover if I didn't?"

"Well, I guess if you trust him, I can too. You pretended you didn't know him in the woods, why?"

"It was just better that way, Eryn. I took care of his obnoxious attitude. Friend or no friend, I didn't appreciate what he said about sharing you."

"I seem to be a little moody now, Uriah. If you trust the man, I do, too. We won't talk about this again, okay?"

"Okay, but what do you mean you're a little moody right now. You always were a little moody," he said, as he sat back on the floor. When he looked up at her, he ducked, but the pillow that was suddenly airborne, still found his blond head. She lunged, landing on top of him. The hot-blooded man he was, he saw an opportunity so he stretched out beneath her. With both hands he lifted her hair from her face, and reached up and kissed her mouth. She parted her lips, taking pleasure in the feel of his demanding yet subtle kiss.

Uriah identified the photographs and told Eryn about her grandparents and her parents. "The brooch was your grandmothers. She gave it to you before she died. You treasured it, Eryn, and I couldn't let it disappear. One night after you were gone two weeks I gathered this stuff for you. I was afraid that once your uncle and cousins came to clear the house out, this would be gone forever."

She hugged a handful of photos to her heart. "Thank you for this." She smiled the smile that Uriah loved and he leaned over to kiss her.

"This makes up for the Chase incident. Thank you for always loving me."

Uriah rummaged through the box as she spoke to him. "Did you see this?" he asked, as he held out a tablet, so yellowed with age that it could hardly be read.

"No. What is it? I didn't finish looking at everything."

"It's your journal, you know, your diary."

She reached for it, fondling it before opening it. Deep in thought, she said, "I don't remember this. Did you read it?"

"Only the last few entries. I wanted to know what happened to you, but you stopped writing the day before the accident."

"Uriah, did I know I was pregnant?"

"You didn't tell me if you did. It might be in your journal."

"Oh, Uriah. I don't like not knowing any of this. Please—let's go back now, please." Lying stretched out on his side on the floor he contemplated what she asked. "We can't bring the past back."

"I have to try. Emmet remembered when he went back."

"That was different. He didn't lose his whole life like you did."

"But it might work." She walked to the window and looked into the dark—it was like looking into her past—she saw only blackness. "Even if

I don't remember, Uriah, it's important for me to see what it was like. I want to walk where you and I walked, I want to see what we saw together. I know this place right here is the same place, but I need to know my own time." Eryn became pensive. "Uriah, I have to confront Taylor, too. I have to go."

"But, Eryn…"

"I have to go, Uriah. Am I still your prisoner?"

"No. You know you're not," he said, quickly taking her by the shoulders.

"Then I am going."

"Okay! Okay, Eryn, we'll go." She wrapped her arms around his neck and kissed him all over his face. He took her hands in his. "Right now, woman, we go to bed if you keep this up."

She kissed him once more, taking a handful of hair and twisting it around her fingers. "Alyce has your ear lobes."

"And they have your nose," he said trying to hold her still because he was already aroused.

"They have that quaint little smile of yours."

"It's a Prescot trait, they couldn't help it. Now be quiet and kiss me."

"No, I want to finish looking at my things."

"No?"

"No," she whispered, "but there's always later." She saw the delight in his eyes, feeling the shudder vibrate its way down her own spine.

Uriah continued to watch as she read a few pages in her journal. With her eyes lowered to the floor, she looked up at him.

"I just read about the day I went to Enchantment with my father to pick up my wedding dress. He nearly fell apart when he saw it in Mrs. Armstrong's sitting room. He must have been a strong man, but that nearly brought him to his knees. I wonder if he would have survived my wedding day without a tear falling."

"Would you, sweet Eryn?"

She could say nothing to him because she was nearly in pieces herself. It was something she didn't want to think about. She couldn't think about her marriage to Uriah, for it broke her heart too much, and the look on his face told her that it cracked his, too.

She took out another journal and began to read. He watched the furrows form between her eyebrows and saw the questioning look on her face. "Did I write this?"

He nodded. "Read it to me, sweet Eryn. I love when you read your poems to me." He reached over and turned a few pages. "Especially that one." Their eyes locked onto each others, both with their own thoughts. Uriah felt like he had the best of both worlds. He had the past and he had Eryn—he now had the present, and—he had Eryn.

Her thoughts were that she had only twenty years of her life to remember and it was all of the present. Now she had an option, a chance to make a choice. She still had a hard time believing it possible to be able to travel to another era, but it was possible. She was looking at proof in the box of memories. She was looking at proof when she looked at Uriah, and she looked at proof when she looked in the mirror.

"The book said once we make the decision, the Portal has to be forgotten."

"Yes, it does. Can you make a decision, Eryn?"

"I think I can after I see the world through my own time period. What would your decision be, Uriah?"

"Where ever you are is where I will be. Don't you know that by now?" He pointed at her journal. "Read, woman."

She smiled at him and continued. When she reread the first part of the poem she looked at him and he smiled, knowing what she was thinking.

"When I came back to Enchantment and stayed with Hanah, I wrote this first verse when I couldn't sleep. I didn't understand where these words came from."

"I know," he said with a sheepish grin. "That encouraged me to take you and keep you until you remembered me."

"How did you get in her house that night?"

"Just an old trick I learned from a friend."

"Sometimes you scare me, Uriah."

"You scare me too, Eryn. I'm frightened you're a dream and I'll wake up and you won't be real."

"Don't be frightened, I'm not a dream... But you were in my dreams...often. It helped me understand you were real. I dreamed about you all these years, but I didn't know you. I always felt like something was missing in my life and I would wake up after an intimate dream—about a man with amber eyes, about you." She lowered her eyes and he saw her chew on her bottom lip. "Uriah, I love you."

When their eyes met it was magnetic. The way they were drawn to each other was uncanny and something special carried over from what they had before.

She put down her journal and rested her chin on her knees, hugging her legs. Uriah still watched her and silently worried that visiting the past would confuse her, not to mention seeing Taylor. Her goal was to find him, and although it wasn't quite like she planned it, find him, she would. Uriah had been through too many years alone and he wouldn't give her up now. Even if Taylor was still her husband, Uriah knew that *he* should have been.

Eryn startled him from his thoughts. "We broke all the rules, didn't we?"

"How do you mean?"

"I stayed here in your house with you. I slept with you." A slight blush crept into her face. "People didn't do that then, Uriah."

"It was more common than you think. You are naive, my dear."

"But what would everyone say about my illegitimate twins?"

"Our twins. We would have been married. Everyone knows twins can arrive early. It would not matter, Eryn, I would've taken care of you, no matter what."

"What would my parents say?"

"They were not ordinary parents, they weren't like everyone else. The weren't, ah—how can I put it. They weren't old-fashioned."

"Are you saying they weren't moral?"

"They would have accepted you and me, and our babies." He looked at her face f or a reaction. "They had to know what we were doing. I had the farm to myself, and even they couldn't keep you away from me. Remember? Your father knew my blood ran hot for you. He warned me that I better not ever hurt you; said he wouldn't stand for it."

"I wonder what kind of things my mother told me."

"You're a mother, what do you tell your—our daughters?"

"To find their dream and follow it."

His uneven smile won her heart. "I'm glad about those girls. Avis is just like me. I can't wait to get to know them better."

Eryn smiled at him, but the pang of guilt cut deep. She stole his chance at fatherhood. He missed so much.

"The radio said it might snow tonight. Are you going to walk in the forest in the wee hours of the morning if it does?" he said, as he stripped off his shirt.

"I don't need to get away from you now," Eryn answered, watching him remove his jeans.

"Good," he said, unbuttoning her blouse. "I think it's later now. Remember?"

She lay back, inviting him into her arms. He stretched his long body along side of her, absorbing every touch. She lay against him, against his soothing warmth. It began with his hot breath against her skin—the fire of his touch, like a branding iron. Eryn wrapped her leg around his, drawing him even closer while she became preoccupied with desire.

His lips moved over hers; the familiar tingle was there when he pressed them against hers, recklessly teasing. The dusty gold in his sly looking eyes was alluring, taking her breath to a quicker pace. His passion excited, delighted her until she couldn't control her own needs, needs that caused her to pull him onto her. Her hands glided down his back to his firm hips, around to his hard belly. She knew by the pounding of his heart that he found the same ecstasy, the same euphoria that she found. Each cry of excitement brought them closer to the summit of passion, until...until she arched upward to meet his desire, holding him there, with her, inside her, moving with experienced rhythm until...until her hunger disappeared.

Knowing her appetite had been completely satisfied he could no longer control his own ravenous need. The final sigh was from pleasure. Totally relaxed he kissed her conquered lips and melted into her warmth. They curled into each others arms, contented while the world around them, past and present, continued.

* * *

The dark was noiseless and not even the wind blew through the pines. Eryn lay awake for hours. The arms that held her meant love. Was this really the same man she was afraid of such a short time ago? Yes! Is he really the man she ran from, hid from, denied? Yes! His arm tightened around her and she heard his breathing, faint as could be.

Her life with Taylor was like a dream to her now. She was where she belonged—with Uriah. Uriah—with his fiery gaze that told her spirit all was well. His, are the golden eyes she would wake up seeing, the eyes she dreamed about. His, are the arms she always longed for, the arms that reached out through the confines of time to hold her. His, is the love that made her feel complete, and complete she would always be. Her search was over the night the terrible fog forced her to walk back into the heart of Uriah Prescot, the night she walked back into her past.

The chime was blowing savagely as it hung in the gazebo. Taylor stood on the step looking up at it. The woman with long, blonde hair blowing in the wind, was standing near. Her gossamer gauze dress blew against her large belly.

"I need to talk to you," Eryn said to the man as she stepped to where he stood. The man with steel-blue eyes looked down at her and put his hands on her shoulders. He started to kiss her mouth, but the blonde woman stepped up and he found her lips instead, and it was long and heedless. He reached back and released the chime from its hook, opened his fist and it fell to the ground, shattered. Uriah came from somewhere and picked up the pieces.

Eryn sat upright in bed. It was the same dream she had before. Her life as she knew it was shattered. Uriah woke instantly and held her. "What is it, Eryn?" he whispered, as he touched his lips to her shoulder.

"A dream—I had it before. Taylor, you, me… The woman." She told him about it and it left her shaken. "Uriah, if I hadn't stumbled through the…rift, the break in time, the Portal, as you call it, we could have been so happy."

"We'll still be happy."

"But…"

"But nothing. Stop feeling guilty about it and get passed it. It happened and I've accepted it. I want you to, also."

She turned to look at him in the night. "You've picked up the shattered pieces of my life. You've rearranged them and you've made this family yours."

"In reality, sweet Eryn, it has always been mine." He wrapped his arms around her and snuggled against her chilled skin. "You and those two beautiful girls have always been mine, nothing can ever change that." He urged her to lie back down beside him and pulled her close. His arms wrapped around her and they finally fell into a peaceful sleep.

Chapter 30

Eryn woke with nervous anticipation. Today she would go back with Uriah—back to her own unfamiliar era. Many thoughts entered her mind as she wondered what she would accomplish. She slipped out of bed and went down the steps as quietly as she could. The box was still on the floor and she took out the book of true stories, fumbling with the knot that held the cloth around it. Finally, she flipped through the pages until she found the entry about her very own life. After reading it once, she reread it again. It said she would find trouble if she went alone. But could she put Uriah in danger? What kind of trouble could Taylor give her? She knew in her mind that she should see him without Uriah, but what about the book, it had been right all along. There was no reason to believe it would be wrong now, but she had to go alone.

She looked to the loft. Her clothes were up there in the trunk. She found herself at the top of the stairs. A smile came across her face when she saw how peaceful Uriah slept. Carefully she tucked the cover around him and kissed his forehead.

Ever so quietly, she went to the trunk and pulled out a brown skirt of fine silk. A yellow muslin petticoat would match it fine. Looking farther inside the trunk she found a sheer blouse with a heart-shaped neckline. As she picked up a silk corset she cringed at the thought of wearing it. She found a pair of brown button-up boots and liked the way they looked, nearly new. Close to the bottom was a cashmere cape with a hood. She looked at the pile of clothes and felt ready.

Uriah turned. She sat on the floor in front of the trunk without moving. His breathing returned to a sleepy rhythm and she continued. Before descending the stairs, she watched him and her heart melted when she thought of how she could love him again so easily. She put her fingers to her lips and blew him a kiss. Stepping down one step, she stopped, looked back and whispered, *forever and always,* Uriah.

As she showered she made it extra hot so the steam would hopefully remove the wrinkles from her clothes. She towel dried her hair then blew it dry. Slowly she opened the bathroom door. Still no sign of Uriah. A blush spread across her cheeks as she thought that maybe she made him work a little too hard the night before. I didn't mean to wear him out, she thought, giggling aloud.

She was ready. Although she hated to do it, it had to be done alone. She convinced herself that Taylor wouldn't do anything to hurt her. After all, they had a life and they were a family, once. Unexpectedly, this time when she thought of him she had a lump in her throat that nearly choked her. Was it all about to come to an end? Did she want that, want to lose him for good? In reality, hadn't she already lost him? She forced the lump down and wiped the wetness that lay beneath her eyes. With her outfit neatly folded and wrapped in the cloak she took the truck key off the hook and went to the barn.

* * *

Traffic was light on the streets of Enchantment. It was nearly dawn and the townspeople were still snuggled in their beds, awaiting another day. Some of the people in the cars she did pass, stared, for they knew Uriah's truck. Suddenly, since he rescued her from Dalton, people were friendlier with him and they looked at him in a respectable way now. They no longer saw him as the strange, loner that owned the Enchanted Inn. One early rising farmer even waved as she drove past him.

Main street was devoid of traffic and people, and she came to a stop when she eased by the Enchanted Inn. She never truly looked at the magnificence of it before. It was of a Queen Anne style, and lovingly kept up. An ornamental tower projected from one side of the house. Bay windows accented the exterior and she saw the balcony outside room 216. Eryn fell in love with it as she pictured its owner tucked in bed twenty miles away. With one last look she scanned the house in its entirety and headed toward the book store.

Fog still hovered over the beautiful Victorian town of Enchantment. This time Eryn didn't seem to mind. She parked in the alley behind Emmet's book store and took her bundle from the seat. Opening the glove compartment she reached for the flashlight. Having all her things together she sat a moment and visualized what she would do. Since the book warned her of danger she wanted to be prepared for anything. Before she opened the door she pulled Uriah's revolver out from under the seat. Looking around, she saw no one and ventured to the wood planks that blockaded the rear door. With the pry bar she popped off enough wood to scoot under until she was inside.

The old clothes laid out in front of her, she looked at the corset and couldn't make herself put it on. She wondered how she ever wore anything that was so padded in the front and had so many laces and ties in the back. A woman had to be crazy! she thought. But then she saw the sheerness of her blouse and decided she must get into the corset, and get into it she did, laughing the whole time.

She wondered if the Portal would let her go through again—not exactly sure how it happened the last time—it just happened. Emmet told her Taylor was now working as a blacksmith and she would use that as a lead. It couldn't be hard to find a blacksmith, could it?

She went to the desk where she stood not so long ago and turned the fragile pages of the album, waiting… Waiting until it felt right. Her eyes closed tightly; she listened to the sounds. A pendulum struck seven times. She didn't remember seeing a clock with a pendulum in the book store. Faintly, a chime tinkled and Eryn cocked her head to hear better. The sun's rays were just shining through the cracks in the stained glass windows and she felt the warmth on her face. She leaned her head to the left to listen more intently. Clang! Yes…she heard it. Clang! Clang! Slowly, she opened her eyes. Books were no longer what she saw.

Eryn slowly turned in a circle, trying to see everything at once. The wallpaper, the pictures on the walls, the lace doilies, a piano near the large window near the foyer, and the perfectly crafted staircase. Her heart beat faster and she felt flushed all over.

Another loud clang brought Eryn out of her thoughts and led her to the front door. As it creaked open she peeked out. A few farmers were going to and fro. As she walked down the front sidewalk she pulled the large hood securely over her hair and around her face, for she didn't want to talk to anyone. At the end of the street she saw the lamplighter extinguish the last street lamp.

The smell of dirt filled her nostrils as a horse and wagon kicked up dust on its way through town. She looked back to where she just came from. The whole house stood where she remembered the book store to be. In the modern time, part of the tower was all that remained which became the book store. This house, as it sat now, was as Emmet had described it before his grandfather died and the house was destroyed by fire. Most of Enchantment's families were well-to-do because of oil and apparently his grandfather was no exception.

Eryn walked to the end of the walkway, noticing the ivy that adorned the wooden fence along the yard's edge. The dew glistened as the sunlight drenched the grass. She walked through the archway, and as she savored the sight of the old house, she heard the sound of the hammer pounding against the anvil. Once again that feeling of foreboding lingered around her.

She went onto the road and followed the noise. As she crossed the park she turned to where the sound rang out, drawn to the clang. The closer she got, the quicker her pace, until she was almost to a run, nearly tripping over the long skirt.

The pounding of the steel matched the pounding of her heart until she suddenly stopped and saw him through the door. His hair was wet and hanging in his face. He was thinner, his hair longer and he had the beginning of a beard. His back glistened with sweat as the early morning sun shone in on him. Eryn was both overwhelmed and torn between love and loss that she couldn't make herself move.

She found him.

She vowed to find him and she did, and she so loved him…once upon a time when she was lost and confused. She took a step and stopped.

He straightened up and swept his hair back from his eyes as he wiped sweat from his brow. The morning sun was hot for autumn and a slight breeze cooled his perspiring body…the body Eryn knew so well. Taylor inhaled deeply, stopped what he was doing and turned toward the familiar scent of perfume. With the sun behind her, he shaded his eyes to make clear the silhouette of a woman. She removed her hood and the sunlight captured the red highlights in her windswept hair.

"Eryn?" he whispered. "Eryn?" he asked again, louder. As he stepped out of the stable the steel blue eyes squinted and he read his name on her lips. He dropped the hammer where he stood as his wife neared him, and not far behind her, a young blonde woman could be seen large with a child growing in her belly.

"I found you, Taylor." It was barely more then a whisper.

"What the hell are you doing here, Eryn?" He gripped her shoulders the same way he gripped the steel he pounded, and his strong hands were hurting her. "How did you find out?" He shook her.

"I don't really know, maybe it was fate. I vowed to find you, but I never thought I'd have to search in a different century. I'm the one that's into that—Remember?"

Taylor looked over her shoulder. "Eryn, you don't understand."

"I know everything about you, but you're right, I *don't* understand." She squirmed out of his clutches. "I need to know why! I need to know why, then I'll be out of your life forever."

"He was tired of your perfect lifestyle," said the other woman when she walked up and possessively put her arm around Taylor's waist. She pulled his face down and kissed him with her mouth hard on his. Eryn held her breath for a moment while her confused emotions tugged at her sanity.

The woman laughed when he pulled away from her. "He told me about you, about your perfect life, your perfect love," she eyed Eryn's full length and looked in her eyes, "your perfect looks." She ran her hand over Taylor's hips. "He was tired of you. You had him since you were a kid.

Give someone else a chance now." She laughed again, while Eryn felt the snap of her heart as it broke a little more.

Quietly she stood there, submissive to the abuse she was so used to. But with some newly born strength from within she straightened and looked directly into his eyes. "Would *my* cheating on you have made you happy, Taylor? Would that have been better than being a faithful wife to you? Would that have made you happy, or only justified your own infidelity?"

Taylor hung his head and kept pushing the woman's hand away. "Eryn—"

The woman interrupted him. "It wasn't easy to steal him away, if that makes you feel any better," said the woman. "I plotted a long time. He tried to be true to you, he really tried. Then I found out about him trying to take you, his precious little wife, to this god-forsaken time. How do they manage without all the conveniences?" She rambled on about how bad it was without her dishwasher and washing machine and anything else she could complain about.

"Mavis, leave us alone a few minutes," said Taylor.

"I don't think I care to, thank you."

He ignored her. "Eryn, she and I didn't have to be tied up with problems of everyday life. She seduced me and made me feel young again. She convinced me this was the right thing to do. And she lets me be reckless, like you used to."

"Yeah, at first it was merely a challenge for me, but then it turned into more, like falling in love." She patted her large belly. "I thought us living here like this would make him forget you." She cocked her head, questioning. "Why are you here anyway?"

Eryn had enough of the whiny woman, ignoring her question. "So what will you do when he gets tired of you? When he gets tired of this *perfect* life he'll change, you'll see, if you haven't already."

Eryn looked at Taylor and his blue eyes flashed angry sparks of steel at her. "Tell her, Taylor. Tell her of the many nights she won't be interested. Remember the nights you forced *me* when the twins were young? Remember you begged for attention and couldn't get it so you abused me. Remember?"

He glanced at Mavis and tried to hide the fact that it was true.

"I remember many times I went out of the way to make it up to you." Eryn moved in front of him, a hands width away. "I remember *many* times I made it up to you." She looked into his eyes and saw disappointment in them, but she saw something more. The metallic eyes had a need that was familiar to only her. Her pain was returning.

"Why did you do this to me, Taylor? Why did you let me think you were dead or injured? Why couldn't you be a man and tell us the truth?" They stared into each others eyes. They were eyes she used to love. Eyes she was once afraid of. Then she was reminded of the hurt she felt over the last few months. No, the last few years! Of the agony she and the girls went through, and now she at least knew he was alive.

At last she found him out.

She looked deep in his eyes again, surprised to see the fire still burned. It was a small burning flame but she saw it, and was confused. But then in place of his blue eyes, amber eyes appeared in her mind, and gave her the strength to turn away. "I don't need you, anymore. As far as I'm concerned, you *are* dead!"

He ran after her, grabbed her arm and pulled her close to him. "Don't leave me. Your fire still entices me. I still need you, Eryn, I love you." He glanced back at his blonde concubine. "It just happened with her. It's you I will always love, but I needed more…more!" He held her tight against him. "I couldn't take it anymore, too much pressure!"

She tried to pull away from his clutches. "You caused it yourself when you committed adultery. Your life was happy until you strayed. You'll never abuse me again. Think about it, Taylor."

"I need the kind of life I've found here." He squeezed harder on her arm and Eryn noticed the smug look on Mavis' face. "You can stay with me." He stared, clutching her tighter. "Stay with me, Eryn, I've found my niche, I have to do this."

"Fine, do it and get your hands off me. You see, I too have found my niche and it's with someone else."

Taylor was grossly insulted by Eryn's revelation. "No! What do you mean?"

The green appeared in her eyes as she burned them into his. Their stares clashed. She was no longer afraid of him. "Just what I said. I've finally accepted your being gone. The girls have too. We don't need you anymore! I won't be at home crying in my tea if you ever need a perfect life again. Good-bye, Taylor, have a nice past!"

She jerked her arm away, but he reached out, taking her by the shoulders, spinning her around to face him.

"I won't let you go. You're not leaving. You're here with me now and I won't let you go back." He embraced her and she smelled his familiar scent…and it hurt, if only, if only…. But then she struggled to get free of him, "Let me go."

He twisted her arm while his other hand grabbed her by the neck, kissing her roughly on the mouth as she tried to push him away from her.

"I suggest you let loose of the lady!" Uriah had appeared out of nowhere. He stood straight and tall with his legs apart and his arms folded in front of him. His hair hung loose the way Eryn liked it. His black shirt was loose fitting and opened nearly to his waist, tucked into his tight black breeches. The leather boots he wore were nearly to his knees, and with the sun behind him, his hair shone like gold.

Taylor didn't release her and he squeezed even tighter as she wiggled to get free of him. He looked down at her with squinted eyes. "You're still my wife. What the hell are you doing with *him?*" he said, through gritted teeth.

Eryn looked over at Mavis who was enjoying the look of Uriah. "You're still my husband, but what did that mean to you?"

"You're *my* wife!" he repeated, pulling harder on her arm.

Eryn twisted out of his grip and went to Uriah, leaving Taylor standing with his mouth gaping. Uriah couldn't help it. He took one short step back then plowed his fist right into Taylor's abdomen. Remembering his earlier threat, he turned around and hit him again. "That's for Eryn." They looked into each others eyes, and the hate hung thick in the air. When Uriah turned to go, Taylor gave a sarcastic laugh.

She walked a few feet and stopped as Uriah took her arm. I have to do it, she thought. Looking over her shoulder she saw Taylor still stood watching her. She turned—"By the way, Taylor. You know how we always wondered whose side of the family Avis took after?" Eryn smirked and enjoyed each painful moment. "Well…she takes after her father's side." Uriah moved in closer and Taylor noticed the golden cat-eyes that looked exactly like his daughter's. Uriah took her hand and smiled and Taylor saw the crooked smile, the same smile he saw on the girl-child for the past twenty years.

"You see, you really weren't the first! It seems I wasn't so perfect, after all, Taylor. Whatever do you think of that?"

Uriah took her arm once more, enjoying her relieved smile.

He looked back at Taylor and relished the sight. He stood with his hands in his pockets, his head down. The woman walked to him and put her arm around his shoulder, but he shrugged it off, taking a step away from her.

And Uriah smiled!

Chapter 31

Eryn didn't look back as Uriah led her away from Taylor and his concubine. The waiting carriage was around the corner of the stable. Uriah lifted Eryn into it, his hands lingering on her waist as she turned toward him. She rested her hands on his shoulders, gazing into his eyes.

"Are you okay, Eryn?" He wiped the wetness from beneath her eyes.

A smile came naturally. "Yes, I'm okay now."

"You handled it better than I would've."

"Thank you, but I don't feel like I handled it very well. I wasn't sure how I would react to him." She took a deep breath.

"Why did you go alone!" he asked.

Eryn looked off to the side, avoiding his eyes. It seemed foolish when she thought about it now. "It doesn't matter because everything worked out and he didn't hurt me. Uriah, the book was wrong. I, I—"

Before Eryn could finish she saw Taylor over Uriah's shoulder in the distance. He raised his arm and pointed it in their direction. Her eyes widened and she screamed, trying to push Uriah back, but the bullet struck him in the shoulder and went through him, lodging in Eryn's side. Uriah fell back pulling her on top of him. He quickly rolled over her, shielding her, but they were both in the open with no protection. He fired again, but this time Mavis ran up and pushed his arm to the side, and the bullet whizzed over their head, hitting the buggy.

With both hands Taylor pushed the woman down on the ground where she clutched her abdomen, screaming. Taylor ran into the livery and came speeding out on a wild bronco.

"No, Taylor, he can't be ridden yet," cried Mavis, as she sat sprawled on the ground. She no sooner screamed the words at him, and the bronco reared up and sent Taylor to the ground. Uriah went to where he lay while his own blood dripped from his shoulder wound. He died as soon as he hit the ground, Uriah thought. He looked back at Eryn ripping off pieces of her petticoat to hold pressure to her wound as blood oozed from the point of entry. She tried to get up, but it hurt too badly to move.

Uriah ran back to check her, but she told him to see to Mavis. He went to the woman that Taylor had so recklessly shunned and knew that the child was about to be born. The town doctor came running with his medical bag, looked down at Taylor then walked to where Mavis waited. He checked the unborn child with his stethoscope. He just shook his head.

While someone ran to get the midwife, two burly men carried her to his office. Eryn saw the blood soaked dress as they carried her past and she truly felt sorry for her. She had been betrayed and it was probably more of a shock to her then it had been for Eryn when Taylor left her. Uriah and the doctor went to examine Eryn. Uriah carried her to his office. He gently lay her on the doctor's table and took her hand in his.

"Ain't seen you 'round here before," said the doctor to Eryn, as he looked at her wound. "Bullet's gotta come out. Where'd you find this pretty thing, Uriah?"

"Oh, she's been around before, Doc."

"She's looking lots like that Miss Matheson," he whispered to Uriah, "if my old memory serves me right."

"Yes, my thoughts exactly."

"Don't mean to bring up hurt feelin's, Uriah, but she's remindin' me of that one."

"It's okay, Doc, you're correct. It is Eryn Rae Matheson, my betrothed."

"Well, high Heaven, where's she been all this time? A body might think she got herself killed or somethin'."

"None of that matters, Doc."

"Will you be staying this time, Uriah?"

"I don't know," Uriah said, as he looked at Eryn on the table as the chloroform took effect. "I don't know."

* * *

Uriah slouched down in the chair beside Eryn. The effect from the morphine allowed him to drift in and out of sleep, but he felt no more pain from his shoulder. It was a clean wound, straight in and straight out without hitting the bone or damaging much tissue. Eryn wasn't as lucky. The bullet had to be removed from her side. It narrowly missed her liver. She would be okay, but was still under the effect of the morphine. She moaned a few times, mumbling his name, but Uriah couldn't do much until his drug wore off. He lay his head back on the chair and exhaled as he succumbed to the drug.

Later, a woman's scream bolted Uriah straight up in his chair. He looked at Eryn but she slept soundly. His head ached and his vision was blurry, but he felt more awake than before. Sobbing came from another room. He peeked through a small opening in the door and saw Mavis. Beneath the sheet that covered her was no bulge where the child had grown. Did she lose everything? he wondered. Taylor was a fool. He had a great life with a successful job, a loving family and a beautiful wife. He gave it all up for a false sense of excitement. But Uriah couldn't be too sorry for the man. Already, he was ready to search the world for Eryn if he had to, but then…then she appeared. With all her beauty, all her pain, she appeared. He heard Eryn whisper his name and went to her side.

"What happened? Where are we?"

"You had the bullet removed, but you'll be okay. We're still in 1882," he whispered.

"How long do I have to stay here? I need to get out and explore." She rubbed her temples. "My head hurts."

"I'm taking you home, Eryn. To my old home until you get better. The morphine probably causes your headache." He massaged her temples and smoothed her hair back.

"Finally, I'm back here. Was the book right, Uriah? Did Taylor really do this?"

"Yes, Eryn, as usual it was right."

"You stopped the bullet from killing me," said Eryn.

"No, you stopped it from killing me, sweet Eryn." He stroked the soft skin of her face. "Now sleep, we'll leave in the morning. We have some unfinished business to see to."

"Are you okay?" she asked, unable to lift her head.

"I'm in better shape than you are…now sleep." He kissed her fingers as he folded them around his hand, and continued to hold her until she fell off to sleep.

* * *

"Miss Mavis is full of grit, Mr. Prescot. She'll be pullin' through. Not sure 'bout that little one, though," said the doctor. "If he's got the guts of his ma he'll be making it. Too soon to tell."

Uriah didn't care to hear about the miserable woman that was responsible for Eryn's pain. "I'll be taking Eryn tomorrow."

"Now, you shouldn't be movin' her just yet!"

"I'll be taking her tomorrow. I don't want her to be staying here in town. We'll be out at my farm."

The old doctor patted Uriah on the back. "Just like before?"

"Sure, Doc. Don't do anything with Mr. Sterling's body until I talk to Eryn."

"What's she got to do with it?" The doctor read the pain on Uriah's face as he spoke and he soon understood.

"He was her husband and I think she should decide."

"Yes, sir. You're right 'bout that. It be kind of a shame. A dad blame shame." The doctor looked at Uriah. The face he had known for nearly forty years, and for the first time in the past twenty years, he saw a sparkle in the eyes of the man.

* * *

The next morning, Eryn was sitting up brushing her hair when Uriah came in with a bundle. She had been crying. He looked handsome and Eryn forgot the pain in her side, and in her heart. His breeches were tight, hugging his strong thighs. His satin shirt was apple green, with a leather bola tie at the neck. This time his leather knee high boots had a shine, probably the first time since he bought them. His left arm was in a sling. She held her arms out, but he didn't know exactly how to hold her, for fear of hurting her. She took his hand and put it around her neck. Running her hands down his back she liked the feel of his muscles under the smooth satin. She kissed his shoulder where his wound was. "We look a mess, don't we."

"Speak for yourself, Madam." He untied the package and pulled out a blue cloak with a paisley print on the inside. She felt the material and remarked how much nicer it was than what she had worn. He handed her another package and when she opened it she found a dark green chemise; she blushed when she saw it was semi-transparent silk. She looked in the wrapping. Uriah smiled when she looked up, ready to question him.

"You wear nothing underneath except your bandage, Madam." The smile was even more crooked when he had a devious thought on his mind.

"Uriah, I don't remember ever blushing as much until I met you. Whatever is it that you do to me?"

"You always blushed, sweet Eryn. Do I make you feel seventeen years old again?"

"Well…yes, you do sometimes."

"Do you mind?"

"I don't know," she answered.

He leaned forward and kissed her then went to the door and came back in with a mixture of fall flowers, freshly cut and wrapped loosely in a square of chantilly lace. She admired their beauty, and the thought behind them. "They look so much brighter now, enhanced in some way." She lowered her head and raised her eyes. "Thank you, I love them."

"I know you do," he said.

"Can we go now?"

He went over and helped her pull the gown off. With only one good hand, now, he tried to help her slide the chemise over her head. He lifted her to the floor, holding her until she was steady. Slowly he slid his hand over her back, stopping at her smooth hips. He didn't miss the chance to brush his fingers against her perfect breasts.

"I'm hungry. The doctor will only let me have broth."

"I'll give you what you want, sweet Eryn."

That smile spread across her lips, the smile that turned Uriah inside-out and back again, but he had to be strong in front of her least she know that she ruled every breath he took.

Little did he know—she knew it anyway!

Chapter 32

Together they sat in the buggy and the late fall morning was cool. Clouds in the sky were heavy and thick, resembling storm clouds, rain or snow. Their trip could very well be ruined. Beneath the blue hooded cape, Uriah saw the angry green leave her eyes and the soft blue was radiant.

"Where do you want to go first, Eryn?"

She looked around town. Down the street she saw the house she came out of from the Portal. "Is that the only way back and forth?" she asked, pointing to the house.

"I believe it is."

"What if something happened to the house or Emmet's book store?"

"Well, the house burned, as you know, but it burned in Emmet's time."

"But the Portal can still be used and the house is gone in our other time."

"Maybe the house has to be destroyed in this time right here. If that happened we would probably never get back."

"Who lives in it?" Eryn asked.

"Emmet's grandfather.

"I wonder how he found the Portal. Did the book ever say? And where is he when we are there?"

"I never read the whole thing," answered Uriah. "I've often wondered myself, why we don't see anyone. I don't have that answer."

"I think we should read it all," she said.

"We will."

"Will you go slowly through Enchantment? I just want to bask in the reality of it."

He pulled a blanket over her legs and clicked for the bay to take them on their way. Uriah turned the buggy and went to the end of town, then turned around and stopped. Eryn looked around, knowing she was at the same corner where she turned into town that fateful night of the fog, a century away. The lamp lights were still standing in their place. She looked at the long dangerous hill. It wasn't much more than a carriageway with a workhorse stationed at the bottom to help carriages ascend the top.

"I remember something about that hill, Uriah. Should I know something about it?"

"Your great-great grandfather was the man in charge of hiring out horses to pull wagons up the hill."

She reached inside her memory for the man's face but grasped nothing. "I don't remember him," she said, sadly.

Slowly, they headed back down the main road, and Eryn took everything in. The red and white barber's pole was still in the same place as she saw in the historical part of town in modern Enchantment. A dry goods store was nestled between a tailor that advertised exquisite care in making, altering or repairing garments, and a shop where shoes and boots were repaired. In front of each place of business was a hitching post. This day was quiet. A large church sat on one corner. As they eased their way down the street, Eryn noticed a buggy in front of a general store and she knew her parents had one like it. She didn't mention it to Uriah.

A little farther Uriah stopped the buggy and pointed. Eryn looked at the Queen Anne style house and except for the colors the only difference was no paved parking lot, or no sign that advertised the Enchanted Inn.

"Your grandfather's?" Eryn asked.

Uriah nodded and shook the reins. "It's ours if we stay here." He said the words but neither looked at the other nor said a word. Across the street was the park, looking just like it did when she envisioned it the very first night in Enchantment.

"Uriah, stop! We have to go to the park." He tied the horse and they walked to the gazebo. She remembered what Lesley told her. "The legend is true, isn't it? You made that chime for *us*." She looked up at her blond enchanter and kissed his smiling lips. "I remember that first kiss now. It was wonderful."

Once again they passed Emmet's family home, and Eryn turned, watching until she could turn her neck no more. A small cafe was where Sweet Nicole's sat in the other time, and still another church down the road. When they were near the church, Eryn saw a churchyard and asked if her parent's graves were there. They were not.

Eryn was in awe of what she was experiencing. "I almost can't believe this is real. How can this be?" Her voice was cracking.

"Eryn," he took her hand, "there is no answer. This is a phenomenon that just can't be explained, let alone understood. We're privileged to be able to experience this."

"Yes, I know, but..."

"But what? I've tried for twenty years to find an answer and explanation. There's not one, girl!"

"There has to be," she said.

"Eryn, stop it. There is no way to find out."

"What if we talk to Emmet's grandfather. Maybe he knows what happened, why I went away."

"Don't be ridiculous," Uriah said, but knew it couldn't be more true.

"What if his father knows then?"

"He's only a little boy. We have to read the whole book, okay? Then let's make a decision." Uriah didn't want to talk about the Portal anymore. It caused him enough pain already.

"Okay, I'll settle with that—For now."

"Good!" said Uriah.

They came up to and passed the stable where Taylor worked. "You okay?"

"No, I don't think I am. For some reason I feel so sad for him. Uriah, I—I think I'll miss him. I did love him, you know."

The only thing Uriah could do was put his arm around her and hold her while she cried, and he wanted to cry, too, for he couldn't bear to see her in agony, and he knew she would be for some time. But he would be there for her, always.

Her sobs were genuine and her anguish was real. Earlier she felt the lump in her throat, but now it felt more like a boulder and it rolled to her chest and sat heavy on her heart. She wouldn't remember the bad times. The good times are what she would hold in her heart. He at least deserved some time of mourning from his wife.

Uriah made the horse gallop away, holding the reins tight with his one good hand. The bouncing made his shoulder hurt and he knew Eryn was hurting. "This isn't a good time to talk about it, but you have to decide what to do with Taylor's body."

"I know, I've been thinking about it." She hesitated. "I don't know what to do. What should I do, Uriah?"

Uriah stopped the buggy and thought before he answered. "If we take him back you can have a funeral. The girls might need one. If you don't, then how do you explain it to them?"

She stared into space, picturing the last time she saw her husband. He was the same man who left her nearly eleven months ago. For so many years she was blinded by the love she had for him. Were they as happy as she imagined? Yes, they were for about the first ten years. He did love her, but the last ten years was clearly a farce. The girls knew it all, and it helped them to accept that Uriah was their real father. But then again, she wasn't going to remember those times.

"He needs to go back. I have to have proof of his death or it will take many more years before we can wrap up his insurance policies and legally declare him dead."

"You don't need his money."

"Taylor worked hard to be sure we had a good life if something happened to him. Besides, the girls are entitled to something."

"They're my girls. Trust me, Eryn, I can make their life financially pleasant, and yours."

"What about Mavis and the baby? Taylor finally has a son. He's entitled to something, too, I guess." She was quiet for a few moments, then said, "I just thought of something. You said I was depressed when I left."

"Yes."

"Maybe that's why I didn't remember anything when I went through, a defense mechanism of some kind."

"It could be possible," said Uriah. "What's your point?"

"Well, Mavis is depressed, too. It wouldn't be fair for her to go through and not remember. Believe me, I know. We have to talk to her."

"What!" said Uriah.

"We have to. Please, let's go now."

* * *

After they visited the doctor to make plans for Taylor, they learned that Mavis had taken his body and disappeared. The doctor put up a fight trying to keep her from doing it, but she brought two large men with her and they insisted he not stand in their way. The doctor knew Mavis had been with Taylor and gave birth to his child. He let her go.

"You can still make up a death certificate."

"How, Uriah?"

"Sweet Eryn, haven't you learned, yet, that I'm capable of doing whatever I need to do. We can leave some money with the doctor. I'm almost sure he knows how to contact Mavis. If she wants to stay here with her child, then some of his money will allow her to live an extravagant life here."

"She doesn't deserve anything, but it's only fair to the boy. My side hurts and I want to put this behind me. I'm sorry Taylor had to die, but I'm glad this is over." She let out a deep sigh. "No more worrying that a cop will come to my door asking me to identify him. No more worrying or waiting." She looked at Uriah and realized what she was saying. "Uriah, I'm sorry. I shouldn't be saying these things to you."

"It's okay, I understand. I know you had a life, two decades with the man, I expect you to feel something." Two decades away from me! he thought, as he gripped the reins until his palm was numb.

"Look around, Eryn Rae. Is this familiar?"

Eryn looked at the seven ridges in the east and saw an oil well pumping oil into a large storage tank, exactly as he described it. To the west she saw a tall windmill and the chimney to a house peeking over a ridge. Feelings of apprehension were in her heart and suddenly her chest felt heavy. It felt like she would vomit. Clutching her abdomen, she made Uriah stop. He lifted her down and went to the spring and dampened his sling, then dabbed her forehead with it. Opening her cloak, he looked through the thin material of her chemise and saw her bandage was clean.

When he looked at her face he saw streaks of tears down to her chin. Her mascara had settled below her eyes. He took the cloth and dabbed at the area and wiped away the darkness, but couldn't wipe away the pain. All he could do was hold her against his body and comfort her while she cried, like he tried a century ago. It didn't help her then but he knew, this time, he would not let her go. She would not desert him again. "I'll see you through it. I'm here, sweet Eryn."

"Uriah, I don't want to remember." She clung to him, her head against his chest. "Please don't let me remember."

"You have to, if you're going to heal, you have to." He stroked her hair and held her for what seemed forever. Then she pulled away from him and walked toward the path that led to her childhood home. As if in a trance she knew the way. Uriah walked close behind, but she motioned him to stop.

"I won't go away, Eryn."

She turned, increasing her speed as did Uriah. Turning again, she screamed at him to stay.

His heart was shattering into little pieces with each glare from her distressed eyes. "No, I won't go, nothing will make me leave you alone again."

Eryn turned and ran down the path, stopping abruptly when she saw the house. The pine trees were singing as the wind whipped through their boughs. The large wooden plank that hung from the monstrous oak branch with rope, swung with the wind's force. Even the mighty windmill spun as if everything was fine. The deacon's bench still sat on the porch, covered with dust, waiting for someone to sit upon it.

She looked to the single upstairs window, her bedroom, and

remembered the long talks with her mother, her beautiful mother who smelled like lavender. Remembering the lectures about Uriah made her smile. She remembered her brother, Joseph, and his freckles. In the mornings he would bounce on her bed trying to get her up, and she would chase him out.

If only she could chase him out now!

Finally, she pictured herself in front of her mirror with a chemise, nothing like the one she had on now. In that room, she dreamed of marrying Uriah, and now she even envisioned her silk wedding dress hanging on the form. The beads sewn on by her. Her father's eyes misted when he saw it. He would be losing his only daughter.

Instead, his only daughter lost him.

Uriah came up behind her, but he didn't know whether to touch her or let her stand alone. He waited and she turned and reached for his hand. "I have to go inside."

"Are you sure?"

She went to the door and it opened. Cobwebs were stretched across the archway and she quickly brushed them away. A light musty odor emanated from inside the house that remained damp and lonely for many years.

She had come home, she had finally come home.

Looking around the kitchen she saw the pump handle remained in the upward position. The cast-iron stove still had hardwood inside it. Dry, dead hardwood. Sadness encompassed her as she thought of the hours spent there making bread and helping her mother make pies. She could almost taste the egg nog that her father loved so. Eryn laughed through her tears when she remembered Joseph drank a glass of Apple-jack and was ill for two days.

She walked into the parlor. All that was left was the fireplace and the large brick hearth. The furniture was gone, but she closed her eyes and remembered. Yes, she remembered. She went down the hall but Uriah took her arm, stopping her.

"Don't put yourself through anymore, please."

"I have to go to their room, I have to remember them." Suddenly she wanted to. He dropped her arm and let her go realizing she had to do it.

In her parent's bedroom the scent of her mother lingered in the walls and the strong smell of her father's tobacco reeked from the room. The tears freely flowed once again. Why hadn't she gone with them that night? she asked herself. As she thought she remembered that it had been Uriah. He kept her in his bed that evening and would not even let her go to church. That must have been when the twins were conceived because she slept with him not again, until....

She went to the window. When she looked out she pictured the carriage in the yard and the horse in the corral near the barn. She pictured her dog, Willy, so wanting to nuzzle her face into his thick, hairy coat. It was more than she could bear, so she sat in a forgotten corner chair feeling as forgotten as the house, and sobbed.

The sun was setting so Uriah lit some lanterns that still had kerosene in them. He went to Eryn's room and waited for her. While he sat on the floor below the window he remembered the night...he wouldn't let her go. She might have died with them. He shuddered to think of it. The feeling was so strong, he couldn't let her leave him that night. He wouldn't take her home until late in the evening. To think of her waiting up for them alone all night tore at his soul. He knew he should have waited with her, but he had to check the fields early the next morning, and Eryn insisted he leave so he could go to bed early.

Eryn came into her room and sat beside him. He warmed her with the heat of his own body.

"There are too many if's, Eryn. I'm tired of saying, if this and if that. Nothing can be changed no matter what we say now."

"Thank you for collecting those photographs and my journals. I never would have them now." In a corner she saw her old pitcher and basin set. Walking to it she saw her pitcher was cracked and the basin had a large chip. The pretty floral design had faded. The dust was thick. "What happened to Willy?"

"I'll fix the pitcher," Uriah told her. "My sister took Willy. He lived a long life. There were puppies."

That made her smile. She collected the pitcher and basin, and put it by the door, then sat beside him again. "Do you know what happened to my wedding dress? I remember it and I'd like to see it again."

"Eryn, would you wear it?"

"I doubt it would fit me now. I wonder what happened to it."

Uriah gently helped her to her feet and removed her cloak. He circled her, and standing with his hand in his pocket, contemplated what she said. He felt her arms and put his hands around her waist, as if measuring. "Hmm, about twenty-two inches. I think it might be a little tight, but you can wear it."

"Thanks. That's a great compliment, I think. My uncle probably gave it to my cousin. It wouldn't fit anyway."

"You don't remember, how do you know what size you were?" Maybe you were larger."

"Was I!"

"No, but you could have been. Back to the question. Would you wear it?"

"Yes, I suppose I would at least try it on, if I had it."

"I have it, sweet Eryn." He looked at her with a look that she loved. His eyes were innocent and he looked like a little boy that just got caught stripping the lug nuts off his dad's car.

She smiled. A wide grin broke out on her face and she threw her arms around his neck.

"How could I let anyone else have that dress. You had it made to marry me. Me! No one else was about to get it!" He had his arms around her waist as he looked down into her soft tropical eyes. "Will you wear it, sweet Eryn, will you wear it...when you marry me?"

Without moving, Eryn didn't know what to do or say. She loved Uriah, but she hadn't thought of marriage since she found him. For one thing, she never thought it would be possible, but the thought occurred to her that she was now a widow and she still felt a pang of sorrow over Taylor. That would take some time. But she saw the love in those cat-eyes....

Eryn looked at the floor, biting her lip. She shivered from the coolness of the evening. Looking back up at him she whispered, "Yes."

"What did you say, I couldn't hear you?"

"Yes," she said again, eyes sparkling.

"Yes, you will what? I didn't quite hear you."

"Yes, Uriah Prescot. I will marry you," she said almost in a shout.

His smile showed the white perfect teeth glistening in the soft glow of the lantern. She hugged his neck, wincing in pain at her own injury, but the pain was minimal, thanks to this ecstatic moment.

"Are you ready to leave yet?"

"I think I am." She didn't move. "Uriah, I miss them so much. Can we return tomorrow?"

"Whenever you want to, Eryn. We'll get through this. I miss them, too," said Uriah.

She gathered up her pitcher and basin and he held the lantern for her to go downstairs. He stopped and looked around. Was it really twenty years ago? he thought—Twenty years plus a century?

One more walk through and she was ready. When she walked from the wash room she recalled a familiar odor. "Grandfather," she said. "Uriah, I just remembered my great-great grandfather. He smelled like...horses?"

"You can say that again," said Uriah, as he took her arm and led her outside.

Chapter 33

Uriah lit the lamps on the buggy and wrapped the blanket around her legs. They were both tired, longing for a place to lie their painful bodies. The road was fairly smooth and faintly bathed in the light of a three-quarter moon.

"Is this the same moon I looked at two nights ago, a century away?" asked Eryn.

"You're a philosopher aren't you?"

"How can you not think about things like that?"

"For a long time I learned to live one day at a time. I couldn't think about things like that, and that *is* the only moon we've ever had."

"But the other night the moon was exactly the same size and in the same place. Do you know what I mean, Uriah?"

"Yes, I know what you mean. Does your side hurt?"

"A little, yes, and I'm hungry."

The doctor gave me some laudanum for the pain, for both of us. I have food at home."

"Good, and I want to rest." Eryn looked around. If not for the horse and buggy she would think it her own time in the future. Funny, she thought, this is my own time. Confusion began to play its part in her mind. She'd been in the modern era for more years than her own time past. In reality, the distant time was her own time now.

When the buggy stopped Eryn opened her mouth in awe. "Uriah, it's almost the same! You built it nearly the same, down to the windmill."

"I had to, Eryn. When you finally stumbled across me you would know it was familiar, and know it was me—waiting for you."

"But, Uriah, *how* did you know I was there?"

He jumped down and went to her side. "The inside is not quite the same. I wasn't that extravagant when I was young." He put his hand out to help her down, but she continued to sit and stare at him.

"What is it?" he asked.

"Why did you build it for me and how did you know I was there?"

"Come inside, it's damp out here."

"Ok," she said, taking his hand. "But I am still waiting for an answer."

Fresh gossamer cobwebs were creatively stretched between the door jambs, but the cabin was otherwise clean and smelled fresh. "Someone comes in and cleans for me. I don't come back very often."

"Who knows where you go, Uriah?"

He helped her sit down then primed the pump for water. After it flowed a few minutes he filled a brass kettle and put pine wood in the cook stove, lit it then started a fire in the fireplace. The dry seasoned logs caught quickly and the warmth overtook the room.

"You're not answering my questions, Sir."

"I know, Madam."

"Why is that?"

"A beautiful, dark haired woman comes in to clean for me."

Eryn didn't realize she was the jealous type until Uriah so nonchalantly spoke of another woman. "Oh," she said.

He saw her bite her lip, and he noticed a look he never saw before. He received the reaction he strived for and he laughed aloud. Sitting next to her, he said, "The beautiful woman is my sister."

A smile as bright as sun shining on the Allegheny River, rippled across her face and she couldn't contain herself. She threw her arms around his neck and hugged him. "Your sister, that's wonderful. I've got to see her, does she know that we found each other again?"

"She knows, sweet Eryn."

The water boiled and he made her a small pot of tea. He sat a white china tea pot on a tray and carried it over with cheese and sour dough bread, and a big slice of apple pie. Then he poured himself a small glass of whiskey.

"You haven't answered my other question."

"Let us have our food and drink in our bed, Eryn."

"No!"

He raised an eyebrow to her as he poured more than half a packet into her tea and the other in his glass. He climbed the ladder and lit candles for light. When he descended the ladder he went to her. "Come up with me. If this takes effect fast I might not be able to help you to the loft, and as you see, the steps aren't as nice as our other ones."

She looked toward the ten rung step ladder and decided he was right.

The tester bed looked freshly made with feather pillows and a quilt. It smelled airy. It was high and she stepped up on the two step bed stool to reach it. When she sat on it she sank down deep into the feather mattress, laughing as she rolled to the middle, holding her aching side. The man went to his chest of drawers and opened a small drawer. He went to the woman lying in the middle of the fluff. Taking her hand he kissed her fingers and held them in his hand. Eryn felt something slip over the third finger of her left hand. When she raised it to see, she saw the gold band, the gold band etched in black, the match. She lifted her eyes to him and no words were necessary between them. At that moment she felt more love for him then she ever thought possible. She reached out and pulled him close. She squeezed ever so tightly, and he gently squeezed her back.

Uriah handed her the tea and most of the drug for her pain. They picked at the food and he waited to drink his whiskey. He took her cup and sat it on the tray on the bedside table. Looking around the room she thought it felt familiar, albeit, not remembering it. Eventually, the feeling brought a memory along with it. She closed her eyes.

Uriah saw a smile on her face and he smiled. "What do you think of?"

"I think of us. I saw a vision of your blond head beside me swallowed up by this bed that feels like a marshmallow." She picked up the pillow next to her and struggled to lift it as she aimed at his head and, as usual, was right on her mark. He flinched when he saw it coming, but it was too late. He could tell by the comical grin on her face that the laudanum was beginning to work.

He looked at her body from her head down to the tip of her toe. There was a yearning inside him. Memories came to mind. Memories of the same woman in his bed, as she is now. He needed her so much when he was but a boy. He never knew a girl could do so many things to his insides. Together they studied each others body until they learned and knew one another like an architect knows his blueprints. They were young, they were in love, and he knew he wanted her to be with him for the rest of his life. He wanted to take care of her, his girl child, his woman.

But then it happened, it happened and his life was changed overnight, as was Eryn's. They were both dealt a hand neither knew how to play. They had loved each other when they were mere children, yet they had to physically grow up away from one another. But mentally there was a bond that stayed connected.

Even though she was away from him he never lost the yearning for her love, for her body to be next to him. She even admitted she had dreamed of him, and yearned for him. Through miles and years, what they had when they were young, somehow, traveled the same road and counted the same days until eventually, finally, they found each other. He gulped his drug laced whiskey and stretched out beside her, holding her close. Tomorrow he would tell her the truth she asked for. Tomorrow he would take her in his arms and love her, and the next day…he would love her… and the next day….

* * *

Uriah stoked the fire before he poured a cup of strong coffee. His thoughts were clouded, his night restless. The small amount of laudanum did little to ease his pain. He quietly opened the swollen door and sat on the back step. Seven forested ridges with deep green valleys stood tall in the east behind the younger forest. A variety of birds sang and chirped, welcoming the dawn. The rising sun was beautiful. He scanned the field, remembering the corn that grew there for generations. The clackety-clack of his oil pump rang out as he smiled at the income he now enjoyed from it. Who would know he would be able to live quite comfortably from the never-ending small well of black gold. Anthracite coal and iron ore were but a few of the minerals on his land that were sought after, and occasionally he would allow mining. When he felt in the mood he would sell hard wood to a hungry lumber company, but only a little at a time and he always insisted they replant, for he didn't want his forest depleted. Yes…they would live comfortably either now or…in the other time. It would be up to her, he would go with her decision, for she had everything there in her time. All Uriah had left was his sister and she lived a happy life with her husband, Graham, their son, Jackson and their daughter, Rebecca. His parents died in the terrible flood in Johnstown in 1889 when they went on a trip there. There was nothing Uriah could do to change it. History couldn't be changed through the Portal. Emmet's grandfather tried, but he learned he could only predict as he did with Eryn…predict and hope heed was taken.

He heard a sound and turned. Eryn stood at the back door smiling. "I didn't know where I was when I woke up. It frightened me when you weren't there." He went inside and looked at her tousled hair and puffy eyes; she was so beautiful to him. She donned a light blue linen wrapper. A long train trailed behind on the floor. He remembered she always wore it before. He scanned her body, feeling aroused just looking at her.

After he checked her wound he poured coffee and they sat on the sofa watching the sun rise even higher.

"You are keeping something from me, Uriah Prescot."

"Yes, that I am, sweet Eryn, Eryn Rae, soon to be Prescot."

She smiled. "I don't like when you keep things from me."

"I won't do it ever again." He tenderly kissed her lips and hugged her. When he looked in her eyes, the eyes he dreamed about, he saw love. He saw the young girl that made his heart sing and he remembered…

Her house was dark when his dobbin cantered up to it. He jumped down and ran to the barn in search of her. The animals were not there, they were running free. Her collie came up to him, whimpering. As he searched the meadow and the orchard his heart pounded, fear turning him into a wild man. He ran into her house, to her room; he inhaled the scent of her, but she was not there. The room was untouched. He waited…and waited, but the beautiful red haired girl he loved, didn't return that night or any night. Then when Uriah thought he could take no more, the old man came to him…

"Eryn, after you left I fell apart, I had nothing, could do nothing. Emmet's grandfather overheard my folks talking about how worried they were about me being alone on my farm. It was two months later and I was still a broken man. Mr. McDanil came to me one day—He found me weakened and sad. What he told me changed my life, again." Uriah tried to read her eyes and he saw hope in them.

"Go on, Uriah."

"He told me he couldn't stand to see you in such pain." He looked up at her and saw anticipation. "Eryn…your great-great grandfather took you through the Portal."

Tears were stinging her eyes and Uriah held her tightly. "Emmet is your mother's father…Emmet is your grandfather." He handed her a handkerchief and she dabbed her eyes, but the tears wouldn't stop.

"He knew when a severely depressed person went through the Portal they forgot their pain. He couldn't understand, but he knew it, and it hurt him so badly to see your sorrow. That was the only way he knew to help you. He vowed to care for you there until he thought you could understand."

"Oh, Uriah, I don't know what to say. Does Emmet know he is my grandfather?"

"No, I'm sure he doesn't. His grandfather died before he was old enough to understand."

"Why didn't my great-great grandfather tell me later?"

"It seems you left Enchantment the very same day you arrived. He lost you."

"What about all the announcements in the paper?"

"He must have been back in his own time then. Your leaving devastated him. It wasn't something he planned on. He regretted it the rest of his life."

"How did *you* go then?"

"After a while he saw that I couldn't recover from losing you. He told me I could go and find you, but first I had to rid myself of my despair or the same thing would happen to me. As soon as I knew I would see you again, I shook it and he led me through."

"But how did he find the Portal anyway? Do you know?"

"All he ever said was that one day he was in his parlor. It's true, he did have visions on occasion, nothing he ever understood. He was looking at some pictures in his album and suddenly envisioned Enchantment, but it didn't look like the town he knew. He said it looked like something from a distant time yet to come. The more he focused on his vision the clearer it became to him. The next thing he knew, he was in what looked like the same room, but not the same. He looked out the window and couldn't believe what he was seeing. He went back to his table and didn't know if he could get back. Knowing it was the future he envisioned to get there, he then pictured his own time and his own town of Enchantment, and the next thing he knew, he was back in this time again."

"But how did he figure out about the sadness taking away a memory?"

"After your parents died he was very sad himself, but not to the point of devastation, like you were. He tried it again and when he went through, he could barely remember how he got where he was, or even where he was. Over a short period of time, his memory came back to him and he envisioned his own time and—there he was again, back home. Apparently, he did a lot of traveling back and forth, more than anyone ever knew. I believe many things happened that he never spoke of. Who knows, maybe another depressed person went through with him once, and that's how he found out. He began writing about the things he saw, knowing that someday it would actually happen. Even his own death."

"That's why he gave Emmet the book the night he died," said Eryn. "Emmet really could have saved him if he read it that night. What responsibility to put on a child!"

"Yes, I agree," said Uriah.

"If he knew, why didn't he save himself?"

"I believe he was still so devastated over what happened to you, he wanted to be free of the pain. Even after all the years."

"But he knew I would return to Enchantment. How?"

"One of his jaunts through the Portal, he saw you had returned. He somehow knew you had the twins and that you were lonely. He knew you were with the wrong man; knew you *had* to be with me. The only thing he could do was write about it. And hope Emmet would figure it all out."

"And eventually he did," said Eryn.

"Not fully until you walked in that day. Thank God you walked in that day." He brought her to him and held her tightly. It felt good for Uriah to finally get this out. It built up for so many years and he had nearly ran out of hope. "But I never could find you. I, too, sought help from the media, but to no avail."

"This is almost impossible to believe, isn't it?"

"I thought the old man had gone over the edge when he came to me and told me," said Uriah. "I know it sure sounds senseless, but we know it's true, girl." While he caressed her arm, he continued. "Then Taylor heard about Emmet's books and he got involved. When he showed me your picture my heart beat again. It beat for you, Eryn, but Taylor left before I could find where he was from. He gave a false license number and address when he checked in so I lost you even before I found you. That's when I began desperately waiting for the day you would search for him."

"But I didn't search for him. I was too distraught. The foggy night...the one my great-great grandfather wrote about led me here."

"He knew it all, except where you ran off to, but he knew you would return, he just knew," he said, while he held her hands.

Eryn stood and went to the door then stepped out. She walked through the wet, dewy grass and looked all around. When she walked back in Uriah followed her wet footprints to the ladder as she reached out to him. "We still have a lifetime together. I want us to live in the other time. Is that okay with you?"

"I figured you would. That's okay with me," he said.

"We have to forget about the Portal, never use it again."

"Yes, my sweet, sweet Eryn," he said, as he became lost in the desire of her eyes.

The feather bed was warm as the heat drifted upstairs. Eryn climbed on it and kneeled toward him. Hurriedly, she unbuttoned Uriah's shirt and outlined his bandage with her finger. He unbuttoned his pants and slid them off. His muscles flexed beneath her fingers as he softly touched his lips to the racing pulse near her throat. She pressed herself against him ignoring the slight twinge of pain in her side. The love she saw in his eyes excited her as much as his touch and she trembled, simply because he was there. They lay side by side. He untied the ribbons and pushed the wrapper open, leaning against her warm skin. The bitter taste of coffee remained on her lips as he delicately kissed her lips.

Eryn stroked his back and the nerves in her fingers tingled at the feel of him. Now she could recall the happiness they had before. She remembered this little log cabin in these same mountains. Thinking about the creek, she now had two wonderful memories, one from the past and one from their future. She knew the man loving her was once her whole life and would always be forever more! He was the only man under the bright planet of Venus that truly loved her, and she believed he was made for her only! He was the father of her children! In some freaky twist it was allowed to happen and it felt so right. Uriah, the golden eyed lover in her dreams. Uriah, the blond beguiler that waited half of his life for *her.*

She felt his hips constrict as he stroked her leg with his. She thought of the handsome, strong man next to her taking her body beyond the boiling point, and she felt lucky. An accident, a freak of nature or whatever it could be called, and an old man who loved her, kept them apart for twenty years, cheated them of the love they both never stopped craving. But now they found each other and the prediction was completed, all was well!

Eryn searched his face, the flame in his eyes intrigued her. A muscle twitched in his cheek as she caressed it and his breathing quickened, as did hers. He held her hair back out of his face as he kissed her, not too gently, but intently and he was lost in her presence.

The urgency in both of them zenithed before they relaxed in each others arms, side by side. They shared the same pillow and looked into each others eyes. The turquoise accented the amber as they lay lost in love. He touched the face of the beautiful, intelligent, submissive woman he loved, "Forever and always, sweet Eryn."

She smoothed the hair behind his ear and loved his courageous spirit, "Always and forever, Uriah, my strong cavalier." They smiled at each other and wrapped up in each others embrace.

Epilogue

All was quiet in the little log cabin that saw a century of love come and go and return again. The walls watched as they slept peacefully, knowing their love would be the mortar that held it all together and would remain together…forever and always…always and forever. As the woman and her man slept, all was right within their soul and their spirits soared. Somehow, while they lay dreaming their dreams bonded together and between them they shared another vision of enchantment:

The park stood in full autumn color. The slight breeze aroused a soft tinkle as a blond haired, amber eyed man hung a crystal chime on an intricate piece of wood trim on the newly built gazebo. It shined so brightly as the sun sparkled off the cut glass. The solid brass "P" in the center stood out in a shadow on the deck, surrounded by the prism of light. He waved to his two grown daughters as they approached with a picnic basket in one hand, and their boyfriends in the other.

A chestnut haired woman sat on a blanket and beside her was a small child with long flaxen hair. When the child looked up at the man, the younger amber eyes sparkled. The man smiled down at the mother and child, playing with a fuzzy teddy bear. Lips curled into a little crooked smile just like the fathers did upon looking at the mother, his wife…the woman they all loved. And the love between all of them would grow and continue forever…and always!

Printed in the United States
77797LV00003B/179